MAX ABADDON

And The Crystal King

Written By Justin S. Leslie

J.S.L

Paperback ISBN: 978-1-7376027-5-0
E-book ISBN: 978-1-7376027-2-9
Hardcover ISBN: 978-1-7376027-6-7

Contact Information
Email: Abaddonbooks@hotmail.com
Facebook: @Maxabaddonbooks
Website: www.JustinLeslie.com

Copyediting by Happily Ever Proofreading LLC

"You can't go back and change the beginning, but you can start where you are and change the ending."

C.S. LEWIS

PROLOGUE

"Mom!" I yelled as a dark shadow stood in my doorway. As always, I needed a good bedtime story to put me to sleep.

The ominous dark figure in the doorway morphed into Mom holding a plate of cookies. "Oh, I know just the one," her calming voice hummed as she set the plate down, pulling a small, flat red book from under her arm.

"Is this story about . . . demons?" I asked, gulping the room-temperature water that had been sitting on my nightstand for the past two days.

Mom sat back in her chair, the smell of baking sweets coming from her clothes. The sound of the chair creaking under her weight was both reassuring and familiar, putting my mind at ease.

"No, not tonight. Tonight, we have a short story about the Four Pillars. This story takes place directly after the Great War in the *History of Demons*. You remember that story?" Mom asked, picking up a cookie taking a light bite.

The cookies were clearly for my mother. "Ye-yes," I stammered, still not sure about what to think of the demons.

"Good. This story is about magic and how it binds the worlds together. Or apart," Mom said, taking another bite of the cookie before turning to the first page, clearing her throat.

"When all was said and done, the Kings and Queens of

the remaining Planes found they had yet another challenge to face," Mom started as I huffed out a question.

"Like demons?" I asked as she reached over to the plate, handing me the other cookie. This was, of course, all orchestrated.

"No, dear. Let me start. The one thing the Lords of the Planes failed to ignore was the magic that surrounded them. During the Great War, the Planes and realms were all connected, allowing magic to flow like water in a calm stream. Natural and fluid.

"After Earth was completely separated from Terrum, the Lords didn't know their realms only had so much magic to give, or take. After a meeting of the Lords, it was discovered that all magic flowed from one place. Do you know what that place was?" Mom asked, pausing as I finished my cookie.

"Earth?" I replied as cookie crumbles fell on my covers.

"That's right. The Lords all found that all magic originated from Earth, the one true remaining piece of Terrum connecting to their worlds. The Lords were smart, and after several years of working on a solution, one was found. Each Realm needed to be somehow connected to Earth. The Plane itself, the Over, the Under, the Everwhere, and Earth.

"From this, four Pillars were created. Magical items of unimaginable power that tied the Realms together. The Lords knew there might be trouble one day and made the Pillars strong, each with its own special power. Taking one out of the loop would not destroy the link, but all had their part to play. The Lords also built the Pillars to shield the realms from the Old Gods, keeping them lost in time and space." Mom paused, seeing if I had any more questions. I, of course, did.

"That's right. In the other story, you said they were not friends with the Old Gods, right?" I said as my eyes started feeling like window shades being pulled down on a rainy day.

"Yes, dear. Let's finish the story. Each of the Pillars was given to the most powerful of the Lords, hidden and protected from nefarious actors. Over time, the locations of some of the Pillars were lost. Wars have been fought while looking for them.

"If all four Pillars were ever removed, magic as we know it would cease to exist. Even worse, the different realms would become easy to find, beacons for the Old Gods, and separated from Earth, the source of all magic. The Pillars are to be protected, the Pillars are to be respected, and most importantly, the Pillars are to never get into the hands of the Old Gods. The end," Mom wrapped up, closing the thin book.

Mom was about to talk when she noticed my chest lightly moving in the twilight of early sleep. She reached down, brushing my hair back.

While I was crossing into dreamland, I could still hear and, as a grown adult, now remember what she whispered to me.

"One day, you will grow to know such things. You will both welcome and hate magic. For now, my son, rest, dream, and be strong in word and deed," she whispered, the smile not fully reaching her eyes. A light breeze full of the baking scents from her clothes finally pushed me over the edge into a deep pool of sleep.

CHAPTER 1

Drag the Waters

"I can assure you the information is correct," Goolsby's rumbling voice came over the speakerphone. Phil, Bo, Petro, and I stood on the beach, overlooking the eerie early morning, mirror-calm waters of Vilano Beach.

Bo rolled his eyes as I held the phone up. "The Council sends teams of Mages or whatever to these *events*, as everyone's calling them, and for this one just us?" I huffed out, shaking my head.

"For the last time. The readings for this event are relatively low. Take it up with the others. And that's another thing: don't call me again," Goolsby said as Petro buzzed down.

"Tell frog face—" Petro started. I swatted at him.

"I'm on speakerphone!" I barked loudly into the receiver, forgetting Goolsby was still on the line.

The back-and-forth from our team was undoubtedly aggravating Goolsby more by the second. Beeping started bouncing off the humid, foggy morning as we all looked at each other. He had hung up the phone.

"What an arse," Phil declared in a library-appropriate tone.

Over the past several months, several magical misfires, for lack of a better word, had occurred throughout the globe: some big, some small. The Council had been working with Goolsby through Mags-Tech to utilize their special satellites to identify the events before they occurred. At least, that was the intent.

These events spanned everything from random eruptions of magic to things floating, and on some occasions, downright monsters appearing. Each event had a specific level and footprint detectable by Mags-Tech's satellites.

Not wasting any time to seize the opportunity, anti-magic groups had been using these occurrences to spread fear and uncertainty about the recent union of worlds. Of course, this was all due to people now looking at things once hidden and the Council not always being able to clean things up, as they often called it.

The Council still kept its secrets, and the regular world was better off for it. At least from my point of view.

"Hey, boss. I don't think the water is supposed to be that calm in the ocean," Petro commented, hovering down to my shoulder.

The calm, still, whisper quiet scene was putting all of us on edge, including Bo.

"I'd be lying If I said this wasn't freaking me out. Hopefully, this is the event," I replied, snapping a picture of the mirrorlike calm waters, sending it to Ed.

"I doubt it, darlings," Bo added, stepping forward while adjusting the round, red-tinted glasses sitting snuggly on his face. "I do think something's under the water."

"Great," Phil blew out in one lungful.

My phone dinged with a reply from Ed simply stating, *"The event has escalated. Be careful."*

"Well, according to Ed, the event has escalated. Meaning . . ." I trailed off as the first signs of early morning regret made themselves known.

Two massive, dark black, spiked crab legs broke the calm ocean surface in an eruption of sand and water. The fortunate yet unfortunate part of the situation was that the sheer size of the massive legs—the height of a ten-story building—allowed the team enough time to shuffle back several feet out of the immediate impact area.

Before Phil could get out a flurry of unidentifiable curse words, the two sharp legs slammed into the sand. The muffled thump shook the ground like two explosions in the distance.

"Looks like a big event to me. *IGNIS!*" I yelled as a smaller leg split off from its bigger brother. This was followed by the lesser appendage smacking Bo, Phil, and myself, sending us gracefully flying through the air.

While I was happy for the embrace of the sand, the blow lodged my body several inches into the powdery dunes as Durundle winked out. If I made it through the next several minutes, I would be spending the next decade removing sand from every crevice in my body.

"Boss!" Petro screamed, landing on the soft sand. It was one of a handful of occasions I had heard him yell.

I opened my mouth to ask what was going on, only to have sand fly out. "Whupft . . . gabath . . . uun."

Petro screwed up his face as I held my hand over my lips, drawing moisture into my mouth from the morning dew.

"What's going on?" I finally spat out, getting to my feet as several more thumps reverberated in the sand.

"Bo's going all native on one of that thing's legs, and Phil is just staring at it," Petro informed me as the ten-story-tall crab came into clear focus. The morning haze coming off the water made its edges blur into the gray sky while the sun hid behind the clouds.

Bo had switched to full-on nightmare mode, trying to claw apart one of the armored legs. The area around the demon was engulfed in a flurry of water and sand, resembling a small tornado.

Using my heightened senses, I scanned the creature, taking note of all its legs, not to mention the truck-sized claws it was slowly pulling out of the sand.

Its belly was white, as with any other normal-sized crab, slowly fading into its armor-like crusted exterior. Unlike most magical creatures, this one simply looked like an oversized version of its normal self. Other than the smaller legs splitting off from the larger ones, there were no extra spiked tails, rows of disproportionate teeth, or evil grins.

I ran to Phil as he started to pull out a pack of cigarettes only to find them smashed. "I don't think Bo's getting very far with that thingy," Phil groaned.

"Any ideas?" I asked, continuing to scan the area.

Out of the blue, Bo, in one leap, jumped from the crab's front legs to its shorter, supporting back ones.

"I think Bobo is keeping it occupied while we have this exact conversation," Phil said, using Abby Normal's nickname for the demon as Petro zipped off.

A wave of water came crashing onto the beach as the creature turned slowly toward Bo. "I'm calling for backup," I stated flatly, pulling out my destroyed phone. The impact of my earlier fall had crushed the device.

Phil chuckled lightly. "You're better off going to the store and getting some Old Bay Seasoning and drawn butter, bruther."

The statement started floating through my head as we watched the creature moving further away from the coast, sinking deeper into the water. The crab was going after Bo, who was entirely under the now angry ocean.

"I mean, it's just a big crab, right?" I wondered as Petro landed on my shoulder.

"Boss, I don't think that thing knows what's going on. It's not a Titan. It's just a big-ass crab," Petro relayed at lightning-fast speed.

The notion of the creature being a Titan hadn't crossed my mind until Petro had mentioned it. One of the many things I had been made very aware of was the existence of Titans, godlike entities with unparalleled power. From what I understood, most of them resided on Terrum. The three of us had run into one on the *Event Horizon* after losing Ned.

To date, most people still didn't fully believe us. We had given up trying to explain the entire situation. The point of the story was they weren't supposed to be here, and they were an absolute sign of the Old Gods making moves.

"Tell you what. You guys get a hold of some help. I'm going to rustle us up a little lunch."

Phil and Petro just looked at me as I formed a mental link with Bo. To this day, it still surprised me how calm demons were when you had a conversation with them in what I liked to call the old head movie.

"*Little busy down here, darling,*" Bo's voice echoed through my mind as soon as I opened the link.

"*I'm going to need to get that thing into deeper water,*" I echoed as Bo loudly exhaled in my thoughts.

"*Water isn't really my thing. Know anyone good with that?*" Bo sarcastically noted, making it clear he was about done for the morning while also telling me to get my ass in gear. "*Oh, by the way, you know this is a regular crab for the most part?*"

"Keep it busy till I get there," I voiced, taking off my

blazer and dropping my pistol.

"Uh, boss? What are you doing?" Petro asked, seeing I was done talking to Bo. The others had gotten used to my mannerisms while talking to him in my head.

"Something stupid," I responded, taking off into the water.

The crab's claws, upon closer inspection, were significantly larger than I'd initially thought. As the large creature slowly turned, its weighed-down death traps dug deep ruts into the shallow waters leading away from the surf.

I shifted my focus to the initial rut from its right claw, springing forward and diving into the deeper water. Upon impact with the salty water, I pushed my will forward, forming a perfect bubble inches away from my face, allowing me to see and breathe.

Reaching out my right hand, I pulled the water in front of me, propelling my body forward at sharklike speed. Murky foaming ocean and general chaos erupted as one of the creature's legs slammed down directly in front of my face.

Dazed, I pulled back, realizing the water was at least twenty feet deep. I had propelled myself forward faster than expected. Refocusing my will, I glanced left just as Bo slammed into me like an out-of-control freight train.

More bubbles erupted around my thinning face shield before we both popped out of the water, the small, watertight seal around my head winking out of existence.

Bo looked at me in full nightmare mode, his chest heaving as deep black pools stared back at me from his deformed face.

"What the hell?" I coughed out as water slapped around us.

"It was about to skewer you. Time for me to leave," Bo

growled, not able to speak in his normal rumbly tone in this form.

"Yeah, can you . . ." I paused. "What are you doing?" I asked instead, knowing the look on his face. "Are you sitting here using the bathroom?"

Bo's grin widened until it finally reached the top of his head, showing his third row of teeth. Not only had the now naked demon tackled me underwater, but he was also taking a bathroom break in front of me, all while grinning.

Before I could start hurling insults at him, Bo vanished underwater. Right as I was about to take a deep breath, the crab let out an odd, high-pitched whine, followed by its front right leg being pulled under.

I stared in amazement as the creature reared back, the front half of its leg now missing. Knowing what was coming, I sucked in a breath and dove again, focusing my will around my face and propelling myself forward out from under the crab's now falling body.

Bo had basically kicked its front leg out from underneath it. With the rapid change in balance, the lack of half its leg lurched the creature forward, effectively making it fall under the weight of its claws. It was clear the crab was not used to its newfound weight, and that pesky little thing called gravity.

Sensing that Bo was now out of the water, I glanced forward, only to see the crab looking directly at me. A mix of panic and lack of interest in seafood for the next decade swept over me as the claw I hadn't noticed popped out of the water, snapping shut around me.

After the initial shock wore off and stars stopped floating around my head, I quickly realized that the creature's claw was so large it couldn't completely close around me. I also realized I was completely stuck, not to mention it had dragged me back underwater.

Mental images of crabs went through my thoughts. *Can it eat me? Does it have large, pointy teeth?* All things someone like myself would think right before they were about to die at the hands of oversize dinner.

I then remembered I had, in fact, watched a documentary on crabs. In it, they described how crabs ate their food. It went something like this:

A crab's mouth is made up of hard, pointy things, which have different uses. One pair of jaws holds the food (ME), while other mouthparts break said food (ME) into small bits and put them into the crab's mouth.

But you may be wondering, *Max, what about the teeth?* That was the part that got my ass in motion. For the most part, crabs had teeth inside their stomachs in what was commonly known as a gastric mill.

This entire train of thought lasted only a handful of seconds, as I quickly realized the creature was slowly moving me toward its fluttering mouth. Much to my benefit, the crab was simply trying to eat me instead of tearing me apart.

Remembering my initial plan, I pulled my hands forward, pushing my remaining will into tendrils of hellfire, and launched them in several directions, effectively turning the water into a boiling pot.

I was ready for this; I slashed upward, cutting the claw in half, before shooting toward the surface. While doing so, I also pushed as much water away from my body as possible without losing any friction.

After a few short seconds, I rocketed out of the water again, forming a bubble around me as the water hissed and crackled while boiling.

The once grayish shell of the crab's back was now turning red under the heat of the water. I did notice the creature wasn't thrashing, meaning my initial push of hellfire had gone directly into its face and mouth, making its end quick and painless. Its back, now floating, looked like an island of spiked, red Georgia clay floating in the surf.

Making it to the shore, a group of marshals, including James, stood by Phil. The looks on their faces made me stop and turn.

The smell hit me before the realization of just how crazy the entire scene looked, or for that matter, now smelled. The air in my lungs kicked and screamed to stay down before my body finally took over, forcing me to take another breath of the warm, rotting, cooked seafood.

It was the type of smell that didn't slowly knock one out; rather, the type that slapped you in the face, then continued to do so.

"Where's Petro?" I asked. Phil opened his mouth, only to lurch up what looked like several half-eaten doughnuts.

James walked over stoically, holding out a can of salve. "It's enchanted. It will make the smell go away. Before Kim left, she handed me a case of the stuff." He sighed, still looking confused by what he was looking at.

Last month, Kim had decided to take a much-needed long-term break from not only the marshals' office but, as it appeared, everything else. We'd had a few good months after recovering from our injuries, but like most times in our line of work, things had gotten busy, and time grew short. We were still fast friends and, on occasion, would have what Petro liked to call adult sleepovers.

After a few seconds of getting myself and Phil back in order, I walked over to James. "This scene needs to be cleared."

"I figured as much when the call came in. Carvel has a group of Mages heading this way as we speak. Is this normal?" James asked, still staring at the water.

"About as normal as Bo the demon running out of the ocean, naked as a jaybird, with a grin on his face—or whatever it's called when he's all crazy," Phil chimed in, now standing up straight, describing Bo as he'd left the scene while Max was still in the water.

"I'm going to have to have a chat with him about that," I said as two gates opened up by the marshal's vehicles.

The Council was now making good use of Mags-Tech's temporary gate ports. I was pretty sure the marshals had brought one with them. These had become known more as portals than actual natural gates.

James, while being a regular, was also a genius. Over the past few years, he had earned a spot on Ed's team, which, thanks to me, was now in the business of artifact retrieval. At least that's what they kept telling everyone. Or better yet, where the checks I cashed for being on retainer always came from.

"Oh, before I forget, mate. Bo said you might want to take a shower and that he will be around later tonight," Phil sighed, turning away from the water.

"I'm not sure what else we can do here," I noted, seeing if I recognized any of the Mages while retrieving my coat and pistol.

James picked up a small seashell, throwing it into the surf. "We're good. I have a feeling you two will be up to your necks in paperwork with this one."

"Ah, well. It's about time for some lunch. Not to mention I bet those crazy animal people will be showing up looking for who did this," Phil replied, losing interest in the entire situation at the mention of paperwork.

"If you say seafood, we aren't friends anymore," I joked as Phil started whistling, heading toward the Black Beast, my old trusty Dodge.

CHAPTER 2

Lucky Richard

"I'm not saying it's all bad," Inspector Richard Holder, better known as Dick Holder, grumbled in his thick British accent, standing in Ed's office in the Council halls, cramming a handful of overly crunchy chips in his mouth.

"Right. I was surprised it took them this long after the incident at Stonehenge," Ed replied, making a face at the grotesque display of eating taking place in front of him.

"Max, what do you think?" Dick asked, licking his fingers.

"Well, just like Ed stated. After everything, it was just a matter of time till the Council offered you a seat at the table," I said, wondering where Jenny and the others were.

Ed had been talking about the run-in with the Soul Dealers in the alternate version of Stonehenge. The entire ordeal with the Kracken and losing Ned was still very fresh on everyone's minds.

While not an end-of-the-world type situation, a handful of hellions and Soul Dealers had escaped into the countryside. I didn't completely understand the logic, but they couldn't leave Britain. Dealing with it was one of the many reasons Inspector

Richard Holder, better known as Dick, had been given a seat on the Council.

After taking down Bruce Teach and Carol Darkwater last year, the silver lining of the entire situation was that things had been relatively calm closing that chapter in the book. Dick had now gained a seat on the Council representing the entirety of the British regular authorities. To be clear, this didn't include MI6 or other military groups, just the old OTN crew, the Dunn, and oddly enough, a direct line to the queen. We still had yet to figure out the logic behind that decision, but as noted, it had come from the queen herself.

"The missus is happy about it, at least. Max, I need to have a word before you leave," Dick insisted as he walked toward the door, laughing at something he was about to say. "Oh, and I heard Carvel's a little crabby today."

Ed and I looked at each other, snickering not at the joke itself but the infectious laugh the man had.

"You know, I still haven't figured that one out," I said, referring to Inspector Holder.

"You do know about his wife?" Ed asked, clearly on one of his paths to explaining something. Mind Mages always had a roundabout way of doing that.

"No, I knew he was married, but other than that . . ." I shrugged.

"Come to find out his wife is a witch. And not just any type of witch, but what they like to call themselves . . . cookers," Ed informed me, walking over with a sealed envelope.

"Cookers? Let me guess, they do their potions through food, and that guy loves food," I huffed as Ed just clicked his teeth, agreeing.

"Here, a letter from Jamison came in via the Messenger the other day. I meant to call you, but things got a little busy after yesterday's events."

Ed walked back behind his desk as Jenny, Phil, and Petro entered the room, all looking at a small wooden board.

"Oi, look at the pretty boy. Check this thing out, bruther. It's an Atticus board," Phil bellowed as everyone circled Ed's desk.

"We just got this in from Greece. It is sort of like a map, but it's not a map. If you are looking for something and know how to use this, it will point you in the right direction," Jenny explained to the group as Ed cleared his throat.

"It also has another neat little trick. It can store, or does store, vast amounts of knowledge. Kind of like an ancient laptop. Every king and queen used to have one of these. Here," Ed added, reaching for the board.

After a few seconds of concentration, burnt words started to appear on the flat wooden surface, a burnt cherrywood smell wafting from the aged slab. The only thing the board presented to the group were two simple words: *The Pillars.*

"Isn't that interesting," Jenny said, pursing her lips in thought.

"Must be about the four Pillars of the Planes. The old bedtime story," Phil added leaning over, making sure the tablet didn't burn his now grown beard.

"Mom used to read me a bedtime story about the four Pillars. I hadn't thought about that in ages," I added as Petro landed on my shoulder.

"Need old Uncle Petro to read you a bedtime story? I just got a new copy of late-night encounters," Petro swooned, doing his hip gyration.

"Casey know about that?" I asked as everyone grinned.

"Ever since Neil was born, we haven't had much time to ourselves. I'm just trying to spice things up, you know. I learned all kinds of new things. My favorite is—" I cut him off.

"We get it, buddy. I'll have to ask my mom about the book she used to read me," I said as Frank opened the door.

"They're ready. We're going to the subchambers. Looks like another one of those secret meetings," Frank stated in his flat, cool-guy tone. I noticed he was wearing the same bland suit he'd had on when we first met at Ed's law office, Rose & Vendal.

"I'm going to stay here and check this thing out for a few minutes. I'll be right behind you guys," Petro buzzed, landing by the wooden tablet.

I had on my favorite pair of dark jeans for today's meeting, and a halfway decent blue button-up shirt with the sleeves rolled up. In reality, I was tired of getting beat up for my choice of clothes when on official business.

The subchamber was just as I'd left it last time. A large U-shaped table curved around the space with a walk-through and several tables in the center. Hanging on the room's far wall was a large board for taking notes and hanging whatever map one thought they would need. While old in style, it was clear that decisions and important conversations occurred here.

Dark stone walls and dull lighting finished the eclectic room off as Ana Vlad looked up from a stack of pictures on the middle table. Davros, Angel, Titus, Lorel, Carvel, Mouth, James, the new leader of the OTN marshals replacing Kim, and a handful of random-looking officials sat around the table mumbling over different topics.

"Ah, we can get started," Ana informed the room in her silky yet authoritative tone.

Phil leaned forward, whispering in my ear, "They don't have any snack cakes or tea out. This must be official."

I nodded, agreeing with his assessment. Not one person in the room was smiling. Except for Angel. She was smirking.

"So, this kind of feels like a holy inquisition," I rattled out, not realizing that things in history weren't always what I believed them to be.

"Excuse me?" Carvel choked out, looking down his pointy nose at me. While I had saved his life and garnered favor with his mom, the man still generally didn't like me.

"Well, you know?" I asked, fishing to take back my statement.

"Oh, I do. I can assure you the Inquisition was substantially more palatable than dealing with you," Carvel grumbled as Ana rolled her eyes unnecessarily.

"Well, not all of us were into that kind of stuff back then," Ana said. Carvel returned the eye gesture.

I had a feeling he was about to bring up her good old brother, the one and only Vlad the Impaler, better known as —you guessed it—Dracula. From what I understood, he'd also been part of the Order of the Dragon, a rather nasty group of religious zealots that rumors insisted were still very active. Ned had insisted I study up on these types of groups when he'd first started as my sponsor.

"Right, enough of that. We're all present and accounted for," Ed interjected as we took our seats around the table. Ana stayed in the center section, leading the conversation. Petro parked on the end of the table in front of me with his feet dangling off the edge, deciding to join us just in time.

"Good. The Supreme Council called this meeting to discuss the most recent event. A few important curiosities occurred with this one, which has garnered some additional attention," Ana told the group, walking in a slow circle. She failed to mention Bo's absence.

"You mean like the small event becoming a crab the size of an office building?" I asked, wanting to get to the point. Ed simply pushed into my mind to shut up.

"Something like that. As I am sure everyone is aware, the initial reading on the event was minor, much like the apparitional events sprouting up all over Jacksonville," Ana continued. Ed, in an odd gesture, raised his hand.

"Apparitional?" he inquired. The room went as still as a teenager sneaking in after hours after stepping on a squeaky floorboard.

"Ghosts," Ana clarified.

"Right, why haven't we been informed of this?" Ed asked, pushing more than usual. He had noticeably not been fully briefed on the current situation.

"Ed, you know with your new position there are some things that are not immediately brought to your attention. It is not on purpose," Ana stated flatly, the truth of her words carrying weight.

Ed nodded in understanding. "Understood. But I have a feeling that's about to change," he noted. Ana nodded.

"Correct as always. There is a reason we have been keeping this quiet. After the event on the beach, it is all but certainly confirmed," Ana continued. Davros interrupted her.

"There are very few things that can explain recent events with the ley lines and other current situations. We hoped it wasn't the case, but as Ana mentioned, after the incident on the beach, it's now very real," he rumbled out before losing interest in the conversation.

"Okay, we get it. What is this 'thing' you all keep saying is confirmed?" I blurted out before Ed or any of the others could. I noticed Jenny sitting with a concerned look on her face.

Titus took a deep breath as Ana sat on the edge of one of the desks. Vs often did this type of thing to make people feel at ease. Much like when Frank would act like he was breathing or huffing out a lungful of air.

"We believe one of the four Pillars has been found, moved, and/or taken," Ana declared. Our group collectively looked at each other after our previous conversation in the office.

"It would make sense," Jenny spoke up, finally breaking from her train of thought. "All the misfires, then the apparitions, and now . . . well . . ." she trailed off, not knowing the rest.

"As you all noted in the report, the creature was a regular crustacean. This would mean that it absorbed an unimaginable amount of power to reach its final size. That is why we believe the event only registered as minor. It might have been a fluke. We don't know," Ana said, laying it all out.

I opened my mouth, only to immediately shut it, not knowing what direction this was going.

Jenny, seeing this, chimed in, clarifying what she had been thinking about. "The Pillars are like drain plugs in the fabric of time and space, or more specifically, magic. It is kind of like uncorking a bottle. With the spikes coming from the ley lines, I was sure the Council would start looking in that direction sooner or later."

"That's a pretty big coincidence from the office," I mentioned.

Carvel slowly turned toward me. "What?" the crusty old Mage huffed out.

"An Atticus board. We were messing with it before coming in, and it noted something about the Pillars," I added as the room remained silent for a few seconds too long.

"Ed," Ana started. "Where is this Atticus board from?"

"It's my understanding it came from the Plane, and more specifically, it's one of Titania's. That is why we were tasked to acquire it," Ed answered as Lorel stood up. She had remained silent for most of the meeting.

"If this is true, that means it is directing you toward the Pillar on the Plane. I'm sure everyone is aware there is one on the Plane, one in the Under, one in the Over, and one here on Earth. I am also sure you are all aware that there is only one we truly know the location of: the one on the Plane," Lorel added with a confused look on her face.

"Didn't you get one of those keys to go see the old queen bee?" Phil piped up. Everyone turned to stare at me.

I had, for the most part, kept that a secret. While I fully intended on going to meet Titania, I was waiting on Jamison or Aslynn to get back in contact with me first. Petro had offered to guide me, but I needed something more official and direct.

The other side of the coin was that unless you had permanent permission from the Supreme Council, any Earthborn Mage had to get authorization to go to the Plane. The trip was highly regulated and watched. In theory, I probably had one of the few back doors to the place.

"Well, since the cat's out of the bag. I was invited a while back to visit the queen. She gave me the gate key to the Plane. Before anyone can ask, no, I haven't been yet. I'm still waiting to hear back from Jamison," I said before anyone could question me. I conveniently left out Aslynn's name.

"We have been wondering about Jamison and his sister's whereabouts for some time. We assume they are both on the Plane. After the situation with Ned, their father, we supposed they needed some time to themselves," Titus belted out. The man couldn't be further from the truth if he got in a Ferrari and drove the opposite direction with the accelerator slammed to the floorboard.

"Yeah, something like that," I replied as Ed, picking up on my mood, took back over the conversation.

"So, what are we here for?" Ed asked, figuring it was time to get to the point. The Supreme Council wanted something.

"Max, Aslynn was a representative of Queen Titania. We were well aware of her gift and request for an audience with you," Ana said, pausing unnecessarily once again. It was getting annoying. "We need you to go to the Plane and meet with the queen. She has to be aware something is going on."

I looked over at Lorel. "So why aren't you taking care of all this, whatever it may be? You have to be in contact with her, right?" I asked, seeing her mood shift to a darker shade of gray.

"Things don't work like that on the Plane. She is the High Fae queen. To put it bluntly, while humans were figuring out how to make fire in a cave, she had already lived a dozen lifetimes. I have only met Titania once. Someone informed her of my role here on Earth. She nodded without a word, then I was shown out of her chambers. I'm not sure you understand how big of a deal it is to be asked to hold court with her. I do get messages, but that's about it," Lorel relayed.

While she was not being completely honest about their relationship, Lorel was right. I didn't have any actual idea. I just knew that it hadn't been on my list of things to do up until now.

"I've been meaning to go. I was just waiting on a few things to line up. So . . ." I said, drawing it out. The truth was, I was still waiting to hear back from Jamison and Aslynn. "Is this another one of those off-the-books type things?"

"When you're involved, it always is," Angel chuckled as the others joined it. I couldn't argue the point.

My relationships and opening of the consulting firm had allowed the Council to navigate some rather gray areas regarding the regular authorities. According to Ed and Jenny, I wasn't the only one. Just the only one with a demon sidekick, not to mention that I could use hellfire.

"I guess I need to pack a bag?" I asked genuinely, not sure what the trip would entail.

"Cute," Carvel croaked out. "I'm sure you have everything you need with you, including how to use the gate. Titania will know you're coming and be ready for you. She is rather hospitable. That is, if you stay on her good side."

"Sounds like I need to read up on Fae courtesy. I'm going to need some backup. If something is going on, I have a feeling things could get sketchy fast. Plus, I don't know my way around," I said, starting to focus on the task at hand.

"Your Pixie companion would be a great guide. I would recommend only taking whom you deem necessary," Lorel added. Again, there was a sense of caution in what she was saying.

"I take it that means no Bo," I noted flatly, already knowing the answer.

"That would be problematic at best, and more than likely catastrophic. Titania may take it as an act of aggression," Lorel again said carefully.

"Alright. Phil? You in?" I asked.

He winked. "You bet, bruther. I hear they have Ambrosia flowing on tap there," Phil accepted, no signs of worry in his tone.

"Right, it's settled. We will work with Max and get things ready," Ed declared, standing up in a show of wanting to leave the meeting.

"Not so fast," Davros spoke up after being silent for most of the conversation. "Max, you need to focus on the other gates in the Postern. We know you have a special bond with the room, but we also know you have yet to work out some of the other gates. Don't forget what I gave you."

He was referring to the coin he had given me, and the one I'd acquired from Penance at FA's after taking my first trip to the Everwhere.

I just shook my head as I stood up, following Ed's lead. After a few more minutes of general back-and-forth about the incident on the beach, we were cleared to go. Ed motioned the group back toward his office.

CHAPTER 3

Here We Go Again . . .

Before making it to Ed's office, Dick grabbed my arm with his pudgy fingers. "A word?"

"Sure, I almost forgot," I replied, surprised by the tone of his voice.

"I got a favor to ask of you. I knew they wouldn't let that Bo fellow go to the Plane. Figured if he's not busy doing whatever it is he does, he could help me out with a little . . . *situation*," Dick said, drawing out the last word for way too long.

"I'm not his keeper; the best I can do is ask. What type of *situation* are we talking about?" I inquired, copying his inflection of the word.

"The Crown has a little vermin problem," Dick replied, wanting me to figure out the rest. Coming from someone who had hated everything magical a few years ago, the now severely balding man had come a long way. Chloe's actions had forced him to accept the Balance and the following Accords, not to mention the irony that he had, in fact, been married to a witch for thirty years without knowing.

"Let me guess. You still have a few rogue hellions running around the countryside," I asked in the form of a knowing statement.

"Something like that, but from what I understand, running around the tunnels under London. I was asked specifically by the head cheese to get some assistance," Inspector Holder stated, the pride at having a direct conduit to the royal family coming through in his voice.

"You know Bo's not really the type to fly under the radar. I'll ask him," I promised as Dick held out his hand, the firm handshake reverberating through my entire body.

"Max, you're good people. A nutter, but still, on the right side of things," the short, fat, pudgy inspector told me as he walked off.

"What was that all about?" Jenny asked when I entered, closing the door firmly behind me.

"Dick needs a hand with something," I said, not realizing the words coming out of my mouth until Phil went on a two-minute joke routine about the good inspector.

"Right, enough of that. Max, are you good?" Ed asked me, knowing I wasn't.

"I guess. Petro, I'm guessing you already heard?" I directed at him as he zipped into the air, dusting. He was excited.

"Did I! It's been years since I went home. My brothers will be super excited. We'll have a party like no other! We'll have balloons and Elf Juice and bug pie, you name it, boss! The Plane is your crab!" Petro exclaimed as I held out my hand, letting him land.

"Oyster, the world is your oyster, ah . . . never mind. We can go see your brothers, but I have a feeling it's not going to be that type of trip," I explained as his wings slightly drooped.

"Agreed," Ed interjected, walking over to his desk. "Phil, I don't see a problem with you going. However, this needs to be official," he said, letting the man know this wasn't a paid vacation.

All joking aside, Phil was a professional through and through when needed. It's just when he was off the clock that things could get a little dicey. But hey, who am I to talk.

"I'm guessing we need to leave as soon as possible," I noted, taking a deep breath. "I just need to get a few things situated first," I finished, feeling Jamison's note in my pocket. Something was telling me to read it later, out of the eye and earshot of others.

Messages often had that effect on me. Almost like I could feel their intent. Bo said it was the demon side of me. The writer left a trail of essence if the message was written by hand, which Fae mostly did, being old-fashioned as they often were. At the same time, a message was just that, ink on paper relaying something.

"Lorel stated she would let us know if it's a good time. We will have a better idea by tomorrow afternoon. That should give you enough time to get ready," Jenny added, putting her hand on Ed's shoulder.

"Max, I wanted everyone in here before things get into motion, which I can assure you they are about to be, to discuss some things. The Supreme Council, including a few of the members we just met with, are holding something back. I'm not sure what, but when I started looking around, there was a ward in place preventing me from going further," Ed stated flatly. He was a powerful Mind Mage and had a knack for figuring things out.

"I picked up on that too. It feels like I'm about to be the cheese in the mousetrap again," I replied as Jenny walked away from Ed.

"I'm not sure that's it. I think they're running blind here. Ana was not her normal self, if there is such a thing. I wouldn't doubt they have others looking for the Pillars. This just sounds like the best lead they have. If someone is messing with the Pillars, it would be disastrous. Magic could disappear or spike, as we've been seeing. Even worse, the Old Gods could use this. We know that's the endgame here," Jenny said, grounding the group.

She was right, as always. The main concern had become apparent, even with all the recent distractions, including the Thule Society, Darkwater, Lilith, and the Soul Dealers. The Old Gods were on the move. Everyone and everything had been jockeying for position since the Balance had been struck and Accords signed.

"That lass was acting different," Phil interjected with a handful of his usual Captain Obvious wisdom. "I think they know a little more about Max's abilities than they are letting on. Think about it. Why him?"

"They need him on the Plane. You guys know what that means with him being . . . you know, a bit of a mixed bag," Petro chimed in.

"You're probably right. Max, I'm not sure how the Plane will affect you. Maybe Petro's correct. They are betting on you having some extra gas in your tank," Ed said, pulling a map out of his desk.

"Bo said something about that. A normal demon on the Plane would be significantly stronger than they already are here," I added, straining to remember the conversation.

"The issue is with your genealogy. We don't really know how it will affect you. Plus, to be clear, things on the Plane are just that much stronger. Think of it as more of a level playing field," Jenny spoke with finality.

I stood up, walking over to Ed as he unrolled the map on the table. "What's this?"

"It's a map," Ed joked, smirking. Ever since he'd started

dating Jenny, according to Phil, *"The arse found his funny bone."*

"It's a map of the main area around the queen's castle," Petro explained, landing on it, dusting lightly.

The map was obviously older than history itself. Burnt edges and faded handwriting adorned the document. In the center was a sketch of a castle surrounded by mountains and a wall. Other geographical features made themselves known as well. These included a large river cutting the map in half.

The top right identified a set of mountain ranges capped in what looked like snow and a dark, shaded valley. On the bottom right, what looked to be open fields made up most of the area, with random waterways and small bridges throughout. A handful of villages peppered the landscape. The bottom left produced a massive forest bubbling up on the map, showing trees, hills, and randomly marked paths.

But what really got my attention was the massive tower surrounded by clouds on the top left of the map. Spiked mountains and blacked-out areas gave this section an ominous feel.

"Is this the entire Plane?" I asked as everyone deferred to Petro.

"Nope. Those are the main dominions. Oh, and don't forget distance doesn't work the same way on the Plane. Beyond the four corners of the map lay vast kingdoms all centered around Queen Titania's palace. That is where the Plane's Pillar is supposed to be kept," Petro said, looking at the forested area with pride.

"Is that where you're from? The forests?" I asked. Petro nodded again, dusting lightly.

"Sure am. There's a village by that path right there. That's where my people are from," Petro replied. It was evident from his inflection that while he loved being on Earth, he still missed home.

"I'm looking forward to seeing Bosley and the others again," I added as he smiled, stroking his majestic mustache. It had become a long-term part of his overall look. Not to mention Casey kept complimenting him on it.

"We need to make sure we are keeping in contact with each other. Jenny, do we have anything that will let us talk while the team is on the Plane?" Ed asked, making a good point.

"The normal communicators won't work. Maybe there's something in the archives. I'll get the girls together and get them to look. Macey and Lacey have been on vacation, so I'm sure they'll want to get back to work. You know those two," Jenny added, nodding at Petro.

"I'm sure Casey will be all over this," Petro added, wrinkling his face. "You know she's always talked about seeing the Plane and where I'm from. Don't forget most Pixies have never been to the Plane. They were born here after the Great War."

"Right. It's settled. Max, Phil, get yourselves ready. Petro and Jenny will work with the ladies to find a way we can communicate. Hopefully, we will hear something from Lorel soon. And Max, before you ask, you are on the clock and will get paid," Ed relayed, laying out the plans for everyone.

"What if anything else pops up? You know, like giant crustaceans?" I added, making a good point.

"I talked with Carvel this morning. Angel was in that meeting because she is being put in charge of the area. The Vs are being pulled in more than usual here. Ever since Cecil and the other Vs were killed, they have been rather dormant. I'm glad things are getting back to normal," Ed answered my question.

Truth be told, I was getting more concerned by the day. The regular population didn't need more excuses not to like or accept the magical community. While comparatively small in size, the community had a rather loud presence.

"I was kind of thinking about asking Angel to go, then I remembered Vs and the Plane don't mix," I recalled, knowing about her alternate persona. She was, in fact, Two, a member of the Night Stalkers, a military group of authorized vampires legally able to consume human blood.

"A V couldn't get there if they tried. It's nasty business. Plus, Titania would have you all killed immediately," Ed said, rolling up the map before handing it to me. "Take care of this," he finished sternly.

"Let's go, guys," I huffed, pulling out an Evergate stone. A gate immediately shimmered to life. It was time to make the doughnuts.

CHAPTER 4

Ghostly Reminders

Petro and I stood in the lab eating cheeseburgers. "You think this is gonna work, boss?" Petro asked, taking a long, slurping draw from his soda as we looked at the sizable, aged book splayed open on the table.

"Maybe. I need to get back to work on the other gates," I admitted, studying a picture of the two coins.

"So you're thinking these have something to do with the Plane?" Petro continued, taking another bite of his burger.

"That's the only thing I can come up with. There's a Postern in the Everwhere, so why not the Plane? Maybe not a mirror, but the Planesgate has to have a solid twin on the other side. Something's just telling me to keep these handy. Plus, they are from the Plane," I said, also having the key to the Timegate on the table.

"I think you're right, boss. Where do you think the Planesgate comes out?" Petro asked as I pulled out Tom's journal.

"Well, that's up for debate. Tom noted it comes out in a set area. What set area, I'm not sure. I was hoping it worked like the Seekergate, but I don't think it does. My thought is it comes out right here," I guessed, pointing at the gate-looking icon located in the middle of what appeared to be a palace.

Flattening out the journal, I pointed to what looked like an identical sketch. "It looks the same," Petro agreed.

"That's what I'm thinking. How big is the palace?" I asked scratching my lightly stubbled chin.

Petro squinted his eyes. "Big as the horses ass that lives in it."

Tom and I had gone over traveling on the Plane. Gating in the regular world was flexible with the right tools; you were fundamentally tearing a hole in the fabric of reality and stepping into the ether, or whatever it was he called it. According to Tom, the Plane was a different story. Gates were property and only placed in specific points. He compared it to a toll road having a much steeper fee to use.

Tom had also mentioned the Fae were more apt to use portals. Confusing as it was, my understanding was that on Earth, we gate, and on the Plane, one uses portals—artificial gates that, while similar, are created differently. Gates were more natural and mysterious, whereas portals were strictly artificial spells. He'd compared them to the new Mags-Tech gating devices that we had been seeing more and more of.

Don't get me wrong; gates are still hard to come by, but as mentioned, one could get just about anywhere they needed to go with the right tools, such as the Postern.

A thought crossed my mind as I clicked my tongue. Jamison and Aslynn were both supposed to be on the Plane. I patted my pockets, searching for Jamison's note.

"I almost forgot about this," I said, taking a bite of my cheeseburger. I inspected the envelope, leaving a grease stain as I held it up to the light.

"Oh, yeah. I'm sure they can help. They owe you one, the way I see it," Petro reminded me.

"Yeah, something like that," I muttered, setting down my food, wiping my greasy hands off on my jeans.

The envelope was closed with the typical old-style wax seal. The paper was a crisp parchment that held weight. We'd learned the Messenger appreciated a well put together note.

I should have known by the official manner the letter had been delivered that it was important. The first sentence confirmed this. Clearing my throat, I read the message out loud.

Max,

Tom is in trouble and being held in Titania's castle. I can't get into more detail, but you need to be careful. Something is going on that even I can't work out. People are worried here, just as I'm sure they are there, about the misfires. I am relatively certain you will be heading here at some point. When you do, I'll know. Don't head directly to the palace. I'll find you.

JD

The one thing the movies about that wizarding school had gotten right was that letters like this had a bad habit of spontaneously combusting.

"Shit!" I exclaimed as the parchment ignited in my hand. Petro snickered, shaking his head.

"Easy, hellfire boy. A little fire get you all worked up?"

"These damn letters do it every time. They scare the hell out of me, like a dangerous jack-in-the-box. Remember when I read that one in my truck and about set the Black Beast on fire?" I reminisced sarcastically.

"Well, it sounds like everything's in motion, boss," Petro said, refocusing. "This is turning into a quest."

"No, I'm not calling it that. Next thing you know, monsters will show up, and all kinds of other crap will go wrong," I responded as Petro grinned.

"Quest. The ladies love heroes on a quest. Casey will not be able to contain herself," Petro declared, doing his usual routine.

I huffed, knowing the actual absurdity of the unfolding events. Overgrown crabs—don't really bother me too much. Big lizard monsters and werewolves—I can work with that. Meeting Benjamin Franklin and realizing he's not only a senior fitness personality but a general asshole—okay. A quest to another Plane of existence to meet a queen in a castle? This made it into a new level of *what the hell am I doing with my life.*

"I'm going to need some time to get my head right. If this is true, it just adds another layer of complications. I need to let Ed know," I said, needing some fresh air.

"He's coming over later. I wouldn't wait too long. This might change things," Petro added, making a valid point.

"One thing at a time. Let's get out of here. I need to get away from this stuff for a couple of hours," I again huffed, needing to take a walk down a normal street and look at normal things.

Petro and I secured the lab and headed out to the downtown area. While still touristy, especially more so due to the Balance, it nevertheless provided an excellent opportunity to refocus.

We walked by the old Casa Monica hotel, garnering a few random stares as Petro hovered over my shoulder. In general, St. Augustine and the First Coast were noted as being one of the primary hubs for the magical community in the US. It wasn't out of the ordinary to see a random Pixie or V in the city. People often traveled here to witness just that.

"You think this is another of Tom's tricks?" I asked Petro as he set his lips in a flat line.

"I'm not sure, boss. He always seems to have the upper hand. You know, pulling strings even if he's in a cage," Petro replied. "Plus, he's supposed to be dead."

A group of small kids pointed at him with a round of *oh*'s and *ah*'s.

"That's what I'm starting to think. It's a little too convenient. It's not like I'm the only Mage around," I reflected as we walked into the main shopping area.

People hustled in random directions as a street performer made flowers appear out of thin air. The noise of the crowd and traffic driving by was oddly calming.

"Last time I checked, you weren't exactly a Mage, you know?" Petro reminded me with a grin, the edges of his majestic mustache not moving with the rest of his face.

I chuckled under my breath, knowing the hard truth he was telling me.

Looking to my right, an older lady walked out of one of those cheap T-shirt tourist traps, the ones with shirts declaring to the world the owner had visited Saint Augustine, Florida, or my new favorite ones proclaiming, "I'm a Wizard." All for the cool price of buy one, get one free.

"Is that Mom?" I mumbled to myself as the woman turned around, lighting up like a Christmas tree.

She was dressed in her normal witchlike ensemble consisting of a floral-patterned dress and flowing blouse, all topped off by an uncountable number of dangly bits of jewelry.

"Max! Such a surprise. Well, not really, but so good to see you," my mother exclaimed, garnering stares from the surrounding crowd. The bag in her hand made it to me first as she reached her arms out, hugging me.

One could say, as a quarter demon, I could move at unnatural speeds. But my mother coming in for a hug was another level of ninja-like reflexes.

"Oomph," I grunted as she squeezed me. I returned the

favor after air made its way back to my brain. "Hey, Mom, what's got you down here?"

In all reality, I was happy to see my mother. Much like with most parents and their offspring, that little thing called life got in the way, often making stints between seeing each other longer than intended by both parties.

"Oddest thing. There I was, drinking tea, and when I was done—*poof!* There they were," Mom rattled off, finally calming down.

"There were what?" I asked as Petro landed on a nearby tree branch.

"The tea leaves. They undoubtedly told me to come here," she said, pursing her lips. "Now, I just need to figure out why."

"Ah, the tea leaves. One day, I'll figure them out. Trust me. I've tried. Was it all blotchy? Is that how you say it?" I asked, getting concerned.

As a witch, my mother had detailed over dessert one night how she could use tea leaves as a form of divination, though she wasn't able to clearly understand what was going to happen or why. She could make out a general direction and overall topic of concern. She was obviously reading the tea leaves on purpose.

"Yes, precisely. Glad you listen to some of the things I say. So, what's going on?" Mom asked as I glanced at Petro.

The aroma of cooking popcorn filled my nostrils; the crowd around us had already lost interest in the scene. Two shops down the street, a performer started playing "Billie Jean" by Michael Jackson on an old beat-up saxophone.

"Let's grab some coffee at the small café on the corner. We can talk there," I recommended as she smiled.

After ten minutes of my mother screaming at my near

deaf father on the phone, we made our way to the café, skipping FA's.

"Let's hear it," Mom prompted as I set down two cups of freshly brewed coffee. They had even made a small cap for Petro.

"Remember that old story you used to read to me about the four Pillars?" I started, sipping the scalding-hot cup of go-juice. "It appears someone is messing with them. More specifically, the one on the Plane. The Council, in all its infinite wisdom, wants me to go save the day."

Mom sat reflectively sipping her cup. Petro dusted lightly, finally moving his wings, waiting on her response. Another long pause and sip followed before she spoke. "I understand why I got the message now. Max, are you sure about this?"

"That's the thing. Not soon after meeting with the Council, I found out that Gramps is being held by the queen, or something to that effect."

Again Mom paused, taking in what I was telling her. "That explains the quest part of the message I got," she said as Petro jumped up.

"See! A quest, I told ya! The ladies are going to love it!" Petro barked as Mom and I both glared at the Pixie, forcing him to settle back down with his cap of coffee.

"The thing is, it might just be Tom's quest. The tea leaves, while full of knowledge, aren't always specific. What was the last thing he was working on?" Mom asked as Petro and I looked at each other.

The more I thought about it, the more I realized I had no clue what he was truly up to. Last I knew, he had been finding a way to travel to Terrum. He had even visited Hades. While I wasn't sure why he hadn't confided in me, I was reasonably sure it was for a good reason. Even Oscar was sketchy on the details of his whereabouts.

"Something about finding what the Old Gods were up to. More specifically, I believe he was looking for a way to Terrum. Look, Mom, I'm not sure he even knew what he was doing last time I saw him. Everyone seems to think he was always looking for fool's gold," I said thoughtfully.

Mom let out a light giggle. "That he was. It makes sense that he was working on the Plane, then. You know, he wasn't exactly the most popular of Mages there. Tom is as old as any Mage I can remember meeting. That means he not only has many allies but just as many enemies. I've never been to the Plane nor met anyone close to the queen. If he is indeed there and in trouble with her, then you need to go. Here," she urged, handing me a small red book.

"Is that the book on the Pillars?" I asked, surprised by her foresight. It was like she was a full-on diviner at times and downplaying her ability to read tea leaves, if that was indeed what she was doing. Witches did have a rather handy knack for using several types of magic in different forms.

"It sure is," she answered.

"You saw that in the leaves as well?" Petro asked, amazed.

"Oh no. To some of us, it's obvious whatever is going on has something to do with the Pillars. So, it was more of an assumption after I received the divine intervention to come here," Mom said, grinning.

"This is perfect. I need to make sure I'm up to speed on this stuff. Do you know if the Plane has a version of the Postern?" I asked as she scrunched her face.

"Max, I know a lot of things, but I've never been to the Plane. All the stories I used to tell you as a child are thousands of years old. Be careful, and whatever you do, don't let them know you are more than a regular Mage," Mom recommended, standing up. "Well, they probably already know. I love you, and before I forget, your father wants to see you. The memory potion has worked wonders. He might even get back into the fold."

With that, we said our goodbyes, and my mother walked out into the darkening evening. While a little loopy at times, Mom was always full of wisdom and guidance; the type that let you feel confident in the decisions you were making, even if absolutely wrong.

After a few minutes of looking through the book, Petro broke the silence. "I think you're right, boss. This thing is a little too obvious. Even if the others don't know it, someone's driving this train."

Taking a deep breath, I shook my head. "Gramps," was all I said.

My phone rang, Phil's ringtone reminding us that he had *too much time on his hands*, a reference to Styx, one of Phil's favorite bands, and a recent potion incident.

What incident, you might wonder? Glad you asked. While working on a time-slowing potion, Phil accidentally spilled some on his hands, which led to several hours of his hands moving at sloth-like speeds. This had led to an evening of laughs as we had taken him to FA's and watched him drink beers at the speed of slow while getting frustrated.

"Hey, man—" I started. Phil cut me off.

"Bruther, there's a bunch of ghosts reported in your area. Like real ones, ooga booga and all. You still downtown?" Phil belted out. I was slightly confused about how he knew my location.

Ghosts were still somewhat of an abstract. From what I understood, only a handful of people had the ability to see them. Even more scarce was the ability to travel to the Everwhere and deal with them. At least according to Gramps.

"Petro and I are at a coffee shop in town. We don't see anything." As soon as the words left my mouth, a crashing wave of people started running down the street in random stages of *oh shit*. Luckily for us, my mother had walked in the opposite direction.

"Hello? Is this damn thing broken again?" Phil asked. He went through at least one phone a month.

I spoke up. "No. I hear you. I think I know where these things are. What makes you think they're ghosts? I didn't think that was a thing people saw?" I questioned, probably thinking too hard about the situation. As of lately, things had been less than average.

"Bunch of normies started calling the coppers, asking if they had any ghostbusters. Next thing I know, I got a call from James," Phil blurted out. He sounded out of breath and was more than likely trying to get to a gate.

"I'll drop you a pin of our location. Get here as fast as you can," I told him. Phil paused.

"You're going to drop me a pen? Like write me a note?" Phil chuffed, still at least a decade behind on smartphone technology. Petro dusted lightly.

"Just let me know when you get downtown. I'm heading to the plaza in front of the bridge. I have a feeling whatever it is, it's coming from there," I sighed, hanging up.

CHAPTER 5

Who You Gonna Call? Maxbusters?

G lowing at random intervals, four hazy forms reached for random screaming people. At the far end of the plaza, a man was attempting to square off with one of the apparitions, his hands held out in front of him as if about to pounce. I had a feeling the spirited young man was about to become the evening's first casualty.

One thing was immediately clear. These were ghosts, or at least, creatures from the Everwhere. Transparent and glowing, not fully in one place.

"Petro!" I barked as he swooped down.

"Yeah, boss. There's four of them. I don't see anyone down yet," Petro spit out.

"See that guy down there trying to fight one? Zip over there and change his mind. I'm going to see what I can do here," I instructed, bringing Durundle to life. "*IGNIS!*"

The glowing blade infused into my own body sprang to life. For today, it had decided to do its best lightsaber impersonation, precise and ready to be put to work.

I finally registered on the closest entity's radar. While not fully solid on good old Earth, its rather disturbing features were clear enough. Pearl-colored skin was stretched over wire-thin muscle. Long, greasy-looking hair sprouted from the top of its head, which was another issue. It had no face, just a blank canvas with various bumps and lines shadowing its skull. Topping this all off were hands with not fingers but claws, looking like they came straight from hell.

Just as the shit show in front of me finally settled into the recesses of my brain, the creature lunged forward, swiping as it moved. I swung my hellfire blade down as the two of us almost passed through each other. Neither of our attacks affected the other.

I noticed that the apparition bounced off me like magnets repelling each other. Taking a deep breath, I scanned the area, realizing that the ghosts were doing more scaring than actual damage. Just as the thought crossed my mind, Petro dove out of the sky, hovering with his sword out.

"Boss, they're getting stronger. It's like they're not fully here yet. I'm thinking we have maybe five minutes tops," Petro informed me as the creature again sprang forward, simply bouncing off me.

"How do you know that?" I asked.

Petro tapped his nose. "Whatever they are, their scent is getting stronger by the second," he chirped, taking back off into the sky. He had convinced the young man that fist fighting a ghost was not in his best interests. Or he'd just threatened to dust him—either option was acceptable.

"Bruther!" Phil bellowed, winded from the short run from the apartment. He was holding what we liked to call his wannabe Thor hammer, which in turn, usually generated a tirade of insults from the man.

Instead of leaping forward again, the creature started slowly backing up toward the Bridge of Lions.

I ran to Phil, pointing at the bridge. "They're not yet solid enough to do any harm, but they're looking for something," I blurted out as Phil scrunched his face, squeezing the handle of his hammer.

"Where are their bloody faces?" Phil asked, noticing the lack of facial features.

"Not sure, but I gotta get to the Everwhere. You good hanging here making sure they don't start messing with anyone?" I asked, forming a plan.

"Why the hell not. James is on his way with some marshals. Mate, this is a new one for me, but I'll hold the fort down," Phil joked, referring to the old fort by the bridge.

I grinned, putting out my hellfire blade and calling for Petro. It was evident the creatures were looking for something, the sounds of banging and yelling telling us they were gaining their footing in the real world.

"Petro! We're gating to the Everwhere then to the plaza. Hopefully, we can take care of these things there. I'm pretty sure Lana or someone already knows this is going on," I said. Phil nodded while Petro took off toward the apartment. He was going to tell Casey it would be a late night.

Phil gripped his hammer as I pulled out an Evergate stone, pushing my will into it before stepping through into the Postern. Since moving to the apartment and subsequent offices of Abaddon and Associates, Devin had somehow created a door connecting to the Postern upstairs in my room. He had also worked a path to Gramps's old lab, which was now mine.

I opened the door to the apartment, having saved myself from running by gating, just as Petro came zooming down the hallway.

"All good, boss. Casey said she'd have food waiting for us when we got back," Petro relayed, smoothing out his still majestic mustache.

Truth be told, Pixie cooking was an acquired taste.

M&M's Spaghetti and several days in a row of Golden Grahams made up most of Petro's diet. Casey had, however, passed the cereal test on the first go. I think she may have gotten a few pointers.

The Postern in the Everwhere was dark, cool, and damp as always, and like the rest of the Atheneum, covered in an odd, foggy haze. Since our final run-in with the Soul Dealers, both versions of the facility were in varying stages of disrepair.

On Earth, the Atheneum was getting repaired and upgraded. In the Everwhere, things hadn't changed. The facility was still heavily damaged.

As predicted, I walked to the door to find Lana standing in front of a row of knocked-over shelves.

"I take it you were down by the bridge and heard I was coming," I guessed as the warrior Elf rolled her shoulders.

"Yes," was all she said, raising an eyebrow as Petro flew out of the Postern.

"Hey, Lana!" Petro bellowed louder than needed. This garnered a smile on the Elf's face.

"It's good to see you, Warrior of the Freeze. We need to get moving. If those creatures slip much further, they will be on your side," Lana cautioned.

"And that's bad?" I asked as we all walked back into the Postern.

"I'm here to make sure these types of things don't happen. And to be completely honest, I'm not sure those things are spirits. I need to get close to one." Lana was pointing out she had trouble dealing with the creatures. This wasn't good, as she was undoubtedly one of the toughest individuals I had ever met.

"Alright, here's what I'm thinking. We gate into the middle of the plaza—those things were almost to the bridge.

Lana, you keep them distracted from a distance while Petro and I get up close and personal," I laid out, looking at the two.

"Your plan sounds reasonable for once." Lana smirked.

"Was that a joke?" I asked, not used to the banter.

Lana just swept her flowing leather armor over, revealing a row of throwing knives as she checked them. Petro looked at me, shaking his head. We had realized all that time in the Everwhere had caught up with Lana, and her people skills had dissipated over the years of fighting monsters and lost souls. She did, on the other hand, have an odd attraction to Pixies.

They were the knives she had gotten from Gramps's enchanted Cadillac DeVille that roamed the Everwhere countryside; I wouldn't be surprised if it decided to show up. Last time I'd been in said car, it had decided to drive down the throat of a giant spider.

I activated the Everwhere's version of the Seekergate, and we shuffled through. The sound of chaos was immediate. Lana quickly dropped to one knee, readying her bow.

"As soon as you move, I'll start firing. Try to stay in the middle of the plaza," Lana instructed as Petro zipped into the air.

Dark-purple waves floated above the ocean, blocking the view of the other side of the bridge. The trees in the plaza swayed like a crowd at a concert, making the area appear alive and breathing.

Taking a deep breath, I whispered, "*Ignis.*" My hellfire blade, as it often did in the Everwhere, crackled to life, spatters of hellfire dripping on the ground. The effect gave the surrounding area a red strobe light effect.

The sound of digging and concrete breaking stopped as I took two leaping bounds forward, several of Lana's arrows whistling by further lighting up the area.

Blank, pale faces shifted in my direction as I landed in front of the group. Two arrows slammed into the closest creature, launching it several feet backward. Its arms and legs flailed as it crashed into the road in front of the Bridge of Lions. The other three acted as if nothing had happened.

I squinted my eyes, seeing the two lions missing from the bridge. This wasn't a surprise, as the Everwhere was, for the most part, a mirror of the regular world, different and yet the same.

I pulled Durundle in front of me as the skin on the creatures' faces stretched as if they were all screaming at the same time. All three of what I had landed on calling the Faceless jumped forward. Several of Lana's arrows thumped into the creature on my far right, sending it flying in the same direction as its still downed partner.

Claws hissed through the air inches away from my face as I swung my hellfire blade up, cutting off the arm and half the head of the attacking Faceless. The last remaining creature, just as its partners, lurched forward. Its attack caught my face with its claws, creating three long, thin slices from ear to chin.

I wasn't going to play nice. "Petro!" I shouted as the Pixie dove out of the night sky, darting his blade into the back of the Faceless creature's head, forcing it to turn around. As it did, I swung my hellfire blade parallel to the ground, and the top and bottom half of the creature separated. Its legs stayed balanced for a few seconds before crumpling to the ground.

Petro hovered over my shoulder, looking at the wound on my face, grimacing. "Yeah, I don't like those things. Super creepy."

"Agreed. All clear!" I yelled to Lana, who immediately walked up beside me.

"I see. Are any of them still alive?" she asked, scanning the shifting buildings.

"Not the two I just finished. I'm not sure about the ones you shot," I replied as we walked toward the bridge.

Lana's arrows were still on fire when we walked up to the other two creatures. "That one's still kicking," Petro huffed. Either the cooler air was getting to him or the smell.

Walking forward, I put my boot on the Faceless creature's throat, which started to writhe.

Lana leaned over, pulling out one of her knives and quickly driving it into the Faceless's arm. Petro shook his head, knowing what she was doing, as the look on her face went blank.

"What's going on?" I asked Petro when he landed on my shoulder.

"She's trying to read its memories," he replied.

Lana gasped, pulling out the dagger before quickly slamming it into the creature's head in one swift motion. With its last spasm, the Faceless let go of all the tension in its body. I lifted my boot off its throat as the Elf warrior leaned back on the ground, a calculating look on her face.

I paused, letting her gather her thoughts. Since turning thirty and joining the magical community, the one thing I'd learned was that manners and patience paid off.

"These creatures are minions of the Crystal King. They are from the Plane. They shouldn't be here," Lana snapped, the disdain at saying the king's name clear in her tone.

"Oh boy. This isn't good, boss," Petro murmured, whistling as he finished.

"Lana," I said, refocusing her thoughts. "You know the Plane's shifting. Do you think this could have anything to do with the Pillars?"

The look on Lana's face hardened in thought like someone staring into Medusa's eyes. Her mouth opened then quickly closed again.

"Yes. If one of the Pillars has been moved, it would explain this and most of the other recent issues," Lana confirmed, getting to her feet.

"You mean like normal people getting powers and the magic misfires," I asked and stated at the same time.

"Precisely that. We've known the Plane is shifting for some time. I'm sure the Council had an idea the Pillars may be involved," Lana quickly answered as Petro cleared his throat.

"The Crystal King is a power-hungry Ethereal from the Plane, but not completely in the wrong from what I understand. No one knows where his castle is. You think he has something to do with this?" Petro asked Lana, who just shrugged, looking down at the two Faceless.

"Lana," I added as she looked up. "Titania has asked me to pay her a visit."

She shook her head, something visibly lining up in her thoughts. "I'm sure you know that she protects one of the Pillars. Only the strongest of Ethereals do; at least the Pillars which locations are known," Lana explained, confirming that a few of the Pillars' locations were either lost or well-kept secrets.

"Petro said this Crystal King guy wasn't or isn't entirely in the wrong. What does that mean?" I asked, trying to put the pieces together. Others often assumed I knew the entirety of the Plane history.

Seeing the expression on my face, Lana clarified further. "The Crystal King was indeed at one time the protector of one of the Pillars. The very one the queen now has in her possession, or did. Titania and the Fae led the charge against the Old Gods—and the other realms, to a point—ultimately winning the fight, but losing their home in the process. The queen's own castle and large portions of her realm became no longer habitable."

"So she just strolled up to this guy's castle and decided to claim it as hers?" I asked, looking for confirmation.

"Over time, yes. Remember, time in their eyes is a long path. It didn't happen overnight. You already know the Pillars were made toward the end of the Great War. There was a reason he was given the Pillar, but I don't think anyone truly knows why he was initially selected. According to history, the Crystal King went underground after Titania took possession, rebuilding his kingdom inside one of the Cavalier Mountains, keeping it hidden and fortified from others," Lana finished.

"Something's fishy about this whole thing, boss," Petro again reiterated.

Lana nodded her head, agreeing with Petro's assessment, before she spoke up again. "Is there anything else odd going on?"

I took a deep breath, about to divulge what I believed to be an important secret. "Tom's not dead. Titania is holding him." The look on Lana's face told me everything. Confusion and clarity all in one expression.

"You must go to the Plane. If the Crystal King is looking for something and Tom is being held, it can mean only a handful of things. The Crystal King could be trying to take the Pillar back, which is causing all these issues, with Tom being somehow involved. Neither is good. The Pillar must be put back in place."

I paused while Petro asked Lana a question. She was, after all, hundreds of years old. "If the Pillar is not in its rightful place, can't the Old Gods find the Plane and Earth after a while?"

Lana nodded, confirming Petro's question. Much like the Pillars, people such as Lana helped control the balance between the different Planes and realms. Everyone played their part to have a relatively normal existence out of reach from the Old Gods.

"All I know is that almost everything that's happened since I joined this rodeo has been due to these Old Gods. I'm getting a little tired of it. Petro, let's get back and make sure things are good back home. Phil's probably waiting for us. Lana, as always, it's a pleasure. I'll check in with you before I leave if time permits. Let me know what you find out, or at least, what those things were looking for," I emphasized, saluting the Elf warrior.

CHAPTER 6

Early Morning Sunshine

T he smell of sweet tobacco floated around the living room as Phil looked at me skeptically, putting out his cigarette. Several months ago, Kristi had gifted him an ashtray which just so happened to be a blended item. As soon as he put out the smoke, every hint that it was ever lit up vanished from the room.

Kristi had turned out to be not only a good friend to the group but Phil's on-again, off-again girlfriend whenever she was around, which was roughly one month out of the year near the holidays. I couldn't say much. My relationship with Kim had become an excellent source of material for others to let me know just how well I was doing in life.

"Bruther, this is a grade-A shit show. I mean, I know the old tales about the Pillars and the Crystal King, but if true, this isn't something we can fix on our own," Phil cautioned. It was clear from his tone he was still computing everything.

Casey flew into the room, dropping off another plastic bowl of Golden Grahams. Truth be told, I was good with it. Phil just shook his head, knowing better than to say anything.

"That's what Petro and I were talking about on our way back. The funny thing is, everyone else seems to think we are

49

good to head to the Plane and sort this all out," I huffed, taking a swig of Vamp Amber.

"Well, count me in there, sunshine. I know you were about to ask," Phil joked, knowing the gravity of the situation.

We spent the rest of the night talking about what had happened in the regular world during my short fight with the Faceless. My already fried brain started melting after a few phone calls and messages to Ed and the Council about the entire ordeal. After a long day, I needed to get some rest. Not to mention I had a trip to take in the morning to see some special youngsters.

***

My phone started ringing around eight in the morning. The smell of coffee brewing was not only sneaking in under my door, but calling me to get moving. Casey must be up getting the day started.

"Shit," I huffed, seeing Kim's name flashing on my phone. I had reset her ringtone a few months ago after she had threatened to kill me if I didn't change it from Eddie Money's timeless classic, "Take Me Home Tonight." Kim more than likely knew I was scrambling to get up, letting the phone ring.

"Hey," I let out coolly once I answered while she just chuckled.

"I totally just woke you up, didn't I?" she accused, the warmth in her voice coming through the phone.

"Pretty much. I needed to get up soon anyway. Uncle Max's presence has been requested," I informed Kim, letting her know I was going to see the children we'd saved from the Thule Society several years ago.

One of the most prominent oddities from the group was that they all aged at an alarming rate. Jenny's projections showed four to five years for every regular year. She had also predicted it would stop when they hit a certain age, more than likely when they turned thirty.

"I wish I were there to see them," Kim added.

"I can pick you up in twenty minutes," I offered. Kim sighed. It wasn't a negative pause, but one of frustration.

She cleared her throat. "You know I need this. I miss you, and that's all you need to know. Anyhow, I called with some interesting news."

I sat up in bed, throwing my legs over the side, stretching them out while flexing my stiff toes. "I'm all ears."

"I think I found a lead on your daughter," Kim said, giving me time to digest the statement.

As of last year, I had been made painfully aware that I may, in fact, have a daughter; the painful part being I had no recollection of the child or her conception. Kim and I had several theories, coming to one main conclusion: whomever the mother was, she had probably been wiped from my memory. This, in turn, made the notion that I had a daughter not as solid in my head.

We had also discussed the idea of it being nothing more than a cruel joke or rumor put out there for some reason. Either way, it weighed heavily on my mind, always just under the surface of what I was doing, reminding me to find her.

Kim's lead would be one of the first we had. "As we discussed before I left, I handed off a sample of your DNA to one of my trusted lab techs who keeps things off the radar and out of other people's hands. While checking your DNA against our records, they also checked that of . . . well, let's just say women you had been close to for a period of time around your thirtieth birthday. Including Sarah."

Kim paused and I stood up, lumbering toward the kitchen like a zombie searching for brains. "Don't tell me it's her," I sighed at the thought, knowing they were just checking random paths to see if anything popped up.

After making his great comeback, Tom had brought Sarah with him, hooking her up with Trish and a job at FA's. She was even dating James, and that appeared to be going rather well.

The thought started to sour in my mind like cheap old wine. It just didn't feel right. I'd had a chance to talk with Sarah, and while I still felt she was holding something back, this wasn't it. Kim had found something else. Gramps had even mentioned there was more than met the eye with Sarah, and she would only be safe in certain places. Come to think of it, I had only seen her outside of FA's on a handful of occasions.

"No, nothing to do with your DNA showing up. It's a little more interesting than that. Do you have your coffee yet?" Kim inquired, knowing I was about to get a shock to the system.

"Yup, I'm good. Lay it on me," I grumbled, knowing Kim was both excited yet hesitant to tell me.

"Did you know Sarah has—well, had a sister?" Kim asked, setting the stage for whatever bombshell she was about to drop.

"No, I didn't. Look, what does this have to do with my daughter, if I truly have one?" I was starting to wonder why she was hesitating.

Kim took a deep breath, ready to lay it all out like Sunday dinner. "Sarah has a fraternal twin sister. According to the files we found after the DNA match pinged in the system, they were separated at birth. Sarah was sent here to America and worked with Tom at some point. Her sister, on the other hand, was sent to England."

"It's Chloe, isn't it?" I asked, already knowing the answer.

"Max, you said Sarah used a powerful mind-block potion

on you after you first met. I called her. Sarah said that potion came from her sister and was one of her specialties."

I took a long slurp of go-juice.

"So you're saying this might be tied to Chloe?" I stated. Hearing the words out loud helped form a clear picture of what Kim was holding back from saying.

"You said it yourself. Lilith didn't mention anything about age. The timing is just too coincidental. Plus, I know you liked her. When I found out about Sarah, it just . . . well, my gut's telling me this means something," Kim wrapped up. The phone hummed, waiting for me to reply.

"I need to talk with Sarah, but it might have to wait. Things are starting to heat up again. You probably left just in time. Kim, thanks for this. I—well, we all miss you. This is going to take some time for me to work through," I lamented, taking a deep breath, the aroma of coffee calming my nerves.

"Take care of yourself and tell the others I said hello," Kim concluded, pausing like she wanted to say more.

We both hesitated, and several seconds passed. Knowing the call was over, I ended it. "I'll call you after I talk with Sarah."

I lightly tapped the end button while staring at the coffee maker. This was the cue for Petro and Casey to zip out of whatever cabinet it was they were hiding in.

"Boss, Sarah and Chloe?" Petro barked as Casey buzzed around my head, dusting lightly.

"Max, do you want me to see if she's working?" Casey joined in the chorus, belting out excitedly.

Everyone became overwhelmingly excited with anything related to my possible daughter's situation. I, on the other hand, was cautious, not knowing if I was being pulled into something.

"Don't you two have a little one to teach how to fly or

something?" I responded, letting them know it wasn't time to dig into this latest revelation.

Three months ago, Casey had given birth to the couple's first child. They'd named the little boy Neil after the detective who had sacrificed himself to help us several months prior. While aging much faster than human children, Pixies still had the same awkward phase as young babies before learning to walk, though for Pixies, this involved learning to fly.

Neil was still in a small crib, not able to take off, but Petro and Casey's son made up for it with a firm grasp around Mama and Papa. Casey had already made it clear that Phil was to be kept out of earshot of their son. They preferred his first words not to be too colorful.

Casey landed on the counter as Petro continued to buzz around the kitchen.

"What's all the bloody noise about?" Phil's voice echoed from behind his closed door.

I eyed the two Pixies. "Nothing. Just getting ready to go visit the kids."

"Tell the little rascals Uncle Phil said to behave," Phil replied, followed by a yawn. He was going back to sleep.

Petro landed by Casey as he smiled at her. Words didn't need to be exchanged. I had struck a nerve with words that I wished I could pull back, but at the same time, it was needed.

"I didn't mean it to come out like that. Phew," I huffed out. "Listen, I just don't want to put my burden on anyone else's shoulders. I'm already asking too much of you two by dragging Petro around when I know Neil needs to have his father near."

They both nodded, knowing I was being genuine. Casey's smile lit up the kitchen as Petro and I looked at each other, confused.

"I want Neil to be proud of his father and grow up in

a world that treats Pixies with respect. Neither of you has anything to prove. Petro is brave, and even if you don't fully know it, has brought great pride to our kind. Lacey and Macey as well. I'll be in the fight soon enough, but today, for now, Neil is my fight. My husband's job is to make sure you don't get yourself killed. It might be hard to find another golden-food provider," Casey finished, walking over to the coffee maker to brew another cup, swagger pouring off her walk.

Again, Petro and I just looked at each other. I could see the pride in Petro as he pushed his chest out.

"Well, boss. I'll meet with James about last night while you're out. You need me to check on anything else?" the Pixie asked, refocusing the conversation.

"I need to talk with Ed later. Jenny is going to be visiting the kids today as well. If I'm lucky, he'll be there. See if you can get a hold of Bo before he leaves with Inspector Holder. He's been flying under the radar lately. I also want to talk with Frank and Angel. Something's been going on with the Vs recently, and I want to know if it's something we need to be concerned about."

"Sounds good, boss," Petro said, giving me a slow wink before he turned toward Casey, flying up behind her as she turned, lightly dusting. I was pretty sure the prior conversation had lit the flames of passion between the two, which for Pixies didn't take much more than a solid smile at times.

CHAPTER 7

Uncle Max

"Well, well, well," I whispered under my breath as I drove the Black Beast through the gate of the house and part-time research facility where the children we had saved from the Thule Society stayed.

The house sat proudly on the beach south of St. Augustine. A gate separated it from the main road, while modern block stones and stylish bulletproof windows gave the impression of a mid-level mansion. That being said, the antennas and nondescript one-story building beside it with no windows screamed official.

Standing at the front entrance were Mouth and Akondo, a Native American Mage that was, according to Frank, *"Someone you don't want to cross,"* which was the main reason Akondo had been assigned to watch over the children and facility.

While he was a self-proclaimed Chief, I had only used that term with the man once. Akondo stood tall at a strong six-foot-eight with pounds of additional muscle layering his already sizable physique. According to Ed, the man had survived some of the most brutal battles over the past two hundred years by using wind magic.

After hours of searching in the stacks with Petro, we had only found a handful of references to the man and the magic he used. Akondo could move like and with the wind, silent and invisible to normal eyes, yet able to unleash all the power of Mother Nature into a cool afternoon breeze and easily turn it into a deadly wall of death and destruction.

Trees shaded the round driveway as I slammed my door shut, disrupting the conversation. Mouth shook his head, letting out ten lungfuls of air as Akondo nodded.

"Mouth, surprised to see you. Here I thought you weren't allowed around kids," I joked, getting the exact reaction I was hoping for. A return insult without a threat.

"Not like any of them are yours. You're not man enough to make a child, let alone bed a woman properly," Mouth growled, reaching out one of his bear claw–sized hands, effectively crushing mine.

"Hmph," Akondo muttered, the throaty growl sounding like a suppressed laugh.

Mouth and I had come to an understanding of sorts. I didn't get in his way, and he didn't beat me into a bloody pulp. We had also formed an awkward bond only people who had been in a fight together would understand.

The one thing I knew was that if he was insulting me and not openly threatening me, things were more than likely okay between us. Plus, ogres loved a good insult.

I paused, cocking my head as Mouth looked over at Akondo. His rumbling voice sounded distracted. "Carvel sent me here with computers from Mags-Tech for the younglings. Waste of time if you ask me."

"Old Carvel going soft on us, huh?" I inquired as Akondo again stifled a snicker.

"He's in charge of the bloody younglings' rehabilitation program," Mouth started, leaning down slightly. "If you ask me, it's punishment for something."

Mouth leaned back up. Even though the ogre had been trying to make the statement away from the prying ears of others, it hadn't worked.

"Akondo, I'll see you later. I'd ignore this one," Mouth rumbled, pointing his stubby thumb at me while walking toward the large SUV parked by the garages.

"I think he respects you," Akondo noted, his voice confident and wise, the man's Native American accent still cutting through despite years of being removed from everyday use.

"Something like that. Odd to see him here. Are the kids out back in the field?" I asked, hearing the sounds of children playing echoing around the large stone house.

"Yes, Jenny and Ed are also around," Akondo affirmed as he pointed toward the garages. Ed's M-Tech edition Lincoln Continental was tucked away in the shadows.

Akondo squinted his eyes at me, causing me to freeze momentarily.

"What?" I shrugged.

"Looks like you've finally got your act together. Not out playing thirty-year-old frat boy anymore," Akondo noted, setting his jaw, the muscles in his cheeks flexing.

"Thanks, I guess? I'll be here for a couple of hours. Oh, before I forget, Petro told me to say hello," I said as Akondo busted out in a full-on belly laugh. He couldn't hold it in.

"You tell Petro he still owes me," Akondo chuffed, walking away.

Petro had a story to tell. Walking out back, I saw Jenny and Ed were playing with the kids on either side of two small soccer goals.

"Right, just in time. I need a breather," Ed huffed,

smiling. He was having fun, Jenny mirroring his smile as both of them swept back their disheveled hair.

"UNCLE MAX!" the chorus of all ten kids came at once as a rush of arms and snotty hands grabbed every piece of clothing I was wearing.

I couldn't help but smile. It was contagious. "Alright, alright, I'm not going anywhere for a while." I got out as the school of hug-happy piranhas released their death grips.

Ed and Jenny walked up, both still grinning. Scanning the children, I looked at the two, shaking my head. It had been a few months since my last visit, yet the kids looked as if they had aged a year.

"How's it going here?" I asked as Tommy, one of the group's smallest boys, politely kicked a soccer ball directly into my stomach. "Oof . . ." I let out, quickly regaining my composure. Even with my heightened reflexes, the kid was fast and strong.

"That about sums it up," Jenny chuckled. "We're going to get cleaned up and talk to Dr. Freeman. When you're done, stop by the lab. And before I forget, Chi asked if she could talk to you privately. She said we can be there, but not the other kids."

Chi was one of the oldest children, and according to Dr. Freeman, Japanese. She was roughly twelve years old, tall, skinny, with long, flowing black hair, and reserved. The young girl also had a unique ability related to divination.

Ed had spent several weeks working to figure it out completely with no luck. Not only could she use divination, but Chi also had the uncanny ability to reveal unknown truths and see several different branches of the future. While not immediately unique in the field, her reach and length of foresight was the type of ability that created respected prophecies.

I nodded, turning back to the kids, pulling a basketball-sized bag of candy out of my enchanted coat. "Who wants some sugar?"

Hands were raised and candy distributed before I took off my coat, running out into the field.

"Uncle Max, tell us about the killer crab," Jake yelled. He was the adventurous one of the group, an obvious ring leader, and often in trouble. I was told he had fashioned himself a long coat to look like mine. Jake was much like myself, able to use several different types of magic. The main difference was that Jake was only twelve—well, three years old, but had aged rapidly.

"Soccer or story time?" I asked. The group ran to the other side of the field where I supposedly couldn't hear and started debating each other.

After two short minutes, Jake walked over with the rest following behind. Piercing, intelligent eyes glared excitedly at me. "Both, but story first. The group also says that you have to bring Petro next time you come to see us. He tells the best stories."

I realized I was in the middle of a negotiation with a group of children. Which meant I was going to lose.

"Alright, deal, but that means I'll have to cut the soccer game short," I agreed, sitting down on the grass as the children mirrored my actions. For the next thirty minutes, I told the story of the Great Crab Boil of Vilano Beach.

After a round of soccer which included one scraped knee and a few well-timed goals to keep my ego intact, it was time to talk to Ed and Jenny.

"I have to go inside. It's been great seeing everyone," I wheezed, still catching my breath.

"Uncle Max, we will miss you!" Trevor, one of the younger children, barked from the back of the group.

"I promise to bring more stories, candies, and let me think . . ." I trailed off, looking up like I was forgetting something.

"Petro!" the group exclaimed. "Bring Petro!"

"That's right . . ." I drawled out, having fun while doing so. I enjoyed my time with the kids, and same as with everything else in my life, I needed to spend more time doing things that brought me joy. The list was long, and talking with Kim this morning wasn't helping me focus.

Ed walked out, having picked up on the end of my time with the children.

"Right, everyone head in and get cleaned up. Ms. Murphy and Leshya will have lunch ready soon," Ed instructed as I looked up to see Leshya floating down the hallway.

I didn't think she could leave the Atheneum, but recent events had proven several of my prior assumptions wrong. Ms. Murphy, on the other hand, was Teen, the witch I'd sat behind a couple of years back in the Council chambers; the one who grew up with my mother. I was betting their cooking was on another level.

"How did Leshya get here?" I asked as Ed put his hands up, obviously not knowing.

"Magic?" he chuckled as we walked toward the main hallway. "That mess with Bruce and Carol did something to the Atheneum. I think she's tied to something in the house, like an item or gate. Last week, I saw her at the Atheneum when I checked up on the wards being set back up. You wouldn't recognize the place. They almost have it back in working order."

"Could it be one of the kids?" I threw into the mix of guesses.

Ed stopped. "Hmm, I never thought about that one. One of them definitely has the ability to shift things."

"Shift things?"

"Not like gating. They can literally think of something or someone and *poof*, they or it appears. We had to talk him out of pulling you here a few times. I'll bring it up with Jenny," Ed noted as Leshya floated out of a dark room in front of us.

"Hello, Max," Leshya murmured in her usual hushed tone.

"Leshya, we were just talking about you. It's the first time I've ever seen you away from the Atheneum," I said, happy to see her.

"Magic," she replied, handing me a brown paper bag with my name on it.

"Is this . . . ?" She nodded, letting a flat smile creep onto her angelic face.

"Always," she boasted, floating past us and heading toward the kitchen.

"I miss that," I said while Ed nodded.

"She's been spending more and more time here helping with the children," Ed relayed thoughtfully, stopping as I confirmed the contents of my sandwich bag. "You need to be careful. You are just a piece of whatever puzzle there is going on. The Council has people all over the place, doing Lord knows what. All I know is they are worried."

"So?" I asked as Ed bit his lip lightly in thought. He was choosing his words wisely.

"I have a feeling you're the one they're sending into the belly of the beast. While the other teams work is important, I believe whatever it is you're setting out to do is part of the endgame. They know the score; don't ever forget that. You think they don't know, but they do," Ed warned as we both nodded our heads.

We strolled to the sterile-looking one-story building

attached to the main house by an out-of-place covered walkway. The sounds of the wind sweeping off the beach and the seagulls greeted my ears as we walked out of the main house under the canopy.

Much to my surprise, the inside contrasted with the building's exterior. The space was inviting and set up to make its occupants comfortable. Light blue walls and ambient, outdoor-type lighting gave the usual shadows of a building no safe harbor. A red carpet with intricate Persian-looking designs created an odd yet beautiful contrast with the walls.

"What's that noise?" I inquired, referring to the gentle hum in the background. Taking a deep breath, I also detected the deliberate smell of cookies baking.

"Ambient noise," Jenny replied, ushering us down the main hallway. "We find it keeps the children calm when they are in here. Needless to say, it's not their favorite place at times. If there is an issue with their gift or we need to work on something, this is where we come. It's a safe place, and as you know, a few of the children are powerful in ways we have yet to understand. Either way, the normal team is taking the day off. That's why Ed and I are here."

The main lab area was comfortable but also filled with tables, chairs, computers, and several other devices one would find in a magical lab.

Chi was sitting in a chair in the middle of the room, drinking a glass of lemonade.

Jenny walked over, smiling as she handed the young girl a lollipop. I cocked my head. "She gets nervous. This helps."

It was clear that Jenny and Ed did not hide things from the children. As Chi unwrapped the sucker, setting down her glass of lemonade, a smile erupted from her face, reaching her eyes.

"I need a pile of those to give to Phil," I joked as the others chuckled.

"Hello, Chi. I understand you want to talk to me. Is now a good time?" I asked. She shook her head, moving the lollipop nervously around, clicking it against her teeth.

The temperature in the room dropped to below freezing as Chi pulled out her sucker, letting out a crystalizing breath. I quickly noticed Ed and Jenny both had on sweaters. They knew the routine.

I shivered, not only from the temperature but because something else had joined us in the room. Whatever it was, it was floating through the air like mist in the frigid Antarctic air, out of place in Florida. The warmer air coming out of the vents started fogging up the area.

Calming my nerves, I watched the entity float around the room, wrapping itself around Chi. Without moving, I looked over at Ed and Jenny. They couldn't see whatever it was now with us.

Being a quarter demon, Mage, human, and witch, I had learned to control my extra abilities and senses. I relaxed my body as Ed looked at me, feeling my mind open.

Ed shifted his eyes to Chi as I formed a picture of what I was seeing. Ed walked forward as I raised my hand.

"Stop," I whispered, not wanting to disturb whatever was wrapping itself around Chi. "It's not harming her. It's a part of her. Chi, what is it you want to talk to me about?"

Chi started talking in a flat voice which was still hers. I had witnessed a possessed person talking. This was something different.

"Max Abaddon Sand, I keep seeing you through the mirror. Something is trying to reach out, but it doesn't know why," Chi slowly murmured, the vapor of her breath getting thicker.

"Okay, what can I do?" I asked, not knowing how to respond to that statement. Prophecies, from what I understood, were often vague.

"Today, something was revealed by a person you care for, which brought me to talk to you," Chi exhaled as I reflected on my conversation with Kim.

"Chi, what is it specifically that has you here talking with me now," I said, looking directly at the entity hugging the child, letting it know I understood who was driving the ship.

Again, I used the skills I'd learned from my days in the army as an intel analyst, asking questions to open the conversation further. My assumption was simple. I was talking to a child, so the other part of Chi was also a child trying to process information.

"Someone being kept against their will knows a truth you seek," Chi urged as I watched the entity untwine itself from the child. The room started to warm up as Chi slowly put the sucker back up to her mouth. Ed and Jenny glanced at me as I stood stoically, staring at nothing.

"I think that was it," the little girl said, crunching down on the sucker.

"It sounds like it. Thank you for talking to me, and it will be our little secret," I assured Chi, making an outline with my fingers of another person around her.

She glanced up, shocked yet comforted. The look on her face was one of relief, knowing she wasn't crazy and someone else could see her other half. While I didn't know precisely what it was, I had a few ideas.

"Run along and catch up with the others. They should be starting lunch," Jenny instructed as Chi jumped up, running out of the room, skipping all the while.

"Right. Jenny, I think we may need to have another conversation about Chi," Ed started as we both explained what had happened.

Jenny's face was blank as the gears in her head were trying to grind out a logical explanation. While she was a powerful Life Mage, Jenny also knew the truth of cold hard science. It made for a lethal combination of intellect and skill.

"I want to have Trish come talk to her," Jenny said slowly.

We both looked at her as I spoke before Ed. "Any particular reason?"

"Trish is, as you are probably figuring out, not a normal Ethereal. I believe she is Celestial, or something close to it in some form. I know she was considered an Egyptian goddess, but that was back in the day. I've heard of something like this before." Jenny hesitated a moment too long.

"I plan on stopping by FA's later. Trish should be there. I heard Sarah is out of town for a few days. What Chi said . . ." I trailed off, shaking my head as I sat on a wooden desk next to a set of chairs.

"I have a feeling you're not here just to see the kids," Ed guessed.

I nodded and spent the next thirty minutes going over my call with Kim, the Crystal King, and Jamison's note. The two stood still with jaws slightly agape. It wasn't a look of confusion but of concern.

"Right, well, this complicates things," Ed stated flatly.

"Yeah, I've told that story at least three times in the past day, and every time I do, it keeps getting more complicated," I said, slapping my hands on the top of my legs.

"We all know you want to find your daughter. You know as well as the rest of us that it's true. Even I can feel it. But you need to figure out what's going on with the Pillars first. Without that, nothing else truly matters," Jenny emphasized while Ed nodded his head, agreeing.

"Things have held off this long. I know you've noticed the Vs being rather preoccupied as of late. Don't think you're doing this on your own. The Night Stalkers are in the background working. While I don't know on what precisely, I do know it has to do with everything going on. Max, I promise we will get to the bottom of Sarah and Chloe's relationship. Jenny and I will talk with her if we have time. I have a feeling she knows more than we thought."

My phone started to vibrate.

"It's Phil. Looks like he's finally up and moving," I said, licking my lips, the cold air taking its toll. "I plan on leaving tomorrow."

The two nodded as I stood up, noticing the condensation on the wall from the drastic temperature change sparkling like glitter.

CHAPTER 8

Happy Hour

"Can you guys believe it?" I asked Amon and Trish as the two gawked at me with the same concerned look on their faces as Ed and Jenny.

I had taken the time to regurgitate the past two days' events once again. It was almost therapeutic as I ran through the information. Reliving the events and conversations I'd recently had was also helping me organize my thoughts.

"I know you said Jenny and Ed were going to stop by, but tell me a little more about Chi," Trish requested quizzically.

Amon followed this with his rumbling support. "Yes. Tell us about the girl."

"All this and you two are more interested in Chi?" I inquired as Trish and Amon both leaned forward.

"Yes . . ." Amon again responded. "Chi."

"Besides what I told you already, Jenny was adamant about the three of you meeting. Well, mostly Trish. She said it was something about who you are.., or...,"—I stuttered—"what you are."

Trish leaned back, crossing her legs. Her leather pants made a stretching sound as she flexed her muscles.

"Yes, well, I guess that puts things into perspective," Trish said tightly as her lips flattened before perking up once again.

Amon chuffed as he often did. "Somebody or a group of somebodies think you're going to make all this right again. Just remember, you are not invincible. When you go to the Plane, you need to remember everything that we and the others have told you. That place may feel like a fairy tale, but if you let it, it will turn into a nightmare."

"Enough, Amon, Max probably knows that he screwed up," Trish joked, lightening the mood as Amon let out a rumbling belly laugh. "Max, follow me to the front. As you know, I'm a little shorthanded right now. I need to get back to work."

I followed Trish after saying my goodbyes to Amon. The retired hellion general, as always, burped a few times and reminded me not to get killed.

Once outside, Trish quickly scanned the bar. Only a handful of patrons looked up as she promptly refilled their drinks. It always threw me off how time didn't really matter when one was in Amon's kitchen.

"Here," Trish offered, setting two Vamp Ambers in front of us, taking a pull from hers.

"No, thanks," I said, shaking my head lightly. Trish perked up.

"Oh my, is the great Max Abaddon turning down a Vamp Amber?" Trish sarcastically drawled out.

"If I tell you something, will you think I'm weird?" I asked, quickly realizing how stupid my question was.

"Are you seriously asking me that?" Trish playfully giggled.

I took a deep breath, about to relay something I hadn't

discussed with anyone else. "For the last couple of months, I've not been in the mood to have anything to drink. Hell, when I've had something, it's not done much," I said, making my confession.

It was a simple truth. It wasn't that I drank too much; in fact, I had significantly slowed down since my initial indoctrination into the magical community. For some reason, alcohol hadn't been affecting me as it used to. More to the point, I had recently outdrunk Phil on three occasions.

Instead of responding, Trish simply smiled, reaching under the bar and pulling out a bottle of Ambrosia.

"You know I can't afford the stuff," I murmured so no one else could hear.

"You should be able to. I don't think I've collected rent in quite some time. Or well, ever. Let's do a little test," Trish encouraged, pouring us both a small glass of Ambrosia.

Ambrosia was rightfully called the nectar of the gods. Whatever flavor or pleasure you so desired, the drink made itself precisely that, including the exact temperature you wanted said drink, the texture, and whatever else you could imagine.

"Ahhh," I let out as the immediate calming effects of the expensive liquor took hold of my body and senses. "Yep, that did the trick."

Again, Trish just grinned at me. "I think I see why."

"And?" I asked, taking another pull.

"I think we will save that for another time. You already have enough on your mind," Trish replied as we sat down behind the bar on two stools strategically placed by the service window.

"You're probably right. Hell, you're always right. I need

you to do me a favor," I started. Trish put her hand on mine.

"I know you said Ed and Jenny are going to talk with Sarah if time permits. I'm guessing you want me to keep an extremely close eye on her?" Trish correctly guessed.

"I've never asked much from you, yet I owe you more than I can possibly repay. But this . . . this is something," I started before cutting myself off, realizing I was mumbling.

"I promise you, when Sarah gets back, I will keep an eye on her. But Max, not everyone is out to get you. Sarah is good. I can feel it. Once this whole thing is through and magic is back to normal, we will help you find your daughter. TOGETHER," Trish emphasized as I smiled at her.

As if on cue, the door swung open as the sound of the light bell chimed behind the bar, informing Trish of new patrons. These patrons just happened to be Frank and Angel.

"What is it with timing and you people?" I uttered under my breath as Trish shook her head.

"You mean us, child," Trish reminded me. I was also part of their messed-up little world.

Without acknowledging the rest of the patrons, Angel and Frank sat down at the end of the bar. Trish raised her hand off mine, letting me know things would be okay. I knew the gesture was full of hope.

I immediately noticed that both Vs were wearing thick layers of clothing as Angel took off a pair of gloves, slapping them on the bar top. "Well, what a coincidence," she purred while Frank shook his head, rolling his eyes.

"It's been a while," I greeted, genuinely happy to see my two favorite vampires.

"You do know some of us have to work," Frank joked flatly, looking around the bar while Trish set two small glasses of synthetic blood in front of them.

I hadn't had a chance to talk to either of them at the Council halls. On both occasions, they'd looked as if they had been somewhere on the opposite side of the world.

"Talking about work, what have you two been up to lately?" I countered. The two just looked at each other.

It was no secret that over the past two years, the vampire community had been working to keep itself flying under the radar, except for the Vs starting themed restaurants and nightclubs who were trying to turn a buck. Though in most cases, if you met somebody out on the street who insisted they were a vampire, they were either lying and trying to scam you, or they were telling you the truth, and you were about to get eaten.

"Besides missing your smug little face," Angel jested as Frank and Trish let out a snicker. "We've been out looking into the Thule Society. Well, or as they're called now, Everbane. You know, figuring out who's involved in all this craziness."

"Last time I talked to Lilith, she wasn't a part of that ragtag group of thick-skulled pukes," I said, taking another sip of Ambrosia.

When spit directly in your face and on one's clothes, synthetic blood had the exact same effect as regular blood. I froze as the viscous material ran out of Frank's nostrils like milk after a well-timed joke.

Stunned, Trish handed me a wet bar towel that had probably lost its fight against some type of spill. Between the blood and the dirty bar rag, the scents were fighting for position to declare themselves the winner in a game designed to make me throw up.

Trish excused herself, walking toward the other patrons in the bar as I continued to wipe off my face and clothes, finally getting a hold of my stomach and preventing it from regurgitating the sandwich that Leshya had lovingly made for me.

After a few short minutes, the inhabitants of the Fallen Angel were down to Amon and the three of us. Bar tabs and food bills remained unpaid as Trish locked the door with a resounding click.

If a V could blush, Frank would be pulling it off. "I-I'm sorry," he stammered before fully regaining his composure.

"Yeah, I'm pretty sure I deserved that for something," I replied, lightening the mood.

Angel tilted her head as Frank took off his jacket. Vs often did things like this when they wanted to put others at ease. Unnecessarily in this case, since in the grand scheme of things, I had killed several, if not dozens, of Vs over the past couple of years, making enemies I had yet to meet.

"We are alone. Let's hear it," Trish insisted as she let out a whistle directed toward the kitchen. It was then and there that I realized neither Frank nor Angel had met Amon before.

After the dramatic clank of locks and the click of gears smoothly opening the door into the kitchen, two thumps echoed in the now empty bar. Angel stood up as Frank's ears pinned back. I immediately noticed both of their nostrils flaring.

"Everyone calm down," Trish insisted as Amon lumbered out of the main kitchen door with an overly toothy grin, holding an odd-looking pizza.

"Hello, I've heard much about the both of you. A Night Stalker and a hero," Amon bellowed before the two Vs could get a word out.

"Amon, glad you could join us," I said, moving out of the way so he could set down one of the most horrid pizzas of all time.

Some would say pineapple on a pizza was a sin. Others

would insist that anything other than cheese was something else, while some were good just as long as it was called a pizza.

Sitting in front of Angel and Frank was a regular crust covered in a thick, purple, gooey substance. I was fairly sure this was some type of raw material out of an animal or— My thoughts shifted as the two Vs finally looked down at the monstrosity in front of them.

On top of the sauce was a layer of paper-thin meat. From what I could tell, there was no fat on the cuts, thanks to Amon's superior knife skills and taste for fine foods. But what truly set my already weak stomach on edge were the raw, fresh bones sliced in doughnut-sized circles with liquid bone marrow inside still moving from being set down. Meat and cartilage were intricately left in key areas of the two-inch thick cuts of bone, which gave the horror its final touch. The strong smell of butter, warm copper, and raw meat topped it all off.

Angel looked up. For the first time since I'd met her, a look of confusion swept across her face. "Your chef is a hellion?"

"Yes. I've been called worse," Amon replied smiling, slipping me a wink. There was something symbolic about the dish he'd brought out. I would bet it had taken him hours to prepare. Which really meant nothing, as time didn't work the same in the kitchen.

Trish grinned, handing the hellion a beer. "Someone wants to make new friends," Trish gushed, understanding replacing Angel's expression.

"I've never seen one of these," Frank said as Angel licked her lips.

"Maybe if you looked more like me, you would have. Hellion, how do you know of this?" Angel asked as I cleared my throat, wanting to get back to the conversation.

"Amon, my name is Amon. Tell Davros we met. I'll let

him tell that tale," Amon suggested as he leaned against the wall, wiping a smudge off the stainless-steel rail on the service window.

"You're . . ." Angel paused. "You're the one that saved him." As the words left her mouth, she walked over to the hellion, reaching out her hand, "It's an honor," followed up by an uncharacteristic bow.

"Bahahaha!" Amon guffawed. "The old blood bag must have played the tale up. Yes, it is also a pleasure to meet you as well. I have heard much about both of you. But I think we need to get back to it before Max explodes."

Angel and Frank looked for Amon's approval before taking slow bites of the pizza, or whatever Amon had made them. Looks of real pleasure crossed both their faces as their bodies relaxed.

"Now that's over with, what about the Thule Society and Lilith?" I asked, getting things back on track.

Frank looked at Angel, who nodded. While we were friends, they both also had jobs and a mission.

"The Thule Society is no longer. From what we understand, Lilith eradicated the entire group of elders. In doing so, the rest of the lackeys swore allegiance to her, or from what we gather, Darkwater. They now call themselves Everbane. There still some Thule Society holdovers though," Frank informed the group.

After a few minutes of digesting what I'd just been told and watching the two Vs finish off their meal, I took another pull of Ambrosia.

"And, what else are you not telling me?" I asked, wondering why the explanation had been cut short. "I'm going to go have a little chat with Lilith later."

"About that. We know about the place on the beach," Angel added quickly.

"What about it?" I asked, confused by the statement. They were clearly talking about the beachside bar and grill that I frequented when I needed to find Lilith.

"My God, you do spend too much time in the Postern or wherever these days. They tore it down last month," Frank told me, saluting Amon while placing his napkin on the tray.

I again took a few seconds to think, slowly speaking back up. "Okay, something else I'll look into later. Something's telling me she doesn't have anything to do with the current situation. I'm sure you've been debriefed on the Pillar."

"Yes, we have. We called Ed before heading this way. That's how we knew to meet you here. Max, there's more. Like everyone else on the Council, we initially thought either Everbane, the Thule Society, or Lilith were involved in the misfires. It appears that's not the case," Frank said in a serious yet flat tone.

"That's three pieces off the chessboard," I huffed. Trish cleared her throat.

"Never take Lilith off the chessboard," was all she said, going back into listening mode.

"Anyway, Davros wanted us to give you something," Frank followed up as Angel pulled out a silver ring, setting it on the bar top with a clink.

"Is he asking me to marry him by proxy? Or giving me his class ring from . . . what? 1492?" I asked as Amon's belly gurgled, stifling back a laugh. Angel even let out a light snort.

Trish stepped forward, picking up the ring. "Interesting. It's a key and a powerful force weapon."

"Not to mention it sends a message to anyone who may want to mess with you on the Plane," Amon chimed in.

"Key to what?" I asked Frank. Angel was the one who spoke up.

"From what Davros told us, which wasn't much, it's a key to his old keep and whatever it is within. Oh, and he also mentioned you bringing a coin he gave you a while back," she said, standing up.

Frank followed her lead, putting his jacket back on. "I don't know where his keep is. We asked around and landed on it likely being hidden."

"When something's hidden on the Plane, that can mean many things," Trish added while Frank walked up to me.

"Max, when you get back and things calm down, Angel and I want to get you in front of the Vampire High Court. Be safe," Frank said as we shook hands.

The Vampire High Court was the Vampire community's ruling group. While Davros was ancient, powerful, and scary, he was, from all accounts, one of a dozen significantly more unsettling senior Vs on the Court. Davros just happened to be their representative on the Council due to him being more . . . flexible, I believe was the term used.

Frank's message was clear. I still had unfinished business to address with the Vs as a whole. My two friends wanted to restore my reputation within the High Court, as well as the Vampire population in general.

CHAPTER 9

The Last Supper

Dishes clinked as the Atheneum's dining room once again buzzed with life. Jenny had insisted we all meet in the ever trusty room that had witnessed many a start to our adventures.

The Werewolves had destroyed large sections of the entranceway and east wing, not to mention all the magic and gunfire that had been used in the fight by both sides. I was still glad Bruce hadn't brought over all the oversized lizards from the Everwhere. We had lost Neil during the siege, and in many ways, the last of my ignorance of the cruelty within the magical community.

Three months ago, the Atheneum had finally started resembling its prior self in all its glory. Certain sections of the east wing, however, were still in disrepair due to what I liked to call "an unforeseen fire event." The one saving grace was the east wing was often unused and left closed off.

"Pass . . . *slurp* . . . the ranch . . . *slurp* . . . please," Phil spit out, along with small chunks of fried chicken that fell onto his beard and the general area in front of him. The group, already aware of his eating prowess, mainly stayed clear of the area around him.

"My God. You could use some proper work on your manners," Inspector Holder scolded Phil as he sucked on each and every one of his fingertips, freeing them from the chicken grease.

I took in the smells and familiar sounds of the group all being back together in the dining room. It was nostalgic, much like eating my favorite cereal.

Over the past few years, I had gotten away from the little tests I used to use on people. That is, all except the music in my truck test. That one still held massive weight. On the other hand, Petro had taken up my cereal test with other Pixies, which didn't make much sense, considering most Pixies could only eat one flake.

Bo sat on the other side of Inspector Holder, also taking in the group. I was quickly realizing why going to the Plane was such a big deal. There seemed to be more rules and reasons for certain groups not to go than there was motivation to make the journey over.

The room was full of the usual suspects. Lacey and Macey were sitting at a small table in the middle of the room with Petro. Casey was doing her motherly duties. The only people who weren't present in the room were Frank and Angel, whom I had already spoken with.

"Right," Ed barked out loudly, bringing the room to attention. "As everyone knows, Max, Phil, and Petro will be leaving tomorrow for the Plane. My understanding is that Angel and Frank have already visited Max. We called everybody together to see if there were any updates for the group."

The room grew moderately silent, only the slurping sounds coming from Inspector Holder and Phil remaining. The light buzzing of Petro's wings also accompanied the two men's assault on the poultry.

Dr. Freeman cleared his throat as the room shifted

its attention to the chubby, balding professor. The stubborn, aging man had finally agreed to take a slowing potion created by Jenny. The spell would allow Dr. Freeman some additional time. While it wasn't enough to slow the ever-sharpening blades of time, it was enough to keep him up and moving, something I had also talked to Kim about.

Most people failed to mention that the professor was a sensitive, meaning there was a mild amount of Etherium in his body, though he couldn't use magic or any type of blended item. Jenny and several others had concluded it was one of the reasons for his vast intelligence. The man could remember anything, at any time, ever told to him.

"Yes. Lacey, Macey, and I spent some time in the stacks seeing if we could find any information on the ring after you sent me a picture of it. We did find reference to the crest on it coming from an old Fae family that, of course, were turned into Vs after the Great War," Dr. Freeman squeaked out as he unrolled the generic map of the Plane on the table in front of me.

Macey buzzed up from the small table as Dr. Freeman handed her a toothpick. "From what we can tell, the crest is somehow related to a geographical area called the Two Valleys. I mean, the origin of this crest comes from a zone where a depression or saddle in the mountain has a valley on either side. Almost as if the center mountain range is an interstate divider. Davros's family were known as the Keepers of the Two Valleys."

Macey stopped talking as Lacey buzzed over, and the two exchanged the toothpick as if it was a baton and they were running an Olympic team racing event. Pixies were highly coordinated and fluid in their movements, their small size often leading to this being overlooked.

Lacey did a short curtsy, as she often did before addressing a group of people. "While we've only had a couple of hours to go through this, we noticed three obvious mountain ranges that look as if they hold two very distinct valleys. These also open up into the area where Petro's home is."

"What?" Petro asked, setting down the crouton he had been eating. "You mean the *very scary, never go to those mountain ranges, Petro* mountains?"

"Yes," Lacey replied with a smug grin on her face. "It looks like you took everyone's advice and never went."

"Well . . . I mean, it was pretty far to fly. I think Bosley and the others went up there once," Petro chuffed, still trying to regain some of this Pixie street cred.

Figuring I had had enough of the girls picking on Petro, I took out a pencil, tracing a line from the gate at the palace, through Petro's home, and finally landing on the two valleys. "It doesn't look that big on the map. I know better, though. Ed, where do you think I need to start?"

Ed looked over at Jenny, who stood up. "After what you told us about Lana, we asked a few of the other Supreme and Senior Council Fae members that exact same question. The answer was unanimous. As you know, the Crystal King's castle is well hidden, and according to the Fae we talked to, Titania does not know its location. It seems there's a specific route to get there. The situation with Tom makes this more complicated. As soon as we mentioned it, the Fae went silent. They will not go against their queen. We believe you need to start with Titania, and you will probably end up having to find the Crystal King or the keep."

"I'm betting Titania needs someone to go fetch the Pillar that she misplaced. It seems to me we have a pretty good idea by whom. Sooo, now what?" I asked, drawing it out, looking around the room.

Sounding like a chorus of concertgoers as the lead singer

pumps up the crowd, the three Pixies in the room yelled, "It's a quest!" all at once.

Phil paused from his grotesque assault on the chicken wings in front of him. He had been oddly quiet throughout the entire conversation, knowing that he was going as well. "If there's some good food and Fae wine, count me in."

I looked over at Bo. "You got anything on this?"

Bo grumbled for a few seconds before speaking up. "There is a reason there are no Fae in this room. Hopefully, everybody has been paying attention lately. Between the Fae and the Vampires, it seems like there's an awful lot of positioning going on. The Fae are generally good, but when they aren't ... let's just say they could give a roomful of demons a run for their money."

The room paused as Bo's statement lingered in the air like sour milk. He was telling the truth and also admitting at the same time that the Fae were just as powerful, or could be, as demons.

That statement was absolutely geared toward me and my abilities. I had asked Jenny and the others how going to the Plane would affect them.

When the Fae had come from the Plane to Earth, or from what I could tell, the Council chambers, wherever the hell those were, they had lost a little bit of their immortality. They were vulnerable, and not nearly as strong as they were back on the Plane.

I paused at the thought. "How many people know we are supposed to leave tomorrow?"

"The majority of the Supreme Council for sure. Other than that, I would guess whoever has found out through word of mouth," Ed replied as he looked skeptically at Jenny.

They knew, between divination and the fact that Mages were worse than gossiping old ladies on bingo night, that word had probably already gotten out.

A fleeting memory of Phil, Petro, and my adventure on the *Event Horizon* a few years ago slammed into my mind. The only reason the operation had been mildly successful—and when I say mildly, I mean only Ned had died during it—was because we had left early. If we had waited any longer and gone when we were supposed to, we would've also never left the deck of the ship.

"I need a few minutes to talk to Phil and Petro," I said in a cordial tone, not giving away what I was about to do.

Everyone in the room looked at me quizzically, except for Bo. A gentle smile that only another creature with demon blood would notice perked up the corner of his lips.

"Look, I want to talk to these two for a few minutes. I'm not saying it's private, but I would like to have a conversation between just the three of us who will be taking this trip. Ed, as you always say, the less you know, the better," I added, grinning as Phil stood up with a chicken leg in his hand.

The funny thing about good friends was that they were either oblivious of what you're about to do or didn't care because they actually trusted you. It was evident by the expression on Phil's face and by Petro quickly buzzing to the door that neither one of them knew what was about to happen. I would've thought they had learned their lesson by now.

"Right, while you are all talking, we'll see if the Council has any updates," Ed informed the group.

Before the door clicked shut, Bo, apparently knowing me better than the others, pushed a message into my thoughts. "*Be safe, and for the love of God, don't get yourself killed.*"

It still took me by surprise when a demon swore to God or prayed. I looked back as the skin around his round glasses tightened, telling me there was probably a wink behind them. Bo was about to leave for England with Inspector Richard

Holder, better known as Dick Holder to his friends.

The full-blooded demon would be no good on the Plane, and was one of the better candidates to handle a rogue hellion hiding out in the Cotswold's countryside.

Larry and Curly followed me down the hall toward the stacks. The Three Stooges were back together again. Petro zipped up, being the obvious Larry of the dynamic comic trio.

"So, boss, what's up?" he asked, dusting lightly over my shoulder.

"I just want some privacy. This entire thing feels a little too planned," I drawled out, spacing my reply as we came to the door of the Postern entrance located in the stacks.

"Bollocks . . ." Phil mumbled with a mouth full of chicken as I opened the door. "This is another one of those thingies where we just go without letting anyone else know."

"Bingo," I replied as he scrunched his face.

"Is this going to be like last time when I got a shiny new boom stick, everyone got all pissed, and we got chewed out a little?" Phil asked skeptically.

"Would I ever trick you into going against the Council's precious schedule without ensuring I had a shiny new toy for you? If memory serves, going early *did* save our asses; plus, we've been chewed out before," I responded, smiling, already prepared for such an occasion.

The truth was, I *had* planned on sticking to the original schedule—up until I saw how many people were involved in the trip and the open conversation about plans. My original plan had been not to leave till the next day, as ordained.

This had changed after seeing the children. Following my detour to FA's, I had taken a couple of hours to prepare, including picking up a rather nasty gun called The Icebreaker.

As with anything involving the Postern, a trip across

the globe was only a few footsteps away. I had found the rifle while looking for Phil's upcoming birthday present. It had been waiting for me after Abby Normal, the one and only lead singer of Planes Drifter, had found it for me after some coaxing.

The rifle would fire bullets and hypercharge them with a freeze spell through some odd enchantment. According to the demonstration I had witnessed, it froze the section of the body or whatever it hit. Phil would probably sleep with it tucked under his pillow for the foreseeable future.

I quickly realized I had already known unconsciously that we were going to leave early.

Phil wrung his hands. "Okay, I'm in. Where's my new baby?" It was that simple. I pointed at the sizable snakeskin rifle case by the lockers we had installed.

Petro, on the other hand, landed on the table, eyeing me skeptically. "You think this is a good idea, boss?" he asked, not pushing back but making sure I wasn't on another crazy suicide mission that involved something other than our main objective.

"Not this time, buddy. The plan doesn't change. We just go a day early and avoid whatever it is someone else may have planned for us," I replied, pulling out a tactical backpack from the locker.

"If we go early, do we get to spend an extra day at my birthplace?" Petro asked. He was negotiating, more than likely feeling left out due to Phil's bribe. I reached down, picking up the weapon's case and setting it on the table, where Phil smoothed his hands over it.

"That's the plan, the way I see it. Plus, who says after this is all said and done we can't go more often," I stated, holding up the Planesgate key.

As the new plan started to settle into our minds, my cell phone chirped to life with Ed's ringtone. Phil, Petro, and I had all set it as the opening theme song of the James Bond films. I hadn't sealed the Postern, meaning our phones were still working. Predictably, Ed was about to do some digging. We had been gone just a minute too long.

"Hello?" I answered in the form of a question. After all, I was one of the few people with the ability to shield my thoughts.

Static greeted me, and I could feel Ed winding up on the other end of the line. "We're ready to get back to it. There's been another magical misfire, and the others need to get going. Plus, Ana Vlad sent us a slightly more detailed map to go over."

I paused, looking at Phil as he made a fist, put it up to his mouth, and stifled a childlike scream. He knew the deal, flashing both hands down to the sleek rifle in the case. Hopping up slightly, he clicked his heels. As I was about to respond, he started walking over with his arms out for a hug, making a kissy face.

"I got to go!" I said quickly, lighting a ball of hellfire in front of me, stopping Phil's appreciative response.

"Wait—MAX!" Ed barked just as I clicked the call off.

"Come here. Give your creepy Uncle Phil a hug," Phil kidded as I turned up the volume on the hellfire, letting out a light chuckle.

"Well, I'm pretty sure by now he knows we're about to leave. He also mentioned another misfire," I responded, pointing toward the weapons locker we had added to the Postern a couple of years back. "Load up. I'm going to lock the door."

After a few minutes of explaining the rifle to Phil and watching Petro buzz around the room nervously, I walked over to the Planesgate, hesitating.

"What is it, boss?" Petro asked, landing on the table with a similar but smaller assault pack on his back.

"It's not me. Why are you so nervous?" I asked as Phil stepped up with his game face on. He had also never been to the Plane, and he knew it was time to get to work.

"Aye, mate. You've been bobbing and zipping around the room like a fat kid in a candy store," Phil confirmed. I was glad I wasn't the only one who had noticed how Petro was acting. This also told me Phil was focused.

"It's just . . . well . . . I kind of left in a rush without telling many people. Bosley and the others told everyone what happened and what I was doing but . . . you know. I'm not sure if other Pixies are going to want to talk to me," Petro stated flatly. He was seriously worried.

"That all? I bet everyone will be beside themselves to see you. Look, if things are not working out or you need more time, we'll just leave and come back. Deal?" I asked, being the voice of reason for once.

"You always know the right things to say, boss. Deal," Petro replied, smiling. What I hadn't said was that I was also nervous.

Phil looked up, nodding for me to activate the gate. Unlike the others, as soon as I turned the key, the gate made a sucking sound, followed by a low rumbling hum that reminded me of a summer thunderstorm in the distance.

Taking a light step, I leaned forward, pushing myself through the gate.

CHAPTER 10

Off to See the Wizard

Falling to my knees, I quickly realized we weren't in the queen's castle as planned, but rather in a wooded meadow shrouded by massive, oddly shaped trees with turf-like grass padding the forest floor. The sound of running water accompanied by the scent of fresh pine took hold of my senses as they came into focus.

The Planesgate, according to Tom and the journal, was supposed to come out in the queen's palace. Not the middle of a forest.

I crawled forward a few feet, still not able to stand up as Phil did the same, catching up to me as we both rolled over on our backs.

Gating had become a general, everyday occurrence for me over the past few years. This one had been different. It felt like a piece of me had been pulled away then suddenly slammed back into my body, much like waking up, unharmed, from a bad car crash.

I cleared my throat, needing a drink of water. "You good?"

"Aye, just a little stiff," Phil huffed as Petro zipped overhead, darting through the trees.

Phil and I started getting up simultaneously as a warming flood of power washed over my body. I took in another lungful of nature, finally steadying myself.

"You feel that?" I probed, going through several stages of odd sensations.

"Yup, a little weak-kneed, but I feel fine. Awake," Phil added just as I was able to fully focus on the area around us.

Petro zipped down, his chest heaving from flying at max speed. "Hey, boss, here! Oh, it's not bugs either; I know you don't like eating them," he exclaimed, handing both of us a small leaf. "Chew on this for a few seconds. It will help your bodies level out."

"Jenny said we would feel a little off at first, but I can't remember why she said it would happen," I lightly grumbled, admitting to not fully paying attention to important information.

"You two knuckleheads are supercharged, baby," Petro barked excitedly, zipping around us.

Phil held up his fist, stretching out his fingers. "That's right. It's like the opposite of when the Fae come to Earth. The Etherium in our bodies wakes up here. I don't think there's any explanation for it. She described it as two magnets with reverse polarity," Phil spit out as Petro and I stared at him.

"Yeah, well, I think it supercharged your brain," I teased. Phil just smirked.

"Good looking and smart," he replied as the sound of a third person clearing their throat caught all three of us by surprise.

"Looks like things haven't changed much," Jamison said as a grin hit all our faces.

"Well, looky what the cat threw up," Phil greeted, getting the insult wrong. Or was he being smart again, noting what cats often did?

I quickly jumped into the general banter, making fun of the fact that I'd had to cart his head around once upon a time. "We were just heading . . . to the queen's castle."

Petro dusted, holding back a laugh as Jamison reached out his hand. We grasped each other's forearms in a Fae handshake representing trust and family. Keeping my promise to his father, Ned, and saving Aslynn from her own actions held more weight than I probably understood.

"It's good to see you," Jamison greeted firmly. "Same to you, Phil," he finished, sharing a lighter yet still meaningful version of the handshake with Phil as Petro flew down.

Jamison held out his hand for Petro to land, stroking his mustache. Jamison's grin widened as he reached into his pocket, pulling out a small glass container full of a lightly glowing green material.

"Is this . . . ?" Petro asked as he sniffed the ampoule. Even though it was sealed, he and other Pixies could still smell the contents.

"I remembered our deal. You help me get cleaned up after our little trip through that big-ass spider . . . I one day get a bottle of wing salve from the far reaches," Jamison said proudly, settling a debt.

Petro had helped clean up the mess sticking to Jamison's disembodied head from not only rolling around the back seat of the trusty Cadillac DeVille, but also the spider guts. In return, Jamison had promised to get him a special wing salve from the Plane, the only thing that could help heal his and Lacey's damaged wings.

Macey and Lacey had constructed a mechanical brace that, while working well, clicked at times, also slowing him down slightly.

After our initial encounter with the Soul Dealers,

Blackbeard had cut off Jamison's head with a soul sword and somehow had it placed in my lab. We had carted Jamison's rather moody head around for months before finally locating the rest of his body, putting Humpty Dumpty back together again.

I actually missed carting his head around. The pure comic relief of it had been a source of night after night of laughs. But that was a story for another day, I thought to myself as the initial mood of the reunion started to fade.

"All right. Now that the honeymoon is over, why the hell aren't we in the queen's palace?" I asked, making a good point as Phil reached down, picking up his rifle and a few other items we had dropped coming through the gate.

"About that. Aslynn had an opportunity to talk to Tom. He said there would likely be complications if you gated directly from the Postern to the palace. Something or someone knows you're coming. After some mild adjustments that will hopefully go unnoticed, we altered the destination on the gate to bring you here," Jamison informed us while he ran his hands through his red hair.

Phil spoke up with his newfound intelligence. "Brilliant, mate. That means all we'll have to do is get back to the Postern from that location, and the destination should be adjusted," Phil declared, grinning as even Jamison looked confused by Phil's newly found knowledge of gates.

The truth of the matter was, Phil had heard this all before. He just didn't remember any of it. The effects of being on the Plane were snapping all the synapses in his brain into overdrive.

"Yes, something like that. We need to get moving. Unlike back home, it's going to be dark here soon. Aslynn is meeting us in a nearby cottage. She should have an update for us," Jamison commented as he turned, pointing toward a dark, shadowy corner of the woods.

"Hey, boss, what do you think is going on back home?" Petro asked.

That was a good question. I hesitated while the others started to walk. "Jamison, do us a favor if you can and find out what's going on back home. The reason we came early was to avoid any surprises. Ed, Jenny, and the others seemed to be more concerned about us being able to make the trip in the first place than what could be expecting us. It felt like something was going on back home as well. There was another misfire a few hours before we left."

Jamison clicked his teeth, a bad habit he often had when he was going through the Rolodex of contacts he had in his mind. "Yeah . . . when we get to the cottage, I'll see what I can find out. Things were rumbling around here as well a few hours ago, and that might just explain it. Whenever a misfire happens on Earth, we get a little bit of it as well."

The rest of the trip was as expected. Alien landscapes and unfamiliar nature colors took hold of my attention as Phil and I both slowly fell behind Jamison and Petro.

"This is it!" Jamison shouted over his shoulder. "If you two are done staring at the trees, let's get inside."

The cottage in front of us melted into its surroundings as moss-covered rocks protruded from either side. It was built into a small row of stones that formed a wall around the area. Ancient trees and spongy moss flowed across the structure as if it were part of nature itself.

Smoke rose from the chimney, resembling part of a tree before flattening out and disappearing within a few feet of its opening. The laws of physics on Earth did not apply here. This was a place of wonder, a place of magic, and most importantly, a place that I knew absolutely nothing about.

Jenny's classes about the Plane and others attempting to explain it to me had done the place an injustice. It was a raw, magical place, full of mystery and omnipotent power. I looked to the right as a tree as big around as a building but only as tall as a water tower forced my brain to accept that I was in a different realm.

The sky was playing hide and seek behind layers of thick treetops. Rays of blue and orange light danced through the green canopy's cracks, making the entire area around the cottage glow as if in some type of trippy, half-cartoonish dream.

Aslynn opened the door with the look of an ex-lover on her face that, while knowing the two of you weren't getting back together, was somehow still in love. "Well, that's one thing that's gone right this week," she greeted us as an eye-reaching smile made its way to her lips.

"Lass, it's been a while. I believe precisely—" Phil started before Jamison cut him off.

"Brain Man here is enjoying the extra dose of Etherium."

"Enjoy it while it lasts. That initial spike only sticks around for a few hours, maybe a couple of days," Aslynn remarked as we followed her into the cozy, tucked-away cottage.

A fireplace filled the house with the cozy haze of sweet wood being burned. Years of constant cooking and smoking permeated the rest of the accommodations as we walked down a few steps into a sitting room half underground. While the front of the cottage didn't give anything away, there was evidently more to the building underground.

Jamison motioned for us to sit at a large, solid oak table surrounded by oversized ornate chairs. Each one was unique, having a story intricately carved into the wood surrounding its cushions.

"This place is something else," I murmured, still taking it all in. "Tolkien would be proud."

"It was once used as a secret meeting place for the local Wood Elves," Aslynn added. She left out the part about the Fae driving the Elves from their homeland thousands of years ago.

From what I understood, while they now tolerated each other, their relationship was superficial at best. I had only really scratched the surface on either culture, my only interaction with Elves coming from Lana.

"We must pay our respects, then," Phil added, not stating why as he pulled out a pack of cigarettes and laid a few on the fireplace mantel.

"I see you understand Elven customs. I'm sure it will be appreciated. Fortunately for us, this place was gifted to our father. He helped several families escape," Jamison proudly asserted. The pride in his voice was evident.

"Well, I'm sure that makes the family balance more than even," I said, looking at Aslynn. Last year, she had been responsible for the deaths of several people. While some were questionably innocent, others appeared to be well-deserving.

After setting up Darkwater's daughter, a gross, dead squid by that point, I had fulfilled my obligation to Ned, my once mentor. I had also informed Aslynn that I wouldn't extend that courtesy anymore. Petro knew, of course, but Phil had not been made aware of the entire story.

"What does that mean?" Phil asked quickly. His newfound, short-lived intelligence was driving him to ask rational questions.

"Oh, you never told him? I thought you two were closer than that," Aslynn said thoughtfully. She wasn't taking a cheap shot; rather, just stating she understood I could be trusted.

"Bruther?" Phil asked, raising an eyebrow while he pulled out a smoke, holding it up to Aslynn, who nodded, permitting him to light it.

"Oh hell," Petro barked, zipping in from the kitchen

94

holding a small piece of bread. "Aslynn here was the one who killed all those folks, including Lucian. Some of those people deserved it, though."

I shrugged as Phil let the smoke roll out of his nose, not pushing it out. He followed this by looking up at Aslynn. "That arse, Beleth, cut off Jamison's head and killed your father. I get that part. Hell, I thought it was you at first. The thing I don't get is, why the others? That poor V and Lucian, for starters."

The look shifted on Aslynn's face. "I'd do it all again times a thousand if it meant I had the chance to ensure those pieces of shit never took another breath. If that meant burning the entire city to the ground, I would have."

Jamison walked over, putting a hand on his sister's shoulder, whispering to her. "What's done is done. What was gained was gained, and what was lost, is forever lost."

I recognized the saying from one of the old storybooks my mother used to read me.

Phil hesitated again before putting the cigarette out in a small wooden cup sitting in front of him. Burn marks from previous cigarettes surrounded its rim.

"Lass, hell . . . I don't know if I wouldn't have done the same thing. Let's just keep this to ourselves," Phil replied, understanding in his voice.

"What she also fails to mention is that taking action in support of the queen gained her significant favor with the Fae Court," Jamison added as the two finally sat down.

"Thus, the ability to send the note and adjust the gate," I said, getting a firm grasp on the situation.

Jamison pulled out the schematic to a large building, laying it flat. "It looks like you're figuring it out."

"What's in it for you?" Petro asked, dipping his wing in the jar of salve. He had taken my ability of being straight and to the point to a whole new level. I enjoyed watching him. It also saved me from coming out of the situation as the asshole. I had a keen feeling the others were starting to catch on.

The siblings looked at each other coolly. Jamison cleared his throat. "I . . ." He paused as Aslynn looked at him. "We owe you in return for not only helping us avenge the death of our father, but saving our lives."

The message was clear; much like Petro, the Fae had an odd way of handling things like this. They felt obligated to repay the favor. It was almost like forming a dysfunctional family with your best friends at the end of the world.

"I appreciate everything you're doing. But I'm with Petro. There's more to it," I said, clearly pulling the conversation back.

"When Titania detained your grandfather, we were bound to help you. The other part is a service for our queen. Things are bad with the Pillar being taken," Jamison stated, leaning over the map.

"You mean the Pillar that your queen stole," I asked in the form of a statement, already having concluded it had been taken from her.

Aslynn cleared her throat, putting several small stones on the map. "Yes, about that. I'm not going to delay this any further. I know you'll appreciate it. The queen believes Tom has something to do with the Pillar being taken. We don't think that's fully the case. Either way, he was at the wrong place at the wrong time. If this doesn't get resolved soon, she will execute him."

"I get it. Damned if you do, damned if you don't. I had a little run-in with Lana the other day in the Everwhere. We ran into something we called the Faceless," I added, wanting to lay it all out on the table.

"Pale, smooth, stonelike skin? Long claws?" Jamison

asked, knowing the answer.

"Yup. She said they had something to do with the Crystal King. They were either looking for something or trying to get out of the Everwhere. She said something about him once owning the Pillar and the palace the queen now occupies," I dropped on the group like a bomb.

"Shit, that confirms our worst fears," Aslynn said, leaning back. "I heard this morning that the Council believes he's somehow involved. We thought this might be the case, but nobody's seen or heard from the Crystal King in thousands of years. Nobody even knows where he could be, other than maybe hidden in the Cavalier Mountains."

"I think that's a little more than a *maybe*. I have a feeling this might help." I smacked the ring and coins on the table, pulling them from my inside pocket.

"You're full of all kinds of surprises today," Aslynn chirped, leaning over to pick up the ring. She knew what it represented.

Phil was going over the map, also listening to the conversation. "I have a feeling Davros is telling us how to find the Crystal King."

Petro was grinning, still soaking his wings. "We go to my village, and I bet we can find a way to Davros's keep. We just go there a little sooner than planned." The group looked at the grinning Pixie. "I'm just saying; everyone ignores us on the Plane, but there's one thing you should know. We have eyes and asses everywhere."

"That's settled then. Queen first, Pixies village, Davros's castle, then we're off to see the wizard," I exclaimed, singing the last part of the sentence.

"Maybe not a wizard unless you mean Tom, but it sounds like a bloody quest to me," Phil said, a slight change in his tone. The initial juice was starting to wear off.

I shifted in my chair, looking at the two Fae sitting across the table. "What's the deal? I'm pretty sure there was some kind of plan for us tomorrow. Lay it out."

"The queen was—or is, for that matter—planning on detaining another one of you. Probably Phil, I would guess. I suggest you walk through the front door instead of gating in. The element of surprise might help. The trip will take most of the day if you leave early enough. As for Tom, we plan to help keeping him alive and ensuring that he leaves the castle in one piece," Aslynn declared, determination clear in her voice.

She would both help Tom and gain more favor in the queen's eyes at the same time. Fae politics, as most politics in the magical community, always ended on a one-way road.

"We're in the jungle, baby," Petro belted out in his best impersonation of Axl Rose, setting the mood for the rest of the conversation as Jamison started going over the map, and more importantly, the detention area of the queen's palace.

CHAPTER 11

Follow the Yellowish Brick Road

Morning came early, as did the smell of coffee and the shuffling of gear. The brother and sister duo had arranged for transportation right up to the castle gates. Aslynn's part was to ensure our approach seemed like any other Fae or visitor traveling to the palace and surrounding city.

The carriage was timeless in its lines, modern and sleek. Nothing physically drivable on Earth could compare to it. A large, round sphere connected to the chassis by two ornate poles that glowed red with some type of internal power, which I was guessing was simply explained as magic. It clearly pulled the carriage along.

Back home, even though the Balance had occurred, things remained unchanged for the most part. Cars still drove on the road, and Mages and Vs alike still needed to get a job to pay for whatever streaming service was the flavor of the month. The magical community was still relatively small and unexplored, with several groups preferring to stay in the shadows.

I reached into my pocket, feeling the stone placed there. Rule one of traveling to a foreign and alien land: always have a plan B. In this case, it was an Evergate stone from the

Everwhere's version of the Postern. From my research, it could possibly transport a person to the Everwhere from the Plane. It was just an extra step that seemed almost impossible if not adequately equipped. I would make sure Phil had the stone if we got separated, and Lana would ensure Phil got back home through the graveyard before he stirred up too much trouble and extra work for her if I didn't make the trip with him.

On the other hand, traveling from the Plane directly back home would be another story. The official gates directly to and from the Plane to Earth were highly watched. The Fae kept the gates they used out of everyone else's sight and only mainly accessible to their kind.

We said our goodbyes, settling in for the day-long journey. Aslynn confirmed the route was clear and, from her perspective, *bland* compared to the rest of the Plane. While her assessment wasn't too far off, the alien landscape was still a lot to take in.

Fields of grain and thick forests rushed by as we rode at blurring speeds, the vehicle obviously cruising on autopilot. The ride was smooth and pin-drop quiet, something I associated to the dark marble-like surface we were riding on. It seemed as if the roads had been carved out of the very ground itself, followed by months, if not years, of polishing.

The high-pitched hum and muffled crackle of the ball driving the carriage started to drop in tone. I leaned forward, peering out the side window. "Holy shit," I exclaimed as the full grandeur of the Emerald Castle came into view.

Phil let out a whistle, under the same spell I was. Petro sighed. "I thought I wouldn't have to see this place again."

We both looked at him as he flew back to his seat in one of the cupholders. "I take it this is one of those places where Pixies aren't treated that well?" I asked flatly, having heard the stories.

"Yeah," was all he said, not followed up by a *boss* or anything.

"It's game time, bruthers," Phil spoke up, sitting up straighter.

"Jamison said all we need to do is show the guards these passes and not act stupid," I reminded the group, pulling my pass out.

Jamison had compared the entrance to the border with Canada at Niagara Falls. Serious yet flexible enough to get through—if you didn't count the dozens of magical wards we had to pass through; though those wards, according to Aslynn, would mostly be shielded by the carriage we rode in.

The wards, from all accounts, covered major spells and offensive-type magic, but one of them identified undesirables such as demons, which made my heritage Aslynn's main concern. Though for some odd reason, that particular ward was being calibrated right now, and would be offline for the next two hours.

Massive barriers and hinged gates the size of office buildings loomed as lofty shadows blocked the still rising sun.

The carriage hummed to a stop as a tall, blonde woman with overly correct posture walked up to the window. She was wearing what looked like a lightly armored set of well-tailored gray-and-green fatigues. An odd, small pistol hung off her hip, along with several other items that looked less than friendly.

"Identification, and state your business," the woman requested flatly as two other guards walked around the security building with indifferent expressions on their faces. I knew the look from my time in the army. They were making the rounds assigned to them while on shift. I would even bet the two men were telling stories about past drinking endeavors.

I handed our passes to the woman, quickly leaning back

in my seat. The vehicle we'd arrived in stated we had some type of status, done on purpose. "We're here for the day to visit some friends for dinner."

This was the scripted plan and the main reason why people came to the city which surrounded the queen's palace. What I had failed to realize was the sheer size of the place.

It was every bit as large as any major metropolitan city back on Earth. More to the point, if you took everything north of Interstate 10 all the way to the Highway 295 beltway in Jacksonville, Florida, it would more than likely fit inside the city's massive walls.

The sheer size of the place made me pause, reflecting on how destructive the prior wars I kept hearing about must have been.

The guard looked around the interior, seeing Petro. "Is he a servant?"

"Yes, he's new. We were just telling him some things we needed before getting through the gate," I replied.

"I see. Make sure he stays in the designated Pixie areas," the stern woman insisted, handing me back our passes. "Have a good eve," she finished, waving her hand at the large barrier in front of us, which slid into the ground.

I smirked, turning as the window automatically closed, somehow knowing the conversation was over. After the carriage hummed back to life, Petro unleashed a flurry of cuss words that made even Phil blush.

"Calm down there, bruther. These people—"

"Fae. They're Fae," I interrupted. Phil nodded and continued.

"These Fae are the least of our worries, Warrior of the Freeze," Phil added as Petro smoothed out his mustache. I could feel he was about to bust out Petro's new title, given to him and his brothers by Macey and Lacey. "Slayer of the Great Wolves, as long as you're with us, you don't have to worry about that poppycock. You brought your swag, right?"

Petro grinned as he pulled a gold-covered sash out of his bag. "Don't leave home without it. For the record, I see that lady again, and I'm dusting her where the sun doesn't shine," Petro promised perking up, his mind shifting off the guard's comments.

After a few more minutes of Petro talking about all the things we were going to do in his village, I realized I hadn't been paying attention to the blazing speeds we were traveling at once again. Buildings zipped by in a blur of gray and gold as we sped along some type of interstate.

The city opened up into a heart of towering buildings and roadways crossing at several different levels in the sky. Looking closer, I could see small vehicles zipping through the air with what looked like Pixie dust trailing behind.

"Where did Aslynn say this thing was going to take us?" I inquired, looking forward and seeing what was obviously the main stronghold of the queen.

"Close to the palace," Phil said, getting the same sinking feeling I was getting. "At this speed and by the looks of the buildings, we should be there in about five minutes." Phil's mind was still firing on all cylinders. While he was getting back to normal, he was still spitting out random pieces of information.

We weren't stopping close to the queen's palace; by the looks of things, we were pulling straight up to the front door.

I leaned back in my seat, reflecting on what was about to happen. "A few years back, I would have sworn I was going crazy seeing this. There was no way in hell I would have believed you if you had told me I was about to meet the Fae queen in a different realm with a Pixie and a kick-ass Earth

Mage."

Petro floated over to the seat. "And I never would have thought I would be hanging out with you two meat bags."

We all smiled, knowing that fun time was about to be over.

"You know what chaps my nuggets?" Phil asked, not giving us time to answer. "The Council knew they would be waiting for us with some bullshite. No Night Stalkers or real help. I wouldn't doubt they sent us to avoid any political fallout in case something goes wrong. That way they can blame us and wash their hands."

"All we need to do is make it out of here and back to the cottage to pick up the rest of our gear," I reminded the group. "We're here to get the situation with the Pillar addressed. I trust Aslynn and Jamison's word on getting Tom out in one piece."

"You haven't seen Tom since we closed that portal to the hellion legions, right, boss?" Petro asked.

It had been some time since I had seen Gramps or been able to confirm he was indeed alive. From what I understood, he had been running around working on something big. Not to mention that he and Lilith had met up on several occasions.

We all looked up as a black, large triangle-shaped device floated out of the sky, wrapping itself around the front sphere driving the carriage.

Phil huffed. "What is it you always say?"

"Gods and graves?" I replied as he shook his head, telling me his newfound genius was slipping.

"No, that Star Fighter saying," Phil continued.

"*Star Wars*. It's *Star Wars*. You mean, that I have a bad feeling about this?" I added in my best Han Solo impression.

"Yeah, that one, bruther," Phil confirmed, shifting in his

seat as the vehicle lurched forward.

Pulling up, the gate surrounding the main palace made several statements, the first being that you were not getting through without a fight. Odd-looking turrets locked onto us. Whatever they fired, I had no desire to find out.

Rows of heavily armed guards peaked over the top of a five-story-high metal wall. The fortification's entrance was melting into a shape large enough for us to pass through instead of opening. In front of the newly formed doorway stood the same female guard who had let us in through the initial checkpoint as if she had been there all day.

"That's never good," I murmured as the vehicle stopped. The hum of the windows quickly sliding open filled the void as the tall woman leaned down.

"I see you found your way to the palace. Excellent," she said as Petro glared at her.

"Was that you at the front gate, Lass?" Phil asked as the woman stood up to her full height, rolling her shoulders back.

"Yes, and my name is Atari," she asserted, walking up to the black shroud covering the front of the carriage, waving her hand over a smooth pale-gray panel.

"You could've just told us who you were when we came in. We might even have played it cool," Petro said, not holding back.

"I see you all are not acting anymore. The queen already knew you were coming. I recommend not playing any more games while you are within the palace walls," Atari cautioned in a more casual tone.

After another few seconds of the vehicle obviously being scanned, another guard popped out of the booth, giving Atari a thumbs up.

"It looks like you're clear to enter. The vehicle will take you where you need to go," she said, and the vehicle rocked into motion while the window slid up.

We sat in silence for a few seconds, taking in our surroundings. Rows of both defensive and offensive weaponry lay in strategic patterns, while groups of guards rushed around in several directions like schools of fish.

The queen's palace was not just her home, but also a fortified strategic location. I hadn't considered that Titania might be building up her armies after the Pillar had been taken.

"Game faces," I blurted out as we pulled up to a massive, shining, silver-and-green building. Squinting my eyes, I quickly realized that the green was, in fact, solid blocks of emerald.

CHAPTER 12

The Queen of Hearts

The vehicle came to a halt as the whisper-quiet doors whooshed open. Lined up on either side of a blazing crimson carpet leading into the building were two lines of what appeared to be high-ranking officials.

Roughly halfway through the line to our right, Aslynn stood, lightly nodding as a small grin perked the corners of her mouth. Just as Petro was about to zip out of the vehicle, he paused, as if hitting an invisible barrier.

"What's up, buddy?" I asked. He turned, wrinkling his nose.

"The red carpet. It's dyed with old blood," Petro replied, the humming sounds of the busy city keeping his words from echoing outside the vehicle.

I looked back at Phil, who just scratched his face. "There will be a lot of that hogwash. We might as well get used to it here and now, bruther."

"Perfect," I groaned, stepping out of the vehicle first while Petro flew up into the air as far away as he could from the carpet without looking overly paranoid.

A slender yet strong twenty-something-year-old man stepped forward, greeting us with a slight nod. While very fashionable, with flowing green lines and streaks of gold, his clothes were also made for utility. The person in front of us likely spent most of his day running around the palace.

The man's snow-white hair contrasted with his tan face. Not a crease or line was visible as he began to talk. "My name is Cliff. I will be your assistant while you are all staying within the confines of the palace. I am to take you to your quarters first. Once there, I will lay out the rest of the afternoon for everyone."

I gave Phil a side-glance, who just shrugged lightly. Cliff was inviting, as was the case with most people in his type of position. Concierges, butlers, and others who ensured everything flowed in the right direction often knew not only more than everyone else around but had favor with important people.

"Cliff, I'm Max—" I started before the slender man cut me off.

"I know who you are and who your associates are. This is not the time or place for introductions. That will take place with the queen and her court later. Aslynn," Cliff snapped, turning around to face the woman. "My understanding is that you know these people from the Earth realm. Please join us."

Listening to Cliff talk, I had the feeling that joining us wasn't a choice for Aslynn. I started walking forward as the ornately dressed Fae on either side of the blood-red carpet lightly nodded their heads in respect.

As if somebody had turned off all ambient noise as soon as we crossed the threshold into the massive crystal-laden entrance, the sounds from the outside world immediately came to an abrupt halt, the echoes of light footsteps and the sounds of our own shuffling clothes taking over.

"Bloody hell, this place is impressive," Phil belted out, voice resonating throughout the space.

"Yes, I'm sure you'll find the rest of the palace just as captivating," Cliff added. I couldn't tell if he was making a smartass remark or genuinely wanted to show us around. The man had an odd aura around him.

Aslynn walked up beside me as Cliff ushered us toward a long hallway to our far right. "He's good. Just be careful what you say around him," she whispered into my ear at an almost tickling volume.

I took a final look around the room. Four large catwalks stacked on top of each other overlooked the entrance hall. Guards dressed in armor made of the same material as the walls melted into the structure, only noticeable upon further inspection.

Hanging in the middle of the room was a chandelier which was its own building. A large, mirrored window surrounded the jewel and metal structure. Light poured from holes in set patterns shooting concentrated light at other reflective markers around the room. It had made me squint when we first walked in.

The feeling of not only being watched but analyzed beamed directly through me from the overhead fixture. There were people or whatever inside.

Stepping into the hallway, we passed through another security checkpoint, finally being ushered into an ornate elevator. Cliff waved his hand over another gray pad as the elevator shot up into the building.

I had not been able to pinpoint the top of the palace when we'd pulled up, lending to it being well over one hundred stories tall; I was even betting it was double that.

After what felt like a hushed eternity, the elevator came to a smooth stop, the buzz of Petro's wings the only noise present.

As the doors opened, the immediate change in the feel

and ambiance of the area was defined by the plush, regal impression and colors of the floor's lobby. Rich reds and deep greens covered the walls and floor, while detailed paintings showed scenes of hunters roving alien landscapes.

Cliff walked us through a large sitting area, finally making it to our rooms as I spoke up, wanting to get my bearings. "What floor are we on?"

"The hundred and fortieth. This part of the main building is reserved for special guests. The queen must think you are important," Cliff speculated, finally taking in what we were wearing, judging us without any hesitation or trying to hide it.

Opening the door to my room first, it was just as nice and posh as the rest of the floor. A large bed sat in a separate section from where we walked into the main living room. The suite was easily the size of a large apartment.

Cliff walked to a sizable crushed-velvet curtain, swinging it open to reveal the literal breathtaking view. We all moved closer. A handful of clouds below us blocked a small patch of the city from our view.

Phil let out a whistle. "Phew, bruther, isn't this some shite? Is there any other way off the floor?"

Phil had a good point. Cliff was showing us how isolated we were this high up in the building, as well as the view.

"No. Let me be clear. While you are all here, you are my responsibility. With that, there will be no random exploring. Not to mention you may run into something less sociable than I am. Oh, and those clothes—or whatever you call them—we will have to change those. We took the liberty of putting some outfits together. I'm certain, now that you're here, we got the sizes right," Cliff snapped, making several points all at once.

The young Fae was reading us the riot act before we headed off to our separate rooms.

"What about me?" Petro chirped. Cliff had been generally ignoring him.

"Oh, yes. As much as I despise saying it, your outfit will do. The no-exploring situation extends to you also. You are not to intermingle with the staff Pixies either. I don't feel like cleaning up the sauna again," Cliff sighed as Petro simply nodded.

I was shocked by Petro's calm demeanor after Cliff had talked to him in that manner. In most cases, he would have threatened him or taken a solid stab at one of his eyes.

Cliff showed the others their rooms—all three were in a row—and made his final comments on us making ourselves presentable after going over the evening's schedule. We would have an initial reception with drinks and an official greeting. Next, dinner would be served with some sort of entertainment. As Cliff had put it, we would retreat for a private meeting if the queen so desired. If not, we would meet in the morning to discuss the current situation.

The purpose of our trip was clear to Cliff, meaning Titania was well aware of our intent. I was also sure the Supreme Council had sent an emissary before discussing how the two powers could work together through—you guessed it —me.

Cliff disappeared into the elevator, leaving us standing in the main sitting room. "I can't believe you let him talk to you like that," I started, falling into one of the plush chairs.

"Who, that guy? He's okay. It sounds like he takes care of the staff Pixies to me. Heard him say he had to clean up the sauna?" Petro said, snickering lightly. "He probably had them do it, but the fact that the stiff didn't mention killing them speaks volumes. Boss . . ." he trailed off. "I still don't think you get how bad it is for Pixies around here at times."

"I know. I just need to understand when Phil and I need

111

to thump someone's head in," I added as Phil threw in his seal of approval.

"Aye, you know all you have to do is say the word."

"You guys are great!" Petro bellowed as he motioned to come in closer. "There are Pixies all over this floor. They will stay hidden for the most part. You want my advice? Cover your private bits when you're in the shower."

"How will we know they are there?" I asked. Petro stroked his mustache.

"You'll hear giggling coming from the walls," he explained, having done this in the past.

"Enough of that bollocks. It sounds like we won't get much time to snoop," Phil interjected as I held up a finger, reminding him to be careful with what he said.

I pulled out one of Ed's famous privacy charms, pushing some will into it before a thin, flowing bubble snapped to life around us.

The charm was extremely harmless, allowing it not to set off any wards. It was also convenient for when you needed to have absolute privacy. The only issue was that you only had as long as there was air still inside the bubble to talk. It shrank as we breathed and talked. Ed had also mentioned it could come in handy underwater.

"That's what it looks like. Phil, what floor was Gramps on?" I asked as he pulled on his waning enhanced intelligence.

"Sub-basement fifteen. Meaning he's in the complete opposite direction." Phil paused. "The plans Jamison let us gander at only had the first twenty upper and lower floors. The dining room we are going to later is about as close as we will get."

While I liked smart Phil, the words coming out of his mouth didn't match his expression. I was sure the last of his gift was almost gone. Part of Phil's charm was his impulsiveness and the lack of ordinariness in anything he did, minus cleaning his guns. He seemed unhappy regurgitating random facts.

"Petro, you know what I'm going to ask," I told him. He nodded.

"The exact opposite of what Cliff told me. I'll see what the Pixies have to say about this place. Guys, listen, I can't end up in a sauna with the other Pixies. Casey would clip my wings," Petro said, getting worried.

Phil and I let out a light chuckle. "I'll make it my personal mission to ensure that doesn't happen. Not to mention I don't want my underwear drawer dusted again," I promised.

Petro snickered. After keeping Petro out late one afternoon on a job, I had found out the next day the effects of having one's underwear pixed. Needless to say, I had run around screaming for a solid hour. There had been some more aftereffects, but I'll keep those to myself for now.

"Phil, I think we should take Cliff's advice and change into whatever clothes they made for us. We need to fit in as best we can. Petro can give them the smell test to make sure they aren't charmed," I recommended as Phil agreed.

"I haven't seen too many tattooed Fae lollygagging around, bruther." He grinned, pointing at the fully stocked bar Cliff had failed to mention.

"No," I huffed, referring to the minibar.

"Yes," Phil replied, standing up, almost popping the now shrinking bubble.

"Shit," Petro added, knowing the evening could quickly devolve into chaos.

"Dammit. Alright, bruther. But I'm not passing up on anything during suppertime," Phil warned, fake pouting as I shook my head.

"You know, we may just need a distraction," I relented. Phil's smile almost reached his forehead.

"I'm just the fellow to do it. I might be able to shelf my inner Irish if needed and bring out the old Texan half," Phil said, referring to his ability to drink others under the table.

"Maybe just a little of the Texan half. Enough to get Cliff preoccupied," I added as we started forming a plan for the evening.

"I need to be on the up-and-up for now. I'll see what I can do," Phil said, pulling out a small vial of his famous sober-up snake oil potion.

"Let's see what Titania has to say first. She may just lay it all out. Listen, I know we're used to these convoluted plans and being the bull in the China shop, but I'm not sure this is the time and place for that. If we can find a path to keep out of trouble, let's do it," I cautioned, thinking once again about collateral damage. "Minus Petro talking with the Pixies."

I was fairly sure we could reason with Titania. After seeing our surroundings, my initial thoughts on stirring up trouble were quickly fading. I looked up to see Phil and Petro's faces landing on the same opinion.

The problem was we immediately assumed there would be trouble. We all seemed to always go down the mischievous-plan path quickly.

While something wasn't sitting right with the group, we also realized we needed to be proper guests. That was, unless something went sideways. In that case, plan B was locked and loaded.

The three of us went our separate ways as I looked at the clothes lying on the bed. No sound echoed or came from the room as I started getting undressed. The gears in my modified steampunk-looking calf started clicking and whirring as I sat on one of the large chairs in the room.

An average person couldn't hear the noise, but I could. The odd thing about it was that I had yet to use the additional functions my replacement leg provided.

I leaned over, clicking open a small compartment in my calf as the ring Davros gave me dropped into the palm of my hand, as well as the coins he had mentioned bringing.

CHAPTER 13

A Cliff Hanger

C liff turned, clicking his heels as the elevator door slid shut behind him. "The queen has chosen to keep the reception to only a few court members. Dinner, not so much. I'm glad to see you all took my advice on the change of clothes."

I looked over to Phil's slicked-back hair which contrasted with the scar he had acquired during the attack on the Atheneum. It was rare to see the man dressed up, but to be fair, he looked confident and regal in his own way. Sensing my thoughts, Phil twisted the end of his mustache.

The shower itself had been something that had taken me several minutes to figure out. Instead of water, the cocoon-like structure closed around you, shooting streams of powerful yet comfortable steam, which did all the work. Even better was the automatic transition from soap to rinse cycle. It was a thoughtless process that had to have some type of spell involved. As the cocoon opened, it sucked every bit of moisture from your body. It reminded me of a microwave for cleaning oneself. And as warned, I had heard giggling while in the steamy shower.

"Who's going to be in attendance?" I inquired as Petro settled in on my shoulder. Cliff's earlier-than-expected return had cut Petro's visit to the other Pixies short. He *had* had enough time to figure out that he was a celebrity of sorts, though, much like back home on Earth.

The doors slid open as we stepped into a smaller, more intimate room. Two apelike guards stood on either end of the doors, staring through us.

"The other people in the room are of no consequence to you or your friends," Cliff quickly explained, looking at Petro and Phil.

I looked at Cliff. "And?"

"Okay. So that you know to be on your best behavior, the captain of the guard will be in there. Her name is Atari. I believe you've already met her. The prince of the Glades, Prince Levert, will be the one lurking in the shadows for the most part, but listening to everything you say." Cliff paused, looking up in thought. "Also, Dr. Van Gully, minister of special projects, will be there. He knows all the dirty secrets, and the clean ones too. Lastly, General Dex. The general is—well, *was* in charge of the Pillar security, along with several other critical items."

"That's it?" Petro asked, reading my mind.

"Those are the only important people you need to pay attention to," Cliff whispered, inferring anyone else in the room wasn't significant enough to mention or for us to talk to.

Cliff walked up to the guards, nodding at them, as the man on the right waved his hand over another gray panel, releasing the doors so they slowly opened. The once silent room was filled with conversation and the clinking of glasses. I looked closer, seeing an odd form of the Mags-Tech logo.

The room paused, allowing Cliff to introduce the group. Heads nodded along, while Atari only smirked.

"I think she's smitten with you," Phil muttered under his breath when the noise picked back up. The change of clothes had been a good call. We melted into the crowd of roughly twenty people.

Titania stood at the end of the room with guards strategically placed around her. The group surrounding her included Aslynn, who was beaming a smile in our direction. She was playing her part. A short, fat man resembling a living sausage sipped from a goblet while telling an animated story with his hands. The look on the queen's face was indifferent as Cliff strolled up to her.

"Hey, boss, I'm going to sniff around a little," Petro whispered, launching into the air. No one in the room even batted an eye as he darted around.

The room's floor plan was open, with several wooden and stone tables erupting from the floor. The usual table legs were replaced by what appeared to be ornate tree roots. Two doors on the far end shifted as the wait staff entered and exited with drink trays and small plates of odd-looking food.

After a few seconds of no one engaging us, Cliff motioned for Phil and I to catch up with him and the queen. We snaked through the room as smoothly as possible through the small crowd, receiving side-glances and envious stares alike. I was starting to wonder what these people knew about our crew.

"My queen," Cliff started as the short, sausage-like man huffed, backing up. I had a gut feeling this was Dr. Van Gully. He had the look. "I would like to introduce you to Max Abaddon Sand and Phil Eces. Petron, Warrior of the Freeze, also accompanies them."

Petro, taking the cue, flew down, landing on my shoulder. His title had carried over to the Plane. Gully, as I would call him now, sneered at the interaction, not liking the trust we had with a Pixie.

Titania reached out her hand, palm down, and I cradled it. Being on his best behavior, Phil followed my lead, only adding a slight wink. It was a habit that even he couldn't break.

She let out a light chuckle as Cliff released the breath he had been holding during the entire interaction. Ruby-red lips and raven-black hair framed Titania's face, cascading into her flowing dress. A mix of undeniable power and millennia of confidence fused with her ensemble, ensuring everyone in the room knew who was in charge.

"How delightful. I've heard much about the three of you," Titania complimented, making a point of acknowledging Petro. "It pleases me you accepted my invitation, and as I'm sure we are all aware, the timing is impeccable. Your Council was smart to send you and not one of their ass-kissing lapdogs."

"Sounds like you've met Councilman Carvel," I jested, testing the waters. She let out a full-on smooth, proper laugh only someone in her position or an evil wizard could pull off.

"Indeed. I think we will get along splendidly," she added, looking Phil up and down as if he were on the menu.

Titania raised her hands, snapping, and a server appeared with a tray of thin wine glasses. The light-blue contents shimmered in the light, reminding me of Ambrosia.

"A toast!" she proclaimed into the room as the group hushed, facing her.

Phil raised his eyebrows as we both grabbed a glass.

"To new beginnings and the health of our guests," she exclaimed as the group echoed back, "TO NEW BEGINNINGS!"

I wasn't clear on the meaning of the pledge. I would have to ask Aslynn or Cliff later. As soon as the toast was completed, the entire room, including Titania, relaxed.

The slight grin on Cliff's face told me we had passed the initial test and ensured he wouldn't fall victim to the whole *Off with his head!* thing, or whatever they did to people on the

Plane.

"My lady, thank you for the hospitality," I started, noticing Phil wandering toward Atari, not to mention another drink-carrying server. "We have much to discuss."

"We do. To the point, I see; I was told as much. We will talk more after dinner. Our immediate concerns are for only select ears," she replied, looking over at Aslynn.

"My queen," Aslynn bowed, nodding.

"Please make sure the Postern and the main Council gate are put back in place so no more of our guests are sent into the deep shire," Titania instructed as a blank look crossed Aslynn's face. "I'm pleased that you ensured our guests' safety," she followed up.

She knew; of course she did. I bet she also knew we'd stayed at the cottage making plans. That notion quickly fizzled out when I remembered it was an Elf's home. The message was meant as a slight warning and genuine compliment at the same time. Titania was letting Aslynn know not much got past her.

I was still debating if Titania was indeed happy we had made it to her palace in one piece. Like everyone had previously said, there was something in it for the queen. After all, she was already holding a few cards up her sleeve, one of which was Tom.

"I'll check the grounds to ensure everything is in working order," Aslynn finally responded.

Me being me, I wasn't as patient. "I think we need to talk now. Is there somewhere more private?" I asked, not taking my eyes off her.

Titania leaned forward. "I like the aggressive types. That being said, don't push your luck. Tom is safe and sound in my holding chambers. If all goes well, we will visit him after dinner."

I stared into her eyes, trying to read any form of emotion. Deep pools of black and brown gazed back as if knowing what I was doing. There was a hush in the area around us, telling me others were watching the interaction closely.

"Fair enough," was all I said, cracking a smile.

"Now that's out of the way, let's take this reception to the main halls," Titania said aloud as Cliff again relaxed. The whole point of the initial reception had evidently been to see if we would be eating dinner or an ax.

I noticed Phil intently talking to Atari. Something had his attention. Atari's posture was relaxed, not matching her earlier attitude.

Cliff walked over to me as Titania nodded, turning toward her security entourage and walking through an opening behind the group.

"That's not our path," Cliff jumped in quickly, stopping me from following as the rest of the room went silent while she made her exit.

"She doesn't travel around the building like the rest of us. It's a security precaution," Aslynn explained as Petro flew over to Phil and Atari. He had also noticed the two talking.

"Hey," I added, nodding over at Atari. "What's her deal?"

Cliff interjected before Aslynn could respond. "She's another one of those Danann. If I'm not mistaken, she's your cousin," Cliff said flatly, looking at Aslynn.

"She is," Aslynn confirmed, smiling. There was more to the situation than I was tracking. I was also aware that meant Atari was more than likely a friend, especially considering what our group had done for her family.

"Good to know," I noted as Gully walked up beside us. Cliff looked lost, apparently not knowing everything about our group.

"Max, it's good to meet you. If we get time later, I'd appreciate a word in private," the short, plump man stated, not asking.

"Anything in particular?" I inquired. He nodded.

"Yes, the Postern. I used to work on it, several years back. It would be good to know how things are going with all the gates," Gully added as I held back my smirk.

He was in charge of special projects—and secrets, as Cliff had put it. But the statement was odd, considering Tom was in their dungeon. What was his angle here? He wasn't exactly being forthcoming, and I didn't trust him. I would have to worry about that part later, but it was clear everyone in the room had an agenda. Had I mentioned I hated politics?

The man had obviously picked up on my mood shift, since he nodded before turning on his heels and walking out the door.

I watched him leave as Phil landed a full-on back smack, making me cough.

"Bruther, my bad. I thought you'd be interested to know Atari here is related to Aslynn," Phil said proudly. He was using the voice he often did when he discovered something no one else knew, or he had a secret.

Upon closer inspection, I also noticed his slack posture and lopsided grin. He had been flirting with her. Petro shook his head lightly when I glanced at him, an entire conversation being had without a word spoken. That's what good friends did. They didn't have to talk or use mind magic.

"I just found out. Pleasure," I said, reaching out my hand to officially meet her.

"Of course. I'm just glad I was on duty today," she replied, giving away a good bit of information with that statement.

I glanced at Aslynn as the skin on her forehead formed lines. Both parties had thoroughly planned our entrance and reception at the palace.

"This is all great, but we need to get going," Cliff interjected while the rest of the room continued to shuffle out.

I got in step beside Phil, leaning over. "Everything cool?" I whispered, seeing what his take on the room was.

"Bunch of egomaniacs walking around like peacocks, chests all pumped out," Phil shared as I pulled back.

"Yeah, I don't trust them either. Titania, though . . . she wants to accomplish something more with all this. Let's play it cool. She promised we would see Tom later," I responded as Phil scrunched his face together.

"You got all that after a few minutes with her?" he asked, already knowing the answer.

"Yeah, something like that."

We made it to the elevator doors, back within earshot of the others.

"Well, you all made it through that without getting anyone killed, so let's keep that up," Cliff encouraged the group with a genuine smile.

It was easy to tell he entertained hundreds, if not thousands, of guests throughout the year. I was betting some of those guests never left. We had made his initial evening fairly uneventful, but the night was still young.

CHAPTER 14

I Hope There's Cake at the End

"Gods and graves," I sighed, taking in the room while Cliff continued to herd us toward the head of the table.

The room was a massive, open colosseum–style structure. Rows of tables sat around an open pit in the middle. The more I continued to stare, the more the space resembled a nightmarish yet sophisticated medieval times restaurant.

Looking up, delicate crystal light strings placed tight enough to conceal the roof swayed lightly. I almost tripped over my own feet when I noticed how they worked. When a person or group walked, the hanging crystals lit up. The effect gave the room an odd radiance, making its inhabitants almost glow. It also created shadows at odd angles.

"Bruther, this place is as crazy as a gassy Pixie," Phil murmured. Petro dusted lightly, not arguing the point.

"I have a feeling those crystals overhead do a little more than light the room," I noted as Petro landed on my shoulder.

"I heard about this place as a kid," Petro informed. "If you're not supposed to be in here, those lights aren't something you want shining on you." Cliff stopped, turning to face us.

"Correct," he confirmed. Petro gasped.

"How did you hear that?" the Pixie asked.

Cliff just smiled. "I hear everything that happens here. You are correct, though. Uninvited guests usually don't make it past the door. If they do . . . well, let's just say having a thousand razor-sharp crystals dropping on one's head isn't conducive to a long life," he warned, motioning us toward the head of the table.

Cliff held his hand out toward Phil, pointing at a seat five spaces from Titania. This was followed by our tour guide walking past, ushering me next to the open seat beside the queen. Off-center to my place was a smaller setup for Petro.

"Really?" I asked as Cliff gave me an *eat-shit* look.

"Mind your manners," he chided, walking back and taking the seat beside Phil. I was fairly certain he had my man Phil pegged as trouble and had opted to sit next to him.

Titania turned from a conversation she looked glad to walk away from and stood behind her chair, smiling at me. She quickly reached down, grabbing a silver bell and shaking it lightly. The sound reverberated from the small, intricate tool, echoing as if it was the size of a car.

A tall woman walked in from the entrance, making her way to the head of the table through the open center area. The room was laser focused, everyone standing behind their chairs.

"My queen. The feast is prepared and clear for the evening," the tall woman informed, bowing her head.

I had a sinking suspicion the food had been checked for poison or whatever they did on the Plane to influential political figures. Petro, sensing my thoughts, looked back, winking.

Titania sat in her chair and the room erupted with noise.

The shuffling of seats on the floor bounced off the walls in a loud, scuffing chorus. Following everyone's lead, I did the same as if I knew what I was doing, which of course, I didn't.

Servers erupted from the walls as if they were part of the building, coming from the shadows in all directions, swarming the guests. Drinks were poured and bowls of what appeared to be some type of broth steamed while Petro sniffed lightly, a smile reaching his eyes.

"This stuff good?" I inquired as he looked up, rubbing his hands together.

"Boss, you're gonna love it," he exclaimed before leaning his head over the cup and taking several slurps.

I looked up at Titania, who was smiling at Petro's lack of table manners.

"He's, uh . . . hungry," I stammered while she chuckled lightly.

"He's a Pixie, and that is serpent bone broth. We served it in his honor," she stated as Petro looked up.

"You're okay in my book, lady," Petro blurted out as the intricately dressed person on the other side of me looked at Petro in utter horror.

I was betting they didn't see too many Pixies at the head of the table talking to Titania that way.

"Little warrior, I'm glad you joined us. You do know you are somewhat famous with the Pixies here?" she asked as the gears in my head started churning.

A queen was, after all, nothing more than a more sophisticated pedigree of politician. She was using this opportunity to gain some points with the local Pixies.

"Trying to get some street cred with the locals?" I asked her. She looked at me, slightly confused by the words. It was easy to forget that Titania, Queen of the Fae, didn't hang out at the Waffle House after midnight.

"You're gaining favor by having Petro here," I explained.

"Smart. Yes, we have had some issues with that, as I'm sure you are aware. But things are changing. There will be a time when we will all need each other," Titania replied, raising her chin slightly after making the statement.

"I'm going to cut to the chase here. Before I do anything, I need to see Tom," I casually mentioned, not adding an edge to my words. My tone was one of concern for my family.

"Yes, after we dine." She paused, taking a sip of the black wine in front of her. "I believe there is more to you than meets the eye. Rumor has it you can wield hellfire and other elements."

After a brief silence, I figured I would lay all my cards on the table to see her reaction. "My grandmother is Lilith."

Her head moved with laser-like precision as her eyes focused on me. As fast as her mood had shifted, she quickly regained her composure.

"I see. That would explain much of what I have heard about you. I would highly recommend keeping that to yourself. Your blood is more than that. If not, you wouldn't have made it past the front door. My staff and I had our suspicions that you were somehow tied to the Under, but if what you told me is true, you will have a part to play," Titania said, relaxing back in her seat.

I'm just saying, telling the queen of the Plane that your grandmother was essentially demon royalty—or whatever Lilith was—couldn't hurt. It was my trump card. Not to mention I had just given her something she definitely hadn't known.

"Since you are sharing with me, I'll share with you. You do, in fact, have a daughter. Even better, I know who the mother is, and if you bring the Pillar back to me, I will help ensure you see her sooner rather than later," she offered, leaving no room for interpretation.

I almost came out of my seat as I fidgeted for a few seconds before regaining my composure. "What do you mean?"

"I'm not going to repeat myself. Let's just say there is a shadow covering your eyes from things directly in front of you," Titania purred.

Since my run-ins with Maman Brigitte and J-man last year, I had grown tired of riddles. They were a work-around not to get directly involved with something in most cases. Knowledge was a currency in this world, and one had to treat it as such. Where it came from, who you gave it to, and the list of questions that could be deemed important.

Steadying myself, I grabbed the glass of water, deciding to skip the tar-like wine. "Let me ask you something. Have you ever taken a trip and realized that you will never truly get to your destination?" I asked, wanting to send a soft message.

She wanted to see how valuable the information she had just relayed to me truly was. I wasn't about to show her my entire hand. There were evidently some gaps in what she truly knew. I had a feeling that was the case with many things between Earth and the Plane.

Titania paused, working to decipher the message in her mind. "Yes, but I always find a way to get where I'm going."

"I don't like taking trips where I never end up where I initially planned. You know, I'm not a big fan of detours and wrong directions. As a matter a fact, if I think I'm going in the wrong direction based on bad instructions . . . I often just say to hell with it," I stated flatly.

She let out a silent huff as a sinister grin perked up her lips.

"I see. Well, let's just hope you know how to follow

instructions," she replied as the main course was served.

I looked over to see Phil being his usual loud self. He was encouraging Cliff to drink with him. Since dear old Phil had taken the sober-up potion before partaking, he wouldn't feel the effects of whatever it was they were serving everyone.

Much to my surprise, Cliff was intently talking with him, leaning in as Phil nodded in response.

An odd assortment of instruments sprang to life from the far end of the room as a small orchestra of sorts started playing. The music was eerie and beautiful at the same time, with sounds and chimes I hadn't heard before.

"Do we get cake at the end?" I asked Titania.

Petro spit out a mouthful of soup back into his cup.

CHAPTER 15

We're All Dying a Little Every Day

Atari ushered me as Titania stood up while the festivities continued. Phil motioned for us to go without him. He was either getting a bunch of good information or had been sucked into braggadocio stories of past endeavors. Petro was going to meet with the house Pixies while Cliff was distracted.

A large door clicked open behind the queen's throne, and we walked through into a long, sterile hallway. The exit shut behind us, completely cutting off the sounds of the dinner party.

Titania stopped, turning to me. "Since the pleasantries are over, I believe it's time to get down to business. We are going to meet with Tom. Things will become clearer for you moving forward."

I smiled, nodding my head as Atari gave me a quick side-glance. Even though she was a Danann, I had yet to figure out her play in all this. "When will the party be over?" I asked, gauging when I would see Phil again.

"At sunrise. Several of the other houses came here to dine with us this evening," Titania responded as Atari opened the elevator door at the end of the hall.

After an awkward ride, the elevator opened into a lobby just as plush as the one in our quarters. The entrance was separated from the main section by heavily warded doors. The familiar scent of burnt hickory that followed Gramps hit my nose.

Titania walked forward as the door automatically swung open. Sitting in front of the lit fireplace was the outline of Tom's head.

"Max," he said, turning with a genuine smile on his face.

On instinct, I scanned the room, also taking in every inch I could see of Tom, looking for signs of mistreatment. I shook my head upon further inspection, seeing a bottle of wine and a plate full of the same food we had been served sitting in front of him, half eaten.

"My compliments to the chef," Tom mumbled around a mouthful of food, taking one last bite before setting down his fork and wiping his lips.

"Indeed. I'm glad you approve," Titania replied in an odd show of mutual respect.

I started to feel like I was either being pranked or, as Titania had noted, not seeing what was right in front of me.

"Alright, I call bullshit here. What's going on?" I asked. Between the surprised snort that came out of Atari's nose and the queen's flat stare, I had evidently been wrong in my initial assumption.

"Here we take care of our guests, even if they have wronged you. Tom has, in the past, earned the respect of this house, and with that, he is also under my protection until certain matters are resolved," Titania said, walking to the fireplace and sitting in one of the plush leather chairs.

I looked at Tom, following her lead. He slouched slightly in his seat, working out where to start.

"Max, Her Royal Highness has every right to hold me here," Tom started, seeing that I was quickly becoming impatient. "Even though I had nothing to do directly with the Pillar being stolen, it was partially due to my actions. Or lack thereof."

"So if you didn't take it or move it, why are you being held here?" I asked, shuffling my gaze between Titania and Tom.

"There is a reason I have remained in the shadows ever since we closed the portal to the hellion legions while fighting the Soul Dealers. Let me show you," Tom said as he gradually stood up.

I quickly noticed how slow he was moving. It wasn't like him. Even though he was old in appearance, Tom had always been ready for a fight and quick to move. This was something different; something was wrong.

Just as I was about to talk, Tom slowly started to unbutton the cream-colored cotton shirt he was wearing. He held out a finger, telling me to hold on as I leaned further forward in my chair. He grabbed either side of the crisp shirt, pulling it fully open to expose his chest. I hadn't been expecting to see a large stab wound covered in some kind of black scarred tissue that spidered across his skin.

"Gods and graves, what the hell is this?" I gasped, shock coming through clearly in my voice.

"When we were fighting Mengele and Beleth, I'm sure you saw the blade sticking out of my back," Tom started flatly, taking in a deep breath. "I was indeed gravely injured that night. The blade that Mengele used on me has done irreparable damage to not only my body, but my essence. You see, Max, whatever that blade was, it seeped into my body and became part of me. Since then, I have started aging, and my body has begun to show the normal stress of a man of my age and experience."

"What does that have to do with the Pillars?" I dug further as Tom started buttoning up his shirt, quickly lowering himself down to the chair.

I'd noticed when he stood there was a deep impression left behind on the cushions. Tom hadn't been moving much from that very spot.

"As you can probably tell, I'm not as sharp as I usually am. I came here to use the power of the Pillar to cure myself through transmigration into another spatial realm," Tom replied. Titania cleared her throat.

"What Tom is trying to say is he was going to use the Pillar to transport himself to Terrum. There has long been a rumor that doing so could cheat even death. Your grandfather is dying," Titania added.

I looked at Tom, still not seeing the connection. "Max, I wasn't cautious with what I was doing. With that, I opened this palace and Her Majesty to attack. I was getting desperate to get here, meaning I had to get the help of others. Titania would not have simply let me attempt to complete my task."

"You are correct. I wouldn't have, as it would've put not only myself but the people of this entire realm at risk. The Old Gods have feelers everywhere and would've sensed the shift. I'm not willing to take that risk. You have no idea of their cruelty and abilities," Titania stated, her mood shifting.

Atari was staying oddly silent, taking in all the information. I had a feeling she wasn't completely aware of everything going on under her watch.

"I'm sure by now we all know the Crystal King has the Pillar," I interjected as all of the room's inhabitants nodded at the same time. "Are you saying that if I go and retrieve this Pillar, you'll help my grandfather?"

"No, not completely. But I will do everything in my power to ensure he stays with us as long as possible. Under our rules of courtesy, we had our best healers and doctors look at your grandfather. The weapon used was celestial, meaning there is no known remedy other than the rumors we think were planted with Tom to help facilitate the theft of the Pillar," Titania said, filling in some additional gaps in her reasoning for detaining Tom.

"And my daughter?" I blurted out, causing Tom to lean forward.

"What deal have you two made?" Tom asked in a hardened tone.

"No deal has been struck. I now know who you were rolling in the hay with all those years ago," Titania teased as Tom stared at me.

The Fae had an odd presence, able to shift moods and topics quickly.

I let out a huff, straightening up in my ever-sinking chair cushion. "I know about my daughter. Bruce Teach dropped that nugget of information before leaving this world and the next. So, I take it you also know. Meaning you also know what Her Majesty supposedly knows?" I inquired, wondering if Tom would fill in the gaps.

Tom hesitated momentarily, gathering his thoughts. "This gets complicated. In a leap of faith, I talked to Titania about your daughter. Max, I promise you, she is fine. But if we don't get the Pillar and put things back to normal, that very well may change for all of us. You know you're special. With that, any child you have will also be different."

My mouth had gone dry. I swallowed, looking around for a glass of water. I couldn't decide if I was angry, confused, or coming to terms with the situation. "How is this all tied together?"

"Is it?" Tom quickly replied. "Maybe it is. Things have been in motion for some time. The Thule Society—or what's now called Everbane—the Council, the Fae and Vampire Courts, the Old Gods, and everything in between has been moving onto a singular path for some time."

"More like on a collision course. And let's not forget Lilith," Titania added.

"I know she's tied to my daughter; I all but figured that out. Gramps, I'm going to get this Pillar situation dealt with, then you, me, and the queen here are going to have a nice, long chat," I said, aggravation finally cutting through my voice.

"It's settled then," Titania started. I cut her off.

"I wasn't talking to you. Plus, as graceful a host as you are, the way I see it, Tom already had favor with you. You are repaying that by helping him, even if it's under strained circumstances. That means you're on the hook with me. Don't forget. He's already died . . . what, three times?" I noted, laying out my terms, leaving no room for interpretation.

Atari had backed up to the door by this point. She was either about to run out of the room to deny her involvement, or she was waiting on the order to kill Tom and me.

"I like this one," Titania added, and I felt Atari relaxing behind me. The queen leaned back in her seat while I stayed rigid. Every nerve ending in my body was screaming at me not to push the woman sitting in front of me an inch farther.

"My lady, shall I make any travel arrangements?" Atari asked.

"You will be going with Max and his team. Get yourself ready," Titania instructed. She stood, turning toward me. "I will leave you two alone for a few minutes to catch up. Might I suggest you leave first thing in the morning?" she all but dictated.

The two women walked out the door, and it slid

smoothly shut. The echo of the elevator taking off told me our time with the queen was over.

"Max, before you say anything—"

I cut him off. The weight of seeing Gramps in this condition was crushing. The dark bags under his eyes told me just how tired he was.

"What is it you're not telling me?" I asked. I wasn't specific, but felt like the universe had lousy news it didn't want to fill me in on.

"Everything and nothing. This is complicated, and I honestly don't know how things will play out. Listen, I know this deal with your daughter has you sidetracked, as it should. But you are being asked to do this for a reason. The Council, as well as others, know how strong you have become. Between that and your ability to use the Postern, I'm not sure anyone else could pull this off without starting an all-out war. We need everyone together in case the Old Gods make a move."

"I get all that. I'm a rogue element in all this; not to mention I picked up on everyone wanting me to take on this Crystal King guy." I paused, recentering my thoughts. "Why is having a daughter complicated? Besides the usual reasons?"

"What if I told you something that has yet to happen is at the center of this? When you get back, we will go over everything. I can tell you that your eventual ability to travel through parts of time with the Postern is part of this. From what I understand, at some point in the near future, you take a trip through that gate, which results in the situation with your daughter."

I blew out a lungful of air. "So you're saying, it's not that I forgot what happened, but that it hasn't happened yet. That is some *Back to the Future* bullshit, and you know it," I huffed out, still not coming to grips with what I was being told.

"Time is a fickle thing, Max, and not to be toyed with.

Even knowing this much could have dire consequences," Tom declared, starting to fall in line with the old movies as Doc Brown's words floated through my mind.

"Like?" I asked, already knowing the answer.

"Like your daughter never being born. Or even worse," Tom trailed off.

I leaned back, starting to put the pieces together even though I didn't want to accept them. Either Tom was protecting me and his family, or he was playing games again, something I had learned he was more than capable of.

"Thus, the reason you're being so damn secretive. This isn't over. Not by a long shot. You've yet to explain what exactly you have been up to over the past couple of years. Shit," I murmured. "I have to go get this Pillar thing. Make everything right. Then, like I said, it's time to get the rest of this situated. Oh, that reminds me."

I pulled out the ring Davros had given me as Tom's face lit up.

"My boy, this is a message and a clue," Tom said, his eyes perking up slightly.

"I figured you'd know something about it. So?" I prompted.

"This is not only a portal house key but a force weapon as well. Not only does the queen not want to go face-to-face with the Crystal King, but they also can't figure out a way to find him. This might just be a way to do that. You see, Davros's old keep in the mountains used to be a portal and was one of the last places the Crystal King was known to be before disappearing. But—" Tom stopped abruptly.

"Let me guess. No one knows where exactly this place is, and I'm betting it's hidden somehow."

Tom nodded. "You need to visit the Pixies. They'll help

you in your quest," Tom said, standing up and holding out his hand to shake as Atari walked back into the room.

I looked down at his hand before I walked off, leaving him standing there without shaking it. For once in my life, I had told Gramps I was at the end of my rope in no uncertain terms. "This isn't a quest. This is me about to finish something I apparently haven't even started."

CHAPTER 16

Big, Scary-Ass Monster
Number Two

The morning came earlier than expected as Atari started banging on the door. When I'd returned the prior night, Petro, Phil, and I had sat around discussing the evening's events and information.

Phil's had been the least impressive, as Cliff had evidently done nothing more than complain about Titania killing a good portion of the guests he had to look after. Though he *had* find out that Tom and Titania had had a relationship at one point, which was likely the reason he was still alive.

Cliff also knew a good amount of information about the gates between the Plane and the other realms. The stone to the Everwhere version of the Postern I had brought—better known as plan B—would not work as planned. I would update the journal later. Phil had exceeded my expectations, still remembering all the details of that conversation.

Petro, on the other hand, had been overflowing with news. Not only had he achieved rock star status on the Plane, everyone's assumption about the Pixies knowing how to find Davros's keep was correct.

He was also now an honorary general in the upcoming Pixie rebellion, which was likely to kick off at any moment. This, of course, had led to a thirty-minute discussion about Phil and I investing in eye patch companies. He had watched *The Wolf of Wall Street* the month prior.

After a long slog of groaning and getting our gear together, we all converged on the Fae honey coffee Atari had sitting on the counter.

"Lass, we may just have an opening for you on the team at this rate," Phil joked, making some funky eyebrow motion.

"Atari, thanks for bringing this. Since we are now in this together, we need to lay down some ground rules," I started. I was surprised when she nodded.

She was wearing the same uniform as the day prior, with the addition of a katana-like sword and several more gadgets dangling from the sleek belt around her formfitting outfit. It looked oddly similar to the uniform the Night Stalker's wore, minus the mask.

Petro hovered by her, inspecting the gear.

"Aslynn told me all I need to know about working with your team," she spoke before I could say anything.

"Then you're well aware that we work as a team. If you have any hidden agendas, lay them out now," I stated authoritatively. I was still slightly pissed from last night.

Picking up on this, Atari walked closer, holding up her hands. "I don't want to be on this little adventure with you. To be clear, I have no agenda other than returning the Pillar." She paused, knowing it wasn't the time to hide anything. "If you don't succeed or you stray from this mission, I am to ensure you are dealt with."

There it was. If we didn't get the Pillar, Atari would ensure we never found our way back to the castle.

"Fair enough. If Aslynn and Jamison told you all about us, then you know that's going to be difficult," I replied, trying to get some type of reaction.

Atari knew we were probably being watched. Her initial response about her relatives had told me most of what I needed to know, but not all of it.

"I have a feeling we are going to succeed in our quest. I wasn't there when Ned died; I have to do this," she threw out to the group. "This may just be her testing my loyalties as well."

Phil and I both sighed as Petro dusted lightly. She had just laid it out on the table, not caring who might hear. After talking with Aslynn and Jamison, I had reservations about their long-term intentions, but I knew our group was a friend and ally to their family. This much I was clear on. I trusted Atari, as would the others.

***

The same carriage we had arrived in sat idly in what equated to a small garage tucked behind the main palace. A few slight modifications had been made to the vehicle, including larger tires and what looked like numerous small boxes now attached to the sides.

Atari had explained the addition of several offensive and defensive spells and weapons inside the boxes. She had also clarified why all the extra muscle was around the palace. With the Pillar gone, so was their primary source of power for several of the larger defensive wards.

What had surprised me the most was the security briefing we had received before leaving. It had reminded me of my days in the army sitting through the same boring intelligence dumps right before going out and doing something both stupid and dangerous.

As soon as the meeting had concluded, we'd reviewed our route and jumped into the chariot-like carriage, starting our journey.

A few short minutes after passing the city walls, I leaned forward, looking at Atari. "So this thing's on cruise control till we get to Ordas?" Ordas was not only a village on the outskirts of the mountains but Petro's home.

"Was," she responded, waving her hand over the small gray panel on the sidewall. The ball and consequent motor of the carriage roared to life as Atari plugged in new directions. "MY understanding is that we have a few things to pick up at the cottage."

"Sounds like you know the score," Phil commented, picking up the newly installed silver box covered in various buttons. "What's this do-flingy all about?"

"Please don't touch that unless we need to. It's the new weapons system for the carriage. The queen had it installed last night to help us along the way," Atari replied as I chuckled.

"What's so funny, boss?" Petro asked.

"I've got a bad feeling about this," I said in my favorite Han Solo tone as the others, including Atari, groaned.

We spent the rest of the trip getting to know our new companion, only to find out she was well versed in our misadventures. It was clear she was still holding back something, but she knew the score. The drumming sound of the new, larger tires in the rough path almost put me to sleep as we pulled up to the cottage.

Standing in front of the door was Jamison holding our gear with an urgent look on his face. "What's up, mate?" Phil asked as we shuffled out of the vehicle.

"There's been reports of disturbances on the route to Ordas. I would change and get moving as soon as possible. The longer you are here, the more ears and eyes become awake," Jamison replied, handing me the tactical outfit I had brought along.

I dropped it on the ground, straightening out my T-shirt and jacket. "I'm good. This old thing hasn't let me down yet," I stated, patting my trench coat.

Jamison nodded as Phil started putting on his vest covered in various pouches and weapons. He wasn't taking any chances on this trip, especially since it was not only his but my first trip to the Plane.

I had the usual: the Judge, my loaded service pistol, fully charged short staff, two of Trish's smoke screen balls, and a handful of dissolution grenades. I also had a gate stone given to me by Jamison. Needless to say, Phil had his usual collection of weapons and blunt, heavy objects, including the new rifle I had procured for him.

Petro zipped over in his ceremonial red armor. "What do you think, boss?"

"Badass, Petro. I don't think I've seen you wearing that stuff since . . . what, when we first met?" I inquired as Jamison handed me a thin silver bracelet.

"Sounds about right. I figured it would be awesome to show up back home with it on. I wish Casey were here to see it all," Petro said, truly missing his better half.

Jamison cleared his throat. "I'm taking it you know what this is?"

"One of those bracelets that connects people. Yeah, we've had a few rounds with these before. Who's got the other one?" I asked.

Jamison raised the sleeve of his shirt, revealing its twin. The bracelet was made on the Plane through blood magic, and on Earth, it was considered outlawed by the Council due to its uses, which mainly consisted of keeping tabs on one's servants or husbands and wives. If needed, the bracelet would give the person access to the other's location and vice versa, depending on how it was arranged. It also meant we had an untraceable method of communication.

After saying our goodbyes to Jamison, the carriage again lurched into motion, and we sped off into the shadowed woods. The clicking of our gear filled the void as, again, the sounds of the tires droned underneath us.

As I floated into sleep, thoughts of a person talking to me materialized like a soft whisper. Lines of a face I couldn't identify kept talking to me, pushing me to respond. The curves of her body were the only thing telling me it was a woman.

The shadow moved, shifting colors to a vibrant red as I reached out my hand. The figure leaned closer as she handed me what looked like a clock. Something flew overhead, drowning the vision in light-gold dust. I looked back down to see the figure distort and turn dark, crumbling slowly to pieces.

Just when the dream was starting to fade, the ashes of the woman came together again, and the jaws of a massive creature clamped down on my head as I let out a scream.

"Wake up, bruther!" I heard Phil call from the darkness as a jolting slap snapped me back to reality.

"There; that should do it," Atari's voice echoed while I opened my eyes.

"What the hell?" I asked, gasping for air.

"Boss, you were having some kind of nightmare. You were like, *ohhh*, and *ahhh*, then all *wahhhh* . . ." Petro relayed as I shook my head.

Looking around, it was clear that not only had I fallen asleep, but apparently, there was also a problem. Phil cradled his rifle while Atari held the box full of the do-not-touch buttons. Petro also had his small rifle full of dissolution rounds.

"Oh, and there's something really big and scary outside

that threw the carriage off the main road into the trees," Petro zipped out rapidly.

"Atari?" I asked. Phil also looked over at her, raising his eyebrows. The sounds of his rifle clicking filled the pause.

"I can tell you being in here, for now, is the safest thing we can do until we figure out what threw us off the road and, more importantly, if we are going to be able to kill it," she replied, pushing one of the buttons on the new security box.

The clang and grind of gears echoed, followed by a loud snap as a glowing blue shield erupted into place around the vehicle.

"Can't those damn things be a little more inconspicuous," I huffed, pulling out my short staff and shifting to get a better view out the back window.

"It doesn't matter," Atari replied as the floor of the vehicle vibrated.

"Petro?" I asked, figuring he might have a good idea of the threat.

"The shield mostly cut off the scent, but I thought I got a good whiff of some kind of big cat or maybe man-thing," Petro said, shrugging.

A loud crash drew everyone's attention to the front windshield as a tree slammed into the shield, causing it to flicker slightly. Since the inside of the carriage was easily twenty feet long and relatively open, the flat, mirrored front windshield gave an almost uncomfortably exposed feeling.

Several massive darts followed the tree, looking like telephone pole-sized needles. Round pools from the shield rippled, still holding firm.

"Petro, did you smell ash?" Atari asked. Petro looked up, remembering the scents.

"Yeah, as a matter of fact, I did," he responded as the

already pale Atari looked ready to lose another shade of white.

"It's a manticore," Atari huffed out, shuffling in her seat.

"A who?" Phil asked as several more massive needles slammed into the shield. The creature was visibly searching for a weak spot.

"Big half lion, half man, half scorpion, or something like that. It was rumored the Crystal King locked several of them away with his people to protect what was left of them. There were reports of one being sighted recently, and I got a slight glimpse of it right before all this happened," Atari informed us as she messaged someone through the box in her lap.

"Meaning?" I asked.

"We have a problem. I can reach out to the wall guards, but it will take them some time to get here," she said, seeing the three of us adjusting our weapons. "I see. The creature will need a little more of a kick in the ass than I believe the four of us can muster. We had one destroy several square miles of the city before we got it under control several years ago. The damn thing is still alive, locked away in a portal."

"Was locked away . . . let me guess, you couldn't kill it," I noted while she nodded.

"My main man Max here kicked a chimera's ass once," Petro bragged, sticking up for my honor.

Atari pursed her lips, raising her eyebrows. "Really?"

"Well, kind of. I'm sure it's still looking for me. Listen, we need to focus on getting this thing moving again, how about that?" I recommended as Atari slowly started to nod.

"Wait a minute there, bruther. She's a Fae warrior on her home turf," Phil said, turning to Atari.

"I may be strong, but I'm not stupid. Someone sent that thing here to either prove a point or stop us from going any further," she replied, leaning forward while pressing another button. A smaller red shield popped up a few feet in front of the blue one getting probed.

"You think we can outrun it?" I asked her while Atari reached for the door handle.

"If we can get a clear shot; nothing short of a miracle will be able to keep up with this thing, but that will only last so long. It knew we would be here," Atari fumed as the team slowly filed out of the vehicle, lightly dropping onto the damp forest floor. All except for Phil; he did so with authority, lighting up a smoke.

I scanned the tree line, seeing shadows and a hazy fog surrounding the shield. From the side of the carriage to the barrier were roughly ten feet, giving us enough room to maneuver.

The vehicle had landed on a tree, shearing it in half. The still rooted section had jammed itself under the large, round, fender-like shell covering the front and top of the driving ball. Phil was already on the move, setting his rifle down as two large, glowing blue eyes erupted from the haze on the other side of the protective barrier.

"Oh shite!" Phil howled, jumping several feet through the air, landing beside Atari. He quickly composed himself as the creature's entire body came into view.

It was precisely as Atari had described it. I landed on big, scary-ass monster number two. The manticore started pacing the shield's edge, making the ground move enough to feel through my boots.

"Phil, time to get moving," I mumbled under my breath, as if it mattered.

Phil pulled out his hammer, slamming the tree's base as splinters of wood flew in all directions. If that didn't work, I'd burn it to a crisp, hopefully without damaging the heart of the carriage.

As soon as Phil got moving, the manticore slammed its spiked tail into the outer shield, popping it out of existence. The impact made the inside of our protective bubble ring like a bell, forcing me to grab my head.

"Phil!" I yelled. He nodded, the rhythmic slamming of his hammer picking up its pace.

"Hey, boss. That tree is Everwood. It's as hard as steel. I'm surprised it didn't completely wreck this thing," Petro informed, landing on my shoulder, his head moving in sync with the manticore.

"I'm done!" Phil yelled back just as the creature once again slammed its massive, spiked tale, now into the inner shield.

This time, the shield buckled, flashing like a strobe light. The sounds and smells of the forest filled my lungs as we jumped back. It was at times like this that I regretted not bringing the Cadillac DeVille O'Doom along with us.

"*IGNIS!*" I yelled as my hellfire blade sprang to life, erupting from my hand. Atari pulled out her sword and a sleek-looking pistol. Petro took flight, dropping back slightly.

The shield started rapidly flickering, showing small, millisecond gaps in its coverage. Phil squeezed his hands around the hammer as a light gray glow emanated from his body.

The plan was pretty straightforward. Throw Phil at whatever big, scary-ass monster was in front of us to distract it while Petro and I threw everything we had at it. Phil was an Earth Mage and able to withstand unbelievable amounts of force and damage. But while he could go toe to toe with most creatures, it could only last so long.

"Atari, can you get this thing moving?" I asked, letting her know we would take care of the manticore as long as possible. Especially since neither I nor Phil had any clue how to operate the chariot-like vehicle.

"Yes, but—"

Another loud, booming crash rocked the already bad situation. Loose dirt and grass flew up from the ground, and even the manticore paused, looking confused.

Blinding, reflective rays of white-hot light exploded in all directions, forcing the group to shield our eyes. Instead of the rhythmic stomping of four feet we had grown accustomed to over the past several minutes, the lumbering thump of something or someone walking heavily on two feet joined the now still scene.

"Boss," Petro drawled out as I squinted, working to pinpoint the origin of the light.

"Yeah, buddy?" I asked quickly as the sound of the manticore's tail swishing in the breeze started back up.

"I don't know what kind, but it's a Celestial," Petro informed the group, loud enough for everyone to hear.

This meant one of two things. It was either a creature like Devin or some other type of deity. To date, I had met Hermes, Hades, and Jesus, not to mention all the others I had surely ran into without knowing.

"Atari, is that bad here?" I asked as she holstered her pistol and sword.

"Yes, very bad. This isn't supposed to be possible, but with the Pillar not in place, who knows. I'm going to get this thing moving. Bigger things are at play," she said quickly, darting inside the carriage.

"Well, boys, it's just us again," I chuckled, trying to calm my nerves. Just as I thought I had done it, the shiny celestial being came into complete focus under the shade of a massive tree.

The thirty-something-foot-tall humanlike figure in

front of us was covered in gleaming, highly polished armor. It was so reflective it almost blended into the surrounding forest, and any ray of sunlight was amplified to the point of eye-squinting pain.

Its gauntlets clanked as large, muscular hands held onto a gladius-like sword in one hand and a shield with a massive etched cross in the other. Not a speck of dust or imperfection could be seen on the enormous figure as it squared off in front of the manticore.

I let the tension out of my body, pulling my hellfire blade back as Phil, also sensing the fight was not between us and the creature anymore, stopped pouring energy into his shield.

Looking up, I could barely make out a set of glowing eyes through the slits of the massive helmet covering the celestial creature's head. Before I could continue inspecting the giant shining knight in front of us, the manticore decided to remind us it was still present, releasing a guttural growl.

The clank of the armor and the sounds of the massive knight moving faster joined the ruckus as the manticore, while still staring at the knight, smashed its tail into the shield one last time. It finally buckled.

The carriage's motor hummed to life as Atari knocked on the window, giving us a thumbs up. I was, unfortunately, frozen in place looking at what I could only guess was an angel.

"Petro, is that an angel?" I asked as Phil jogged over to us, getting closer to the door.

"Never met one before, boss, but from how Belm and Bo always described them, I would say yes. Oh, and they also used to say the ones in armor were the big, mean ones," Petro said, dusting lightly.

"Jesus Christ almighty," Phil breathed out, making the sign of the cross while saying J-Man's full name for once.

"You think he can help here?" I asked, being slightly

behind on the gravity of the unfolding situation.

"I hope so. If that thing is pissed at us, I don't know if I can dance with it, bruther,"
Phil admitted, chewing his lip.

The blur of motion that followed as the others piled into the vehicle was jarring and swift. The manticore, sensing it had a fight on its hands, leapt through the air at the knight. The tang of a blade slicing through flesh and the following thud of the manticore's head smashing into the ground several feet away was the next thing we heard.

The creature's eyes were still alive, scanning us frantically, taking in its last sights, before the cloud of death sunk into them.

I stopped at the door, looking at the knight to gauge its next move.

Atari grabbed my shoulder. "We have to go," she whispered as the knight slid the long, heavy-looking blade into its sheath.

"No, you guys stay here. Button up the ride and be ready to leave. If that thing wanted us dead, I have a feeling we wouldn't be sitting here talking," I whispered back. Atari nodded.

"Told you, Miss Fancy-pants. It's never a dull moment around this lot," Phil interjected as Petro snorted lightly.

As if ordained by the gods, the knight lifted the front shield of its mask, exposing his face. Pale porcelain skin covered the man's face as two glowing gray eyes stared down at me. I had never met an angel, but figured this was precisely what one would look like.

"Max Abaddon Sand," the authoritative yet soft voice echoed in my mind and out loud.

I took a deep breath, taking several steps away from the

vehicle to give the others room to move if needed.

"It seems I'm at a loss for your name," I said as the knight moved forward, taking a knee. He was still ten feet taller than I was as he looked down at me stoically.

The air stilled as he opened his mouth and also pushed into my thoughts. "I am Metatron. Some people know me by my past human name, Enoch," the angel replied. I looked over my shoulder at Petro hovering by the window, giving me a thumbs-up or down sign.

I nodded, holding my thumb up before turning back to the knight. "So, Metatron, mind if I ask you a few questions?"

"Straight and to the point as preordained. Yes, you may," he accepted. His voice slowly stopped reverberating in my mind.

"How did you know we were here, and why did you help?" I asked. The thing about beings such as angels and demons was they followed their creed not to get involved in the working of humans—or Ethereals, for that matter.

It was also clear that angels were reserved for specific tasks and only allowed to make their presence known if ordered or permitted to do so. Thoughts of my meeting with J-man came into mind as I looked at the warrior angel in front of me.

"I know many things. As for this beast, it was sent here by a divine presence. That is why I am here," Metatron replied. The stoic look on his face softened slightly.

Much like demons, I figured angels could only answer certain things and get involved to a point, bending the rules to meet their end goal. I was starting to think the manticore had been the perfect excuse for an angel to have a little chat with me. It was clear he wanted to talk.

Metatron shifted as rays of light reflected off his armor. I took a clearing breath, gathering my thoughts. "While you are here, is there anything we can talk about?" I pushed, seeing if that would clear a few hurdles. "Oh, and thanks for saving our asses. I'm pretty sure we could have handled it, though."

Metatron gave a nod, a smirk washing over his face. "I'm sure you could have. That's not what I believe would have happened, however. There is something I would like to talk with you about."

He brought his large, gauntlet-covered hands to a delicate-looking pouch hanging off his waist. "Here, take this."

The angel deposited a small hourglass with a note attached on the ground in front of me. His big yet precise movements reminded me of Amon. "Max Abaddon Sand, you need to understand that time is not to be toyed with. We will meet each other three more times."

Metatron stood up as grass slid off his armor. "What does that mean?" I asked, figuring he was seconds away from leaving.

"I suppose you should read the note. Peace be with you," Metatron finished, his voice again echoing through my thoughts as a flash of blinding white light and a snap pushed me to my knees.

I dropped on my back, staring up at the pinkish-blue sky. The head of the manticore, only a few feet away from me, let out a gurgling hack, followed by the sizzle of e-core dissipating into nothingness. The sounds and smells were pushing my stomach to revolt.

Looking up, I saw Atari and Phil standing outside the carriage, doing their best to look away. Due to the smell, Petro had retreated into a dark corner of the vehicle's interior.

"Bruther, you done lying down on the job? What the hell did old mirror face give you?" he asked, not stepping any closer to the piles of rotting e-core.

The smooth feel of the paper reminded me Metatron

had given me something important. "I just needed a few seconds," I said, regaining my composure. It wasn't that I was exhausted. My mind was simply trying to compute what had just happened.

I stood up quickly, realizing that whatever Metatron had done while talking had taken a mental toll on me. Jenny, at one point, had explained that being partially demon was the reason I could communicate with Bo and the others in what I called my head movie.

This likely meant the demon part of me was not in-tune enough to communicate fully with an angel. I shrugged it off, thinking about my conversation with J-man.

The door closed, the click of it sealing extinguishing the sounds of the bustling forest. Atari pushed a button, and a table lifted out of the floor between the seats.

"Aslynn was absolutely right about you guys," Atari said as the carriage lurched forward, moving once again. The automatic system was taking over, getting us back on track. I immediately noticed we were moving faster than before.

"What's that, about how good we look?" Petro replied, pulling the string off the letter attached to the small hourglass.

She shook her head, grinning. "Never a dull moment. Let's just leave it at that," she said, copying Phil's earlier comment as I grabbed the note from Petro.

"Thanks, Petro. I can read the letter written to and for me," I told him as Phil leaned forward.

"You think we're meant to hear what's on that letter?" Phil asked, knowing messages could be problematic at times.

"He didn't say otherwise. I have a feeling he would have let me know. He said something interesting, though. I asked how he knew where we were. He just said something about the manticore. That's why he had an excuse to show up. I know Atari mentioned the Crystal King had them at one point, but

I'm not so sure this was him," I responded, reading a few lines to myself before starting over out loud.

Max,

Hey, man, I hope all is well. It has been some time since we last talked. Great job handling those Soul Dealers. I had faith in you and your friends. Now to business. I spoke to my old man a few months ago, and he mentioned you had been tasked to retrieve the Pillar taken by the Crystal King. He also mentioned this situation with your daughter. My good buddy Metatron, as I'm sure he told you, knows, well, just about everything.

I can't tell you much, but I can tell you that time is on your side and that nothing you do now can change your fate—or at least that of your offspring—till this task is complete. When the time comes, take this hourglass with you. Never be on the other side of the Timegate longer than the grains of sand last. It's nothing fancy, but it has a way of letting you know when it's time to come or go.

Peace Be with You. Your Pal,

J-man

P.S. Don't let Metatron fool you. He's a big softy.

"Who is J-Man?" Atari asked as I looked at Phil.

"Jesus; you know, the son of God. The main one, not the others," Phil explained, picking up the hourglass.

Atari looked shocked as Petro spoke up. "Hey, boss, he's . . . kind of . . . looked at differently here."

"He and his angels destroyed entire realms during the Great War. I must inform Aslynn and Titania of this immediately. Him being here is a sign," she said as a strained, angry-looking vein started dancing on her forehead.

"Hey, let's just calm down. He wasn't here. It was an angel. An angel that saved our asses back there. Between that and this letter, it looks like he's trying to help while staying out of the way," I pointed out.

"Lass, J-Man's not all that bad. I know that the Celestials did cruel things to keep the peace, but from what I understand, it's one of the only reasons we are here able to chitchat. He's not going to get involved unless there's a damn good reason. Instead, I think we need to worry about whatever arse sent that ugly man-lion thingy," Phil added.

She started calming down. "You have a point. A small one . . . but a point. I need to talk with Aslynn when we get to Ordas," Atari huffed out as she finally leaned back in her seat.

"If anything, what happened back there probably has nothing to do with you or this realm. It's something to do with me. Every time something goes haywire, there's always someone in the shadows, waiting and watching. When it gets a chance, *boom*," I exclaimed, not fully aware of what Aslynn and Jamison had filled her in on.

"So you're saying the Pillar has something to do with you?" she asked.

I was starting to see how others viewed me. It was probably good that people didn't know I kept running into gods and other higher beings.

"Me, no; Tom, yes. I'm starting to think the world is telling me to pump the brakes on looking for my daughter. This whole time thing has me a little confused, but things have a way of making themselves clear," I said, opening up to Atari.

Phil and Petro had already gotten bored of the conversation and were in various stages of falling asleep.

"It sounds like the gods have bigger plans for you. I'm not telling you something you don't already know or suspect, but family is something that, no matter what state they are in, are still just that," Atari said, letting out a breath as her body relaxed.

"What?"

"Family," she replied, leaning forward, still relaxed.

"Neither my family nor I will ever forget what you did for us. What I can't do, though, is watch my people die or get hurt. This thing we are doing is important and needs to be completed sooner rather than later. To be clear, if this is a one-way trip, so be it," she replied, making a good point.

"Yeah, I kinda had a feeling we were sent here under that pretense. Just remember one thing about me and those two," I said, pointing at the now snoring and drooling dynamic duo. "We won't go down without one hell of a fight."

"So I've heard," Atari said, crossing her arms over her chest as she closed her eyes.

CHAPTER 17

Village of the Pixie King

"Then there's the old tree I used to practice sword fighting on. Oh, and the date bushes, let me tell you," Petro babbled, telling us everything and anything we needed or thought we might want to know about Ordas, his hometown.

"I think we can go without hearing about the date bushes," I chuckled while Phil shrugged, looking interested.

Atari looked up as the engine's hum slowed to a calm purr. Over the last eight hours, we had concluded the carriage had been going well over one hundred miles per hour.

Every now and then, the mysterious box would beep and a button would light up, only to have Atari press it, accelerating the vehicle even faster for a short amount of time. According to our host, this was some type of danger the sensors were detecting, or an updated security report.

"This is it!" Petro exclaimed as a large tree hanging over the road shaded our path. "Let's start with dinner. It's getting late. Treek and Bosley have it all set up. Gran is hanging with some Elf lady and won't be around, but I'm sure he will miss seeing you. My bros!"

I cocked my head at Phil and Atari; we all knew

there was no way out of it. While Pixie hospitality was well documented, not everyone saw the display of courtesy the same way. We had already informed Petro that we didn't want to eat bugs or be greeted by hundreds of naked, drunk Pixies.

Luckily for us, Petro's family lived in the provincial governor's house. Even though Ordas was primarily known as a Pixie town, most of its structures were normal-sized and inhabited by what Atari called *Outlivers*. I equated this to suburbanites back home.

Atari pushed another button, taking control of the vehicle when a joystick popped up. Clearing the trees, a vibrant, eclectic city painted itself under the dimming sky.

Pixies zoomed around in all directions as people and small cart-like cars slowly puttered in and out of the narrow streets. I leaned forward, taking in the structures.

Many, if not all the buildings were roughly three stories high, resembling an old European village, with cobbled roads surrounded by modern conveniences. The best way to honestly describe it was a steampunk mid-sixteenth-century nightmare.

"You think this thing is going to fit?" I asked as Atari pushed another button.

The sides of the vehicle started sliding together while she grinned. Looking forward, the ball started shrinking, and the long arms reaching back to the carriage narrowed.

"Is there anything this magic buggy can't do?" Phil asked as she swiped her hand over the gray pad in an off gesture.

A small door popped open as a bottle of brown liquor slowly rose out the top. It went without saying we all could have used a few sips after our little run-in with a manticore and subsequent angel.

"You've been keeping this a secret the whole time?" Phil accused with a mix of mild aggravation and relief.

Atari quickly grinned, pulling out three small glasses from underneath the seat. "I don't think anybody would be stupid enough to do anything in this city. An angel is scary, but one million angry Pixies is an entirely different story."

She quickly poured three small glasses and a cap for Petro. We all took a sip from the evidently human whiskey. On the Plane, liquors from Earth were extremely extravagant and rare, catching unprecedented prices even for the cheap stuff. That's right, even Wild Rose, Night Train, and Mad Dog 20/20 had their place on the top shelves of revered drinking establishments on the Plane.

"We're not too far, guys," Petro said nervously, buzzing around the now snugger interior. "She's right. There's some nefarious ball-slapping stuff that happens here, but I doubt any big, scary-ass monsters are going to show up. Oh, before I forget. Remember, my brothers and remaining family are staying with a new keeper. This isn't the prick bucket that gave my folks a hard time back in the day. Just remember, this is one of the only places where a Pixie can get a fair shake."

I had the feeling he was directing his comments toward Atari, whose expression of indifference swept across her face. While she was related to two friends of ours, she had spent no time on Earth.

We took several more sharp turns as the taller buildings began to thin out, giving place to several rows of trees just as tall. A small yet still imposing gate leading to a private drive slid open as the crackle of gravel vibrated through the floorboards.

"Hooray for the Warrior of the Freeze! Hooray for Petron, the bravest of all Pixies!" a group of several hundred Pixies exclaimed, exploding from the shrubbery while throwing confetti in front of the vehicle seemingly out of nowhere.

Petro was getting an honest-to-God ticker-tape parade. Looking to my right, I could read various small signs from several Pixies professing their undying love for Petro. One even proclaimed to be an Earth Pixie.

"Phil, for the sake of our eyeballs when we get back home with Casey, we need to make sure Rambo here doesn't get into any trouble," I noted as Phil readily agreed.

"I love you, Petron! Ahhh!" a random female Pixie yelled, pressing up against the window.

"Me, get in trouble? Would I do that? Look, they love me, boss. I'm going to have to sign autographs and do that one thing politicians do," Petro busted out rapidly.

"You mean creepily hold babies for the camera and tell fibs?" Phil replied.

"Yeah, that first one," Petro said as a swift, strong wind slammed into the front of the vehicle.

The wall of Pixies went flying ass over teakettle as small signs proclaiming how awesome Petro's mustache was flew behind the vehicle. The Pixies were all still in flight and not hurt.

"What the hell was that?" Phil asked as Atari pointed at the front windshield.

"It was an air cannon. We use it to politely remove Pixies from areas and places they are not supposed to be," Atari explained as Petro stuck his tongue out at her.

A business idea quickly crossed my mind; this could be the solution to handling Pixies and other airborne creatures during outdoor concerts and festivals. The thought had bothered me since the Dark Carnival the year prior. I quickly shrugged off the idea, storing it for later as the carriage finally came to a halt.

I hadn't paid much attention, but we had been inside the vehicle without stopping for a restroom break for roughly half a day. My legs creaked as I stretched, snapping like dry rice cereal being doused in milk.

"Look at that," Phil said, pointing at hundreds of splatter marks and small darts sticking out of the wheels.

"Rogue Pixies while we were on the road," Petro replied, shaking his head, raising an eyebrow at Atari.

We all turned when we heard steps behind us to see a man wearing what appeared to be a cape, with several Pixies hovering around his head like a halo. Bosley and Treek zoomed forward, Petro meeting them halfway. Phil and I grinned, happy to see the two Pixies.

Last year, we had fought side by side, finally putting an end to the Soul Dealers. They were smart, brave, and much like Petro, a handful of trouble.

"Gents," I greeted when Bosley zipped around me, dusting heavily.

"You are here! You saved our family once from the freeze, and now you will save us all!" Bosley exclaimed as the mob of Pixies again got blown back by the air cannon.

Treek grinned, being the calmer of the two, as he hovered in front of me, waiting for me to hold out my hand so he could land.

"Treek, it's great to see you in one piece. How's life?" I asked as he grinned.

"I see you didn't bring the Elf. Is the Fae her replacement?" Treek asked, winking at her. Last year, he had professed his undying love to Lana, the Elf warrior who protects the portion of the Everwhere around the Atheneum. Unfortunately for Treek, it appeared his brother Gran had already won Lana's heart, or whatever it could be between a Fae and a Pixie.

"She's off the market there, killer," I replied as he set his lips in a flat line.

Atari walked forward. "Who said I wasn't available?"

Treek and I looked at each other, shrugging. I still didn't understand the odd banter between Pixies and the other inhabitants of the Plane. I was guessing it was more of a taboo subject. The cape-wearing man walked forward, beaming a warm smile and even more welcoming posture.

I had already been informed the Fae outside the city were different than the rest. Here, the Fae were a little bigger around the waist, a little tanner, a little less official, and from what I could tell, a little faster to smile at a stranger.

"My goodness, Max Abaddon Sand. I'm Gaseous, overseer of this town. It's a pleasure to meet you," the man said, reaching out a sincere handshake.

"Your name's Gaseous?" I asked, trying not to overthink it. Of course, I was too late. Phil turned in the other direction before outright laughing.

"That's right!" Bosley interjected. "Keeper of the City, Master of the Rubber Stamp, Protector of Pixies, and Lord of the Gas."

I again looked blankly at the man while Petro spoke up. "Keeper Gaseous is from the swamplands. His family harvests swamp gas and sells it to fuel hover balloons."

Those, according to what Aslynn and Jamison had told us when we'd first arrived, were the flying blimp-like machines we would be seeing from time to time.

"Ah, yes, the flying machines," I replied while he beamed as only a man proud of his family business could. I was betting there was a reason we hadn't taken one.

"Please come in, mind the rules, and dinner will be ready soon. The king will be here shortly," Gaseous exclaimed, referring to the Pixie king.

After a few more high fives and hellos, we eventually

made our way into the house. The walls were covered with paintings of alien landscapes in earthy tones. The rest of the house felt like a hunting lodge confused about its purpose.

Hallways and doors spidered out in all directions as Bosley, Treek, and Petro led us into what appeared to be the main sitting room. The space was much like something you would see in an old manor house on a TV show about royalty.

Couches and lush yet comfortable chairs sat at random intervals, arranged to support conversation. In addition, an oversized fireplace large enough to walk into sat dominantly at the far end of the room.

"This place is cozy posh," Phil noted while Gaseous directed us to the large table near the fireplace. While the temperature wasn't exactly cold, it wasn't warm either. Flames flickered as everyone finally settled around the table, the Pixies having a smaller version in the center. Small cookies and drinks had already been placed there for Petro and his brothers.

"Where have I heard the name of this city before?" I asked, referring to Ordas, the city's name.

Petro zipped over, grinning. "You know, boss. The lions."

"You mean like Ordius? The Keeper?" I replied, already knowing the answer.

Gaseous cleared his throat. "That's right. Ordius. He was the original keeper of this city, and thus it was named after him. During the Great War, he was tasked with a heavy burden and left for your realm."

The math started adding up in my head. I nodded. "I would like to hear more about it sometime, but right now, we are here on business," I stated.

He let out a breath. "Yes, understood. You are under my protection and under no obligation while in my home. So, what is it we can do for you?" Gaseous asked, flipping his mood to businesslike. I had a feeling he had been prepped on my manner of working through things.

"Most of this I think the Pixie king will be able to help me with. The rest is just making it through in one piece." I proceeded to tell them the story of our trip so far, leading up to Ordas.

As the story concluded, a bell rang throughout the house, stilling everyone. "He's here!" Petro exclaimed, buzzing into the air.

"You and the king pals?" Phil asked.

Petro just dusted, replying, "Well, I mean, I've seen him before," while Gaseous stood up, snapping his fingers. Several Pixies that had been out of sight flew from behind the fireplace toward the front door.

"I'll be right back," Gaseous spoke.

"Petro, I thought there were no Pixie servants or whatever here," I noted flatly.

"Oh, these aren't servants. They're here working off a debt or trying to get something in return. Gaseous is the man! He will take on a Pixie family's debt from some asswipe and let them work here in an open, friendly environment. The only way he keeps it going is still having them work out of the house. He even lets them bump uglies," Petro said.

"I don't need to hear about that," I commented, shaking my head. "So it's like an honor to be here. I just want to make sure this guy is on the up-and-up," I stated as Petro gave me the thumbs-up.

I looked over at the entrance, seeing Gaseous walk in with several heavily armored Pixies flying in sync by his head as what was undoubtedly the Pixie king sat perched on his shoulder, a position Pixies only took on people or things they respected and trusted.

Upon closer examination, I noticed two of the Pixies that had helped defeat Carol Darkwater in the group of guards surrounding the king.

"All rise in the presence of his Royal Majesty, King Toto the Thirtieth," the closest guard exclaimed.

King Toto cleared his throat. "His friends call him Toto," the guard again exclaimed in an off yet still regal tone, making a horn sound as he finished. *"Pum, pum, pummm."*

"The thirtieth?" I asked as Toto flew down, thumping on the table. Needless to say, the good old king had not missed a meal in several years. He looked vaguely familiar, and thoughts of Willy, Benjamin Franklin's Pixie partner in crime, came to mind.

"Yes, I am one of many in my bloodline who have ruled over the Pixies. As they say, 'God bless the rains down in the Planes,'" Toto proclaimed, looking down at the plate of cookies on the small table.

"I bet they hear things echoing as well," I followed up as Phil snorted, the melody of the song coming out.

"Oh, you know our songs," Toto replied, and I now had questions for a particular band back home. Maybe Abby Normal would know.

"So, your family has held the umbrella over the Pixies for thirty generations?" Phil asked.

"I'm the thirtieth in my bloodline named Toto. It just stuck, from what I can tell," Toto responded, cramming a cookie in his mouth while talking smoothly enough to make Inspector Holder proud.

"Leave us," Toto ushered his crew of guards. Only the two familiar ones stayed, knowing their place. "First things first."

One of the armored Pixies actually pulled out a small

horn this time, tooting it out of key as the other one spoke. "Petron, Warrior of the Freeze, Slayer of the Eye, and Whizzer of the Great Smoke Stone, you are hereby awarded the honorary title of Prince of Ordas."

Again, the other Pixie let off a few notes as Toto pinned an emerald medallion on Petro's chest.

"You are an inspiration to us all. May your wings be true, and your dust be forever flowing," the king stated, bowing slightly.

"I'm a prince now? Casey is going to love it! All the ladies are going to love it! Does this mean I get into movie theaters for free?" Petro asked, looking at me as if I had some type of clue.

"Here, if there are theatres, I would think yes. Back home . . . sorry, bud. You still have to have a job," I answered while he pushed out his chest as far as he could, quickly taking out his miniature cell phone, which didn't work on the Plane, and snapping several selfies of him making a kissy face. I couldn't stop grinning while watching Petro.

"Casey's going to love those," Phil noted.

"Alright, is there anything else?" I asked Toto, who shook his head. A serious expression formed on his face. He knew it was time to talk.

"No, we just needed to get that out of the way. Are those your brothers?" Petro nodded. "That means they are now part of the royal family as well. I will ensure they get the appropriate armor."

The two guards clearly knew Bosley and Treek, as high fives and wing smacks were exchanged.

Before landing on my main questions, I again spent the next thirty minutes walking Toto through our current situation.

"We need help on where, or how to find the Crystal

King," I concluded as he grabbed another cookie.

"Yes, I can help you. Please sit," Toto ushered as Gaseous poured a glass of wine. "While I can't give you the precise location, I can set you on the right path."

Atari shuffled in her seat, staring intensely at the small king. I was starting to think that while the queen was all-knowing, managing to get help from her kingdom's inhabitants was another story. To be fair, I understood why.

"There are no obligations tied to what I am about to tell you. You and your group are doing what others can't," Toto started as the room became whisper quiet.

After another handful of cookies, washed down with a glass of grayish milk, Toto cleared his throat. "On the path to the Cavalier Mountains, if you follow the westernmost route, you will find two bridges crossing the Black River. Do any of you know it?"

"Yes, from the old rhyme. *Where two bridges cross the river black, choose wisely or never make it back*," Atari recited while Toto nodded.

"Yes, and Petro?" he prompted.

"Yeah, never go there," Petro replied, stroking his glorious mustache.

"I can tell you these bridges are very real and very dangerous. Unlike most paths, you must choose the correct bridge. If you don't, well, your trip will be much shorter than initially planned," Toto informed the group, lowering his voice as if telling a scary story to a group of kids.

"What happens if you don't take the right bridge?" I asked as Petro lightly dusted.

"There is a troll that lives under the bridges. He travels between the two of them. Whatever bridge he is on is the one that will allow safe passage. The troll also protects the bridge from something; I'm not exactly sure what, but from what I understand, it will make your quest much shorter than planned," Toto said, nodding.

"It's not a quest," I huffed, still not liking the label.

"Bruther, I think at this point it's fair to say it's a quest," Phil chimed in.

I blew out a lungful of air as Toto started back up. "You see, this troll is precisely who you need to visit. As you mentioned earlier, the portal to the Crystal King's domain is through Davros's old keep. The troll can send you there."

Atari interrupted Toto. "And you've never bothered telling Titania this?"

"The last thing a slave wants to give its master is another whip or field to sow," Toto answered, wisdom coming through in his response. While he was a unique Pixie, as they all were, he was also a king.

She nodded, knowing anything she responded with would be meaningless.

"Then what?" I brought Toto's attention back to me.

"Then you figure out how to make your way to the Crystal King," Toto replied flatly.

"Oi, that's it, mate? You're saying you don't know from there?" Phil asked, making a damn good point. I felt like we had been told half the story, and the middle of the book was missing.

Reaching into my trench coat, I pulled out Davros's ring, clunking it on the table. Phil and Petro were already aware of the ring; the others' eyes widened, not only surprised but shocked.

Davros was a story that traveled in the wind to people on the Plane. A myth here, while back home, he was a very real, scary-ass old Vampire who happened to like hellhounds.

I always judged people on how they treated their pets. That meant he was okay in my book.

"Where did you get that?" Toto inquired thoughtfully, examining the ring.

"I got it from Davros," I replied, not realizing what that meant to the group at the table. "Well, from a couple of his constituents."

Gaseous looked at Toto as if they were both keeping a secret. "Alright, guys, spill it," I insisted, picking the ring back up.

"You see, a lot of people have tried to enter Davros's keep. The bridge troll, whom neither of us has met directly, will indeed get one to the keep," Gaseous started, getting interrupted by Toto clearing his throat.

"That's mostly true," Toto interjected. "But only if you meet certain parameters of the troll. If not, well, I'm not too sure if he eats you or not."

The two looked at each other, shrugging lightly. Gaseous continued. "From what we understand, without that ring, the keep remains invisible."

"Shite, meaning no other buggers have ever actually seen it or made it in. Davros took the ring with him, so unless you know this Crystal King fellow, there hasn't been a way to get there since?" Phil trailed off, seeing the depth of the statement.

Petro took flight, hovering in front of the group. "Meaning no one's been in the old crusty farts's castle since the Great War."

According to my understanding, that meant several thousand years ago. Before what I had learned was considered "current history" had been recorded. Yeah, Atlantis and all that good stuff, if you're asking.

"Correct," Gaseous replied, grinning at Petro. "I would have thought Davros would have long since perished."

"Nope. Vampires on Earth have a tendency of sticking around a little longer than anticipated. According to some of our V friends, they can even live longer than the Fae," I added as Atari pulled out a map, effectively changing the subject.

"What route will we need to take?" she asked, flattening out the parchment before placing cups on the four corners.

Toto waddled over, pulling out a small staff from his belt. Smacking it on the ground, it tripled its size. "Well, barring any more manticores, you will still have to travel by land if you want to keep your vehicle with you. It also goes without saying, air travel is too dangerous that close to the mountains. There is a gate close by, but you would still have to travel a ways. I recommend taking the five river roads all the way north."

The small king snapped his fingers, causing his two guards to buzz over. "Take the prince's brothers," he started, using Petro's new title. "Check the route as quickly as you can. Ask around, but don't let anyone know why. If anything comes up, let us know."

"How will we know there's an issue?" I asked quickly.

"We will put a communicator stone in the vehicle. I will have them leave before nightfall," Toto replied as Treek and Bosley nodded in affirmation.

This reminded me I needed to check in with Jamison and Aslynn at some point. I was reasonably sure Atari already had, but I trusted the two as well and would fill them in. The good thing about the bracelets was their iron-clad ability to be secure, attributed to the blood magic used to create them.

I was still shocked they didn't have cell phones on the Plane with all the other technology they had.

"It's settled. We'll stay the night, then take out at first

light. That should give us a heads-up if there's anything in front of us," I stated, looking around at the team to make sure they were good with settling in for the night.

I wanted to check out the city, but had a feeling Petro wanted us to meet some of his other acquaintances.

"Oh, and one more thing," Toto spoke flatly, squaring up in front of me as if the rest of the room wasn't involved in our conversation. "You know, the Crystal King never truly gave anyone a reason to not like him. It wasn't until Titania and the Fae Court came along that things changed. Just remember that. After all, how truly dangerous is a wasp until you cram your fist through its nest."

The message was loud and clear. The Crystal King, at one point, had not been hated or feared. It wasn't until the Fae had come along, taking over his palace and kingdom, that he had indeed done some egregious things.

I had also picked up those vibes from Titania back at the palace. My stomach started to sink, the same feeling I got when I unknowingly helped Goolsby setting in.

The little king hovered as his two guards took their positions on either side of him. "I'll take your advice into consideration. Thank you for the guidance and wisdom," I told him. Toto let out a loud fart, dusting the table in front of me.

After a few minutes of getting recomposed, the front doorbell rang again. Petro flew like a dart out of the room, leaving a light trail of dust behind as Gaseous rolled his eyes. Bosley and Treek started lightly singing and dancing a little jig, knowing who was about to show up.

"What's all this about, then?" Phil asked when Petro returned, flanked by two identical female Pixies.

Treek spoke up first while all the Pixies collided in a shower of high fives, hugs, and butt bumping. "They are Petro's twin sisters, Carla and Darla."

"Alright, ladies, I'm going to lay down some rules right now. Rule number one, I'm so happy to see you. Hugs and celebrations will continue for ten more minutes. Rule number two, no flirting with the Earthers," Petro barked out quickly, giving both Phil and I side-glances. "Rule number three, we will all take selfies to show Gran! Rule number four, since I'm a prince now, that means you're both ladies."

The five Pixies all broke out in some kind of weird dance, celebrating the new titles. "Wait a minute," Carla said, pausing, as did Darla. "We're already ladies, you grape brain. That means you will address us as super ladies."

"That's not a real thing," Petro huffed out as Carla stepped forward, raising an eyebrow while poking a finger at his chest.

"Do you want me to tell this big hunk of handsomeness"—Carla nodded in my direction—"about your first girlfriend, Brunhilda?"

Petro stammered lightly, "Uh . . . no, that's okay. Super ladies it is!"

With that, the five Pixies again rejoiced in a chorus of squeaks, pointing jazzy fingers and performing the Pixies' go-to move, the hip gyration.

"What about the rest of your family?" I asked. The words got out of my mouth before I remembered. I had forgotten the stories about his parents and the price that had been paid to get him to Earth.

The Pixies saw the look on my face, and Petro spoke up. "You know, boss, if it weren't for you and for what my parents did, the five of us would probably not be here right now. Here on the Plane, we look at that as a celebration."

Gaseous spoke up after taking in the Pixies. "That means it's time for some libations," he echoed, clapping his hands again. Several pixies flew down with cups and what looked like a significantly nicer bottle than the one already sitting on the table.

While it felt awkward to have the Pixies serving us, when they were done, Gaseous nodded at the group, and they all pulled out small caps, taking a serving of the neon-green liquor. They gave Carla and Darla a couple of high fives as well before darting off into what I could only guess was the kitchen.

"They should only be here a couple more weeks," Gaseous noted, pointing to the dark area where the Pixies had just flown back into. "I hate to say it, but I'm going to miss this group. From what I understand, they're all heading to the Elf lands."

I had no clue what that meant, but it sounded exciting, and more importantly, like freedom for the group.

The one thing I had noticed was Atari's quietness during the interaction with the Pixies. It was clear she wasn't completely sold on the idea of helping the Pixies out. *That's an issue for another day,* I thought. Shelving it for later, I smiled as Petro's sisters started telling unflattering stories about him.

CHAPTER 18

Long Dark Teatime for
Tom's Soul . . . Part 3

"**A**re you bloody sure?" Phil asked as Treek's voice flowed out of the box beside him. The communication stone was lying on a small speaker cabinet covered in wood.

"*Pam, parmph, pam dum, boom,* yes," Treek replied, sounding like a broken fast-food drive-through speaker.

Petro buzzed over, shaking his head. "Say that again, in the old wing click code."

Several rhythmic clicks echoed out of the speaker, sounding like a professional tap dancer getting busy. Petro nodded his head, mumbling to himself. "I see . . . yes . . . okay. Alright, thanks, see you soon."

I looked over as the carriage shook on a rough patch of cobbled road. It didn't help we were going well over seventy miles per hour. "Spill it there, prince," I urged Petro as Atari slowed the vehicle down to a crawl.

She glanced over. "Just in case."

"Well, boss. It sounds like they ran into someone who wants to talk to you. Some lady," Petro responded, shrugging, doing a calmer version of the hip gyration.

"Did Treek sound concerned?" I inquired quickly, figuring Petro would be able to tell from the tempo of his wings. I chalked that thought up to the now random pile of Pixie trivia I knew, which would make me win on any given Sunday.

"Nope, he sounded fine to me. Plus, if it were bad, Bosley would have been sending the message," he replied.

I sat back while Petro flew over to Atari, grabbing a small pen to scribble down a set of numbers for her to punch into the navigation system. After a few clicks, she looked up. "We aren't far. Looks to be an old boarding house in the middle of nowhere. These are fairly common in this area, and they close and reopen often."

Atari put the vehicle back into motion, veering off the main path heading east. I had reached out to Aslynn and Jamison earlier, finding nothing had changed back at the palace. Atari had joined the conversation in a show of trust.

Getting Tom out of the palace was becoming glaringly problematic. Aslynn had spent some time going back through our conversation with the queen, feeling there had been a lot of room for interpretation; not to mention I hadn't gotten the queen to tell clearly what she was going to do. "Look at this place," Phil announced, snapping me back to reality.

The road was mostly grass with two well-worn ruts in the middle. Trees concealed the wooden edges of the old two-story building, making it look like it grew out of the forest, much like everything else outside the main population centers. We also noticed the lack of people or anything else outside.

"Let me guess, bruther. You got a bad feeling about this?" Phil joked, also trying to steady his nerves.

"Something like that. There's light coming through the

front window, and if I'm not mistaken, that's Bosley heading our way," I replied as Atari opened the door.

"Hello, fellow questers," he greeted. I had given up on my disdain for the word by that point. The task Toto had given them made them a part of the journey.

"Hey, bro," Petro greeted, buzzing around before he finally landed on my shoulder.

"Prince Petro and associates. There is a rather powerful older lady in there who insists on talking with Max, and Max only. She stinks like high magic," Bosley again huffed. He sounded winded.

"What does this lady look like?" I asked, not sure where this was going.

"Tall, black hair, older, but not too old. She has some crazy golden thing wrapped around her arm that stinks of weird magic," Bosley replied quickly.

"Lilith," I murmured as Phil let out a curt, "Shite."

"Who?" Atari asked. Petro let out a whistle, pointing down.

"My grandmother. If she wanted us hurt or dead, we wouldn't be standing here. She wants something, and I want something from her," I explained, refocusing on my daughter. She was here either as a distraction or because she truly needed something. I felt Petro jerk around, and I turned back to look into the carriage. "What?"

"You see that, boss? The hourglass Metatron gave you just flipped over, and sand started coming out."

I climbed back inside, grabbing the celestial device.

We had spent several hours trying to get the sand to move like a regular hourglass would. Except this one wouldn't. It just stayed put no matter how many times you flipped it.

The note and message had been clear. When the sand

ran out, it was time to leave.

Complaining, I put the device in my pocket. "Damn it. This thing is going to either be really helpful or annoying as hell."

Atari stood silent with a lost look on her thoughtful face. "What is it, lass?" Phil asked as she leaned against the vehicle.

"We need to get the Pillar back and reactivated. The manticore, the angel, and now . . . well, a demon. I'm sure Petro's explained this, but it's not that they shouldn't be here. It's that they *can't* be here," Atari said flatly.

"I heard that but never thought it was real," I replied as the sound of loose gravel crunched under Atari's feet. The fact that Lilith wasn't physically supposed to be here, much like Metatron, wasn't lost on me.

"It's the same as why Vs, as you call them, can't come back to the Plane. The Pillar kept everything in balance. It prevented certain beings from coming here and leaving in many ways. It won't be long before the Old Gods show up. That goes for Earth as well," Atari noted, reiterating some of what Aslynn and Jamison had already told us.

"True, but I think they would have already shown up. Bruther, get this over with and let's get back on the damn road. That damn sand thingamabob seems to be telling us the same," Phil noted again. I still had a feeling being on the Plane had his mind on overdrive.

Like a dark cloud foreboding a storm, we all started to feel the pressure of time creeping in on us. I realized that the hourglass wasn't only a gift for the Timegate, but Metatron's way of giving me something we needed without being directly involved. Yes, I wouldn't say I liked these weird-ass rules, but the more I thought about it, the more I realized we needed to get moving.

Just as I started to talk, time and space froze. Bosley's wings stilled as the usually blurry dust that came off him stilled in the air. Phil had been pulling out a smoke in midstride, while Atari's eyes remained alert. Lilith had stopped time.

I could see the calculation in Atari's eyes, telling me that unlike the others, she knew precisely what was going on and was unable to do anything about it. The sounds of the forest also disappeared as my heartbeat started pounding, filling the void. It was time to talk with dear old grandma.

The cozy building felt warm and inviting as I strolled up to Lilith sitting at a dusty table, eating what looked like a bowl of cereal. This was personal for me, and she knew it.

"Cut the shit. I want to know why you're here. No games, and while we're at it, where's my daughter?" I barked louder than planned, my frustration coming out.

Lilith set the spoon down in the bowl. It sunk below the flakes. "Sit," was all she said.

I refocused, calming my nerves, and pulled out the hourglass, setting it in front of me. This, of course, caught Lilith's attention, who reached for it.

"No, that's close enough. Talk," I demanded, not in the mood for pleasantries.

"Mister impatient," she replied as I glared at her. "Fine. Have it your way. I'm here to give you something and take something in return."

Again I glared, not speaking.

"You're being serious for once. Good, it's about time. I'll keep this short. I want you to give this to Tom when you see him again," Lilith requested, handing me the gold sash from around her arm.

We had taken it from her at one time, only to have Tom

give it back. I was still foggy on the details as to why.

"What do you want?" I asked tightly.

"Not what I want; what I need. I am sure by now Tom has told you about the Timegate and its importance—"

I cut her off.

"No games. As you can see, we're on a tight schedule," I noted as she again stared at the hourglass as if she knew its significance.

"Before you say anything, I can smell angel all over that thing, and I'll give you back the time I've taken. Unlike the thing that gave you this, I'm more flexible with my moral compass. Anyway, to answer your question about your daughter, the key lies in the Timegate. I . . . " She paused, catching herself. Lilith wasn't showing her usually composed, authoritarian personality. "We need to ensure you learn how to use that gate.

"There is more at play here than you know. Dark, light, the in-between, and so on. Davros knew you would come here, and he also knew you would be able to find his keep. There, you will find your answers on how to use the Timegate. Your daughter must be born. That's all I can tell you."

I hesitated, contemplating her request. While I knew Lilith was working with Tom, I also knew she had gone back to the remnants of the Thule Society, now called Everbane. Even though she had basically nuked the entire place, killing most of the shithead senior leaders, she was still up to something I had yet to understand. Not to mention Darkwater still being a part of her circle, from what I gathered.

I leaned back, saying one simple name. "Chloe."

She twitched lightly enough for me to see. Lilith and the Thule Society goons had killed her several years ago after what appeared to be some sick punishment.

"You have everything you need, grandchild. When this is all over, you will look at me with more understanding. Oh, one last thing. When the shit hits the fan, don't go up against Titania. That would be bad for your health. She's much stronger and wiser than you can imagine," Lilith warned. I nodded, picking up the almost drained hourglass.

"Well then, one last thing for you while we're at it. I'm done playing games, but I'm sure you already figured that out. Whatever it is you're doing with Darkwater needs to stop," I proclaimed, letting hellfire dance through my eyes. This wasn't the time to get into that conversation, but I knew Darkwater was still causing issues behind the scenes, yet to be held accountable for Ned's death.

While Lilith and the others were immortal beings, they hadn't planned on how strong I had and might just still become. For the first time while talking with Lilith, I saw hesitation and uncertainty.

I retook my position, standing in front of Bosley as the door to the building slammed shut, followed by a whoosh of air. Holding up the hourglass, the last sands of time floated to the other side as everything started to slowly turn back on, sounding like a record player on half speed.

The rustle of Phil reaching for his lighter brought me back as Bosley looked at me sideways.

"Time to go," I barked, waving my hand in the air while everyone stared at me.

"Did she do that time-freeze stuff you keep talking about?" Petro buzzed out. I nodded.

"What does that mean?" Atari asked as Phil patted her on the shoulder.

"Ah," Phil started, rolling the now lit smoke around his mouth as plumes of sweet tobacco billowed out. "He was probably in there for a good thirty minutes. Who knows with

Lilith?"

I was surprised by the seemingly lack of experience with Celestials, demons, and angels they had on the Plane. Atari had hinted that it had been millennia since it had occurred. Knowing some of the folks in my family, I highly doubted it.

"Shotgun!" I barked out of instinct. For some reason, talking with Lilith had giving me the impression that the situation with my daughter was being closely watched by her and Tom. Even though I didn't trust Lilith, I was getting the impression things needed to happen in a specific order.

Tucking the gold sash into my pocket, I once again drifted off into a deep, unrelenting dream.

CHAPTER 19

Eenie, Meenie, Miny, Moe

"**F**or the love of the gods," I exhaled, the four of us staring at the two bridges. "I mean, it can't be that hard."

"It's as hard as Petro at a disco club," Phil joked, making Atari groan.

"You guys are about as funny as a pile of passed-out Pixies," she blurted out, sounding frustrated at the childish banter.

Petro smirked at Phil. "That's not what Kristi said."

"Oh no, he went there," I whispered to myself as Atari grunted, trying not to laugh after hearing about Phil's on-again, off-again crush. We had, after all, been stuck in a carriage together for well over a day. Petro's response had made her unwantedly giggle.

"Well, we will just see about that, Rambo," Phil chuffed back while Petro started doing the hip gyration.

"At least I can tell which bridge the troll's under," Petro stated. We all turned to stare at him. He shrugged, pointing to the bridge on the right. He immediately corrected this by shifting to the bridge on the left, looking confused.

"Oh shit," I blurted out, knowing something was wonky.

"What?" Atari asked, composing herself.

"Well, Petro here has about the best nose there is." He corrected me by shaking his head. "Correction, second best behind his brother Bosley. We have this thing where we sit around and talk smack while he figures it out, as you just witnessed. The issue is, he's never hesitated before."

Phil spit his cigarette on the ground. "Aye. Petro, what's up, bruther?"

"I don't know. I-it's like it moved," Petro stammered. "But, something else is—" He stopped as the water under the bridge on the right started shifting, forming some type of figure.

"I'm guessing that's the issue with choosing the wrong bridge," I huffed, yelling, "*IGNIS!*"

Hellfire erupted from my arm, forming Durundle's blade. Atari hesitated, taking in the weapon. While she had witnessed the event once, this time my hellfire blade was crackling, letting off drops of what looked like lava.

"What?" I asked as Atari pulled out a pistol.

"I've never witnessed magic like you wield," she replied flatly as the pitch-black water shifted over the edge of the bridge, forming a goo figure that could only be described as a blob man.

"I think we caught the troll during shift change," I declared, walking toward the bridge as Phil's body started glowing a familiar shade of silvery gray. Petro had taken his place ten feet above and slightly behind us.

"Atari, Petro? Any ideas?" Phil prompted, walking to the left as I shifted right.

Atari didn't say a word, leaping forward and shooting several hushed rounds into the mass. The glowing blue bullets hissed as they sizzled through the air.

I swept my blade right, pulling a ball of hellfire in my left hand as a ball of black goo flew toward Atari.

"Phil!" I yelled and he bolted forward, slamming Atari out of the way.

The ball of dripping hellfire rocketed from my hand as Atari lost her footing. She iconically fired several more rounds directly into the blob before hitting the ground.

Hellfire slammed into the black blob, creating a wall of hissing, yellowish steam. Gurgling sounds followed the hissing of smoldering hellfire. Atari's rounds also mixed into the chorus of sounds.

"BOSS!" Petro screamed as a rocket of black goo slammed directly into my dwarf-made biomechanical calf, forcing me to the ground.

The whistling noise of Petro diving toward the blob took over the sound of the raging black water below.

"PETRO!" I yelled as he flew into the yellow cloud of steam still pouring out of the creature from my hellfire mixing with whatever the hell it was.

I found myself on my feet, Phil's glowing hand letting go of my shoulder. Atari was standing by his side, the three of us looking into the fog.

Just as we all moved forward, Petro flew out of the cloud, finally stopping several feet behind us. Black residue dripped from his wings as his chest heaved.

"Guys, I think whatever that is, well . . . it's melting like the wicked witch," Petro panted, having gone at max speed.

"Time to use the new boom stick," Phil purred, wrapping five rounds from Icebreaker, his new rifle, into the now fog-covered blob.

The sounds of steam and something crackling as it

froze mixed while Phil looked down at the rifle. The barrel was covered in ice shards, dropping the temperature several degrees around us.

A confusing mix of hellfire and whatever freezing spell the gun had fired had crashed into the fluid creature like a fat kid into a candy store.

Graying sky's shifted slightly, giving us a view of the mountains as a loud boom, followed by a shower of black rain, erupted from the fog. Frozen chunks of whatever material the creature had been also smacked the hard pavement, several pieces rolling to a stop at our feet.

Unfortunately for us, the new creature that walked through the initial blob of death was just as disheartening.

Atari pulled another magazine from her belt as Phil pushed more will into his shield. I focused using my enhanced sight and noticed the slight grin on what could only be described as a troll standing in front of us covered in the black sludge-like material.

The standoff lasted several seconds in which I took in the creature's features. Spiked, worn ears protruded from a brown leather skull cap, keeping a nest of long hair in check. The troll's features were not as distorted as I had been led to believe. They were more exaggerated in odd places than anything. A large, bulbous nose protruded from a round, mostly human face.

The troll's body was another story. Short legs and long arms, much like those of a hellion, supported a large, thick torso covered in layers of country-strong muscle. A leather trench coat with padded shoulders overhanging his already massive frame finished off its look.

I released the tension in my posture, seeing the creature staring at my hellfire blade. "Guys, hang on," I whispered as the troll lowered the large blunderbuss he had blasted the black blob with.

"Was that you slinging hellfire at Black River?" the nasal, deep voice of the troll echoed across the bridge as rain started to spatter lightly.

"If you are the one who shot that thing in the back, then yes," I replied as Petro hovered down to my shoulder due to the rain.

"Very well. What are your intentions here?" the troll asked, holstering his oversized weapon.

Phil huffed, letting the energy out of his body as a plop of rain hit the cigarette he was about to light. "Bloody hell, we're going to have this conversation in the bloody rain?"

The troll paused, exploring the others with intelligent yet tired eyes, his focus still primarily resting on me.

"Fine. Follow me," the troll relented, trudging over the now dissipated blob. "Black River will be back soon."

We looked at each other, hesitating. The thickening rain finally pushed our bodies into motion. I noticed he had called the creature Black River. A proper name rather than the overall label for the river on a map. Hopefully, I hadn't just added to my growing list of enemies.

By the time we reached the far underside of the bridge, the rain had turned into a torrential, tropical-like, proper Florida downpour.

The troll led us around a stone wall and down a neatly cobbled path to a hobbit-like entrance nestled snuggly under the bridge. A lamp swayed in the also growing wind, flickering like butterfly wings.

Petro leaned against my ear. "He smells okay, boss. I don't think he's going to eat us yet."

The troll cranked the large handle, opening the creaking door just as I was about to speak. "Please follow me."

Atari stopped our advance, quickly asking, "How are we entering your house?"

The troll stopped, visible flecks of fluid flying from his nose. "As guests . . ." he drawled out.

"Hmph," Atari puffed out, walking in front of the rest of us. Nothing was more sacred to the magical community than the rules of hospitality. This included being invited into someone's home as a guest. The old adage about a Vampire not being able to enter a home without permission was largely based on this rule and not much of anything else.

It was always good to remember that a home and a house were two different things. This was the troll's home.

We entered a plain, yet homely room built into the earth lit by a large fireplace and several hanging lanterns full of what appeared to be exceptionally bright fireflies. The floor was made of worn wooden planks knotted and rutted with age. A clear path the troll used could be seen, leading off into a long, dark hallway. What appeared to be a kitchen was on the other side of the large room.

The troll ushered us to a large table sitting in front of the fireplace as I shook off the last of the water from my trench coat.

In typical Phil fashion, he leaned back in one of the chairs, slinging his leg over the side.

"My name's Max Abaddon Sand," I introduced myself when the troll sat down, staring at us speculatively, lighting up a large corncob pipe. The smell of sweet tobacco was oddly calming.

"I am Ian, the keeper of the bridges and the gate to the keep," he replied, taking a long draw from his pipe.

"Okay, Ian," I said, figuring I was speaking for the group. "What was that on the bridge?"

"Black River. Or, more like a part of Black River. I keep Black River from destroying the bridges, and with that, growing more," Ian answered, leaning back as he offered up some of the sweet tobacco.

We all waved off the offer, and Phil pulled out one of the black, burnt rubber–smelling cigarettes from a dry pocket. Ian nodded approvingly, flicking Phil an oversized box of matches.

"So that was just a piece of the river?" I continued asking as Ian simply nodded. "Is that how you usually handle that type of situation?"

Ian's chest heaved as he set his pipe down. "No. In most cases, Black River doesn't show themselves. I handle the situation by using a special ward. Something's got everything out of balance, that is why Black River attacked you the way they did," Ian explained, scratching his nose. "Why can you use hellfire?"

At times like these, I sometimes figured laying most of my cards on the table was the best course of action. "I'm part demon. We are here to fix the imbalance," I replied, pulling out Davros's ring again and clunking it on the table, again getting an odd look. Atari looked at me as if she hadn't heard this before.

"I see," he let out. He picked up the ring, rolling it in his fat fingers. "This is the first time anyone has come here seeking the keep with the actual key in their possession. At least that I'm aware of."

"What does hellfire have to do with Black River?" I asked, getting as much information as possible in case we ever crossed paths again.

"I've never witnessed anyone, or anything hurt Black River. Now I know the way," Ian answered. I was starting to notice the abrupt ending to his statements. It was like he was stopping halfway to think.

"I'm glad we could help. We, in return, need your help," I stated. He grinned, knowing the game I was playing.

The others shuffled lightly as a gust of wind shot down the chimney, stoking the fire and letting embers fly around the fireplace.

"You want to go to the keep?" Ian inquired.

"Yes, and nothing more, mate," Phil confirmed, leaning forward, making sure we kept between the lines of a straightforward negotiation.

Ian rolled his eyes as frustration flickered behind his heavy gaze. "Max and the Pixie, yes. You and the Fae no."

"Excuse me, bruther? I'll have you know I'm up for the challenge," Phil declared louder than needed, pronouncing each syllable, clearly offended. I could see the tension building in Atari as well.

"Guys, hang on," I said, playing peacekeeper for as long as Phil's pride would allow. "Why is that, and why are you acting like you don't really care about anything other than Black River? I thought trolls were all about travel and safe passage.

The gurgling laugh that came out of Ian would have made a twinkie-eating Inspector Dick Holder proud. "I got bored of trolling centuries ago. Everyone only comes here to travel to the keep or try and find the Crystal King. Protecting my home, however, is another thing. My family has controlled these bridges for as long as Black River has been here. I am all that is left of that legacy."

In one of the books Jenny had made me study, I'd read that trolls were, above everything else, violently territorial, willing to go to extraordinary lengths to keep their homes safe.

If this included having a running liquid monster making the bridge necessary to justify everyone leaving the troll alone, I wouldn't doubt the relationship was more symbiotic than anything. I shifted gears in my mind, leaving that thought for later, adding it to the pile of things I would figure out at some point.

"So what is it you do now besides fighting this Black River creature?" I asked.

Ian stood up, walking over to a small metal box from where he pulled out an older Polaroid camera from the 1980s. "I collect faces and keep track of everyone who I've ever gated to the keep. Well, at least gated to try and find it. No one who has made it to the front door has ever returned to let me know what they found. A few have gated there only to jump right back through."

Petro made the universal sign for crazy with his finger as I spoke back up. "You're into photography?"

"AGGHHH!" Ian yelled, slamming his fist on the table. "That's what it's called! I'd forgotten and have been trying to remember for decades."

We all again looked at each other. I cleared my throat. While I was curious about how he had a camera from Earth, I would save that one for another day. "I'm glad we could help again," I stated, seeing if I could rack up some more favors. It was all about delivery.

"Your friends still can't go with you," Ian deflected, not paying attention anymore as he pulled out a knife to carve the word *photography* into the wooden table.

Phil spoke up at that point, seeing as this involved him. "Let's talk this through. Why can't sunshine and I go?"

Ian looked up once he was done writing on the table, slamming the blade's tip firmly into the wood. "Of all the people who could have decided to come here on this day, I got you lot," he grumbled. "If you must know, there are a few things you need to understand. First, and the main reason I'm saying this, is that Max has Davros's ring, which tells me you all might just have a chance of finding what you're looking for. If that is the case, I can tell you this: the gate from the keep to the Crystal Castle is more of a portal. A portal that will not allow an Earthborn, let alone a Fae, to go through."

"So why Max and Petro?" Atari asked before anybody else could.

"As you are aware, Pixies aren't considered in these types of things. As for the mutt," Ian paused, giving me a loving nickname which happened to ring true. His tone was not one of insult, rather a generalization. He had seen his fair share of oddities.

Ian tapped his fat fingers on the word he had just carved on the table, sweeping away the chips. "From the smell of him, the portal's likely to ignore him as well. Very unfortunate for whoever is on the other side. Secondly, I know who sent you. I'm not going to be responsible for not sending at least one of you back to the queen if the others fail in their quest.

"Third, if all of you did, in fact, theoretically made it to the Crystal Castle, and more importantly, in front of the Crystal King, he would have those two killed immediately. I'm sure, young lady, you fully understand why."

While all three reasons made some sense, they also had significant gaps big enough to drive a truck through. It was clear the troll in front of us hadn't witnessed the three amigos, plus one, fully in action. Ian raised his stubby index finger just as I was about to speak up.

"My decision is final. I will gate you to the keep after I get a meal in your bellies and your faces on my wall." Ian stood up.

"Mate, what about the two of us?" Phil asked, frustration evident in his voice.

"Do I look like your father? You are allowed to do as you please. Might I recommend staying here for a few days in case something happens? I'll need some help scraping all that muck and mess you all made off my bridge," Ian noted, walking toward the kitchen section of the large room, banging and clanking several pots and pans.

"This is some shite. Well, if you're not going to gate us to the keep, can you at least get us a drink?" Phil requested, scowling.

Ian looked at me, figuring out I was the band's lead singer. "I mean . . . I would if I were you. Just don't get him wet, and if you can, absolutely under no circumstances feed him after midnight," I said, referring to Phil as a Gremlin.

Petro busted out laughing, knowing the movie. Phil had never partaken in what I considered a Christmas special, *Gremlins*.

"No eating after midnight? Don't get me wet? What kind of bollocks is this?" Phil asked.

"Relax, Gizmo," I replied, chuckling, realizing that Ian was preoccupied banging pots and pans in the kitchen. "Let's not play all our cards yet. Plus, I think he's got a good point. If Petro and I can sneak in and figure out where this Pillar is, we might be able to do this under the radar," I whispered, handing Phil a small gate stone and one of the linking bracelets from home.

Topping that off, I pulled the end of the gate rope out of my inner pocket as Phil cocked a wicked smile. "You sly devil you," Phil muttered, getting some of the wind back into his sails.

I had come prepared with a plan C. Well, sort of, if we couldn't get one of the stones to work in either direction. Simply put, I didn't trust any of the gating and/or communication methods we had with us.

From there, your guess was as good as mine. I just knew I didn't want to travel through any portals or gates without options. The curveball Ian the Troll had thrown us had put my mind into overdrive.

While I trusted Jamison, I wasn't clear where the gate stone had come out of or if it had other uses. I also considered Davros's ring might give us a leg up. I intended to wear it for the rest of the trip, as it was also a powerful enchanted item.

The one issue we had yet to work through entirely was how to get the Pillar back to Titania's palace. Atari was supposed to have that piece covered.

My understanding was we were to locate the Crystal King, find the Pillar, and she would get its location to the Fae leadership directly. We had also been informed that if the Crystal King were to fall, the wards protecting the castle would also be disabled.

"Atari?" She turned. It was apparent she was also thinking about the conversation. "How, precisely, are we going to get the message and location back to the palace?"

"Don't be naive. We both know the endgame here is to take out the king. Max, I . . . my family owes you and your companions more than we can ever repay. This you know and can trust. I hide no secrets from you that would change that," Atari started. I paid close attention to how she had worded her last sentence. "We all have one of the beacons, as discussed before. The fact that I'm not there won't change anything."

Ian started singing in a mix of grunts and sniffs. He was genuinely enjoying the company. Apparently, he liked to entertain guests.

He turned to the large pot hanging over the fireplace, dropping what looked like a chicken into the steaming hot water, followed by carrots and celery. The smell of freshly cracked pepper, basil, and sweet onions joined the chorus of aromas making my mouth water. If I wasn't mistaken, he was making us chicken soup.

I lowered my voice, leaning into Atari. "I'm in a little

more of a rush to get this thing back. Titania made it clear that the Pillar needed to be returned first."

Petro flew to Ian, landing on his shoulder as the troll grinned, reaching into the pot before handing him a carrot. Petro was hungry and obviously comfortable around trolls.

"I have a plan, but depending on what we run into, it may be risky. You ever heard of a gate rope?"

She squinted her eyes.

"I know what they do, but as a Fae, we don't have much use for them. Plus, I'm pretty sure there isn't one anywhere to be found," she replied as Ian again started singing.

"*Gargle belly house, and pan on fire, turn Black River into a mire. Bridge of gold, and foot of large, tell my lover I left with Marge,*" Ian belted out while Phil nodded his head, enjoying a large growler of mead.

I grinned again, showing my plan C as Atari looked up with intelligent eyes. "You're full of surprises."

She knew precisely what I was planning to do. Get Ian the Troll to gate us to the keep, and then pull them along for the ride with the gate rope once at the Crystal Castle.

The rope's one trait was that it didn't immediately work once bound to it. The primary holder of the gate rope had to activate it. This meant you could gate all day and travel for weeks before being sucked through, which in turn meant you could get someone or a group of someones to a specific destination without others knowing.

"Food's about ready," Ian's nasal voice came from the kitchen as Petro darted toward us.

"Hey, boss. The food smells great. He's not so bad. Stinks a little like a troll, but has all kinds of stories about the keep. I'm just worried he's batshit crazy," Petro noted, flying back off to the table once Ian pulled the big steaming pot off the fire.

CHAPTER 20

Say Cheese

Ian became much less animated as we walked down the long corridor into a large room with pictures plastered all over the walls surrounding a rather bland-looking gate. He was not enthusiastic about performing his duties as a troll.

After a much needed nap, prep, and the team quietly binding to the gate rope, it was time to go. On my left, two rather familiar faces stared back at me. It was Tom and Ed, both looking relatively young.

"Hey," I blurted. "I thought you said these were people who went through the gate?"

"Oh, right. Those two. They only wanted to see where the gate came out. Nothing more. Plus, they had a young lady with them. She didn't come back. They jumped right back through. Those pictures on the left wall are folks who did that or just came here to ask me questions. Most of the others took off on foot toward the mountains," Ian replied as Phil picked a stretch of wall to look over.

"What happened to these blokes?" Phil asked, pointing to one of the walls away from the gate.

"They probably died," Ian replied. "Alright, line up individually. Or do you want to take a group face capture?"

"You mean picture?" Petro asked as Ian again let out a joyful howl.

"Gahhh! Yes, of course. I also forgot what that was called. I'll need to carve that down on the table. Yes, let's take a picture," Ian responded, smiling once again.

"What do you say, gang? A group photo? We can use it for our Christmas cards," I joked as Atari, Ian, and Petro glared at me. "Okay, I keep forgetting old Saint Nick is a little bit of a jackass around these parts. Let's just get it for the office then," I followed up.

In all fairness, the accounts I had been made aware of concerning Chris Kringle, as he was also known, weren't precisely all presents, cookies, and cute workshops. According to the others, the only thing he liked to give out was a solid swift kick in the ass to anyone in his way. Kim and a few of us had even gone after him a couple years back. But that's another story for another time . . .

Ian motioned us to stand in front of the gate as he held up the Polaroid camera. It was the old type that opened with the push of a button, exposing the lens as the flash popped up with a quick click. Topping this all off was the small rubber ducky he held out as he deadpan asked us to say, "Cheese."

The click of the camera and blinding flash were quickly followed by the sound of the film rolling out of the magical image box—Ian's name for the device before our arrival.

"That wasn't so bad, was it. Now let me see," Ian mumbled to himself, scratching his nose.

"What's he doing, boss?" Petro asked me. Ian interrupted before I could answer.

"Ah, right here!" he bellowed.

"Why there?" I asked as he patted me on the back, noticing it didn't budge me.

"The far-right wall beside the gate is where I put the maybes," he responded in his nasal voice.

"As in maybe coming back?" Phil joked. Ian glared at him with an obvious nod, agreeing.

"No worries. We'll be back in time for breakfast," I said as Ian again nodded.

"Or not," the troll followed up. "Well, it's time."

I sighed as we all gave each other the look, knowing we would see each other again. Minus Atari; she didn't look reassured.

"I'll see you on the other side," I huffed, doing one last check on my gear. Feeling for the communicator Atari had given me, I patted it just to make doubly sure.

To be clear, I was loaded down with about every weapon I had and could carry. Davros's ring sat snuggly on my right index finger, and the Judge's weight made itself known. Pulling out my short staff, I was ready.

Ian activated the gate as Petro spoke up, jokingly referencing *Poltergeist*. "Don't go into the light, Carol Anne!" I regretted letting him use my streaming accounts to watch movies.

"Who is this Carol Anne?" Atari asked. I let out a snort.

As brave as he was, Petro had had Casey checking under their bed for clowns and the closet for monsters for well over a month. She hadn't been particularly happy about the situation. This had been followed by the odd occurrence of my socks all going missing simultaneously.

"Bruther, be safe. No shenanigans . . . without me, that is. Petro, bring fire boy home in one piece," Phil instructed, playing off his concern. While he was one of the most kickass Mages I had ever met, he was more like family these days.

"Will do. Atari, keep Phil out of Ian's liquor cabinet," I

joked. Ian chuffed, looking concerned, swiftly glancing at Phil.

A few hours earlier, we had set as much of a plan B in place as possible. While it still wasn't much to work with, the main task at this point was not only finding Davros's keep but also getting inside.

Since I'd had oversight of the Postern, one of the most powerful room of gates on Earth, a few things had become profusely clear. Every gate had a slightly different feel to it. The distance it sent you, the oddity of the location, and more frequently, what was waiting for you on the other side all had a slightly different reverberation.

The gate in front of us crackled like a Fourth of July sparkler. Colors flowed throughout the veil of the gate as if not entirely knowing where it would end up dropping us. While we didn't know where precisely the Crystal Castle was on the Plane, we had a fairly good idea where Davros's keep was.

I felt the light push and Petro's feet on my shoulder as he pointed to the inside of my trench coat. He often hitched a ride in the inner pocket when we gated together in unpredictable situations.

Nodding, I pulled it forward, and he quickly slid into one of the two pockets, hanging his arms over the side as his wings folded inward. The energy coming from the gate was different. It had a flavor that you could taste as Ian activated it. I gripped my short staff and readied myself to walk through, taking a deep breath.

CHAPTER 21

Davros's Keep

The crunch of frozen ground and slap in the face of Mother Winter's cold embrace greeted us like old lovers as I walked out of the gate. Gusty winds and flecks of snow mixed with fog ensured we wouldn't be seeing much more than a few feet in front of us.

A sheer wall reached into the muffled sky to our backs and right. To my left, a drop-off filled with pillowy clouds invited us to jump into the cushioned abyss.

I chuckled lightly to myself, thinking it probably dropped all the way to hell; a quick way to warm up. We were in the clouds above, out of sight and out of mind. If this was where Davros was from, he was more complex than I'd thought.

Knowing the effects cold weather had on Pixies, I pulled my trench coat together, opening the collar to speak as Petro squirmed, yelling about something.

"It stinks in here. You using that hippy deodorant again?" Petro asked. I let out a freezing huff. The air was unnaturally cold. Even with my heightened senses and hellfire core, it was quickly taking its toll on me.

"Yeah. Every time I use Old Spice, it burns. Hey, you're

going to need to stay in there," I mumbled, trying not to take in too much razor-sharp cold air.

"No shit, Sherlock. Man, I should have worn two pairs of underwear. Casey packed some extra just in case. You know that human deodorant has metal in it. Probably why . . ." Petro noted before trailing off, blowing warm air into his hands as he rubbed them together.

I closed the collar of my coat, figuring now wasn't the time to talk with a cold Pixie about deodorant, which usually involved lots of cussing. Again pausing, I cleared my mind, focusing on our surroundings.

Davros's ring started pulsating on my finger as I pulled it in front of me. "It can't be this easy. Hot and cold?" I asked myself, lifting my hand. It started pulsing warmly in front of us.

I shook my head, figuring it couldn't be that simple. After only a dozen frigid steps forward while holding onto the wall, I realized it wasn't. Random objects lay strewn on the ground, frozen in time. A canteen, a sword, and a boot that looked like it still had the foot inside it sat on the path.

Ian was right. Some of the individuals that had passed through his gate had only made it a few short feet. I could feel Petro rustling around as I started walking forward again.

The wind howled in some type of song as the path opened up into a field. My hand slipped off the rocks to my right as I looked up at another sheer stone wall covered in massive, deathly icicles which dissolved into the misty gray sky.

A light shimmer of ice had already formed on my shoulders after a few short minutes, and light snow started to accumulate on top of it. The humid yet freezing environment was sticking to my clothes. I was either going to have to set the place on fire or find shelter soon.

Trees frozen in time, looking like giant monsters, stood angrily beside me as I walked forward. The wall in front of us had twelve or so distinct slits in them large enough to squeeze through. Piles of bones and frozen bodies sat in heaps of different sizes in front of each.

Petro jabbed me, and I let out an, "OUCH!"

"What?" I said, opening my collar.

"Why did we stop? And your heart rate just went up. Are there ladies out there?" he asked as I looked up, refocusing on the open area. It reminded me of a video game level. A puzzle for us to figure out or join the frozen piles of bones.

"There's a large rock wall covered in ice with twelve or so slits big enough to go through. I'm thinking the icicles don't let unwanted travelers pass. There are bones everywhere," I relayed as Petro paused again, blowing in his hands.

"Sounds like Hades's place. You know, with all the gate passages," Petro replied.

"That's why you get paid the big bucks, buddy," I said before again closing my collar.

"It can't be this easy," I mumbled to myself again, lifting Davros's ring.

A subtle yet present pull was directing me to the far-left slit, close to the edge. I noticed the piles of bones thinning out the farther left one went. I was starting to think people showed up and went for the closest opening with the fewer bones in front of it. There was a puzzle to solve, and I had a hunch the ring was just one part of it.

I stood as close as I dared to the edge, away from the spiked ice wall. A tree stood frozen in time to my left, looking razor sharp and edgy, as if it were about to attack. I held up the ring, noticing that it was still pointing in the general direction I was going. While it was enough to lead me to the proper opening, the piles of bones sitting around and in front of the crevices were pushing my thought processes into overdrive.

Taking two steps forward, a cracking sound reverberated from the wall. I froze in place. "Gods and graves," I groaned, looking to the pillowy layer of clouds just below the edge of the drop-off.

Steadying myself, I again held out my left hand, slowly moving it in the general direction of the far-left crack. Again, the ring pulsed more, signaling from the drop-off all the way to the far side of the left opening.

Without thinking, I held up my right hand, yelling, "*IGNIS!*"

A wave of hellfire erupted from my hands, scorching everything within the area the ring had identified as hotter. Ice crackled and fell to the ground as steam hissed and clouds evaporated. For a brief moment in time, the frozen, dull earth in front of me showed its true disposition. More surprisingly, it also showed a roughly 4-foot-wide path directly to the left of the wall leading over the drop-off. It would take a coordinated slide down the steep embankment to ensure we didn't die.

This was the trick the openings had been playing for hundreds of years. Since everybody had focused on the twelve obvious routes, they had not tried the path less traveled—or seen it, for that matter.

I opened my collar as Petro's eyes gleamed back up at me. "Hey, boss, I don't like it when you get all quiet and give me that look. Are you about to do something stupid?"

"On a scale of one to ten, it's a steady nine. If for some reason you don't feel us hitting hard ground, figure a way out and take flight," I said, enjoying the warmth my hellfire produced.

"Boss, do I need to come up there?" Petro chided, shaking his head east to west as he spoke.

"It's all part of the quest, buddy," I nervously chuckled,

taking ownership of the ridiculous situation. Petro reached up, smoothing out his majestic mustache.

"You know . . . the ladies love a good quest, and more importantly . . . the heroes," he finished as I closed my collar. I could feel Petro getting situated in my pocket as my heartbeat started to accelerate.

I set my jaw as a gust of wind and snow reminded me how dangerous the small drop would be. Taking one last calming breath of frozen air, I dropped to my knees and delicately turned around, sliding onto the small path.

The sound of cracking ice overtook that of my heartbeat. I looked over, only to see the trees starting to move violently. They appeared to be spearing and stabbing, looking for anything within reach. My initial instinct was to blast the entire place with hellfire to allow safe passage for anyone who might follow, but the thought was replaced quickly as another gust of fog, snow, and wind blocked out the scene. I lightly patted my trench coat, letting Petro know everything would be okay, at least for now.

I focused on the path, noticing the wind was pushing me against the side of the rock wall instead of away from it. The next several minutes were filled with light shuffles and cracking rocks dropping from the edge of the footpath. I could hear them tumble below before the sound was muffled by the fog and hungry clouds.

Just as my nerves started to fray, a large crack appeared in front of me. A ledge intersected with the path, forming another solid opening. I held up Davros's ring, and it pulsated for me to move forward, the rhythmic beat of the device speeding up.

Squinting my eyes, I noticed water trickling from the stone wall in front of me. I also noted my breath no longer turning into instant snot-cicles on my face. I could hear Petro talking, which made me regain my focus.

"If horm . . . tafe thaf path," was all I could make out. Feeling comfortable enough to open my coat, I asked, "What?"

He zipped out. He was still stiff, as the air was close to freezing.

"It's warm. Take that path," Petro blurted out. He was sensitive and could feel the change in temperature through my enchanted coat.

"You picking anything up on the other side?"

Petro shrugged. "Still too cold. All I can tell you is it's warm," he said, landing on my shoulder and fluttering his wings to knock off the snow.

I looked around, noticing the soft edges of the gray, snowy mist act as if they were going to eat the warm patch of mountainside. I stepped forward as the ring settled on a low, steady, humming vibration. Taking a final look behind us, I entered the dark path.

Awkward warmth greeted us as I pushed my will into the short staff, lighting the tip. The surrounding area started glistening. Moisture hung on the walls, not knowing where to go, and the sound of my footsteps turned into wet crunches of gravel.

"Boss, you see that?" Petro whispered as the light from my staff reflected off what looked like a heavy, metal door, much like the ones back at the Atheneum and Postern.

Looking at the ring, the marking intricately etched in the door matched. "Yeah, I think we made it. Any ideas from here?" I asked as Petro darted over to the door, doing what could only be described as sniffing for clues.

Petro shrugged, zipping back behind me. "See that small round gap? Push the ring into it."

I shook my head, pressing the ring into the small indentation. More than twenty other notches told me this was another puzzle to solve, and we had hit the easy button again.

The sounds of gears grinding and small rubble dropping bounced off the walls of the small room we stood in as light flickered off the moist walls. When the door started to grind open, the air from inside lashed out, more humid than an old lady's breath whispering to you at church

Steam erupted from the entrance. "It's all clear," I said after a moment, and he came out from behind me. The dark mouth of the room in front of us gave away no secrets. I shrugged, raising my staff to light up the space.

What greeted us was hard to explain. A now glowing pool of bubbling water flowed in several directions from the center of the massive room. Large banners and random furnishings sat in a stylish manner, telling me this had once been the home of someone with power.

"You smell that, boss?" Petro asked as he flicked around several torches, lighting them quickly.

"Sulfur?" I replied as he landed on the small stone table next to the door. I had only stepped a few feet inside the room.

"This place is either inside or on the side of a volcano," Petro guessed, not making me feel any better.

"Why couldn't we see the pool of water?" I asked. Petro paused, thinking.

"I guess it needed some type of light to get it going. Who knows. This place stinks to the high heavens of magic," Petro replied as the torches finally started fully lighting after what appeared to be hundreds, if not thousands of years sitting dormant.

"That's the thing. Do you notice anything familiar?" I asked as Petro wrinkled his nose.

"I see what you're saying, boss, but I can't put my finger on it," he replied as I stepped forward, looking up at the catwalk.

"This place, minus all the fancy curves and darker vibe, is almost identical to the Atheneum," I whispered as the sound of something falling echoed down the long main hall.

"You're right, boss. Look," Petro said, zipping over to the door to our left on the other side of the main stairs. "The dining room's in the same place."

Walking forward, I started to feel hidden eyes staring at us from odd shadows at the far end of the hallway, which would led to the stacks back home. Petro turned quickly, confirming my suspicions. We weren't alone.

A loud squeal echoed throughout the building from the dining room door as I turned the aged handle after putting a little heat into it and pushing lightly.

"Well, I guess there goes the element of surprise," I whispered as we both quickly entered the room, closing the door behind us. Petro was already lighting aged candles.

"Wow, boss, look at this place," Petro said in amazement.

The table was covered in treasure and other important-looking artifacts while exhaustingly detailed paintings hung on the walls.

"Petro, look at this one. Does that look like Angel and Davros?" I asked, pointing to a lifelike painting of two Fae.

"That's Davros, alright. The lady, though . . . I bet we just figured out who Angel's grandparents are," Petro added.

"She's stunning. Look at the intelligence in her eyes," I noted.

After a few more moments of contemplation, we both started scanning the room. There had to be a king's ransom in here. Petro landed on a few jewels, sizing them up.

"Later, buddy. This stuff might belong to Davros, or hell, who knows. I'm starting to think we can already guess where the gate is," I stated thoughtfully, clicking my tongue.

Petro nodded his head, agreeing. We had spent so much time around each other we had started to vibe. My train of thought was simple: if this was a mirror of the Atheneum, it would stand to reason it also included some version of the Postern. Between the Everwhere, back home, and here, I was starting to see a pattern.

"Look, man, something's in here with us. I don't want to start any trouble, so I say we haul ass as fast as we can, then figure out the gate or portal?" I stated in the form of a question.

Petro sniffed, closing his eyes. "I don't think whatever it is, is planning on making that easy."

I pulled out my pistol loaded with special ammunition, and without saying the invocation, ignited my hellfire blade. Red light started dancing off the paintings.

Petro dropped the emerald in his hand, scowling, as I spoke up. "I agree, but now is not the time. This place is something we need to come back to."

With a nod of his head and flutter of wings, Petro zoomed into the air, taking his usual position behind my right shoulder. The lawn dart of death would, if needed, zip forward, addressing any issues and/or eyeballs we encountered.

I wasn't as careful with the door, slamming it open this time around. If something was going to make our trip hard, I wanted to ensure it had second thoughts.

I stepped out, walking along the wall. The light from the entrance dulled the further in we went, replaced by the rhythmic flames of my hellfire blade. Again, the sounds of something clacking from the far end of the hallway kept the hairs on the back of my neck standing at attention.

Petro flew up to my ear. "Whatever it is, it's behind the doors at the end of the hallway. I can smell a ward or something."

It was either another layer of protection or the door was there to keep something trapped. Nodding, I stepped into the middle of the hall. I could sense the magic holding whatever it was inside.

The door in front of us was in the same spot as the one back home, again affirming our suspicions. "Let's try this the easy way," I said, taking several steps back before pointing my blade at the door.

"*EJECTOS!*" I yelled as a ball of pointed hellfire flew from my blade, crashing into the door.

There was a brief pause as the now lodged ball of hellfire blazed, starting to eat through the door. In doing so, a ring of glowing fire like a lit cigar started racing to the edges of the frame, evaporating the ward. I needed to remember to put one back in place on our way back.

"Watch out!" Petro exclaimed as one of the Faceless we had encountered in St. Augustine leaped from the dark room.

I ducked as its razor-sharp claws slashed through the air overhead. "We must be getting hotter!" I exclaimed as another of the creatures exploded from the room.

"They don't have eyes, boss!" Petro yelled, figuring he would have to change tactics.

I hesitated, gathering my focus. The creature that had come out first had put so much effort into the leap, it had crashed into a pile of old armor stacked in the middle of the hallway. It also had one of Lana's arrows sticking out of its chest.

"Shit. I thought these things were dead," I said, confused by the creature's apparent resurrection.

The three cuts from my previous encounter with the Faceless were still fresh in my memory. The fact that the other two were still able to move told me they were not the same ones I had killed with my hellfire blade, proving that hellfire was a Do Not Pass Go life ender.

Petro picked up on the same thing, flying in the opposite direction and diving as the one now in front reached out, the skin on its face stretched as if it wanted to let out a scream without a mouth to do so.

I swung my blade just as a sting rocked my modified calf. The Faceless behind me had already made its way back to us. Shifting my body weight, I slammed my boot on its clawed hand as it pulled back for another swipe. With the quick squeeze of my trigger, I fired three fast rounds directly into the creature's face, which exploded in gore and black e-core.

I pulled up my hellfire blade as a wet thump caught my attention. Petro had driven his small saber through the back of the creature's skull, stunning it temporarily, same as our previous encounter.

Without hesitation, I decapitated the faceless monster; it fell to the ground.

Silence took over the madness as we both scanned the door for more Faceless. "Was that the last of them?" I asked as Petro sniffed the air.

"I think so. These things stink like burnt, moldy, dirty baby diapers," Petro replied, wrinkling his nose.

"It looks like these were the ones that somehow survived our little scuffle in the Everwhere. At least that one. I don't think they were here on purpose. It was like they were lost or something. Maybe they were somehow shifted to the Everwhere, and well, they figured a way back here, but not the rest of the trip," I guessed thoughtfully, quickly stepping forward.

The more time we spent there, the more time others had to figure out what we were doing. We entered the stacks to find it full of armor and weapons instead of books and artifacts. Armored chariots with giant catapult-like weapons were lined up as far as the light allowed us to see.

"Right here, boss," Petro yelled, having flown several feet ahead, dusting by what looked like the same door to the Postern as back on Earth.

I scanned the entrance, looking for any wards or possible traps. If it weren't for the fact that I had been trying not to freeze to death, I would have been more cautious on our journey to the keep.

Holding up Davros's ring, I balled my hand into a fist, placing it on instinct inside the dragon's mouth etched into the door. The opening clicked, followed by a dusty thump letting us know we had done a significantly good job at guessing since arriving to the keep. The design and similarities to the Atheneum had certainly helped us along the way.

If someone were to walk into the massive building not knowing their way around, it could take days before they even checked out the area. Not to mention they would be running into several uninviting wards along the way.

"How'd you know to do that?" Petro asked as I slowly pulled the door open. Centuries of stale, cool air hissed out. I walked forward, quickly extinguishing my hellfire blade and lighting the end of my staff instead.

"It just felt right. Can you get those torches lit?' I asked Petro as he buzzed around the room. Instead of fire, he was dusting the small, encased fixtures.

"These just need a little juice. They're the same as the ones at Ian's place," Petro replied. Once he finished, we both stood in the middle of the now lit room.

Unlike the Postern back home and the almost identical one in the Everwhere, this room only had three gates. A round table sat in the middle with a few books stacked on top of each other. The top volume grabbed my attention immediately.

An hourglass and old-style sundial lay embroidered on

the dusty leather cover. I had been told that I would find what I needed to use the Timegate here. My plan had been to get the Pillar situated, then work through the rest of my compiling list of things to do.

"What is it, boss?" Petro asked, seeing my eyes staring a hole through the book as I picked it up gently. Dust and tiny flecks of disintegrating paper fluttered to the floor.

I opened the book, seeing a sketch much like the one in Tom's journal of the Timegate.

"Bingo," I exhaled, shuffling through the pages, seeing pictures of not only the key I had in my possession, but the hourglass Metatron had given us as well. "That reminds me," I followed up, pulling out the hourglass.

The sands had not moved, telling us we had time. Just as the thought crossed my mind, an individual fleck dropped into the empty portion of the container.

"Look at that, boss. It means we need to get moving," Petro said, holding up what looked like a Pixie sword also lying on the table.

"I hate this damn thing," I complained, noticing that it was only moving one piece of sand at a time. It would take several hours to empty at this rate, if not days. "I don't think it means we have this much time here. I'm betting it's for the entire trip."

Petro nodded, agreeing, as he pulled the short, pointed blade from its sheath. "Wow," he echoed as he slashed it through the air.

"What's up?" I asked, walking up to the one gate that looked out of place from the other two.

"It's an Elf-made Pixie sword. I've only heard about these. It must be from the war," Petro observed, giving me what could only be called puppy dog eyes.

"Geez, yes, you can take it," I said. He dusted lightly, doing the hip gyration before acting like he was spearing the deadly weapon through an unsuspecting eyeball.

I squinted as two round indentions sitting snuggly to the right side of the portal's or gate's frame came into focus. I clicked my tongue. Reaching down, I pushed the small compartment on my leg open.

"I think all we need to do is put these in that matching inlay, and this thing should rock," I noted, holding up both of the coins. One coin was from Davros, and the other I'd received from a crusty old guy at FA's on my first trip to the Everwhere.

As with the rest of our assumptions since entering the keep, I was correct, and the portal sprang to life. While similar to gates, portals were more of a made item. Gates were parts of nature manipulated to go and/or do certain things. A portal, on the other hand, was made entirely from magic. It was easy to tell the difference simply by the feel and resonance of the shimmering veil.

"Hey, boss. I think it's time to try the gate rope," Petro reminded me.

I pulled it out, as well as the gate stone from Jamison.

The logic was simple, if not wholly sound. Activate the gate and the rope, pull the others through, then get on with the quest. Yes, I was still accepting the fact that I was on a quest.

I pulled out the gate stone, pushing my will into it. Nothing happened. The clack of rock against the stone floor was disheartening, and Petro dusted lightly, shaking his head.

Since stepping through Ian's gate, I was positive that until we fixed the situation with the Pillar, our secondary plans were off the table.

CHAPTER 22

Hole in the Earth

We stood gawking at the scenery around us as if we were in a museum looking at a work of true art. Massive spiked gray mountains protruded from the ground and pierced through the lightning-streaked clouds.

The space in front of us was an enclosed world. Massive crystals erupted from the rocky landscape in a mix of random yet seemingly manicured patterns. The glow from the lightning was only interrupted by random, distant splatters of lava, creating a dull, silvery gray light.

The clouds pulsed, covering the mountaintops above us, making the area look more natural. Sticking out like a beacon of light in the middle of the open-cave world, atop the tallest mountain, was something that could only be described as a Crystal Castle.

"Keep an eye out for big gorillas or oversized lizards," I muttered to Petro, who looked up from my shoulder.

"Is that a King Kong and Godzilla reference?" he asked, turning back, locking his tiny, glistening eyes on the castle.

"Yeah, something like that. Just when I thought I'd seen everything, we walk into some shit like this. Sometimes, I just want to wake up and walk to the gas station for coffee and stale doughnuts," I reminisced, thinking about the smells and sounds of a busy gas station in the morning.

"You know, boss. There are some amazing things on the Plane. We ever get some time, I plan on showing you and little Neil around," Petro replied, drawing out his newly acquired sword.

Pulling out the hourglass, I saw several more grains of sand had floated to the other side. It was time to get moving. "You see that opening down toward the bottom, a few stories off the ground?" I asked Petro as he squinted his eyes.

"Yeah, it looks like a little bit of a climb."

I reassured myself, shaking my modified leg. "This thing will give me a little boost. As long as it's not an optical illusion and we aren't that far away, we should be fine."

Petro took flight, and we finally scanned our immediate surroundings. What I'd initially assumed were small mounds of earth when we had stepped into the surprisingly warm, dry air, transformed into something more ominous. Piles of fossilized bodies sat stacked on top of each other, crystals growing from the skeletal structures. I wasn't in the mood to investigate why, but figured they had been there for a very long time.

"What do you think, boss?" Petro asked, staying close to my shoulder.

"I think we don't need to stay here too long. It reminds me of old pictures they used to show us in the army. After the battle, medics and other soldiers would pile up the dead bodies to either burn or bury. Here . . . I just don't know," I replied as a few small rocks fell from the sky, clacking on the trail in front of us.

Petro dusted lightly as we started walking down the footpath. There was a plus and a minus to the trip in front of us. Being fairly open, there was little to no chance of an ambush. The downside of that was the path being out in the open.

While we would look like ants in a yard at first, we would be more visible to others as we got closer. Not to mention, I was already assuming activating the portal had alerted someone, somewhere.

We started walking at a brisk mall walker's pace as the mountains grew in front and around us. Lightning traced the sky in different colors, lending to a slight strobe effect every few seconds.

The closer we got, the more the size of the fortification grew, which meant more space we needed to cover to find the Pillar, and at this point, the Crystal King.

Like every time I started thinking random thoughts, I stopped.

"What is it, boss?" Petro asked as I pulled out the hourglass.

"You want to know something that's been bugging me? The only time this thing worked before getting here was with Lilith, when she slowed down time. Metatron mentioned I would need it to use the Timegate. Hell, with just that quick flip through the book, we found pictures of this thing all over it. Why did it start working again?" I pondered.

"What are you saying, boss? The thing only works when time is involved?" Petro asked, landing on my shoulder.

I nodded. "Well, we just assumed that it worked by telling us how much time we had left, but I don't think that's it. I think it means there is something related to time in what we're doing or where we are," I noted.

"It could be, boss," Petro responded, starting to hum an old Hootie & The Blowfish song about how time punished people.

That trail of thought stayed front and center as we continued walking. If I was right, this meant we had either somehow traveled in time, or time was either slowed down or accelerated back home. A trip to Amon's kitchen would confirm my theory if we made it back.

After another two hours of walking, the last leg of our journey curved around several large boulders into an opening. We had been so focused on the main route we had failed to notice the dip in the moonlike landscape.

Petro and I let out a hissed, "Ssshiiit," simultaneously.

"We're totally getting ambushed here," I murmured just as dozens of Faceless creatures and what looked to be a handful of larger rock monsters dropped in front of the small opening we were about to go through.

One of the bigger rock monsters landed directly on top of two Faceless, crushing them in a spray of gore. I could feel the thump of their bodies through my boots.

"Hey, buddy, I want you to scout that opening. Let me handle this. I'm not sure you're going to be able to do much to those rocks," I said louder, knowing it was useless to hide.

Petro winked, pulling out a small dissolution grenade from his waist. "It might slow them down if they have any type of magical enchantment on them," he proclaimed, immediately zooming forward, lobbing the small grenade into the Faceless moving toward us.

The surprisingly large flash stunned the creatures, a light pop of sparks and ozone wafting from them. By the look of it, something was driving them or at least had them shielded. They had already proven to be mindless creatures.

On the other hand, the rocky monsters continued to lumber forward, unfazed by the minor blast. I glanced up as Petro disappeared into the cave.

"*IGNIS!*" I yelled, also pulling out the Judge. While

hellfire did the job against the Faceless, I wasn't willing to take any chances with the crystal monsters heading my way, which I would now forever refer to as rock gorillas.

As I started to focus, two of the Faceless dove from the giant boulder to my right. I swung my hellfire blade up, missing the first as it slammed into the rocks behind me but taking a portion of the other's shoulder and arm off.

The thump of the rock gorillas forced me to turn quickly, only to have several finger-sized crystals fly from their hands, whistling through the air like oversized razor blades.

Using my enhanced strength, I leaped several dozen feet backward in three large bounds, clearing the first of the boulders and giving me a chance to funnel the oncoming wall of nightmare fuel.

Dropping my hellfire blade, I again refocused, changing to ranged attacks quickly and launching two balls of hellfire at the initial Faceless. The first ball slammed into the one with the missing arm and effectively started melting its neck and head.

A screech emanated from the other Faceless as the ball of sticky hellfire wrapped around its leg, instantly reducing everything from the knee down into charred meat. This was the first time I'd heard the creatures make any noise.

Squinting my eyes, I noticed a rip in the skin around its mouth, allowing the creature to scream. Dark-purple, oozing blood poured from the opening, covering its body in a chaotic mess of gore and pale skin.

A thump pounded against my enchanted trench coat. I looked down to see one of the crystals lodged into it, piercing a small section under my ribs. I gasped, feeling the searing pain of either a broken or cracked rib. A cold sensation flowed from the small area where it pierced my skin. The shot would have blown a hole through me if it weren't for my coat.

The now flopping Faceless missing a leg had shuffled back to the rocks, working out another method of attack.

Gathering a larger than normal ball of hellfire in my hand, I launched it at one of the rock gorillas at the same time I pulled up the Judge, firing at its partner.

The hellfire slammed into the massive creature, and its once rocky exterior burned away, exposing a layer of quartz-like crystal underneath. From what I could tell, the rock gorilla was solid crystal.

What was left of the hellfire ball was now sliding off its newly exposed interior. The second rock gorilla, on the other hand, was frozen in place. Its arms looked as if they should be moving as large cracks traced every line of its body.

I again gasped as the penetrating cold from my injury spread to my upper arms and legs. "What the hell!" I barked as two more Faceless exploded through the now shattered rock gorilla.

I quickly launched another round from the Judge to the closest one, slinging a ball of hellfire at the second, only to miss. The first one disintegrated, while the other regrouped on top of a boulder. I again jumped back as two more of the rock gorillas dropped from the opening.

My vision blurred as voices started swimming through my mind. "*Boss . . . hey, boss . . .*" the voice echoed.

I quickly focused, realizing Petro was buzzing in front of my face. "Hey, buddy," I slurred slowly.

"You don't look so good, boss," Petro chirped frantically as I pulled open my trench coat.

"I got hit by something," I said.

Petro urgently shook his head. "We got to go, boss. That smells like some kind of stunning spell—" was the last thing I heard Petro say as a silver-infused net fell on top of both of us.

My body finally gave up as the graying sky turned black and the sounds of the thumping rock gorillas rocked me to sleep.

CHAPTER 23

I Let Them Catch Me . . . I Also Lie Sometimes.

Sounds of a conversation trailed through my thoughts as my eyes continued to reflect the darkness of deep, unnatural sleep. Noises became whispers, which slowly turned into words.

"Yeah, he's a big lug head, but he's the best lug head," Petro's voice echoed in my dream.

This was followed by the sounds of a young woman's voice piercing the veil of sleep as my eyes finally fluttered to life. Light beamed through my clouded vision as the harsh bright light pulled me further out of sleep.

"Boss!" Petro exclaimed as I slowly pushed my body up from the hard, cold glass-like table I was lying on. The only cushion under my head was my trench coat.

"What happened?" I mumbled. What actually came out was, "Waf happened . . ."

"What happened? You went all badass on those monsters. You were all like, zip, boom, pow," Petro started, acting out cheesy karate moves. It was clear we had an audience.

"Alright, alright. Give me a minute," I moaned as the sounds of a thirty-something-year-old woman came from behind me.

"Cover your head. It will make it easier," she suggested, her voice creating an odd reverb effect.

My eyes focused as I held the trench coat over my head, noticing the lack of anything that could absorb sound besides our clothes. Crystal and slick, polished marble covered the entire room. Hard lines and sharp angles floated in and out of focus, melting into the matching scenery. Even though we were clearly in some type of holding cell, it felt angelic, if not regal. "Where are we?" I mumbled, finally putting some weight on my feet, lifting my shirt to inspect the damage.

The wound was light blue and silvery as it spidered off into various directions. The tendrils were already moving back toward the initial impact spot as I watched. The spell I had been hit with had not been intended to kill.

"You're in the holding cells of the Crystal King," the young woman's voice again echoed. I turned to see her.

Gray, piercing eyes and a familiar-feeling face smiled back at me. She had the type of smile that made you feel as if you knew each other even though you didn't.

Her clothes were tattered from months of wear and tear with little to no attention. Whoever she was, there was no doubt that she was in control of not only her emotions, but herself.

"You are?" I asked, walking over to the transparent yet cloudy wall made out of crystal, facing the woman. Between her holding cell and ours was a wide corridor leading off several dozen feet in both directions. The echo of our voices carried with every breath and word spoken. I grabbed the large crystal slats, pushing my strength to its limits to no effect.

"I wouldn't waste your time, boss. Magic doesn't work in

here. That Crystal King guy has this place all figured out," Petro noted as I again looked at the unassuming woman.

"My name is Destiny. You're Max Abaddon Sand," she stated, again following it up with a smile.

"I'm guessing Petro filled you in on me and my preferences in pajamas, I'm sure," I replied as Petro snorted.

"No, boss. She knew who we were. She even knows who else is in the soup bowl with us. I might have talked about your dating life for a few, but that's about it," Petro said, referring to Atari, Phil, and the others.

This was surprising but not unusual. We had, after all, gained a rather known and at times frequent reputation for finding trouble.

I reflected, gathering my thoughts as I patted down my coat and pockets, finding all my gear missing. "Do you know anything about the Pillar?"

Destiny also placed her hands on the crystal bars. "Yes. I also want to add to my prior statement about where we are. You might also want to consider *when* we are."

Petro slowly flew over to the bars, looking at Destiny.

"When? So you're saying, what? Time's slowed down or sped up?" I asked as I stopped patting myself down.

"A little of both. You might not understand this, but this place is almost impossible to find. The fact that it is in another timeline might be hard to explain," the young woman said thoughtfully. She was trying not to break the bad or unbelievable news.

One of my skills was reading people and being straight to the point. I understood that places could be subjective, and that time could be manipulated to a certain extent, which was against every rule ever made due to the possible repercussions.

"Are we in the future or the past?" I asked. She turned the

volume up on her grin, the cracks in her smooth face showing through the dirt that had accumulated over time.

Something attracted me to her. Not a physical attraction, but one of genuine interest and the feeling I needed to help and protect her. Maybe all the recent talk about my daughter had me confused.

Destiny smiled, shrugging. "That's a good question. Let's just say a little bit of both. For me, I would say the past. For you, more like the here and now. The both of us meeting somewhere in the middle," she said as I tried to digest the statement.

"Gods and graves, of course. I figured this place would make no sense," I breathed out as the loud click and clack of heavy footsteps echoed from the end of the hall.

"That didn't last long, boss," Petro noted, flying to the far end of the cell, sniffing the air. "Interesting," was all he said as he coasted back a few feet from the bars.

I followed suit, taking several steps back. Destiny stayed next to the crystal bars. The figure that materialized from the long, bright hall could only be described as a crystal knight. Much like Metatron, the person walking toward us was clad in mirrorlike armor from head to toe, the only difference being their armor was made from crystals creating the mirrored finish.

The knight stopped in front of our cell, turning to face me with a sharp clicking of their heels. The thing standing in front of us was easily seven to eight feet tall and looked to have a slim and agile build under the armor.

Reaching up, the knight snapped a bracket from his helmet, pulling it off and placing it snuggly under his arm.

"Max Abaddon Sand, you are to come with me," the aristocratic, authoritative knight requested. His voice was sharp as a razor's edge, the threat of violence hinted in every word. This was a warrior and not someone to be taken lightly, unlike some of the armored political figures we had met at Titania's palace.

"Will there be bagels? Doughnuts, preferably?" I requested, knowing the jab was probably not a good idea.

"If either of those items involves possible death, then yes," the knight responded, obviously not knowing or caring about food from home.

"I don't like this, boss," Petro whispered, taking his place on my shoulder.

"Me neither," I murmured before clearing my throat, putting on my trench coat, and smoothing out the front. "What about Destiny?"

"She is to remain here. Her future is none of your concern," the knight replied flatly, smirking in his first showing of genuine emotion. "The past, though . . ." he said under his breath.

I finally accepted that the knight was in no mood to talk further as the crystal bars in front of our cell neatly melted into the floor. Whatever magic ruled this place was enough to keep my powers shut off and the knight in front of us unflinching.

It was as if he wasn't concerned about us harming him in the slightest. If Phil were here, he would have taken the gesture personally. This would have, of course, then led to lots of cursing and more trouble than we were already in.

To be clear, I had let them capture us. Our plan had worked perfectly, landing us directly in the heart of the Crystal Castle. I was also known to be full of shit at times. While I had not gone full demon or whatever on our initial attackers, I had been trying.

I chuckled lightly while everyone looked at me. "What? Just thinking about something," I said, glancing at Destiny, who nodded at us. Again, something about her made me not want to leave. She reminded me of someone.

The knight, who had yet to give us his name, motioned us in front of him as two of the giant crystal gorillas walked up.

"Great . . . rock gorillas," I exhaled to Petro. He repeated my name for them under his breath.

"Rock gorillas. I like it, boss. Everyone will love it when we tell them," he said, feeling confident. His mood rubbed off on me, and I pushed my chest out a few inches.

Petro was right. Now wasn't the time to show weakness. If anything, we had been sent here because we could handle the situation. Or because of the glaring fact that we were expendable in the Council's eyes.

While the Plane had been a place of curiosity and wonder, this place was something different. In many ways, I was starting to realize how precisely big the other side of things was. Thoughts of my life back in my North Florida beachside apartment started to feel more and more distant as we walked down the long hallway.

For once, I was feeling in over my head. Without my gear or companions to lean on, I would have to be hyper focused.

It was at times like this that I wished Phil, Bo, Angel, Kim, and the others were about to bust in to save the day, followed by Ed walking in, melting everyone we disagreed with brains.

Looking back at the knight, it was clear this would not be the case.

After several minutes of walking through locked doorways and odd, darkened corridors, we finally stopped in front of a set of massive iron doors. Instead of the ambient bright white crystals in the holding area, the gray of rock and stone seeped through the glass-like surroundings, the dulling effect in contrast to everything else.

"Say it, boss," Petro whispered as I shook my head.

"Yeah, I've got a bad feeling about this," I replied as the knight walked up beside us. I hadn't noticed his sword before. The hilt was almost identical to that of Durundle, the mythical sword that had bonded with my body.

The two ogreish rock gorillas pulled open the doors. The room in front of us looked eerily similar to Hades's humble abode. Massive columns held up a crystal-covered pointed roof. Stones jutted out at odd angles, forming geometrical designs.

Several less decoratively armored knights stood on either side of the colossal figure sitting in a throne made of gemstones. Behind the throne was another open space full of larger rock gorillas.

The sight of the Crystal King took a few seconds to digest. While the knight was tall, the king was enormous. His armor was dulled metal covered in crystals which looked like they grew from the material. As he shifted forward, several small gems fell from his armor, only to be immediately replaced.

I huffed, pulling my shoulders back. The creature, king, or whatever it was in front of us was significantly scarier than I had expected or planned on him being. Petro landed on my shoulder, his feet firmly planted in my skin, telling me he was just as concerned.

We all stood silent as the king again shifted. He started speaking, the growl from his voice rumbling like an engine before words came out.

"I know who you are and why you are here," he thundered, his crushing voice forcing me to turn my head.

He paused, and I quickly scanned the room, looking at the other creatures now frozen in time. It seemed as if he had flipped the switch, shutting them down. The sound of small, dropping crystals echoed as I took a step forward.

"So . . . does that mean we aren't going to be friends?" I asked, figuring I would see how short his fuse was.

Instead of laughing as most dialoguing bad guys would, he pondered the question. "Perhaps," he replied, snapping his finger. One of the rock gorillas started moving.

I noticed the knights seemed to be completely independent of everything else. The more I looked, the more they seemed not to fit the rest of the ensemble.

The room was silent as the rock gorilla walked back out with a tray of clear drinks in intricately designed glasses. I tensed as the once violent monster came closer to us, now seemingly docile. I side-eyed Petro, who nodded. It was rude to turn down a drink from a host.

As with everything in the magical community, if the host offered hospitality, it was only polite to accept it. The thought faded once I realized the creature in front of me probably didn't give a damn about us, the rules, or what I was there to do, like most immortals.

Taking a sip of the smooth, cool water, I shuddered as the experience caught me off guard. As far as water goes, this had to be the best of the best. Letting out a smooth, "Ahhh," I looked up.

Since I couldn't use hellfire, I focused on the remaining liquid in the glass, seeing it lightly shift. I had a feeling the Crystal King might know my name and why I was there, but being as secluded as he was, there was a good chance he didn't know what I was. Hell, I didn't entirely know the answer to that myself.

"Okay, then you know I can't just leave here," I said, taking the remaining sip of the refreshing water.

"Yes, and that is where the problem lies," he agreed, shifting again in his seat as more crystals fell from his arms. The massive king stood up slowly, the true breadth of his size coming into focus.

"Shit, boss," Petro whispered as I let out a breath.

"I am not going to hand over the Pillar to that freak," the king hissed. Petro and I were about to get a monologue. I loved a good, bad guy monologue.

"Freak?" I asked, knowing the answer.

"Titania. She took it from me after the Great War. Did you know things were just fine when I had control of the Pillar before?" He was trying to see how much I knew.

"No, I didn't," I replied, being honest.

"Just like everyone else who's made their way here, or tried. You think you know what is going on. You have no idea," the king rumbled.

"What's your name, big guy?" Petro chimed in, catching me off guard.

"My name is Dire Caspian. I have been known by many names, but that was my birth title," he answered reflectively. I noticed the knights shifting as he spoke.

I could tell he wanted to talk. The issue was why. "Caspian, you say you know why I'm here, so you know what I am expected to do."

This was the first thing that produced a reaction from the immortal god.

"Kill me and take the Pillar back to that harlot," he scoffed quickly as a new crystal formed on his arm. "She wants power more than you know. Titania almost destroyed an entire race of people to gain it. My people."

His face was stoic and regal. Muscles sat on top of his frame as if made in a forge. The closer I looked, the more I realized his eyes were made of crystal and devoid of empathy.

"Something like that," I replied as he nodded.

"At least you're honest. I'll give you and your little warrior that. He's brave amongst his people," Caspian noted.

"How are we going to handle this?" I asked, figuring being up-front was the best course of action.

The large knight that had escorted us to the chamber delicately shifted. Luckily, the movement was enough for my heightened senses to notice, along with the light sensation of magic being used.

"Handle this? Ha, you will go back to my holding cells, then you will die like the rest," Caspian replied, sitting back down before snapping his fingers. The rock gorillas came back to life.

"Yeah, I don't like that plan," I said as Petro dug his feet further into my shoulder. "I'm thinking we need to talk about this. The way I see it, we have something to offer each other."

Caspian paused, slamming his fist on the throne. "What's that? Redemption? Honor? A chance to take my revenge on the merry old queen? I don't think you have anything I need or want."

I started to talk, but he cut me off. "The queen wants this Pillar back to gain and keep her power. I want it to ensure my people survive. Magic must flow freely. She's power drunk; you know it. She wants the Old Gods to come back. It will give her a reason to take full control of all the Planes. Well, until he gets involved."

"He?"

Caspian shook his head. "God. If she has her way, she will take over his realm, and with it, his mantel." He pointed to the three rock gorillas to our right.

"Listen, I get it. We can help each other," I insisted, seeing if there was any room for negotiation. It was like he heard what I was saying but was not fully computing it.

"You will die here. I don't care what you think or want, or what your problems are. My people have suffered long enough. If the Old Gods find their way here, so be it. I welcome them to purge the rot on the Plane and return it to its rightful people," Caspian spit out, finally laying it all out.

He was going to war with the world; not just against the Old Gods, but everyone and everything he could. The Pillar was a simple way for him to accomplish this task. He could, if it came to it, let the Old Gods do all the work while he sat back, only to put the genie back in the bottle when it was done. Centuries of solitude and his surroundings had driven him seemingly mad.

I reflected on his statement. From my perspective, he had a point and plenty of motivation to be angry. But this was something different; something engrained and intertwined through every part of his being. The timing also wasn't lost on me with all the other recent issues concerning the Old Gods.

If time permitted, I wanted to have a little chat with his head knight. The massive figure seemed out of place. He was sharp and groomed. Upon further consideration, so were the other knights in the room.

They appeared to be new additions, and from our brief conversation, possibly in control of the king's actions. I would try to reason with Caspian and see if I could jar something loose.

"The Faceless. Those creatures. Your people," I pleaded as the rock gorillas stepped in front of me, moving us slowly toward the door. "They aren't your people anymore. Let me help you. Just let me take the Pillar back, and I promise to help make things right."

The truth slapped the immortal in the face like a dead fish. He knew the truth. His people had long since left, replaced by terrifying Faceless creatures with a singular train of thought.

The Crystal King sat unmoving as our favorite knight sidestepped in front of me.

"The time is almost upon us. The Plane and its queen will soon pay the price for her injustices. May God not have mercy on your soul," the leading knight scoffed as we walked out of the chamber. Dire Caspian lowered his head in thought as the doors slammed shut.

CHAPTER 24

The Not-So Hogan's Heroes

Destiny listened as we recounted our brief yet telling conversation with Caspian. She looked concerned as I sat back on the cold slab in the middle of the cell.

"I agree. The knights are not supposed to be here; they only showed up recently. The Crystal King stayed out of sight and mind for thousands of years, only to pop back up suddenly. He was content to live out his days here," Destiny noted.

"Back home, things have been getting heated. Every time something big happens, the Old Gods come up in conversation. Something's not right here. Listen, I don't think they're messing around. Any chances you know a way out of here?" I asked, figuring it was worth a shot.

What I was failing to ask was precisely why the young woman was here. That would be a conversation for later.

Destiny's grin stretched the span of her entire face. "Well, now that you've been sentenced to death, none of us have anything to lose. You have to promise to take me with you, though. I have a place. It's close. Can you use any of your powers?"

I nodded my head, having more questions. I pointed my finger as the bowl of water sitting in the corner shook. While

I could work water magic, the brief gesture was excruciatingly draining of my will. The small effort in front of the king had been just as taxing.

"Okay, I think we can work with that," she assured, shuffling around her cell.

We had already attempted to get Petro through the bars, only to have some type of ward shock him into second thoughts. Destiny grabbed a handful of hair, pulling it violently from her scalp. A tearing sound reverberated through the empty hall as she let out a hushed whimper.

"What was that for, lady?" Petro asked, concerned. While Pixies could seem rather brash at times, Petro was, contrary to popular belief, a gentleman. He didn't like seeing people get hurt.

"The bars. Living beings can't pass through them. Here," Destiny said, tying the hair in a knot, attaching it to a button, and flicking it perfectly between both sets of crystal bars. It clicked on the floor on our side.

Petro and I looked at each other. "I'm not eating that," I huffed. Petro sniffed it, getting a confused look on his face.

"No, it's not that dramatic. Though I guess you could if you really wanted," she joked, letting out a giggle. "I know you're not from here. Magic works a little differently. Take it into your hand and pull from it. I pushed all my remaining energy into my hair. This will sound a little crazy, but I think there is a way to get Petro out of here. After that, it's as simple as him flipping the lever at the far end of the hallway. It will get everyone's attention, but it will work," Destiny informed the group quickly.

"Do you know where they would keep our stuff, and more importantly, the Pillar?" I asked, seeing just how much she knew.

"I believe so. Your stuff should be down one level. The

Pillar . . ." Destiny paused, thoughtful. "It will be at the very top of the castle."

I let the thought marinate like an Italian grandmother's homemade tomato sauce.

"Boss?" Petro spoke up after a couple of minutes.

"Destiny, how do we get Petro through the bars? Lay it out for us," I finally stated, committing to the plan.

"There is enough water in that bucket to cover your friend long enough to pass through. You just have to hold it in place. The ward will see it as nothing more than water. From there, I have a place close by. We can stop and get our stuff on the way," Destiny explained as Petro flew between us.

"Does this mean I have to hold my breath? What if I have to pee? Boss, you know how I get with water," Petro spit out in a jumbled sentence. He didn't like being underwater—or wet, for that matter. It was a Pixie thing.

"Relax. I'll see if I can make some room for you to breathe. Plus, we get through this; the Golden Grahams are on me."

Petro smoothed his slightly ruffled mustache. "Alright, I see what you're cooking, boss," he said, followed by a less animated version of the Pixie's favorite thing to do—the hip gyration.

"What is this golden food?" Destiny inquired while I picked up the small bucket of water, walking to the cell bars. Even a short amount of time encased in water would be a significantly emotional event for Petro. I was also not going to mention the water was from the chamber pot.

"Cereal of the gods," I replied as Petro looked at the still unused bucket.

"Boss?"

I nodded. "Alright, guys. We're doing this now," I

exclaimed, picking up the ball of hair. I looked at my hand, seeing the wear on the button and the likelihood that Destiny's hair hadn't been washed in months, if not longer.

"Destiny, once he's out, you're going to have to take the lead. If something comes up, let me handle it. Just keep focused on getting us to our stuff," I indicated, lifting my pant leg to expose the biomechanical portion.

Our newfound friend squinted her eyes, looking at the odd addition to my otherwise normal body. I reached down, clicking open the small compartment. The two coins and Davros's ring dropped into my hand.

"What is that?" she asked as I put on Davros's ring, feeling a slight surge of power. While I couldn't manifest my hellfire blade or do any heavy casting, the ring itself could still function.

It was a powerful force ring able to knock back or knock over things significantly larger than me. I wasn't under any illusion that it would budge the cell bars, but it could buy us a few precious seconds if needed.

"The key to Davros's keep," I told her, focusing on my inner core.

Destiny again grinned as if she were on an elementary school playground and knew a secret.

Petro nodded as I kept the focus on the water. He squinted his eyes, puffing out his cheeks. He looked like that creepy monster from the old movie *Mac and Me*. Yeah, avoid that one.

The liquid started to flow toward Petro's feet as the power from Destiny's hair coursed through my body. It was strong and rhythmic, feeling like music beating to a perfect tempo. She was powerful, giving me the feeling we were in sync with each other. Her magic felt familiar.

Within a few seconds, Petro was covered in a thin,

moving layer of water. Tiny droplets floated off before I pulled them in. Back home, this would have taken nothing but a passing thought. Here, I was struggling not to pass out.

"You can open your eyes," I told Petro's now bluing complexion. I had created a small helmetlike bubble around his head. It would only last long enough to get Petro to the other side, so I slowly pushed him onward.

Petro opened his eyes, nodding slightly. We had already discussed him not moving his wings, staying perfectly still. The less water I had to move, the more energy I would be able to keep. More to the point, I wouldn't pass out.

Destiny stared, leaning forward. The tension was as thick as Florida rain in the late summer.

The floating water bubble slowly started to melt into the bars as we all held our breaths. I pushed again as several droplets came off the bottom of the bubble, immediately dropping to the floor. If any more came off, it would expose Petro.

We were being so quiet you could hear the sound of the water shifting around the bars. I took another deep breath, starting to feel the pull of exhaustion in my chest. I was fighting the wards, and only had a few short seconds left.

"He's almost there," Destiny whispered, not breaking my concentration. From her angle, she would be able to tell me when to drop the spell.

"Now!" she barked quickly. I dropped the bubble, water splashing to the floor as I took a heaving breath.

Petro dropped immediately, catching himself just before hitting the floor. His wings had been wet for a few seconds, causing the brief fall. We all paused, listening for any signs of our captors. Silence greeted us like old friends as Petro smoothed back his hair, giving us a thumbs-up before zooming down the hallway.

Within a few seconds, the bars in front of our cells started melting, just like before, followed by an odd pulsing of the crystal walls, floor, and ceiling.

"Looks like we set off the alarm," I noted, no longer being quiet. "Ladies first."

I motioned for Destiny to take the lead while Petro flew back, taking position slightly overhead. He would warn us if we were about to run into any company.

"Let's go. Stay close. We're going to be taking three left turns, then down the stairs," Destiny stated as we started moving. Banging sounds began emanating from behind us, and Destiny turned, smacking another lever. The door slammed behind us as we left the long hallway.

We moved as quickly as possible on the slick crystal floor. Movement echoed from all directions, pushing us to move faster.

"There's the stairs," Destiny panted, pointing to the small opening in front of us. "We'll go down a long flight of stairs which ends in a long hallway. From there, all of our stuff should be in one of the rooms to our right. We're not going to have a lot of time. As soon as I grab my things, I can get us out of here."

More crashes and bangs erupted behind us, telling me there was nothing but open air between us and our pursuers. Petro, also figuring this out, darted forward, ensuring things were clear in front of us. Even though he couldn't use any magic or weapons, he still had a Pixie's keen sense of smell.

After a few short seconds of leaping several stairs at a time, we came to an opening. Petro hovered in front of the second door to our right, motioning us to hurry our asses up. Walking through the door, it was evident not many people had ever found their way back to their belongings.

Piles of armor and swords sat in neat stacks on flat

inspection tables. The odd thing about it was the layer of dust covering the items. Nowhere else in the facility had I seen even a speck of dirt, telling me that whatever was in that room had been brought in from the outside world.

Petro had already located our gear. I quickly grabbed my short staff, service pistol, the Judge, and the rest of my stuff. Destiny's items were right beside ours. She quickly grabbed a long staff, a small pouch, and a wand. We started heading toward the door, and I noticed her looking around the room.

"I don't think we have enough time to go window-shopping," I joked while she scanned all the other items lying on the tables.

"There it is," she said to herself, grabbing a smooth black stone.

"We gotta go. Where to?" I prompted, the sounds of our pursuers slamming into the walls amplifying as they came down the stairs.

Destiny reached into her bag, pulling out a vial of glowing blue liquid. Without saying anything, she immediately downed its contents as a shudder rippled through her body.

After just a few short seconds, a silvery glow started weeping from her eyes. She held up a hand, pushing energy into the stairwell opening. There was a loud, reverberating thump as a solid chunk of the crystal ceiling slammed to the ground, effectively sealing off the entrance.

"She's got magic pouring from her, boss," Petro noted as I quickly realized what she had done. Whatever she had taken had been either some type of magical ward inhibitor or an enhancer, much like Kracken.

I didn't respond as she held out her fists, pulling the black stone into the air. It hovered between her hands as if sitting on a hard surface. The silvery mist snaked from her eyes, slowly hugging the stone. A round purple-and-orange halo started growing around its center. Destiny backed up, finally breaking her concentration.

"This will get us to my place," Destiny let out as the almost angelic silvery glow continued to swirl around her eyes and face.

Petro and I glanced at each other when she turned, walking through the portal she had just created.

CHAPTER 25

Honey, I Shrunk the Mage

Destiny's living arrangements were just as intriguing as the young lady. We came out in an underground cave opening full of moss, grass, and oddly enough, trees. In the center of the space was a simple house built into a tree trunk that grew from the floor to the top of the cavern.

The trickle of water could be heard from a small stream flowing in front of the cottage. Like the ones in the Crystal Castle, crystals lit the area in a dull, ever-present glow.

Entering the house, I scanned the insides as we sat at a small table obviously not used to company, taking in all the odd trinkets and books.

"Your magic should work here. Before you ask, we are below the castle," Destiny informed us while she placed several small bowls of soup on the table.

"How far under?" Petro asked, not liking tight underground spaces after watching a documentary about mining incidents one late night, which was partially my fault.

"Far enough," was all she replied, finally sitting at the table. I still couldn't pinpoint why she felt and looked so familiar.

"How do we get back?" I continued, still focused on my

initial task.

"That was going to be the tricky part, but now we have this," she said, dropping the black rock she'd picked up from someone else's belongings. "It should let us come back here in case we get stuck."

"How did it bring us here?" I asked, being interrupted by the sound of Petro gulping his soup, which lightened the mood. He looked up at our silence.

"What, can't a guy slurp his soup in peace?" he demanded sarcastically, going back to it.

Destiny took in a deep breath. "I have a few tricks up my sleeve that forced the stone to bring us here. I knew the person that stone belonged to," she said as a longing expression swept across her face. It was one of lost love. "Now that I think about it, I doubt it will take us to the main chambers of the primary tower. They have to have more wards up by now. That is where I believe you will find the Pillar, among other things."

"What about the people Caspian kept mentioning?"

Destiny looked reflectively into her soup.

"There's nothing left of them but those things. They crawl all over the place, like animals. Years ago, a few thinking creatures remained, but when the knights arrived, everything changed. I used to travel freely, for the most part, in the castle. Now, well, I'm more of a wanted entity," Destiny explained as I steepled my fingers, resting my chin on my thumbs.

"How hard is it for the knights or the king to get to the Plane or anywhere else?" I inquired, landing on the right question.

"That's the thing . . . they can't. From what I gather, Caspian invited the knights with open arms. Something went wrong, though. I still don't know how they got here or who they truly are. When I was taken before Caspian, they wanted my help to get something," she said.

"The Pillar," Petro interjected, slurping soup from his mustache.

"Yes, to free them from here, but something happened. It appears someone else was also looking for it, looking to use it. That gave the knights the window they needed to get the Pillar and bring it here. I don't know much more than that. I think you may know the other party," she noted, referring to Tom.

"I'm pretty sure this was all planned. His eyes; it was like he wasn't all there," I recalled as she nodded.

"Agreed. It's as if one of those knights has some type of mind control over him. I don't think it's all the time, though, or fully in place. More like a suggestion or light push," Destiny added. I took a sip of the bland, steaming soup.

"Meaning he still put all those souls to death," I said, working to justify my upcoming actions.

"Hey, boss," Petro chimed in. "If your magic works now, can we pull the others over?"

"I tried the communicators. No luck there. Will this work here?" I asked, pulling out the gate rope.

Destiny ran her slim fingers over the rope, grinning as if patting an old friend on the back. "I'm sure it will. The only issue is time," she noted.

"You've used one of these before?" I asked. She grinned.

"Yes, long ago. What's that?" she inquired softly, seeing one of the bracelets as well.

"It's a linking bracelet. I tried it also with no luck. I figure it has something to do with this time thing you keep mentioning."

"If your friends are with Ian the Troll, as you stated, I would think they should both work. Being in a different time is more of a shifting type of issue. If we can get to the Pillar and shut it down, I would think the Crystal Castle and this place would stop moving, if even temporarily," Destiny stated flatly as it all came together.

The reason everyone had so much trouble finding the Crystal Palace and the king was that they constantly shifted through time and, possibly, space. If you followed a specific path, as we had, you would sync with the location and have safe passage.

I was starting to think other quest lovers had attempted the trip before many of the Fae had been cursed like Davros to remain on Earth as Vampires. Which, in all fairness, wasn't half that bad of a gig. It had been, unfortunately, hundreds if not thousands of years ago.

"How did you get here? You're clearly not Fae?" I asked as Petro stopped eating, also having the same question.

"Thomas, that man who had some role to play in all this, and a companion of his named Edward Rose pulled me through the portal once upon a time," Destiny stated as I shook my head.

Thoughts of their picture on Ian's wall took hold of my mind as I pondered the statement.

"It's always something with him. That must have been decades ago, if not longer. Petro, that had to be the picture we saw. You've been here this whole time?" I directed at her as she looked around the small living area, pointing at the aged space.

"Yes, I had almost given up hope. The future, the past . . . it all starts blurring together at some point, but it is the world in which I live. For years I survived here in relative peace. I would go topside to the Crystal Castle now and then to get things. Then the knights arrived. I evaded them for several months, staying here, until I was forced to go up for supplies. Like I said, it was as if the king didn't care I was running around until they arrived," Destiny reminisced, standing up.

"Boss, you thinking what I'm thinking?" Petro asked as

Destiny walked into the other room.

"That we have a fifty-fifty chance of getting out of here alive?" I breathed out tightly.

"Well that, and that this lady seems awfully familiar?" he stated in the form of a question.

I paused reflectively again, trying to focus. "I'm sure since she knows Tom and Ed, we've probably seen a picture of her or something. I trust her, though," I followed up as she walked back in with three glowing silver vials of liquid.

"I think I have a plan," Destiny informed the group, placing the vial holder on the table.

"We taking shots? My old lady doesn't like me drinking if I'm in another time. Which I've never been. But she said something about how even if she hadn't been born, it still counted if I got into trouble," Petro said, looking concerned. He smelled something in the liquid that he didn't like.

Destiny and I grinned at his words before she cleared her throat.

"This is a shrinking potion. My thought is we use it to become Petro sized and sneak up to the room where they are keeping the Pillar." She paused, waiting on my response.

The thought of downsizing brought up childhood memories of the old Rick Moranis movie *Honey, I Shrunk the Kids*. While the idea was sound, the logistics slapped me in the face.

"How long does it last?" I asked.

She sighed. "Maybe thirty minutes," she stated while I leaned back. "Before you ask, there is a way to get around since we will be small enough to fit into the air shaft that runs up the length of the building."

"I'm taking it this potion doesn't make us grow wings." I stated.

She pointed at Petro. "You do know how strong he is, right? He could carry us no problem if we shrink down small enough." Petro chuckled.

"This is going to be awesome!" he exclaimed, flying in front of me. "I can't wait till you take a ride in my pocket. I'm going to go wash off my deodorant," Petro said with a thinking look on his face.

"That was one time, Petro. I made up for it," I replied, talking about one of our prior misadventures.

"We won't shrink down that small, just enough for him to pull us along. The only thing is we'll have to leave any enchanted items here. They won't shrink. Once we get the Pillar turned off, I'll be able to gate back and grab them," Destiny stated, answering the majority of my questions.

"I'm starting to think we need to handle these knights just as much if not more than the king," I concluded. She nodded her agreement.

"Petro, how're your wings holding up?" I asked, talking about his reinforced wing. It had been repaired more times than I could count.

He clicked his wings loudly. "Good as it gets after using the stuff Jamison gave me. As long as I can stop every couple minutes, we should be good," Petro said, the excitement coming through in his voice.

After another hour of talking, the plan was set. I set several of my items on the table as Destiny did the same, only keeping her staff. I looked at the hourglass which was now half full.

While Destiny and I would drink an entire vial and a portion of the third, Petro would only take a few sips. The overall idea was to get as small as possible not to trigger any tracking wards, yet still travel at a decent pace.

"Are you ready?" Destiny asked, handing me one of the

vials.

"Will it hurt?" I returned, starting to have second thoughts.

"What doesn't," she countered, bottoming up her vial.

CHAPTER 26

Fly Me to the Moon

I gawked at Petro, taking in his features as he hugged me tight enough to pop my head off. I stood what would equate to two feet shorter than he did, about two inches. His features were striking and scary at the same time. If human-sized, he would be a one-Pixie wrecking ball.

"Look at you boss, all grown down. I better make sure no Pixie ladies see you like this, or it's all over but the crime," Petro said, winking at me.

Shaking her head, Destiny pointed toward a small opening at the top of the tree in the center of the cavern.

"Hold on to your goodies," Petro exclaimed as he grabbed us by the shoulders, launching into the sky at face-tearing speed.

I focused on Destiny, grays and milky-white crystals blurring in my vision. While she was just as jolted by the pace as I was, her jaw was set with steadfast determination.

Just as I went to say something, Petro completed several 360-degree barrel rolls as sharp angles jutted from the side of the air shaft. At one point, Petro dropped speed, forcing my body into a weightless state before being yanked back into motion. His flying skills were not just impressive but more articulate than I had ever perceived.

"Break time," Petro huffed as he slowed down, putting us down as gently as falling feathers on the small ledge.

"That was amazing, Petro," I praised while he grinned.

"You need to go on a diet, boss. You're solid as a rock," he huffed as Destiny flattened her back against the smooth wall. The sounds of our conversation traveled endlessly in all directions.

"Petro," Destiny said as I looked down, only to see a black void. "How far did we travel?"

"Maybe a mile," he replied, looking up. "You weren't joking about you living under the castle. This place is huge. I'm thinking we have another couple to go. Oh, and we passed a vent that smelled like those knights just now."

Destiny uttered an incantation, rubbing her long staff on the sidewall. She was marking the spot with a tracker spell. While I still couldn't manifest my hellfire blade, I could still do simple magical tasks. She was using the power in her staff to mark the area.

"I'm not leaving till they're gone," Destiny flatly promised. Petro cleared his throat.

"Alright, time to go. Do you think they know we're here yet?" Petro asked, directing me to stand by Destiny.

"No. We would have heard something by now. Since they know there's a Pixie with us, they'd probably have cranked the heat up to max in these air shafts," Destiny said. She had left out that little detail.

"Whelp, guess we will just have to fly fast. Hi Ho, Silver! Away!" Petro barked as he launched into the shaft, snapping my head back.

I was slightly more prepared this time as I anchored my arm on his waist. Petro, being a more skilled flyer than I'd given him credit for during his missile-like rise through the shaft, shook his hips while singing MC Hammer's immortal song of youthful power and love, "U Can't Touch This." He often sang songs and blurted cheesy movie lines when he was nervous.

Another minute passed as we bobbed and weaved through several more gaps and twists in the shaft. This time, Petro all but dropped us on a flat, protruding rock that looked out of place.

Destiny squinted her eyes, looking at Petro as he flexed his shoulders, rolling them in a circle. I also noticed something looked off with him.

"Hey, buddy. You doing good?" I asked as he returned the odd expression.

"Yeah, boss. How about you? It looks like you guys are shrinking even more," he drawled out skeptically.

"Did you touch any of the small containers in my kitchen?" Destiny asked.

Petro smacked his lips. "Maybe. Would it be bad if I did? I was thirsty and needed a drink," Petro replied, playing it off.

"I'm betting you grabbed the small green jar that looked and smelled like Elf juice," she followed up as Petro tapped his index finger on the tip of his nose.

"Is it bad? Am I going to live, doc?" Petro asked, a small bead of sweat forming on his forehead.

"Let me guess, you're feeling a little warmer and anxious," she continued as I realized he *had* been on edge.

"Yes, and affirmative, ghost rider," Petro replied. She looked over at me.

"We aren't shrinking anymore. He's growing. That was the counterspell for the shrinking potion," she said. I quickly noticed his wings could now stretch to either side of the shaft.

"Meaning . . ." I drawled out as Petro sniffed the air.

"Meaning, if we don't get going, I could get stuck like a cork in here. I never got to watch the last season of *Magnum P.I*! What do I do?" Petro asked frantically.

"Time to go. Listen, you can't stop no matter what you do. Don't stop. Hell, you're probably stronger now too. Destiny, should we be worried?"

She looked at me blankly.

"I have no clue how big he's going to get or what that stuff will do to a Pixie," she finally replied. Petro launched into the shaft more aggressively than the prior two neckbreaking takeoffs.

Just as I was getting acclimated to the more aggressive flight patterns Petro had started, I made the mistake of looking down. Small glowing orbs fluttered at random intervals under my feet; I looked over to see Destiny noticing the same thing.

I pulled in a lungful of air, screaming, "Is that bad?"

Destiny didn't immediately reply. She instead turned, hugging closer to Petro's body, and quickly climbed up the side of his waist and chest. Within a few quick seconds after she reached his ear, Petro hesitated slightly, glancing down, only to rocket faster up the shaft.

I quickly noticed that Petro's hand was growing around my shoulder as Destiny slid down the other side of his body, holding on to his belt as a smirk crossed his lips.

"They know we're here!" Destiny bellowed as the whooshing rush of air and wind continued to howl like a runaway freight train.

Just as I was about to respond, we erupted through what appeared to be the final opening, darting into the open air. Petro released me into the sky and pulled off Destiny in a single sweep of his hand.

Time slowed as I tumbled ass over teakettle, staring

directly at the glowing crystal floor below us. A blur of wings traced underneath us as several of the luminous dots popped out of the hole, only to be cut down by three or four surgical sweeps of Petro's new sword.

I was about to start praying to whatever God would take me while rocketing to the hard floor when Petro again snagged me by my shoulder, swooping around and picking up Destiny before curling into a ball and rolling on the smooth floor.

Once we stopped, Petro lightly deposited us on the ground and flashed forward, leaving a trail of dust, to slice into three of the small orbs now spinning around his head. If I was not mistaken, Petro was roughly the size of a baby now. The one thing that hadn't changed was his coordination and ability to move quickly.

Destiny and I stood up, finally getting ourselves together. She stood stoically with her long staff as I pulled out both my pistol and short staff. The Judge and my trench coat, as well as a few other items, had had to stay behind.

Petro dropped in front of us as another group of small orbs shot out of the vent. Focusing on the closest creature, I immediately noticed their resemblance to glowing ladybugs. Except this version of a ladybug had razors for feet and blades gleaming from its fluttering wings.

"Seekers. They know we're here, just not where," Destiny noted as I pulled up my pistol, firing two shots into the lead ladybug of death.

The special ammunition slammed into the creature, which immediately dropped to the ground and started moving forward, the sounds of its sharp legs scraping as it moved.

Before I could line up another shot, Petro slashed down, beheading the bug, while Destiny launched several small green tracking balls from her staff. Each of the spells stalked the flight patterns of the orbs as they dove away from Petro's swinging attacks. I noticed the longer the spells she launched were in the air, the faster they moved. It all came to a crashing end as one of the bugs dove directly at me, only to be caught by her leading spell, slamming it several feet away.

The smell and sound of burning bugs told me whatever she had shot at the creatures was slowly disintegrating them. I had done nothing but fire a couple of shots into one.

"I think that's the last of them, boss," Petro announced. At this point, he wouldn't be able to fit back into the vent.

"I think the potion is starting to wear off as well," Destiny noted. I looked down. It's hard to explain the feeling of shrinking and growing at a steady pace. This was subtle, strong magic, unlike the awkward cracking and snapping of a shifter growing into its most prominent form. Precise and to the point.

"Well, it doesn't seem to be doing so with big boy here," I joked while Petro shrugged.

"Does he often just go into people's homes and drink whatever he finds?" Destiny asked. We both shrugged.

"Yup, and I wouldn't have it any other way," I affirmed. The moment was quickly interrupted by the sounds of banging from the far hallway.

"The Pillar should be directly above us," Destiny noted as I pointed toward the direction the noise was coming from.

"Of course. Petro, you feeling up for an old-school distraction?" I asked. He reached into his pouch, grabbing a somewhat maddening blended version of a flashbang grenade.

"I'm your worst nightmare," he smirked, getting into Rambo mode.

"Destiny, when that thing explodes, we have to be out of sight. As soon as it goes off, we can haul ass to the Pillar. It might not be much, but it should give us enough time to figure out our next move," I stated as she nodded.

The item had grown along with Petro, meaning it would have a significantly angrier effect on whoever was about to join the party. I was assuming they would be more of a problem than the ladybugs of death.

"I'm sure they know exactly where we are by now. All we have to do is move the Pillar off its holder, and it should pull enough power to drop all the wards holding our magic in check," she said as I followed up with a curt, "And keeping our backup away."

I pulled out the bracelet and gate rope. While neither item was enchanted, they were strong, blended objects able to accomplish amazing feats of magic.

CHAPTER 27

We Merry Few...

Blinding light followed by several bangs was the signal for Destiny and me to get our asses in gear. We had pressed ourselves against the wall waiting on the now teenager-sized Petro to let off the stun grenade he had so graciously remembered to bring.

"Go!" I exclaimed at the clattering sound of armor smacking into crystal rock walls. A group of knights had been guarding the door to the stairwell leading up to the Pillar. Petro had not only set off the magical stunning grenade but, with his newly found size, had also crashed through the door like a missile. I would be hearing about his heroics later.

I was now roughly the height of a toddler as I scurried past the knights lying on the floor. Petro stood above the two guards, looking at them, as glowing red blood slid down his blade.

"Any more between us and the Pillar?" I asked, figuring his nose was also now supersized.

"No, I don't think so. They're coming, though. Not sure from where, but I smell them. Hey, boss . . . you see that small symbol on that guard's sword?" Petro pointed out.

I let out a breath when I saw it. The symbol Petro was

indicating was one associated with the Old Gods in all the texts in the Atheneum that I had looked over.

Destiny spoke up, climbing a handful of stairs, still not taking them in full steps. "These are knights from the Old Gods. I haven't seen one wearing that symbol until now. This means we are about to really piss them off."

"I've read about these guys," I said as Petro picked us both up, pulling us up the remaining stairs. I finished as he set us down in front of a massive door made of iron and steel. "The Old Gods, I believe, sent thousands of these knights out hunting for Earth. I bet this group figured they'd hit the jackpot."

"I had my suspicions, but this confirms it," Destiny added while Petro squinted his eyes, looking at the door.

"Any idea?" I asked. He took a deep breath.

"Stand over there. Super Petro, ACTIVATE!" he bellowed, launching down the stairs, only to turn around and blur past, ramming into the door with a bone-crunching smack. The blow was followed by a creak of metal and the following buckling of the door inward.

I ran over to Petro as he sat still on the ground, looking up. "Is this heaven?" Petro asked in his melodramatic voice.

"No, buddy, those are just stars. You rammed the hell out of that door, and if you can answer me, that means you'll be just fine," I responded, knowing his usual *tell my wife and kids I love them* routine. The ironic thing was he now had both.

"Oh, that's good. I think I bent my wing again, though," he said, sitting up. "I had this dream I was all big, and then I shrunk again, but my winky stayed big."

I looked over at Destiny, trying not to grin. "I'll hang with him for a minute. See what's going on in there, but don't go too far. He'll be fine in a minute or two."

She nodded and went inside while I stayed with Petro.

"Petro, shake it off. Your winky will be just fine. We got a bunch of really pissed-off knights from the Old Gods heading our way. I can't carry you out of here," I stated as he started moving. If I wasn't mistaken, he was still growing.

"I smell more of those knights . . ." Petro trailed off as a muffled whimper came from inside the room.

I knew better than this. I should have had Destiny wait till we got Petro moving. I was shocked he hadn't been able to smell them before.

"Come out from the hallway," a gruff soldier's voice boomed from inside the room.

After Petro's race to knock the door down, I hadn't looked inside the room other than to give it a quick glance. I turned to look through the opening now. Instead of beaming white crystals covering all the surfaces, solid ruby-red gemstones filled the space with deep, rich light.

The room was the size of a basketball court with several arches and columns all leading to the center of the space. In the center sat a rugged, precisely cut six-foot-long stone. Pulsating light seeped from its bottom and top, appearing to flow into the building like blood pumping from a healthy heart.

Destiny, who was now close to her original size, was on her knees as one of the guards held a rather nasty-looking ax behind her head.

I leaned close to Petro's ear, whispering, "Hey, buddy. They have Destiny in there. They aren't playing."

Petro looked at me, his eyes still dilated. "You mean the lady that made that amazing soup?"

"Yeah, she's in there," I said as Petro set his jaw.

"Hey, no . . . you need to sit—" I demanded with no luck.

Petro exploded in a violent leap through the air. His

wings clicked and failed, as he had bent the brace on his repaired wing. This didn't stop Petro, though, who landed with catlike precision in front of the visibly confused knights.

I wasn't going to sugarcoat things. A Pixie wasn't that intimidating when it was buzzing around talking about their dating life. But a now six-foot-tall Petro was on another level of scary.

"You messed with the wrong lady," Petro growled in a tone I had heard only one other time. "If you had ever tried her soup, you wouldn't be treating her like that."

Petro not only had a concussion but was also monologuing about soup, further confusing the two knights.

I reached down, pulling up my short staff as Petro finally made his move. Time seemed to freeze, and all I could see was the trace of lines and dust where his body had once been.

The violence Petro displayed on the two knights was something I hadn't witnessed before. Maybe it was the concussion, or perhaps the fact that he was just fed up with the entire situation. They didn't have a chance in hell of reacting more than the slight upswing of one of the knight's axes.

Petro stood with his back facing us. In one hand, his blade. In the other, the head of one of the knights. He dropped the appendage as the head from the second knight slid off its body with a wet splat, the two figures crumpling to the ground simultaneously.

Destiny slowly turned as I finally made my way to her, glowing red blood starting to pool under the bodies.

"Petro . . ." I said. When he didn't seem to hear me, I spoke up. "PETRO!"

"What? Hey, oh," he replied, realizing that we were both staring at him.

"You okay?" I asked when he turned to look at me. I

noticed his bottom lip was turned up and a small tear streaked from his right eye.

I walked over, noting he was starting to shrink, finally. "Boss, I'm fine. I'm a little dizzy still, but these ass rabbits are one of the reasons my people are treated the way they are."

It wasn't the time or place to question the emotion he was showing. It wasn't anger, but sadness. Not sadness for himself, but for everyone else around him.

"Hey, man, there's a lot of other people who's done that. I get it. It all started with the Old Gods destroying your realm, and with it, your world in many ways. Let's get this done, and we'll go to the Fallen Angel for a cold one with the crew. What do you say?" I asked. I wanted to ensure he was ready for what was inevitably about to arrive.

It was clear these were not the knights that Caspian had had in his chambers or their smug leader. These were grunts. Frontline fodder, meant to do the one thing they had accomplished: stall for time until the adults could come and take charge.

"Ah, hell, boss. I'm good. I just promised my folks I'd do great things one day, and here I am. Picking a fight with the knights of the Old Gods. That one on the left, the one that I dropped his head, was for my aunt Judy. She made amazing cookies. A little loose in the skirt, if you know what I mean, but used to tell me the old stories," Petro interjected, completely switching his mood. He was back to his old self.

I looked over to see Destiny circling the Pillar as light tendrils of electricity crackled off it at random intervals, reaching for her.

"I'm thinking we use that ring of yours to push this thing off the energy stream," she suggested, pointing at the glowing light holding the Pillar in place.

"Get out of the way," I barked, taking a deep breath to

steady myself.

Just as I was about to release the energy spell from the ring, an octagon-shaped cage erupted from both the ceiling and the floor. The shimmering walls crashed shut in the blink of an eye as Destiny was slammed inside.

"Shit, shit, shit!" I shouted running forward, only to have several of the knights rush into the room, moving to take position.

"Boss, it's about to get messy in here," Petro mumbled, still unable to fly. I nodded my head in agreement.

Destiny continued to bang on the inside of the protective barrier with no apparent effect. What I did notice were the tendrils of lightning coming off the Pillar now reaching her. Destiny's skin and clothes started glowing.

Without thinking, I pulled out my pistol, firing several shots into the knights. Rounds went in various directions, bouncing off their armor. A few shots landed as the knights pushed forward, only to stop in front of the barrier surrounding the Pillar.

Petro and I backed up several feet, reassessing the situation, noticing that they weren't moving any closer to us.

"They're stalling," I said as the sound of heavy footsteps echoed from the stairwell.

"Boss, I don't know if we're going to be able to get out of this one," Petro noted. I again agreed with the sentiment. It was odd seeing eye to eye with him, literally, though he continued to shrink.

I glared at the knights guarding the barrier, noticing one of them had blood trickling down their arm. One of my rounds had found its home.

Destiny stared at me when our eyes finally met. She had an indescribable expression on her face as the silvery tendrils from the Pillar continued to wrap themselves around her like the warm arms of a lover on a cold December night.

It wasn't an expression of worry or fear, but one of regret. Destiny was about to do something that she knew she would not be able to take back.

"I see your true intentions and abilities should not have been underestimated like the others," the arrogant, sharp-nosed lead knight bellowed, his voice echoing off the walls. The clicking of his armored boots on the red crystal floor was just as irritating as fingernails on a chalkboard.

Without shifting my focus, I turned my body, still keeping eye contact with Destiny while shaking my head, telling her not to do whatever it was the woman had planned.

It was time to draw the conversation out to give us enough time to switch tactics. Like I always said, give a bad guy a chance to brag about their plan and all the big bad things they were about to do, and they'd make your ears bleed every time. Unless the bad guy was a demon. In that case, they'd probably be eating your liver already, and would just have a conversation with what remained of your carcass.

"This is my last warning. You and the rest of your knights leave now, go home, and tell the Old Gods they better try harder next time," I belted back in the manliest tone I could summon. In most cases, I would let a little hellfire dance through my eyes and hands, but that wasn't an option.

The lead knight flung his head back in a show of arrogant emotion, chuckling as he began to speak. "You are a naive brat. Going back without a victory is not an option. Your threat is meaningless to us. You think you know the Old Gods, but you don't. If it weren't for that thick-skulled Crystal King, Dire Caspian, we would've already made our way through this Plane and to your world. We will break him fully soon. Yes . . . I can smell Earth on you."

I paused, rethinking my approach to the conversation as I once again glanced at Destiny. She was still looking at me as if she wanted to say something before playing whatever hand she had been dealt.

"There's a lot more of those king types where I come from. Things have changed, and with that, I don't think you or any of your goons are ready for the fight you have in front of you," I replied as the lead knight walked closer.

"Perhaps. I actually agree with your statement, mortal. Or should I say . . . false god," the knight finished, staring at me intently.

Just when his statement started to register, I noticed Destiny quickly spinning around, followed by a loud, cracking boom. She had lept onto the Pillar, wrapping her arms and legs around it as what appeared to be glowing, red hellfire erupted from her body.

The rods of light flickered as the knights surrounding the barrier turned to face it. The lead knight was no longer in a chatty mood as he pulled out his sword, leaping dozens of feet through the air, landing in the middle of the room.

Two knights broke off, heading toward Petro and I, one with the spear, the other with a large, rather used battle-ax.

I glanced again at Destiny, seeing her face pointing toward me while it disintegrated to ash. Small flakes floated into the Pillar, looking like she was becoming one with the stone.

"NOOO!" the knight bellowed as he sliced his glowing blade through the barrier, turning it into vapor as the light holding the Pillar finally shuttered.

Embers swirled around the Pillar from whatever it was Destiny had done. As I squinted, I could still see an outline of her body as the glowing ash finally pulled the rest of itself inside the Pillar.

The large stone dropped, crashing into the crystal floor, forcing shards of the red material to spray in all directions. I looked up as one of the guards pulled back their ax. Leaping right, I pulled up Davros's ring, pushing everything I had into it.

"*EJECTUS!*" I yelled as a wall of unbridled force slammed into the guards, flinging them in several directions. The power of the ring also threw me back several feet, my back crashing into the wall.

I shook my head, looking up, and my heart sank. Not only was Destiny gone, but dozens more of the knights started pouring into the room. It was apparent several of them were significantly more experienced than the handful we had already run through.

"BOSS!" Petro yelled. I looked down at him running toward me.

"Yeah, I know. I don't think anybody's going to be able to tell any of our wives and kids that we love them," I huffed, getting back on my feet as several of the knights finally honed in on our location.

"No, you big meat bag, look at your hands!" he again barked at me. I looked down.

Hellfire danced on my right hand, as if a friendly reminder that Destiny had sacrificed herself to deactivate the Pillar.

Without thinking, I reached for the gate stone, the bracelet, and the rope simultaneously. While I didn't have enough time to gate back and get the rest of our gear, some of my friends were about to have a rude awakening via an unexpected trip.

CHAPTER 28

The King of Kings

I gathered my thoughts, yelling, "IGNIS!" as my hellfire blade sprang to life. "Game time, buddy," I told Petro, who pulled out his sword. Even though he couldn't fly, he would stand and fight, still large enough to do some serious damage.

My first action was to sling several balls of dripping hellfire in the direction of the knights, scattering them. The leading two got splattered with the sticky, lavalike material.

I dropped the gate stone, not caring where it opened, and pulled out the gate rope, yelling as I pushed my will into it. The gate shuddered, rocking the room, as a couple of knights that had jumped out of the way pulled forward, squaring off with us.

With the sucking sound of a flushing toilet, Phil and Atari flew out of the gate, sprawling out on the floor. Again, this caused the oncoming attackers to pause. Meanwhile, the head knight was trying to lift the Pillar, working to put it back in place.

Okay, let's take a deep breath, everyone. When you pulled someone through with a gate rope, they may or may not know they are about to be gated out of their current situation.

Phil was now probably the best example of this.

He had apparently been in the middle of his daily constitutional when he was sucked through the gate.

"What the shite, bruther!" he yelled, spitting out a cigarette as his bare ass flashed the knights. He slung the paper he was reading, rolling over to complicate the situation further. I grimaced while Petro grinned.

Phil had been using the toilet when we'd pulled him through. I would be hearing about this for a long, long time.

Luckily for us, he shifted gears just as quickly, pulling up his pants, setting his jaw, and pushing his will to flow over his body. He was now effectively a one-person wrecking machine, weapon or not. Phil had quickly figured out the shitstorm he was in the middle of.

Atari was more prepared, having what looked like all her weapons and gear. She already had both her pistols sitting firmly in hand, ready to reign out death.

They took in the room, sizing up the issue, while the main knight, sounding frustrated, barked out several orders. "Kill them all!"

That was enough to put the four of us into motion. Several spatters of gunfire barked in the echoing room as bullets both ricocheted and landed with wet thumps.

Phil jumped forward, grabbing the battle-ax from one of the already dead knights and swinging forward as the clang of weapons joined the chorus.

I leaped forward as one of the larger knights lunged with a massive sword, swinging down. Their blade smashed into the crystal floor when I dodged. Swinging up, I sliced their sword in half, also cutting a perfect line in the front of their armor.

The knight jumped back quickly, pulling out a small

dagger while slinging the melting armor off his body. Pearl-white skin reflected back with a charred line streaking the length of his chest.

We stood walking slowly in a circle. The crash of Phil dealing a killing blow pulled the knight's attention long enough for me to plunge forward. I swung my hellfire blade around, slowly pulling the creature's attention while slinging a ball of concentrated hellfire directly at its chest.

The impact of the hellfire stunned the knight, who again swung his dagger blindly in my direction. We turned, squaring off, as the hellfire finally reached what I assumed were his heart and lungs, viscous material erupting from his mouth. Without flinching, I threw another small ball of hellfire at the knight's mouth as he reached up to feel what was coming out.

The resulting effect was horrendous as the ball ripped through his fingers, landing inside his open mouth. I turned away, not wanting to see the rest, as two more prominent knights leaped forward.

Taking a quick glance around, I noticed Petro was significantly smaller, now backing up against the far wall. He had three of the now dead knights strewn across the floor in front of him.

Before I could react, one of the approaching creatures slammed a spiked mace into my left arm. The searing pain dropped me to my knees. I brought up my hellfire blade just in time to block another attack while trying to get my other arm to move enough to sling a spell.

Looking down to see my limp arm, I pulled my hellfire blade back in without thinking and, just when both knights were about to strike again, I swept my arm up, screaming, "*IGNITO!*" as a wave of indiscriminate hellfire washed over them like a crashing ocean wave.

The two knights flew back, not only due to the heat but

from the force with which I had projected the casting. I shook my head, feeling the draining effects as Atari yelled, "There's more coming through the door!"

Phil was still fighting three of the knights, holding his own. He hesitated, turning at Atari's announcement, and one of them landed a crushing blow with a large hammer, knocking him back as several teeth flew from his mouth.

While I had knocked the two knights on their asses with my casting, they were already getting back on their feet, ripping off pieces of burning armor. The gear they wore would only protect them from one or two direct strikes of hellfire. I had a feeling the main asshole's armor would be slightly more problematic.

I pulled the linking bracelet from my pocket. Jamison's main reason for giving it to me had been its ability to allow us to communicate. The other nasty part of the bracelets that people didn't like was their uncanny ability to simply bring the other person to you.

The item was much like the gate rope, with the additional ability to link the two persons' minds to communicate.

I focused as Jamison's thoughts snapped into my mind. The sensation was immediate, surprising me.

"*Need help . . . we are in the castle. The knights of the Old Gods are here,*" my mind echoed as Jamison gathered his thoughts.

"*Give me five minutes. Pull me through then; focus on the area around me as well,*" Jamison replied. I fully clicked the bracelet back onto my wrist in time to put a water spell together, launching it under the feet of the two knights getting up, quickly crashing their large frames back on the hard floor.

"Arhgg!" another knight yelled, swinging down a claymore-style sword as I pulled up my hellfire blade without speaking the invocation.

The knight's sword was different from the others, and the force of the blow caught me off guard, pushing me back a few feet. Much like a soul sword, this sword would stand up against mine. Our attackers were getting stronger.

I shook my left arm, traces of blood pooling in my hand, as my fist finally opened and closed. This meant I was healing at an accelerated rate, even if I still didn't have any feeling in it.

A deep, thundering horn echoed throughout the room, freezing the onslaught of our attackers. I looked around, realizing Atari, Phil, and myself were all in a line with our backs to the far wall. Petro was now in the corner keeping out of the way, almost back to his normal size.

The knights had been herding us away from their leader as he worked to put the Pillar back in place.

"Bruther, this is total bullshite," Phil spat out along with a spray of blood, his chest heaving with exertion.

"Whatever that horn means, they don't like it," Atari added. Just then, the wall opposite of us exploded inward, forcing us to shield our faces.

Shards of crystals sliced into my skin in random places; nothing piercing like a bullet, but enough to create several trickles of blood.

"You okay, mate?" Phil asked, seeing the condition of my left arm.

"I think so. But if he gets that Pillar back in place, we're toast," I replied, flexing my left hand.

Petro took the time and distraction to regroup with us, climbing up Atari's leg and resting in the ammo pouch on her waist. While Phil had been hanging out, Atari had been patiently waiting to be pulled through. My guess was she'd had her gear on the entire time we had been gone.

"Boss, look, it's Caspian!" Petro yelled as the Crystal King lumbered out of the dusty opening. He held a massive scimitar-style sword in one hand and a double-sided battle-ax the size of a small car in the other.

"Bruther, is that bad?" Phil asked slowly as he spit more blood from his mouth, his eyes wide open. I was sure Jenny could repair his teeth. Whether we had a dental plan to pay for it was another story. Ever since the Balance, all magical medical procedures had to be reported. I was fairly certain we broke that law at least once a week.

"Little of both. No time to explain, but I'm thinking with the Pillar shut down, whatever they were using to control him is probably gone. Everyone against the wall," I instructed, looking for the fastest path to the center of the room, pulling out the linking bracelet.

"He looks really pissed, you guys," Petro said as the first swing of Caspian's ax sent four of the lesser knights flying through the air, two of them crashing in front of us, forcing the wall of knights to dodge out of the way.

Even with that, there were still more than a dozen knights between us and the Pillar. More were also still pouring in from the stairwell. There were now around twenty or so of the hulking figures in the room by my count, the majority now squarely focused on a very emotionally distraught Crystal King.

While not a full five minutes had passed yet, we were quickly running out of options and needed all the help we could get. I paused, looking at the chaos in the room. The leading group of knights had shifted to stop Caspian, while a handful remained behind to distract us.

I didn't want any more blood on my hands. Anyone or anything I pulled through with the bracelet was not going to make it out of here unscathed. I had already pulled Atari and Phil through.

The thought quickly melted as visions of the news and the beachside crab boil came into laser focus. More people would be hurt or killed if I didn't do everything I could to end this here and now.

Pushing my will into the bracelet, my fingers tingled as bolts of lightning erupted from the device, shooting in all directions. At first, I thought it was some type of misfire until I realized every bolt of lightning coming from the bracelet was depositing a rather pissed-looking armor-wearing Pixie in a pop of ozone.

I gasped as the final part of whatever was tied to the bracelet deposited itself on the floor in front of me. Jamison, wearing his father's yellow robes and silver armor, stood up with a solid black wand in his hand.

Toto, the Pixie King, flew down from one of the lightning bolts, landing on Jamison's shoulder. Phil bellowed an ear-crushing yell as he ran forward, cutting off two knights as Atari let loose a round of bullets. They were finally making their move on us.

"We are here to bring peace to these lands," Toto proclaimed as I looked over his shoulder at the oncoming wall of knights, his crown slightly cocked to one side. The other Pixies hovered in the air overhead, unflinching. "Today, we show all the ladies who has the goods!" he yelled, pointing at the wall of oncoming knights. The Pixies followed his speech with a round of midair hip gyrations, finally showing some type of emotion.

I could make out a few female Pixies rolling their eyes, yet still excited after the proclamation.

A hurricane is something you're ready for. You know it's coming, and you plan accordingly. A tornado of Pixies, on the other hand, was another level of unsuspectingly messing your shit up.

The unholy wrath of roughly a hundred plus glory-seeking Pixies exploded from the sky in what I liked to call an aerial Pixie blender of death. I looked over as Bosley and Treek flew in Atari's direction, causing her to pause fire when Treek held out his blade toward her eye. Bosley pulled Petro out of her holster, and the newly crowned Prince Petro pulled out his sword. Treek grabbed his other side as Atari bowed her head in respect, quickly pulling her pistols back up and unleashing a flurry of bullets.

Petro's two brothers had scooped him up and were now diving toward one of the knights, about to drop Petro on his head like a bomb. I glanced at Jamison, who was grinning. "Two birds with one stone," was all he said. I smiled back, springing my hellfire blade back to life while pointing my short staff into the second row of knights.

While I didn't understand the meaning of the Pixies being here, I knew we had to end this now. Crashing into a rather round knight, I slashed up, cutting through his armor and catching the chin of his helmet. I pushed my blade inside, turning the creature's helmet into a furnace.

Flames shot out from the eye openings as he fell to his knees, grabbing his head. The Pixies had every one of the knights distracted looking up. They were keeping their eyes on the sky while I moved.

After a few more brief encounters, I finally cleared a path, only to have the lead asshole staring at me with his arms wrapped around the Pillar.

"You know this is over. Caspian will not let you leave here alive," I breathed out, my chest heaving. I at least figured if we couldn't finish the job, the jolly old king would. The longer I kept the lead knight talking, the more of a chance Caspian had of eventually making his way to him. Well, us. I was still on the fence about whether he would let us live.

The knight shifted his weight, placing the Pillar on the

ground. "My name is Abigor. You will remember me in death. I can still feel your companion's essence on the Pillar. It was all in vain. Killing my manticore, her sacrifice . . ." the knight bragged as Caspian threw several random body parts of knights overhead. Glowing blood lightly sprinkled the area as I moved a few steps closer.

I noticed the slight hesitation in Abigor's taunt as he pulled out his sword. Light and power erupted from the sheath, taking my attention off his face.

Before I could fully react, Abigor swung his sword down, clashing with my hellfire blade. The two collided in a hiss and pop, pushing us both back a few feet to regroup. Caspian let out a guttural howl as a crashing boom rocked the room.

The Crystal King had been injured, dropping to one knee, as several of the knights crawled up his back, only to be knocked off by a group of Pixies. I pulled up my short staff, barely able to aim it, and let off a stunning spell which deflected off Abigor's armor. He smirked, seeing my damaged left arm. Lunging through the air, his blade hissed by my head.

My enhanced abilities were the only thing saving me as I turned, swinging my hellfire blade around wildly. The tip caught Abigor on the back of his shoulder, and he turned, smacking my sword into the air as I lost grip of my short staff.

Another howl came from Caspian as the crunching sounds of Phil plowing through the room echoed. We squared off, and I noticed Abigor looking over my shoulder a second too late; a crushing blow hammered me to the ground. I pulled Durundle back inside, pushing my hand palm first behind me.

A quick flash of hellfire, and the smell of burning flesh caught in my nose as the sound of a body thumping to the ground slapped the hard floor. The smell reached me before the sound. By the time I'd refocused my efforts in front of me, Abigor had his blade inches away from my face.

This time, the lead knight was in no mood to talk as blood flowed from his shoulder, covering half his body. Just as he pulled up his sword to deliver a killing blow, time felt as if it had frozen.

I looked around, taking in my surroundings, asking myself fast but steady questions. Had I failed my friends? Were the Old Gods going to make their way to Earth? Was this the end?

My vision went red as I fell back from the force of the explosion in front of me. I lay there face up, the familiar tang of iron and blood making its way through my mouth.

Seconds passed as I lay in what I assumed was my own pool of blood. More seconds passed as the sounds of battle started to thin out. More loud bangs and crashes, echoes of screams, and then silence.

When you realize you're not quite dead yet, you have a habit of sitting up. As I opened my eyes, the carnage in front of me started to come into focus.

Jamison stood over Abigor's body, covered in what I assumed was the knight's blood. His hands were red with gore as he stared at the disfigured body lying on the ground in front of him.

Several Pixies zoomed overhead as numerous wet thumps caught my ear. They were taking care of unfinished business.

"Jamison . . . JAMISON!' I finally yelled so he would look up.

"Max, thank the gods," he said, rushing over to help me to my feet. This was followed by a loud, booming, "Hell yeah, bruther!" from Phil. I didn't have the heart to tell him he was missing several teeth and looked like death.

The Pillar lay on the ground as Atari continued to fight, heading toward the stairwell. "Caspian—I mean, the Crystal

King?" I asked. Phil and Jamison both pointed at the large, hulking mass leaning against a wall on the far end of the room.

Just as I was about to inquire, Bosley and Treek dropped Petro on the ground in front of us. All three Pixies were covered in wounds and dirt. They had been in the thick of the fight and made it. I focused on the ground, seeing several small mounds with wings sticking up at random angles.

Not all the Pixies had survived the fight. Petro picked up on this, nodding at me. "It will be okay, boss. These are heroes." These were not my deaths to mourn, but I still would. I would just keep them tucked away for another time.

"Jamison?" I asked.

As if he knew the rest of the question, Ned's son stood stoically, looking at Petro. "The queen will see this as an opportunity to bring the Pixies out of servitude."

Jamison had known what he was doing when he'd stated it was two birds with one stone. He would make a good, genuinely caring politician, like his father, Ned. He had come a long way since our first meeting at Riverplace Tower.

The Fae didn't want to be tied to the assault if it failed, but if it succeeded, it would be a chance to bring the two societies together once again.

I looked over at Caspian, seeing his chest heave. Taking off in a sprint, I made my way to the Crystal King while the others joined.

His voice boomed before I could talk. Caspian's head wobbled as dozens of spears, swords, and other weapons stuck out of him at random intervals.

"You . . . you are welcome in my kingdom," Caspian rumbled as a slight grin rippled through his pained expression.

I bowed my head as Toto flew beside me, depositing a tired-looking Petro on my shoulder. The two Pixies looked at each other with respect in their eyes.

While I usually didn't use titles, it felt like the right thing to do. "My lord, thank you for the reprieve. But I am still here to take the Pillar back to Titania," I finished, getting to the point and seeing just how much control Abigor had on him.

"Yes, take the Pillar back to the queen. Bring balance back to our and your lands," Caspian said as gray concrete-like material oozed from his lips. "I have not been myself of late. My people will be glad this is over."

I hesitated as Phil joined us. The truth was, he had sentenced all his people to a mindless life of servitude under the control of the knights of the Old Gods.

"Your people . . ." I paused again, concluding Caspian would not be getting up. This room would be his final resting place. "I will do what I can to help." He was either avoiding the truth staring at him or didn't fully remember due to the hold Abigor had had on him.

Caspian nodded, several crystals breaking off his face and armor. This time, they didn't immediately grow back. Phil looked sheepishly at the ground, also knowing the end was near.

"I see that in you. We are not much different, you and me. I can see it in your soul," Caspian mumbled lowly. "Kings and gods from another time and place."

I looked around as Toto and Phil both watched me. "I need to get a few things before we leave. With your permission, I would like my friends to tend to you."

"Tend to me. Ha, I'm dying. As long as my people are here, this place will carry on. Though I wouldn't mind sharing one last drink before I see my final dream in this realm," Caspian painfully declared.

His message was clear. He knew he wasn't getting back up. With the condition of his people, when he passed, the

Crystal Castle would fall. I was still surprised by the lack of Faceless and rock gorillas, as I had dubbed them.

I realized I had spoken too soon when the rhythmic thumping of massive, hammer-like fists echoed distantly. There were more than likely other knights still fighting the now unbridled creatures in the castle.

"Well, I know just the guy," I replied, looking at Phil, who tapped the end of his nose. The blood crusting on his mouth from his now toothless smile was extremely off-putting and absolutely on the table for jokes in the future. I was already planning on calling him Madonna.

Toto snapped his finger as every remaining Pixie in the room hovered to attention. "King Caspian, I am King Toto. With your permission, we will bring you drinks from your stores. Um . . . where are they?"

Caspian grinned as much as a dying king could. Reaching into his upper armor sleeve, he pulled out a slim flask. Dozens of Pixies lurched forward, grabbing the flagon and quickly unscrewing the cap, putting it to the dying king's lips.

"Phil," I whispered. "I need to grab a few things we left at —" Her name caught in my throat. "I need to grab a few things. I have a feeling we'll need to get out of here in a hurry. You got this?"

"Of course, bruther. We can talk later," he said, walking over to the flask, letting out a whistle.

Jamison walked up as I pulled out the gate stone Destiny had handed me to get back to her underground home. The trip would only take a minute or two but had to be done. I would grab whatever else I could of Destiny's as well.

"Jamison," I started, handing him the stone Titania had given us to signal the location of the Pillar. Atari came closer, finally putting her last pistol away. "Here's the stone the queen gave us to signal her. We don't have much time, by the looks of things."

"Are the wards down?" Jamison asked Atari as she squinted her eyes.

"I don't feel any. The magic here is different. It's..." she trailed off.

"This place used to shift in time," I interjected. "That's why the queen could never find it or Dire Caspian. That's his name, by the way. I need you guys to get everyone out of here as fast as you can. My gut's telling me as soon as you set that beacon gate stone off, we're going to have company. Hell, I bet Titania already knows this place is here with the wards down."

"How are you getting back?" Atari asked, pulling out the gate stone directly tied to Titania's palace.

"Once you ensure everyone's through, wait for me. I won't be long," I replied, activating Destiny's gate stone, glancing at what was left of her and her belongings before finally walking through into the dark.

The sounds of several portals materializing echoed behind me as the sounds of Dire Caspian's final stand went silent.

CHAPTER 29

The Steps We Take to Avoid
Destiny Often Lead Us to It

T he smell of moss and cool, wet stone replaced the foul, burning stench of the battle I had just left. Water trickled through the small stream as a light breeze from an unseen opening ruffled the leaves in the tree holding up the roof of the large yet cozy cavern.

Spongy damp ground muffled my footsteps as I leaned over, squeezing through the small door to Destiny's cottage. Without thinking, I immediately dropped into one of the chairs next to our gear on the kitchen table.

I leaned forward, seeing the hourglass nearly empty. A handful of slowly moving grains of sand sluggishly floated to the almost full side. By my estimate, I had anywhere from five to ten minutes left before my time was up.

Looking at my trench coat, I decided to clean up a little before putting it on. The coat would appreciate the effort. I pulled a cloth off the small stone counter in the modest kitchen as I examined the room, walking around while I cleaned my arms and face.

Earlier, I hadn't noticed the lack of pictures or anything else overly personal. My gut told me to turn left, and I pushed a hanging blanket out of the way, walking into Destiny's room. Much like the rest of the house, the room was basic. A bed, a long wooden rod holding various pieces of clothing and, as I pushed some of the garments out of the way, a small trunk was all that materialized.

"Bingo," I whispered to myself, clicking the latch open.

Sitting as if alone in the world was a key with an empty coin-sized oval in the middle. The only other item in the trunk was a small clock identical to the one my mother had gifted me on my thirtieth rebirthday, the one I had subsequently broke.

I gazed at the contents of the container, finally reaching down and tucking them away in my trench coat. A wave of unfamiliar emotion washed over my body as I took one last look around the room.

Destiny had been alone in this small underground cottage for decades. The only things she had to show for it were the contents of the container I had just taken and her long staff still sitting on the floor by what was left of her ashes in the Pillar room above.

The woman had sacrificed herself for not only me but everyone else. She had mentioned Ian the Troll, and with that, I would be visiting him soon. The future, the past, thoughts of her, and Abigor's statements about time flailed in my thoughts like a man trapped under ice.

Did I know her, or would I at some point? Questions kept springing up, not finding a break in the hard ice. She was from my future but had arrived at the Crystal Castle from the past. There it was, clear as day, as the man in my mind broke through the ice gasping for air.

I pulled out the clock, looking closer, noticing the small crack on the front glass and what looked to be a repaired hour hand. I had taken the original hand, as it was part of one of the gates in the Postern.

I stared at the clock, still feeling as if I was missing something. The weight of the book I had taken from Davros's keep made itself known in my expandable enchanted pocket. The coat had a way of doing that. I reached into my pocket again, this time pulling out the coin Davros had given me.

"Son of a bitch," I belted out, clicking the coin into the slot on the key I found in Destiny's room as a pop of ozone let me know I had done something either good or bad. Either way, I felt one step closer to unlocking more of the gates.

Not only did I have what I believed to be the answer to the Timegate, but also one of the other gates in Davros's keep. I had a feeling it wasn't another portal like the one we had used to get to the Crystal Castle.

Reactivating the portal, I stepped back into the Pillar room where Atari stood resolute by the still open gate to the palace. Phil was by Dire Caspian, and I spotted Petro on his shoulder. Random Fae soldiers scurried around picking items off the fallen knights, obviously on the orders of the queen.

I shook my head, pulling out the hourglass in which two small particles of sand remained. It was time to go. I turned to Atari. "Head back. We'll be right behind you," I insisted while she shook her head, not agreeing with me.

"Oh no, you guys are stuck with me. Plus," she cautioned, leaning closer. "I'm not going to take any chances with these other goons in here."

Atari was now officially on the buy-a-drink-for list, and would be welcomed at the dining room table back at the Atheneum if it was ever put into full-time use again. You get the point.

I made my way to Phil as Petro cleared his throat. "Hey, boss, something on your mind?"

"Later, Petro. How's Caspian?" I inquired, knowing his final breaths were nearing as the last grains of sand hovered dangerously close.

"Yes," Caspian slurred, the growl in his voice still present.

"You said kings and gods like us. What did you mean by that?" I asked him. While I didn't want to take away from his final moments, I knew he had much to atone for.

"You don't see it, do you, Max. Do you, warrior?" Caspian asked, nodding at Phil.

"I mean, he's good for an all-nighter and has great taste in music," Phil replied awkwardly, taking a deep breath. "Aye, I do."

"The mark of a true leader is not knowing you are one until you're forced to become one. That holds true with gods and kings. That time is here. I . . ." Caspian faltered. The last grain of sand dropped in the hourglass as everything shuddered.

Dust lifted from its resting place, floating in midair, as all the crystals on Caspian's body and armor dropped to the ground, shattering. The floor felt like it was floating as large cracks spidered in all directions. The Crystal Castle was in its last few minutes of existence.

"Damn it!" I barked. "We got to go. Where's Jamison?"

"He went back with the others to make sure no shenanigans happened with Tom," Phil replied as we headed to Atari.

CHAPTER 30

The Queen of Now Bleeding Hearts

"**A**bout time," Cliff snapped as several other guards and Fae stood around the room, going through the dead knight's belongings. One of the knights awkwardly sat in the corner covered with a silver sheet.

Several Pixies flew over, picking up Petro before they took off to undoubtedly fix his broken wing.

"Phil," was all I replied with as Cliff walked between us.

"Hey, Cliffy boy, great to see you again. Are those new pants?" Phil inquired while I walked toward the far end of the room, being joined by Atari, only for us to be stopped near the door by Dr. Gully, the queen's minister of special projects. He was there to keep us from going anywhere.

"Captain Atari, Max. Glad to see the both of you," the knowing yet in control voice of Gully ventured.

"I need to see Titania," I replied, following up with a curt, "Now."

"Of course. She is, as you can guess, very busy. Not to mention very pleased with the work you have all done. Captain, this room and its contents are considered classified. Max, I'm going to need you to understand what that means," Gully, as I liked to call him, explained.

"I get it. I say something, and it's big-time trouble for me," I snapped. It wasn't that I didn't like the Fae. I just didn't have time. "You have my word. That is, minus whatever I report back to the Council."

Dr. Van Gully squinted his eyes. "Very well. I'll reach out to our member on the Supreme Council," Gully replied reluctantly, moving out of our way just as Cliff started shouting.

"Excuse me, you two!"

We shuffled past the doors. The reflective mirror polish of the elevator doors in front of us gave me a good idea of how crazy I looked. My body was covered in bruises, with streaks of dried blood matting sections of my hair. Several scrape marks lined the side of my face, adding to the others from the crystal wall exploding outward, making me look like I'd lost a fight with Oscar.

Atari picked up on this. "We can rest when we ensure Tom is safe," she noted, swiping her hand in front of the gray pad to the elevator.

Security was evidently on high alert, as two Fae guards stood in the elevator placed there for this very occasion.

"Stand down," Atari commanded. The guard on the left, having more intestinal fortitude, spoke up.

"Ma'am, I'm sorry, but these orders came from General Dex. We are to escort you up to the Pillar room," the guard explained, stiffening again, knowing Atari would have words with him later. They both wore the same patches, and she visibly outranked them.

The doors slid open to more guards and a smaller room similar to the Pillar room in the Crystal Castle. Titania stood with her arms stretched around the Pillar in the middle of the room. Two beams of light pulsed as she turned, walking away.

"I am pleased with the outcome here," Titania purred as

she looked at Atari. "You are, as a result of this, promoted to the rank of general. You will report directly to Senior General Dex."

This was apparently also a promotion for Dex, since he corrected his posture. The old general bowed while Atari stared straight at her.

"This is an honor, my queen. I must insist on Thomas Gabriel Sand's location?" Atari stated in the form of a question. Titania let out a purring chuckle.

"Mmm, he is in his quarters. I will take you to him shortly," Titania replied.

"Now. You will take me now," I blurted out. The room went silent, the cold glance coming from the queen piercing through me.

"Max, you have also done a great service to the Plane, and with that, to me. Let me finish here. Then we can go see Tom. I'm curious what he has to say about all this," Titania stated as if it were a fleeting thought.

A knock at the door drew our attention as a guard let in Toto, along with a now fixed Petro.

"Hey, boss. Good as new," he announced, clicking his now repaired wings.

"Good to see you up and flying," I said, turning my attention back to Titania. "There's blood on that stone. We lost someone."

Titania looked thoughtfully at it. "Yes, I could feel a fresh essence on the Pillar. It must have been a rather heroic sacrifice to leave that type of energy." She was dancing around the fact that she possibly knew who Destiny was.

I was, in my own way, pushing to see how transparent Titania was going to be about the whole situation. It wasn't lost on me that there was more at play than just the Pillar.

"Dire Caspian is dead," I declared, making a point of

using his name.

"Yes, and for that, I am especially grateful. That is the reason I called Toto here," Titania started, snapping her fingers. General Dex walked over with a small box. She spoke up again. "I hereby decree that all Pixies, from this time forward, are free of obligation and, with that, will be paid for any and all services rendered."

Petro's and Toto's jaws dropped as Jamison marched into the room with a grin on his face. He walked over to General Dex, opening the small box and pulling out a royal-colored emerald-green cape the same color as Titania's, placing it on Toto's shoulders.

"This is . . . this is . . ." Toto started as a light tear streaked his face, only to be quickly sucked back in. "My lady, you will have the full backing of the Pixie delegations."

There it was; the political play. While this was a significant step in the right direction, I watched Titania as a snakish grin took hold of her lips.

She had, in a matter of days, rid herself of the Crystal King, gained the full support of all the Pixies on the Plane, and become the face of warding off the Old Gods, wrapping this all up in a neat bow without mentioning a damn thing about our team.

Jamison started grinning before he quickly corrected himself, seeing the expression on my face. "My lady, I believe it's time for us to go to the under chambers," he said, reminding her to let us go see Tom. He hadn't seen him since returning.

"Tell you what, Max. Why don't you get a head start? And we will catch up shortly. I'm sure you have some things to talk about," Titania directed, and I immediately walked to the door, Atari and Petro following close behind.

Toto stayed, giving Petro the okay to leave as Jamison

also turned to join us. "No," Titania said flatly. "Jamison, we need to discuss a few items concerning your needed attention on the Council."

Jamison stopped, giving Atari a quick, reassuring glance. I had the feeling he was about to get more responsibility on the Council.

The ride to Tom's holding area was quiet as we all took the time to digest the last couple of hours. A loud ding snapped us out of our peaceful trance as the doors slid open.

There, sitting in a chair alone, was Tom, facing out one of the large windows overlooking several smaller buildings. He slowly stood up, observing me with a mixed expression on his face. It was a mix of relief and the same look a doctor gave a patient when there was bad news.

I stared at the two guards by the door. "Is he free to leave?" The two guards looked at each other, not knowing the answer.

"Yes, he is," Atari declared as the two guards noticed the new shiny general stars on her lapel.

"Of course, Capta—I mean, General," one of the guards let out.

"My boy, it's such a relief to see you," Tom said, walking toward me as I held up a hand.

I had no intention of letting him off the hook. While I was glad to see him, I could tell this wasn't over yet. He had more up his sleeve, as always. I loved my Gramps, but this was another level of me needing to understand what this all meant.

Lilith, the Pillar, Terrum, Destiny, the Postern, and more importantly, my daughter. He knew the glue that tied all these pieces together, playing both the dark and light side of the fight to get whatever it was he was, in fact, after.

"Atari, Petro, I need a word with my grandson," Tom

requested. The aging lines on his face seemed to deepen as I stood there. The two left, and I walked over to one of the chairs, again dropping down, exhausted.

The weary look on Tom's face started defusing my temper as I took in his thinning skin. He was beginning to have trouble moving.

"Has Titania helped you yet?" I asked, wanting to get that piece out of the way.

"She has made a promise to me that I believe she will keep," Tom said flatly as he sat back down across from me. "That's not what's important now. I need to ask you something."

I stared blankly at him. He cleared his throat, letting out a lungful of air as if releasing a long-kept secret. "Did you run into anyone else while at the Crystal Castle or the keep?"

"We did. A woman named Destiny."

Tom's eyes lit up as he nodded. "Is she okay? Did she come back with you?"

"No, she didn't make it," I replied, and a dark cloud swept over Tom's face. "I saw a picture of Ed and you at Ian the Troll's place. Destiny mentioned that you and Ed brought her to the keep. She kept saying something about her being from the future. It was like I knew her."

Tom sat in reflective silence. "Yes, we did take her to the keep. Max, I need you to understand something. I have met your daughter twice. I only realized who she was recently, when I first met her."

I leaned forward, getting a sinking feeling in the pit of my stomach. "What's her name? WHAT'S HER NAME?!"

Tom glanced away. "Destiny . . ." he murmured. My chest started to heave as heat radiated from my hands, creating a haze of smoke coming from the chair.

"You wait till now to tell me this bullshit. More games and lies," I accused, my temper flaring like a spot on the sun.

"No, it's not like that. If I had told you, the path you chose might have been altered. Destiny was just a young woman who asked for our help back then. A rather knowledgeable one at that. It was only recently, when I found out your daughter's name, that I realized," Tom replied as I let out a breath. This time, it turned to mist, almost freezing in the air. My body was going haywire.

"Destiny died saving my and everyone else's asses. She wrapped her arms around the Pillar and burned herself to dust." Tears started freely flowing from my eyes, only to fizzle out of existence from the heat my body was now letting off.

Reaching into my pocket, I pulled out the sash Lilith had given me, throwing it at Tom, who wrapped his gnarled hands around it. He simply nodded, understanding how I'd gotten it in some weird, unspoken manner. I wanted nothing more to do with Tom and his games.

"She did what?" Tom asked, a slight shift in his tone.

"She grabbed the damn Pillar and turned to fire. I can fix this. I have to," I rambled to no one as Tom stood up, placing a frail hand on my back.

"My boy, if what you say is true, I don't believe she is gone. Just in a different place," he reassured us both, his tone now completely changed. He was calculating and working through what had happened.

"What do you mean? Destiny used the Pillar as a gate like you were planning to?" I asked, rage and pain still coming through in my voice.

"Precisely that. Max, Destiny is a special child. I know it's confusing to hear me talk about her this way, but she is in the Everwhere as we sit here talking, a child being raised by someone you know and who is not who you think they are.

Chloe, as of last year, is now alive and partially well," Tom noted, and I found myself calming down.

"Chloe was nothing but a killer. I need to find them. Tell me where," I said as I finally regained control of my body.

Tom spent several minutes walking me through Chloe's betrayal of Lilith and the Thule Society. It still confused me how Lilith was part of this, but the more Tom explained, the more she seemed to be the lesser of two evils. The-Devil-you-know type of situation, literally.

I listened as Tom laid out everything. This included his belief that she had used the opportunity to gate to Terrum through the Pillar just like he had intended to do. Tom still danced around Lilith's part in all this, but kept insisting she had done what she had to do with the children for a reason.

Lilith wanted control of the Plane. To unseat Titania and bring change and possible war to the Plane. With the storm coming, the Plane needed a strong, calculating leader. Someone not afraid to make hard decisions, even if it involved causing unimaginable pain. I knew both Titania and Lilith were capable of such things.

The rest of her actions were not excusable, and Lilith would have to pay for what she had done at some point. In Tom's eyes, he was not the judge of her actions. It was blind love and family clouding his judgment. I understood it, but made it clear that moving forward, I wouldn't accept it.

"That, Max, is why you must not try to change what has already happened. I believe no matter what occurs, the events of today will still stand the test of time," he concluded as I pulled out the clock and gate key.

Thoughts of Chi's message to me floated through my mind. While I'd initially figured the message was about Tom, as had Ed, I was starting to think it pertained to Destiny.

"The key to the Blackgate. You have been a busy boy. This

will allow you to gate to and from Davros's keep. Which, I'm sure you understand, is in the Plane but to a point not exactly on the Plane," Tom said. The sparkle was coming back to his gaze. "The clock should allow you to use the Timegate. Max, you must promise to use it with great caution. You already know from the journals that it only goes to a few certain times and places. Davros has the knowledge you seek."

I sat there only hearing two key points. I now had the ability to use the Timegate, and moving forward, I had a type of secret hideout that no one else could access. It wasn't the time to work through the rest of the issues, but I still needed one final piece of information.

"How do I find Chloe in the Everwhere?" I asked, as he had obviously been avoiding that piece of the conversation.

"Sarah has a way to find her. Just be aware, she did take the final journey. I brought her back to help get Destiny away from Lilith. This is where we meet in the middle. The rest of the journey has yet to be had. From what I understand, Chloe has, as of this week, taken the path set for her away from Lilith," Tom noted.

"So you're saying Lilith's on the warpath, then. I talked with her a few days ago. She seemed fine. I'm guessing that's when Chloe made her move," I replied as Tom nodded.

"I could only speculate. You would know," Tom said just as Titania walked into the room. The others were now gone from the entranceway, I noticed, looking around her.

She stopped. "They went to the main hall. There are still some things that need to be addressed. Tom," she greeted smoothly, holding out her hand. "It's time."

"Time for what?" I asked as Tom looked at me with a smile that could only be described as final. The decision had already been made and discussed between the two.

It was the expression someone gave when they knew

they would never see you again. The look of a hero going off into an unwinnable battle. One of pride and just cause. Just like Destiny's.

"Titania has agreed to send me through the Pillar," Tom answered. She smiled.

"This is how you're going to repay me? By sending him off somewhere he can never come back from?" I asked, confused by the gesture after everything she had said about sending him through the Pillar.

"The Old Gods know we're here now. It's only a matter of time," she replied as I stood still.

"Wait, why can't you just gate an army to Terrum and fight them?" I brainstormed out loud. Titania bowed her head slightly, looking at Tom.

"Max, the energy it will take just to push me through the Pillar is enough to power most of this city. It doesn't work like that. Destiny was only able to do so—and I'm only guessing —due to the amount of power she herself held," Tom said as Titania looked skeptically at us.

We took the ride up the elevator again to the Pillar room, where Titania made everyone leave except for the three of us. The hum of the Pillar droned as the room emptied.

"Are you ready?" she asked Tom. He looked over, taking a few light steps in my direction.

I walked over to Gramps only to have him sling his arms around me in a deep, meaningful hug. "I love you, grandson. Max, tell your mother I love her. You will find your daughter, and we will one day meet again. Maybe not in this world, but the next. You have a gift. Use it. Whatever happens next, you must not hold it against anyone. This is the way it has to be," Tom conveyed calmly before he walked over to the Pillar.

Titania leaned over, placing a longer than comfortable kiss on Tom's lips, and shivered slightly. "We would have made such good lovers," was the last thing Tom heard before Titania slid a glowing dagger into his chest.

I stared at the scene, both chaotic and serene. Tom smiled while pieces of his body floated away just like Destiny's, only to be pulled into the Pillar.

Titania walked over, handing me the dagger. "He will make the trip. The energy used from that dagger was more than enough. It could have fueled an army. I'm sorry for how this ended, but there is much work to be done. We are on equal footing now. My favor is complete." She paused, looking reflectively at the Pillar.

"Those things are coming here, and when they do, there will be more of them—countless legions, stronger, faster, and better equipped than those rogues. You've done well," she finished, placing a much more platonic kiss on my cheek before she turned to walk off, leaving me to reflect.

"Wait, you promised that you would help me find my daughter," I barked as she again paused, looking back over her shoulder.

"I did. How was it?" Titania stated, void of emotion, walking out of the room. She had known the entire time.

CHAPTER 31

These Are the Things I Can Do Without

F at Florida rain spattered on the roof of the outdoor pavilion as I slouched in my seat. Sounds of bottles clinked as an older, overly tanned bartender with a name tag reading Bill walked up.

"You've been sitting here staring at the rain for the last hour. Everything okay?" Bill asked as he wiped off an oversized margarita glass.

I was sitting at a bar on the beach I used to frequent before leaving for the army. It was the type of bar only locals would know about. Tucked away enough to stay private, but good enough to get a steady stream of good-tipping customers.

Gray sky melted into the dark blue waters of the Atlantic ocean, the contrasting tan sand reflecting the dark sky as rain pooled on its surface.

"As good as it could be, I guess. Let me ask you something," I pondered as Bill leaned over the bar, setting the already clean glass down, a habit bored bartenders had. "What do you think about things since the great Balance occurred?"

Bill reflected thoughtfully, as did most bartenders when asked a legitimately good question.

"Well, at first not much. You know, it was all over TV, but that was about it. Then everything went crazy around here." He paused, taking a closer look at me. "Every now and then, I get someone in here I can tell is . . . well, you know. Anyways, for me, in my little slice of the world, I still have bills to pay, and my girlfriend's boyfriend still thinks I haven't figured it out. So there's that pile of shit I'm dealing with."

I nodded, taking a pull of my now warm beer as Bill started back up.

"Some days, I wish I could just wake up and have powers, you know, like a V or something. That would fix that relationship. Hell, it would fix everything. Look, I'm sorry to dump on you like this. It's just been a long week. Here," he followed up, taking my warm beer away before handing me another one.

"Shout" by Tears For Fears kicked on from the small digital jukebox at the end of the bar.

"Thanks," I said, taking a refreshing pull as a gust of wind launched my napkin into the air. "There are days when I wish I didn't. Magic does nothing more than create bigger, more complex problems," I sighed as his eyes opened wide.

"I knew it. You're that fire guy. Man, you're sort of famous. Can I get a picture?" Bill asked, picking up his phone. Too bad I was famous for the wrong things.

"Sure. I would give anything some days to be behind that bar serving drinks and nothing more," I replied as my phone buzzed with a message from Sarah. *I'll be there in five minutes.*

Bill, seeing the sincerity of my statement, set his phone back down. He was a good bartender, and knew I was going through something. What that something was, I had yet to figure out. All I knew was that I needed to get back into the Postern and work on the other gates.

I had already planned a trip to the Everwhere, and

hopefully, with Sarah's help, would be able to find Chloe and Destiny. It was more of a chicken-before-the-egg type of situation, as I still needed to figure out the Timegate. I would be seeing Davros and the Council in the morning.

Since returning from the Plane, I had spent a reasonable amount of time with the others, telling them as much as I was comfortable with. Of course, Petro, Phil, Ed, and Jenny were privy to the entire shitstorm that had occurred, since I would need their help. But I was keeping most of the situation surrounding Destiny, Chloe, and Gramps off the table with everyone else.

After hearing we had returned, surprisingly enough, Sarah had booked an early flight back. I was even more surprised she had decided to fly, since she had a gate permit and stone to the Atheneum, which was starting to look reasonably livable again.

When I'd laid everything out to the others, it had been like talking to a room full of people I didn't know. Either things were getting too complicated, or I sounded like a madman.

When Petro arrived home, news of his actions and new position spread fast in the Pixie community. Not only was he a hero for a second time around, but Petro was also now a standing member of the Council, representing the newly established Pixie Plane Delegations, P.P.D. for short.

This, in many ways, pulled power from the current Pixie Council members. The good news was, they didn't care. Petro had noted all they did was a little dance before flying off to go party. Casey would not be allowing such behavior, and the Warrior of the Freeze knew it. It was a new era for Pixies, both on Earth and the Plane. I was proud of the little guy.

After some more small talk, I landed on liking Bill. He had impeccable taste in cereal, not to mention how it was supposed to be served. He had also explained how he'd installed all the Planes Drifter songs on the jukebox. I decided not to tell him how well I knew them.

"Hey, stranger," I greeted warmly, standing up as Sarah ran under the cover, trying to keep out of the thickening rain. The rhythmic sound of it beating on the tin roof was intensifying.

We hugged lightly before I motioned her to sit down. I had set up our meeting away from the usual locations to give us some breathing room to talk openly. I had even considered taking her to the Postern. Without saying anything, she pulled me back in for another hug. "It's good to see you."

"You didn't have to come back so fast. I'm not asking you to get involved," I blurted out, not thinking the statement through.

"That's the reason I'm here. Max, you know I care for you and your family. I also care for James, Trish, Amon, Phil, Petro, and the others. This thing with Chloe means a lot to me. And if what you hinted at is true, I will do everything I can to help. I understand Tom told you everything," Sarah stated quickly.

She finally sat down, shaking off the remaining water from her coat.

"Looks like you got in a fight with a cat," Sarah noted as her smile beamed, forcing me to grin.

"I wish. More like slicing, crystal thingies," I replied, seeing her shifting uncomfortably in the barstool. She was nervous.

Most of my wounds had healed, as my ability to fix myself had accelerated rapidly over the past year. Jenny attributed my healing abilities to me being able to use magic that had been used on me. Not fully, but enough to help. The fact that I frequently needed a healer was not helping.

I took another pull from my beer as Bill dropped off a glass of ice water. "Anything to drink?" he asked Sarah, who pointed at a bottle of red wine sitting behind him.

We settled into our beverages before I took the leap. While I was usually straightforward, that wasn't always the case with my friends. "Chloe's alive. She's in the Everwhere, and I'm going to find her."

Sarah's lip quivered as she held back her emotions. "And your daughter. My niece. Does everyone else know?"

"I gave everyone the abbreviated version. I wanted to talk with you first before saying much more to the group," I replied as thunder rumbled in the background.

"There are some things I want to tell you, and I promise I will. It is true that Chloe is my sister, but I want to be clear on something: I haven't talked or seen Tom since he left with you to fight the Soul Dealers," Sarah pointed out as I leaned back. She wanted me to know there may be some gaps in what she knew. Sarah also wanted me to know she was being honest.

"This isn't about trust. You already have that. I need to know where to find her," I followed up. She nodded.

"I think I know where to start. But this isn't something we can just jump into. Tom and Chloe set something up before she disappeared," she said. I leaned forward.

"You mean before we found the Fountain of Youth?"

"Yes," Sarah confirmed lightly, pulling a small wooden stick out of her purse. "Here."

I took the hand-sized piece of wood, noticing the tiny runes carved into the grain and what appeared to be dried blood.

"Is this a tracking charm?" I asked as "The Red Queen" by Planes Drifter came over the radio.

"Tom told me this would open up a way to find her. When they were working together, I was on the Plane. It's a long story, but you need to understand they set up many things I was not fully aware of. I would start by going to Chloe's old house. That's what Tom stated when he gave me this. It was like they knew what was going to happen, and planned for it."

The statement shouldn't have taken me off guard, but it did. I'd never thought about digging into her prior living arrangements. "And I'm guessing you know where it is and that it wasn't ransacked after she was tied to Jayal's murder?"

"Oh, there's no way they found this place. Her apartment for sure, but not her home," Sarah replied, pulling out a slip of paper with a simple address on it. "This is all I know."

I pocketed both items as Sarah's phone began to buzz. "It's James. He knows we are talking, and I think it's driving him crazy. Not in a jealous way, but I sort of told him a few things—not everything," she corrected herself. "Just about Chloe and how that was why you wanted to meet."

The term *meet* echoed in my mind. I called it my head movie jokingly. The problem was there weren't many jokes to go around lately. Minus Phil showing up to the fight with his pants down; that was a classic. The thought tucked itself back away. It had been a little over four years since I last remembered looking into Chloe's smiling face.

"Tell James I said hello. I might see him tomorrow at the Council chambers. I've got some things to get sorted out first, but I'll let you know before I go check out Chloe's place," I promised as we both stood up.

Saluting Bill, I dropped a fifty on the bar. I would be coming back here.

CHAPTER 32

Knights of the Round Table

Mouth, Kristi, and Nora, Goolsby's accountant, stood outside the chamber doors in the same spot as last time I had come to brief the Council during the fiasco with the Dark Carnival.

"This is becoming quite the exclusive club," I chuffed, walking up to Kristi and shaking her hand while looking up at Mouth. "Hey there, big guy."

"I almost went an entire week without having to look at your ugly face. It sounds like everyone in there wants to kiss your smelly ass," Mouth grunted as I grinned. Again, the lack of any threat of immediate physical dismemberment was a positive sign.

"Good to see you too. Hey, I need to get with you sometime. I want to get schooled up on trolls," I noted. Mouth rolled his eyes, barely moving his massive overhanging forehead.

"Great, the only thing you need to know is they are more stubborn and annoying than you," Mouth responded, pointing his fat stubby finger in the general direction of his phone, telling me to call him.

"Max, great to see you. We were just out here talking

with Nora," Kristi noted. Nora shifted, not liking the lack of attention. Every time I was around her, I did it on purpose. It was mainly due to Nora not telling me her name for well over a year. "Oh, and Phil's picking me up later. It sounds like we are meeting for drinks. That includes you, by the way."

"I wouldn't miss it for the world," I replied, shifting my focus to Nora. "So, what's up?"

"Here," she snapped, her feelings obviously on display. She liked being the center of attention. "It's new access codes to the Mags-Tech NCTS computer systems."

"Mags-Tech, huh. It sounds like there is a security concern," I commented, putting the plastic credit card–sized note in my pocket.

Her mood shifted to professional mode as she cleared her throat. "Yes, there has been a recent uptick in external penetrations into the NCTS systems database. I know this is a sore subject for some, but the files from the Transitions Office never really went away."

I stood still with my shoulders slightly raised. Mouth spoke up, getting tired of the conversation. "What she's saying, you twit, is that some unauthorized regulars have been trying to access files on prominent Mages and Ethereals."

"Oh, well, why didn't you just say that? I would bet anything it's tied to Darkwater and his new goons," I replied, getting another jab in at Nora.

"Everbane. Yes, that reminds me. Mr. Goolsby would like a word with you after this. If that's clear enough to understand," Nora added quickly.

"I'll find old grumpy Goolsby later," I said. Mouth snorted out a short laugh as Petro's voice came into focus from down the hall.

"I'm here, boss. Do I look good? Do I have any bugs in my teeth?" Petro babbled, hovering a few inches from my face. "Oh yeah, check it out."

Petro turned around, showing off his newly embroidered cape. It simply read *Prince Petro*. "Is that the cape Titania gave you?" I asked, getting the others' attention at the casual mention of her name.

"You betcha. Casey did the stitching. I wanted her to add all the other stuff I'd done, but it would get sloppy. Let's go," Petro urged, buzzing in front of us.

Several years ago, I had introduced Petro to professional wrestling. It had taken me a subsequent year to convince him it wasn't real. But he had become obsessed with their outfits during this time and stated how badly he wanted a cape.

Now that he had one, I was fairly confident I would also be seeing the rest of his costume at some point. To be fully transparent, we used to get hammered and make up our wrestling tag team personas.

We all walked into the main Council chambers. The guards, this time around, smartly avoided any conversation. Phil, Ed, Jenny, Bo, and Inspector Holder sat at one of the tables below the general seating areas overlooking the main floor.

Bull stood at the far end, his bald head reflecting the dull ambient lighting as only his could. Carvel, Goolsby, and James, all members of the intel community, sat across from our group's table, looking up at the crowd.

Davros, Lorel, Titus, and Ana Vlad sat in the Supreme Council thrones, conducting the orchestra. It still struck me that there were ten other members of the Supreme Council I had yet to meet.

Petro landed in front of Phil as I took my seat. Mouth and the others filed into the nosebleed section. In all fairness, I wished I was with them. Ed cleared his throat.

"Right, Petro, I do believe you need to be in the Senior Council members section. Just for today. People need to see that you're the new sheriff in town," Ed noted as Petro pushed his chest out a little further. We were only on the floor due to the content of the meeting.

"You're right. I'm now in charge of the Pixie delegations. Plus, I think the guy I replaced was caught flying around a movie theater naked last night dropping popcorn on people," Petro said confidently, flying to the small raised platform. Several of the other Senior Council members greeted him as he kept turning around, pointing out the embroidery on his cape.

I leaned over. "What was that all about?"

"He needs to be making new friends. It never hurts to have more eyes and ears. Petro will do great. Look, they like him already," Ed said, pointing up as the people around Petro all looked captivated by whatever story he was telling. "His predecessor was not too popular."

I leaned back as Bull brought the room to attention. "Please be seated. Ms. Vlad," he gave her the word. She stood up. Davros sat still with the same indifferent look he always had on his face unless you were discussing hellhounds with him.

"Thank you all for coming today. As some in this chamber are aware, we had an encounter on the Plane with several of the knights of the Old Gods." Ana paused as the room erupted in gasps, murmurs, and outright conversation.

She knew hiding this information would be problematic. I was curious to see just how much she would reveal to the public.

"Silence!" Bull's amplified voice slammed through the room.

Ana was skipping all the juicy parts about our team's role in ensuring the knights were no longer a threat. Looking over, Bo pulled out a small, dainty handkerchief, chuckling lightly into it. I smirked at him, as I was sure he was rolling his eyes behind his round, old-timey tinted glasses.

I needed to show Bo the hourglass and tell him about Metatron when this was over, since he had just arrived back from England.

"We are here to inform the Council that the immediate threat has been addressed. With that, I will be handing the floor over to Frank," Ana announced.

In a short amount of time, Frank had gained a significant foothold on the CSA team, basically leading it at this point. I was also confident he had a secondary role working with the Night Stalkers.

Frank glanced at our table, giving us his typical *I hate this shit and would rather be at home listening to The Cure* glare. Vampires. He knew what he had given me with Davros's ring, and what our trip had entailed. Davros sat up slightly, simply out of respect for Frank.

"Thank you, Supreme Councilor Vlad. As many of you have been briefed, the CSA and Night Stalkers have been working behind the scenes on several projects. I am only able to discuss one of them today. We will be holding a secondary meeting with the Intelligence and Artifact Retrieval teams afterward." Frank paused briefly before Ana motioned him to continue.

"Last year, we received reports of an entity armed like a knight appearing on a small island off the coast of Florida. The Night Stalkers were deployed and, after deliberating, decided the entity was hostile and dispatched it. I have just released the remains to the Artifact Retrieval Team for study and testing. We were able to use traces of Etherium from the armor to create an alert, much like that used to detect demons."

Bo coughed. It was well known by many in the room that Bo, like Belm, was not trackable. It was also evident that by *deliberating*, Frank had meant fighting. He was just trying to put everyone's mind at ease with the situation, letting them know it was under some sort of control. It wasn't.

Lorel stood up. "We have also coordinated with the Fae Court to work with the team from the Atheneum on comparing the secondary remains retrieved from the Plane. Jamison will be arriving soon to review this with the Council. I would also like to formally announce Jamison's new position on the Senior Council."

Lorel continued playing political word ninja for several minutes, seeming to avoid several key issues. I also found Jamison's absence curious. From what I understood, he was taking on Aslynn's old role with more direct influence.

Aslynn had been assigned to work with the Elves and Pixie delegations when we'd arrived back at the palace. We hadn't had much time to talk, but I was sure Jamison would fill me in.

After several more minutes of general follow-up, Bull called the end of the session, which didn't include the two groups of tables on the main floor. Petro joined us as Bull motioned the Supreme Council members and us into the subchambers, a more intimate and private place to talk shop.

Frank bumped into me as we filed into the room. "Hey, I hear you guys are going to FA's later. Mind if I join?"

"I was hoping you would. I just let Trish know we would need some space to ourselves, so I'm sure she's going to shut down early. I don't even know where to start," I said as Frank grinned a toothy smile.

"When time permits, Angel and I are dying to hear . . ." Frank paused, seeing me smile. "We really want to know about the keep."

We took our seats as Davros stood up next to Ed. "Max, good to see you in one piece. We are here to discuss the Round Table."

Several people looked at each other knowingly. Phil, Petro, and I looked at each other unknowingly. I spoke up.

"Look, I'm not sure you need me here."

Carvel interrupted, cutting Ed off. "Oh no, you are specifically who we need here for this conversation."

"It's not another quest, is it?" I asked, feeling like my old self for a few short seconds.

Carvel scowled as he looked at Ed with a *get your kid under control* stare.

"Right," Ed started. "The Vampire Courts have been working with the Council on recent reports of these so-called knights showing up randomly on Earth. From what I was briefed this morning, the Courts believe this is random, and much like you stated, Max, some sort of scouting group. We believe these were part of the same group of knights you encountered on the Plane. We will be able to confirm that shortly."

Ed motioned at Davros, and the old V walked to a large wall-mounted monitor, clicking a button. Nothing happened. He clicked it three more times before Frank quickly inserted himself into hitting the proper control.

Davros let out a muffled growl. "You push that button," Davros commanded Frank, who took control of the presentation clicker. A schematic depicting a round shape with several lines and designs marked on its surface popped up on the screen.

By the look on Ed's and the others' faces, I could tell this was all relatively new information to the group. On the other hand, the Vs seemed comfortable with the picture on the screen.

"We're good," Frank informed Davros, who unnecessarily cleared his throat. "While many of you in this room have been around for decades, if not centuries," he started, glancing at Ed. "During the Great War, when my people were cursed and sent to Earth right before the connection to Terrum was severed, this gate—or portal, if you will—was a crucial part of ending the war with the Old Gods."

I raised my hand as if needing to go to the bathroom.

"Yes, Max," Davros slithered out.

"I thought the Great War was also fought between all the realms?" I asked. While it was a stupid question, I seemed to be missing something.

"By the end of it, yes. The Old Gods did try to play their hand along the way. This device was used to prevent that, or well, finish it," Davros started back up, hitting his stride. Frank clicked the button as a new picture popped onto the screen. This time, several knights were wielding swords, all standing around a round table resembling the previous slide. I hated PowerPoint presentations.

Ed stepped forward. "Yes, the knights of the Round Table, before anyone else asks."

Davros turned back to the picture. "Yes, Edward. It's not so much the knights but rather the table itself. Max, does that small piece at the bottom look familiar?"

"Let me guess. I have a section of this table, and the Night Stalkers have been looking for the rest while I was away?"

Phil smacked his hand down. "Told you the shite was real, bruther. You owe me a bottle of the good stuff," he bellowed as I groaned.

"Ah hell, we did make a bet. But my table is square," I stated flatly, getting a sinking feeling.

"Your piece, yes. The others, no. The Round Table was created from the very same material as the Pillars. If the knights of the Old Gods are coming, the Old Gods may not be far behind. Mind you, there are thousands of these knights searching across the cosmos," Davros finished before sitting back down. The old Vampire was done with his piece. My guess was he was the only one old enough to understand the connection entirely. Frank turned, taking over.

"The Night Stalkers and a special CSA task force are working to track the other pieces down. According to the information gathered from the knight we encountered here, they are looking for the pieces of the Table."

Jenny, in her infinite wisdom, spoke up. "It was used to send them back. They want to use it to come here now. The Pillars were more of a smoke screen, while the Round Table was more of a hammer."

"Precisely," Davros added drily from his seat. "It was not a coincidence the knight on Earth was found close to your home, Max."

"So, this Table is tied to the Pillars?" I clarified, making sure I was reading the room.

"Exactly that. From what we gather, the knights of the Old Gods you ran into just happened to find one of the Pillars. They are also most assuredly looking for the Round Table, or as it's officially called, the Eye of Merlin. Its name comes from the center of the table," Jenny explained.

I sat up, remembering my conversation with Titania's team before leaving the Plane. "The Fae seemed to believe that once Abigor found the location of the Pillar, he was using it to bring over one knight at a time. They believe they were coming from somewhere else other than Terrum. It almost sounded like they were lost and just got lucky. Abigor couldn't take on Titania, so he worked out a way to get the Pillar and build up whatever army he had. I would bet that knight was one of his. He must have gathered enough energy to send him here."

"Noted," Davros sighed.

"Right, Max, we will need to secure your part of the table," Ed explained as Carvel scribbled down a note, handing it off to Mouth, who just grinned at me.

"It doesn't sound like I have a choice. Listen, there's a lot more to worry about than just the Old Gods. We don't need to lose sight of everyone else," I cautioned. Several people in the room nervously shuffled in their seats.

"Max is right," Petro spoke up. "Half you people on the Council want to be in charge. We need not lose sight of ourselves. Just look at ex-Councilman Dipshitdarkwater," Petro noted as Ana walked over to him.

"You are a good addition to this Council. Titania was wise, or maybe careless, putting you in place, but I believe we are lucky," she said, taking control of the meeting as she usually did when things were about to wrap up.

"As of now, the Night Stalkers will continue to hunt down these pieces. We already have two out of the twelve remaining sections. Max, we know the sacrifice you, Phil, Petro, and the others have made. We are not asking you to engage here. As stated, these were just some of the thousands of scouts. We are, however, asking that you restrict your travel to the Plane for now." With this, Ana concluded the meeting. Everyone stood up, starting their own conversations.

Something wasn't adding up with her statement. While I was good with taking a short break from the Plane, they would be hard pressed to stop me unless they took the gate key or somehow destroyed the Postern. There was probably a reason I would have to figure out.

The Vampires were making it very clear they didn't want me or possibly anyone else helping them hunt down the Eye of Merlin.

"Max," Carvel called, catching me off guard as my mind raced. "Again, good work. Sorry about the mess," was all he said, chuckling to himself as he walked off.

The son of a bitch had probably had someone trash my

apartment, having the Table removed while we sat there. "Your mom's pies suck," I mumbled to myself as Phil looked at me.

"No, they don't. You said they were some of the best pies you had ever wrapped your gums around." Phil took a deep breath, and I felt my chest move with his. "Ah, this isn't our problem, bruther."

"Yet. It isn't our problem *yet*. Something was off about that meeting. It's like they don't want us poking around," I added while he shook his head. "I have other things to get to anyways."

"Yes, we do," he replied, emphasizing the *we*, before refocusing on the subject of the meeting. "Maybe, maybe not. Let's get to FA's. Kristi is gating back with me. Oh, and Goolsby keeps giving you the side-eye. I heard he wants to chat with you. Have fun with that ray of sunshine," Phil joked as he walked over to Kristi.

"Petro, you got a few minutes?" I asked, wanting him to join me while talking with Goolsby.

"Sure thing, boss. I only have two other people to show my new sexy cape to," he replied, quickly darting over to Davros.

I let the room thin out, forcing Goolsby to walk over to me. "Max, we need to talk. In private."

"It's a package deal," I countered, pointing at Petro.

"Yes, fine, let's go to my office," Goolsby relented, walking out at a brisk pace, catching Nora off guard.

After a short five-minute, noncommunicative walk, we entered a rather bland set of offices which looked a lot like they belonged back home. Goolsby closed the initial door, followed by the secondary entrance to his private office.

Nora took her usual position by the door, lurking in the background.

"Alright, you've banned me from every other place you own or manage. How long is it going to be before this place is included?" I chuckled, getting no reaction. This was more telling than the stone-cold serious look on his face.

"The evening's not over," Goolsby chided. He slid his hand over one of the gray pads precisely like the ones on the Plane. Of course he would have something to do with that technology.

Goolsby set two glasses and a cap on the table, ignoring Nora. I had a feeling she didn't appreciate the gesture. I would pocket that one for later.

"Let's get to it," I huffed, taking a sip of the overly expensive, smooth wood-flavored whisky.

"Yes, I appear to be at a bit of a crossroads. That being said, appearances can be deceiving. I know you have other things preoccupying your thoughts," Goolsby started.

"Right, like what I'm doing later this evening," I interjected, pushing back on the notion that he knew what was going on in the background, not to mention my plans on finding Chloe and Destiny.

"You mean going to FA's and drowning your sorrows, followed up by a bunch of storytelling to make yourself feel better about the fact that when you did find your daughter, you didn't have a clue who she was," Goolsby stabbed back.

I froze, and even Petro set his cap down. "You listen here, mister gooley pants," Petro barked as I held up my hand. His newfound title and position was quickly loosening his tongue.

"Thanks, buddy. I got this," I said, calming Petro down before eyes became an issue in the general vicinity.

"I'll give you that one; I know a good amount about what happened in Titania's palace. You even met one of my constituents. I'll let you figure that one out," Goolsby explained. I swiftly guessed Cliff was probably on the payroll.

"I don't think the others on the Council truly know how much you've done, not only for their kind but for us."

"By us, who do you mean?" I asked, digging deeper.

"Regulars, the civilian population of Earth. I know you might not see it, but ever since the Balance, things have been changing. Not only are there more magic types popping up everywhere, but the civilian population is also getting restless. They're worried, or should I say, concerned that they are going to become slaves to some ill-mannered demigod." Goolsby paused, taking a sip of his drink.

While he wasn't off his usual game, he had a tired look behind his eyes. "I get that. We knew that would happen at some point. Last I checked," I said, pointing at the gray pad on his desk, "business was good."

"Contrary to popular belief, I do care. Well, let's just say I need customers. I'm not interested in ruling the Earth or the Plane. Did you notice the Vampire Court not wanting your involvement? With this being so close to you, it seems suspicious," Goolsby pointed out as I sat up straighter.

"I did," was all I responded, knowing he had the answer already.

"In that room were probably the only V allies you have. You do recall your involvement with Cecil and the death of several other Vampires over the years?" Goolsby asked without giving me time to respond. "It did not go unnoticed by several factions within the community. Davros and his cronies are trying to protect you; I would heed their advice."

"You know, when one person tells me I can't do something, I might not do it. When two people tell me not to do something, I'm absolutely going to get my hands dirty. I appreciate the heads-up. Hell, I would say it's been a crazy past few days, but you already know that. So what's the endgame here? Yours, more specifically?"

"My loyalty lies here. More precisely, in Jacksonville," Goolsby replied, referring to regulars, pointing at a map of the United States on the wall. "As much as I hate to admit it, without you running about, I have a feeling things would not be as calm—if that's what you call it—around town lately. The Vs are going to make a move on you, and with that, my city. When the time comes, I want you to know who you can trust."

"By telling me you know my dirty little secrets. Yeah, I get it. You need me to do more of your dirty work. Petro, it's time to go," I declared. He flew to my shoulder as I stood up. "You know, the way I see it, I just saved all your asses. It's time for me to handle some personal business."

I was referring to finding Chloe and Destiny, and hopefully, putting things right. This also meant taking the Council's advice and staying out of current affairs for a while.

I looked at Nora as I reached the door. "I'd recommend dusting off your resume." She just scowled while Goolsby stood up.

"Max, family is something you have to fight for. Just be careful how hard and who you're fighting. You fight too extremely, you know, get your emotions into it, and others will start to worry about your intentions. I know what's going on with Titania and Lilith. Maybe you should focus on that."

I turned, giving Goolsby the universal finger sign for friendship, then Petro and I left his office. The problem was, I agreed with everything the man had just said, and he knew it.

CHAPTER 33

The Same Old Song and Dance

"**I** didn't see this coming," I whispered to Trish as she led us through the packed bar back to the kitchen.

"Well, it was about time we all got comfortable around Amon. Plus, he's been a little moody lately," Trish teased as we all piled into Amon's sitting room.

Not much had changed since my last visit, minus a few of Bo's things. Considering he was Amon's new roommate, that was to be expected.

Ed, Jenny, Phil, Kristi, James, Sarah, the Pixie crew, and Bo all took seats around the large open firepit in the middle of the room. Petro and Casey had found a new babysitter, the one and only Leshya.

The smell of freshly cooked pizzas covered with exotic flavors floated around the room as everyone stuffed their faces with appetizers while in mid conversation. Everyone was patiently waiting on the pizzas to be finished.

Ed walked over, handing me a beer out of the coolers Amon had set up around the firepit inside his apartment, or whatever the hell it was. Besides being a former hellion general, Amon was a fantastic cook, and apparently, a good party host.

"Are you okay?" Ed asked, not having talked to me since the previous day.

"Yeah, I'm getting better. I still have a ton of unanswered questions, though," I replied as Bo walked in holding an oversized pizza tray wearing a flour-covered apron.

"Darlings, pizza is served," Bo said bombastically, doing a slight bow after setting the tray down.

"You didn't cook that, fart brains," Petro noted, flying over to the table. Bo did the fake fly-swatting routine to save some of his demon dignity.

"He added the toppings, and that counts," Amon bellowed as he walked into the room. His smile stretched from the end of his tusks to whatever was hanging on the side of his crooked head.

"Fair enough, bruther," Phil belted out, grabbing two slices of pizza before quickly driving them into his mouth, only to stop midcram.

Kristi looked at him as he slowly pulled the pizza out of his mouth, setting it down on the table, making matters worse. "I always cock this up. Would you like a slice?"

Kristi snickered as one of her top teeth anchored itself behind her lips, sticking out more than the others. "Not one of those, but yes, please, and a plate," she replied as the group started throwing napkins at Phil.

"Bloody hell! Okay, okay, calm your tits, everyone," Phil said as everyone let out a much-needed laugh.

Phil was one of the most badass Earth Mages you would ever meet, but when it came to manners . . . well, let's just say he needed some help. At least his heart was in the right place.

I turned back to Ed as he let out one last huff. "I spoke with Davros after the meeting while you were off with Goolsby. He wants to meet tomorrow to talk about the keep and a few other things he said would be better discussed with you. What did Goolsby have to say for himself, by the way?"

"Goolsby thinks the Vs are after me," I told him. Ed's face didn't look reassuring.

"Well, we already knew that, to a point. Davros has your best interests at heart, I can say that much," Ed stated flatly. We both took a bite of pizza, followed by a slow pull of our beers. The sounds of Amon laughing and Bo making sound effects in the background were keeping everyone entertained as we talked.

"I believe you. I didn't talk much about it, but his keep is almost a mirror, albeit a creepy mirror version of the Atheneum. More put together than the one in the Everwhere, though," I informed him.

"The one in the Everwhere is a mirror of ours. The keep, from what I understand from talking with Davros, is one of, if not the first, Atheneum. If it weren't for everything else that needed to be sorted out, we would be talking with him about it now. It might be a good thing everyone is preoccupied," Ed noted as I took the final pull of my beer.

"You know what I've got to do. I told you about Tom, and even though it was messed up, I feel like he is where he wants or needs to be right now. I almost forgot," I added, remembering the dagger Titania had given me. "Titania gave me the blade she used. It looks like a smaller version of Durundle before it, you know, did its thing."

"When we get back, I'd like to take a look at it. I went by Tom's old place, and, well . . . his room was open. There are some things in there for you, I believe. We all know where your priorities are now, and we will help you in any way we can," Ed promised as I genuinely smiled for the first time in several days.

"Thanks. Gramps is always up to something. Knowing

my luck, the dagger is now cursed with his ghost or something." We both paused, looking at each other slowly.

"I've got a bad feeling about that dagger, now that you mention it," Ed said, making a good point. The energy it gave off was slightly off.

I turned to see Frank and Angel walking in just as Petro started telling the story of his magic water bubble ride.

"Max, Ed," Frank greeted us as Angel winked, heading over to the bottle of synthetic blood sitting on Amon's bar.

"I'll catch up with you shortly. Jenny went into the kitchen. I have to see this," Ed noted, leaving us alone.

"What a ride," Frank huffed, sounding frustrated as I handed him a Vamp Amber. "Thanks. I need about ten of these."

"How's it going on your end?" I asked as he took the beer down in one swoop. *Do Vampires burp?* I thought to myself, only seeing him not flinch.

"Politics and more politics. It almost feels like all this Old Gods stuff was made up to position people." Frank ran his hand through his hair, a gesture not needed by a Vampire and done more out of habit. "You know, *give me more power, and I'll protect you* kind of bullshit."

Frank was in a talkative mood. It reminded me of the first time we'd had drinks in Gramps's old office when I first took it over before his third or fourth fake death. I had lost count at fake death number three.

"Talking to Titania, it feels the same way. If you had been there, you would understand," I said in a reflective tone, not jabbing but relaying the ludicrousness of the situation.

"I believe you; out of anyone, I believe you. We just want you to know . . . Angel and I are here to help. Don't let the Council or the other Vs get under your skin. Everyone is failing to say that it could take a thousand years for another of those knights to show up, or for anything to happen. Remember, time's nothing to those types. We just wanted to come by and say hello," Frank said as he did the oddest thing. The moody emo Vampire leaned forward, hugging me.

"See you later, Max," Angel purred, giving me a light peck on the cheek as the two walked out of the room.

"What was that all about?" I asked Phil while Kristi continued to stare at Amon. She was still coming to terms with the whole hellion thing. I noticed she hadn't touched her pizza either. Once she did, Kristi's perspective would change.

"You found Davros's keep, bruther. That place is sacred to them. Rumor has it they can actually go to the Plane through the keep. Not go anywhere, mind you, but get some of the old hometown vibes, I'm guessing," Phil pondered. I was starting to see why Davros wanted to talk. I was also starting to wonder if some of that extra mind power Phil had picked up when we first hit the Plane had stayed with him.

This suspicion was dispelled when he let out a loud, echoing belch.

Amon sat in the largest throne in the room, doing so with authority. The loud thump of his oversized body hitting the cushion made a whooshing sound, catching everyone's attention.

"Max," the hellion bellowed. "So, what's your next quest?"

"Another quest!" Petro burped out as Casey, Macey, and Lacey all let out an excited, "Wow!"

This was followed by Petro winking at me. "Told you so, boss. The ladies love a good quest."

The word made me grin as we all sat down around the fire. The Pixies flew to the table, landing in front of Ed and Jenny, and Kristi leaned on Phil's shoulder.

Bo leaned back, crossing his legs and steepling his fingers. Trish, doing the most Trish thing ever, bounced on Amon's massive knee, taking a seat, while James and Sarah sat nestled together, sharing a chair.

Looking around the room, I saw every eye and ear pointed in my direction. I hadn't told everyone fully about Chloe, or much of what had happened over the past two years, for that matter. It was time. I leaned forward, taking a deep breath as I left no stone unturned, or fact left to witness.

There's something about telling your friends, and now family, everything. Stripping your soul down to its bones and not picking and choosing who to tell what or whose feelings it may hurt.

We all sat around the fire as it danced off our eyes. At that time and place, us merry few, us band of not only brothers but misfits, worked out precisely what we were about to do.

EPILOGUE

Supreme Council Chambers - Fae Offices

"I'm not buying any of this," Lorel barked as Jamison walked out of the shadowed corner of the Fae Council offices.

Jamison had finally returned from the Plane to officially hand over several private documents to Lorel from Titania. Some documents even Jamison had not been made privy to. In all reality, he didn't care.

"Me neither, but it is what it is. If the queen hadn't said it in front of my face, I wouldn't have believed it," Jamison responded.

He was, in many ways, telling the truth. The son of Ned and once prominent information broker had been forced into politics.

"She trusts Max?" Lorel sneered, slamming a stack of papers on the desk.

"You mean to ask if she trusts me. I'm not lost on everyone knowing about our connection. I would be stupid to think otherwise," Jamison relayed in a calm, soothing tone.

Lorel let her shoulders drop before she finally sat down. "All these years and the sacrifices I've made, for what? Nothing?"

"Lorel, I was there. I saw the Crystal Palace," Jamison started. "You're looking at this the wrong way. Titania, if anything, needs your help back on the Plane. We all know you wanted to go back home. I don't think it's permanent, anyway. Plus, I can't fully sit on the Supreme Council. Titania needs you."

Titania had instructed Jamison to be her lead emissary and represent the Fae as the senior-most Fae member. Her instructions had also included sending Lorel back, leaving her seat on the Supreme Council open. Jamison was almost certain she was about to fill the role with someone more aligned with her future goals.

"Yes, but this just seems out of sorts. You do know Max and Lilith are related, right?" Lorel stated. That caught Jamison's attention. For the most part, that connection had been kept a secret. Seeing this, Lorel dug deeper, now with the knowledge Jamison already knew. "Then you also know Lilith wants to take the throne from our queen, and with that, our people. She's done enough damage on Earth. Think what she'll do on the Plane."

Jamison paused in reflection, thinking about the cruelty Titania was also known for at times. "I know, I know. Listen, I'll do my best. You know I have our people's best interest at heart, at the end of the day. Plus, we have bigger things at hand."

Lorel let out a light chuckle. "Yes, I heard Max's little speech. I'm also aware that it may be decades, if not hundreds of years, before we hear anything from the Old Gods again. Jamison, don't lose sight of the Fae. Being on Earth or in these halls will do that to you. Max is powerful beyond measure, and according to this report, which is not meant for your eyes, this has now been proven. He must be dealt with at some point. It is now your duty to protect the Fae and the Plane. Feel free to look over your friend Max's file. I'm sure you will find it enlightening."

Jamison took the stack of papers, acting like he was about to open pandora's box, already knowing where she was going with her statement. He also already knew the contents of the package, as he had been responsible for its contents. That was the part Lorel didn't know. All adjusted and put in place by Jamison himself. While mentioning Lilith, it also decidedly left out several other key details that would have otherwise been included.

Lilith and Darkwater in an Undisclosed Location

Furniture shattered as Lilith threw another electrified spell at the farthest wall. Books, dust, and what was left of the table in the middle of the room were all reduced to rubble.

"Calm down," Darkwater politely requested as rage occupied Lilith's gaze.

"Where is she?" Lilith again demanded while Darkwater shook his head, not knowing.

"I kept you alive and gave you power for one reason, and that was to keep the child safe," Lilith screamed as Darkwater calmly stepped forward.

The one miscalculation Lilith had made with Darkwater was just how powerful he may become. With the shifting of the Planes—which Max had just stopped—energy and power had affected things differently than before.

When Darkwater had drank the water from the Fountain, it had had a rather different effect than initially planned.

The once Councilman was in many ways now immune to magic. Which often included lethal spells. He had also gained the ability to control people's actions.

"I've been sitting in your shadow long enough. I know

you want to take over the Plane, and I wish you well on that endeavor," Darkwater stated flatly while Lilith stood frozen in the room. He had somehow taken control of her body, but as always with this little trick, not her mind. "I want what was taken from me. I will destroy the Council, including your precious Max. Yes, I have been stirring the pot with some of the Vampires."

"You will not harm my grandchild," Lilith spat through gritted teeth, still not able to move.

"I've already sent the remaining holdovers from the Thule Society back to Earth. Everbane will rise to power, and from the ashes of the old, we will prosper again. We made a deal with the Old Gods, and I plan on seeing it through," Darkwater roared as if giving a speech to a thundering crowd.

He let go of his grip on Lilith, who stood with death in her eyes. "Remember; what I give, I can always take. If I see you again, I will take everything," Lilith promised as she relaxed her posture.

Darkwater had failed to remember that Lilith was not only a demon but a demigod. She would fulfill her promise. Not only did Lilith see his ambitions as shortsighted, but they could now get in her way.

While the deal with the Old Gods still held in the eyes of Darkwater and several others, Lilith knew better. She recognized the Old Gods were not to be trusted in their promise to hand the Plane over to the Thule Society in return of softening the agreement between the Plane and the inhabitants of Earth, which Mengele and the others were supposed to do before the former was handed over to Hades by Tom.

The truth of the situation was that Mengele had worked out a deal with Abigor, who had been just as power hungry. Abigor had convinced several others that he was speaking directly for the Old Gods. The deal he had made was self-serving, and as of two days ago, no longer relevant. The agreement was now lost in the sands of time, along with Abigor and his missing army of knights. Lilith had, of course, already figured this out.

It wasn't even clear to Lilith if Abigor had truly relayed any of this or his location to the Old Gods.

Darkwater went to walk out of the room, hesitating. "Oh, and you can keep those rejects that you somehow managed to bring back."

He was referring to the handful of children Lilith had gated when she lost her arm and had her first run-in with Max several years ago. In some odd way, these were the siblings of the children back on Earth that had been rescued.

What he didn't know was just how powerful those children would not only become, but already were. As Darkwater walked out of the room, a wicked smile swept across Lilith's face. She had let him take control of her. In reality, she had tested the man's loyalty, only to find him failing. Lilith, as always, had planned for either way.

Darkwater would keep the Council occupied, separating from her, while she focused on finding Destiny and taking control of the Plane.

The one thing she didn't realize was Destiny's role in the fall of the Crystal King, and that Max was now more focused than ever to ensure her fate didn't happen. Only a handful of people knew he'd even met her, and that was a secret he and his companions would keep.

ACKNOWLEDGEMENT

First and foremost, I'd like to thank everyone that's joined me on this ride. I have been overwhelmed by the support and acceptance of Max into the world of Urban Fantasy heavy hitters.

When I started this journey, I wanted to break the mold ever so slightly and write a well-thought-out series in a genre that frequently has trouble finding its identity.

From the fans who dig into the overarching themes, to the apparent wizard and demon that often sends me emails, the thought put into some of your questions and observations amazes me.

A few folks I'd like to give a shout-out:

The latest addition to the Max Adabbon world, Gene Mollica Studios. You and your team are one of the best at what you do. The new covers have exceeded my expectations.

Hunter, as always, for helping me kick this off. 1LT Moss, I owe you a call, man!

Luke Daniels and team as always…, thank you for taking the time to bring Max's world to life. Yup, I'm still a fanboy.

To my family, my wife, and two sons. This book is part of my legacy to you. When I am but a memory in time, you will always be able to pick this book up and remember what a nerd I really was and, well, still am...and will probably be some more. Then when you think I'm done, I'll pop up again, being even more of a nerd. When that's done, nope, more nerd from the grave.

BOOKS BY THIS AUTHOR

Max Abaddon And The Will

MA 1

Max Abaddon And The Purity Law

MA 2

Max Abaddon And The Ghost And The Grave

MA 2.5

Max Abaddon And The Gate To Everwhere

MA 3

Max Abaddon And The Dark Carnival

MA 4

Sheltered

The Sinking Man Series: Part 1

Awakened

The Sinking Man Series: Part 2

Released

The Sinking Man Series: Part 3

Fractured

The Sinking Man Series: Part 4

Made in the USA
Columbia, SC
16 July 2022

63453167R00202